Ghost People:
Death in the Mines

SANDI C. KNAPP

Copyright © 2013 Sandi C. Knapp

All rights reserved.

ISBN: 1484112024
ISBN-13: 978-1484112021

DEDICATION

To June Farmer and Hershel Lewis

CONTENTS

	Acknowledgments	i
1	Ghosts and Creekstone House	1
2	Death in No. 5 Mine	7
3	The Death of Floyd Wilkes	24
4	The Wakes	41
5	Bart Asher	57
6	Rumblings of Trouble	61
7	A Visit from Big Brock Asher	69
8	Granny Lee's House in Putney	77
9	A Visit from Uncle Purl	90
10	Amity Smith	103
11	Stolen Watches	111
12	Floyd Wilkes' Ghost	122
13	The Blizzard	130
14	Rose	145
15	Daddy	149
16	The Revelation	153
17	Christmas at the Lodge	158
18	The Confrontation	163
19	A Visit from Uncle Larkin	167
20	A New Year's Celebration	174

21	School and Amity Smith	176
22	Floyd Wilkes, Where Have You Gone?	179
23	Visions of Death	185
24	A Death in the Family	191
25	Introduction of a Union	197
26	Indianapolis	204
27	More Death at the No. 5 Mine	209
28	A Note from Bart Asher	215
29	There are no Ghosts	217
30	History Repeats Itself	223
31	Mama's Missing Parts Revealed	229
32	Rumors of More Trouble	237
33	The Strike Begins	240
34	Rose's Secret Revealed	248
35	A Birthday and Celebrations	250
36	Injury on the Picket Line	252
37	A Trip to town	254
38	Just Like Floyd Wilkes	259
39	Cry for Your Daughter	261
40	"Vengeance is Mine," Sayeth the Lord	264
41	Sometimes God Don't Make no Sense	269
42	Little Brock Asher Concedes	273
43	Bonzelle Creech and Pea Salad	275

44	Just like Rose	278
45	The Photograph	282
46	A Visit from Mama	286
47	Ghost People	297
48	Just an Accident	303
49	Retribution for Rose	307
50	Unfinished Business	311
51	Floyd Wilkes is Dead	315
52	Faces to Remember	319
53	The Divorce	320
54	The Return of Floyd Wilkes' Ghost	323
55	God Gives us What we Need	325
56	Goodbye, Floyd Wilkes	328
57	Ghosts at Peace	333

ACKNOWLEDGMENTS

Although based in fact, parts of this work have been fictionalized. Some names and locations have been changed, but the plights of many countless Kentucky coal mining families – including the author's own family – are undeniably true and have served as the inspiration for this work.

The author wishes to acknowledge the guidance and support of the English Writing instructors at Indiana University Southeast; your encouragement over the years has been truly invaluable. The author also wishes to thank the many family members and friends for their continued support. Without these people, this book would not exist.

SANDI C. KNAPP

1 GHOSTS AND CREEKSTONE HOUSE

It seems my most vivid memories of childhood always come back to the summer of 1948 when the coalmine disaster occurred. I had just turned fourteen years old that May, and Daddy worked for Little Brock Asher in the No. 5 mine. Our rough-hewn log house that we all referred to as "the lodge" belonged to Little Brock Asher and stood in the middle of Wilder Field in a valley where the Wilder Creek emptied out into the Cumberland River. The little city of Evarts was only a few miles from our home, and the town of Harlan was just over the mountain.

During that sweltering month of August, the lack of rain had caused peoples' crops to wither in the fields. The grasses paled and the very earth cracked in places. The shoals of the Cumberland River seemed to disappear beneath the rocks, while the surface of the river wore a kind of sickly white film and stunk of rotten fish. Near the fence in our yard, the tall poke stalks were dying. Once a lovely dark purple, the intense heat had caused the berries to shrivel and their leaves to droop, finally turning them dark around their edges.

I recall another summer when my then eight year-old sister, Rose, had picked a handful of the purple berries and eaten them. Worried, I'd told Mama, who quickly found Rose and stuck two of her fingers down her throat and made her throw up the berries. "How many times have I told you that poke berries are poison? If Pearlie Johnson was still alive, she'd tell you all about them! Her daughter almost died after mixin' up a batch in sugar and milk. It killed the baby she was carryin' inside her belly, which God forgive me was probably for the best. But if a doctor hadn't pumped her stomach, she woulda died too!"

I recall Rose gagging violently as Mama forced her fingers deeper down her throat. Rose recovered but ironically never lost her fascination for the little berries. She couldn't believe anything that looked so pretty could be that poisonous. Afterwards, I asked her how they tasted. She wrinkled her little nose and said, "Not good at all. I thought they'd taste a lot better."

Daddy called the dry hot season "dog days" and said that during mid-July and early August, the earth was poison. Both he and Mama warned Rose and me to stay away from the river and to make sure we never went barefoot because a cut or a bruise could be deadly. However, neither of us had listened and had gone barefoot whenever we got the chance.

When I was five years old, I learned about dog days the hard way after nearly dying from an infected cut on my heel. I had developed a high fever and my foot soon turned black. Mama applied bacon fat to the wound but even its powerful drawing effects failed to pull out the infection. When the baleful red streaks started up my leg, old Dr. Abel from Harlan informed Mama and Daddy that he might have to amputate my foot. For days, I lay in a kind of feverish stupor and was in and out of consciousness.

During this time, it was said that my Granny Martha Lee, along with several women from both the church and the Salvation Army (with whom she was heavily affiliated), held a vigil at my bedside. Granny Lee and the women took turns praying and reciting passages from the Bible. Although I remember nothing about the women and their prayers, I do recall seeing the ghost of Mama's little brother Floyd Wilkes for the first time. After that, my fever subsided and almost overnight, the red streaks disappeared, and turned into pink healthy skin. Granny Lee gave all the credit to God, but I believed in the power of Floyd Wilkes' ghost. I remember my dream and reaching out to the same little blonde-haired boy whose face I had seen in Grandma Ivy Haley's picture album. He was standing about midways on the weathered planks of the Wilder Creek Bridge, dressed in faded overalls and a plain shirt. His curly blonde locks stood out in the bright white light. I recall the sensation of warmth spreading throughout my body as I stood waiting for the ghost of Floyd Wilkes to help me cross over to the other side of the bridge. Instead of coming to embrace me, the ghost motioned for me to turn back. I remember some sort of pulling force inside me yearned to stay near him where the air felt warm and good to my skin. I had never felt such comfort or lightness of body. My limbs turned into feathers, just waiting for a breeze to carry them off to some wonderful place. However, somewhere inside of my brain, some conscious thread told me to turn back and that it wasn't time yet to cross over. That night, the ghost of Floyd Wilkes was absorbed within the bright light but would reappear many times throughout my childhood.

Granny Martha Lee was the only person I told about Floyd Wilkes' ghost and the dream or vision I had of him holding me back from death. I trusted her because I knew she understood ghosts and spirits almost as well as she understood the living. Having my own personal ghost seemed special at first, but as time passed and I grew more knowledgeable, I realized that ghosts weren't that much of an anomaly.

For as far back as I can remember the ghost story was part of my everyday living. It seemed that everyone I knew claimed to have either seen or heard a ghost at least one time in his or her life. Older folks referred to these ghosts or sprits as "haints." Around well-lit grates, wide-eyed children gathered in suspense listening to the wizened, skillful storyteller talk of ghosts roaming through the age-old houses and spooks living in mountaintop caves. One of the most popular haint stories involved a pack peddler. Robbed of his precious goods, word had it that he was murdered, and then his body weighted down with rocks and dumped in the Cumberland River where he eventually sank to the bottom. .

In those days, it seemed that every old house, cliff, bridge, or hollow was haunted by ghosts or discontented spirits. Even the Wilder Creek Bridge had a story behind it. According to Granny Lee, right after the bridge was finished, a little six-year-old wondered off from his home near Wilder Creek. Nobody ever found his little body but everybody guessed that he had fallen off the bridge into the water and drowned.

Even the stately Asher house was steeped in tragedy and made a perfect ghost story because of the strange and eerie ways its past dwellers had met their deaths. I was to learn about the Asher house when I was nine years old. Granny Martha Lee was spending the night with us while Mama and Daddy sat with Mama's sick cousin, Sophia, who was dying of tuberculosis. It was near dark and the river frogs had already started their night croaking. Granny Lee and I were sitting in the front porch swing trying to catch a cool breeze, while Rose sat on the steps hugging her knees. To the left side of us on the hill, the Asher house was lit up like a Christmas tree. Pole lights shaped like old-fashioned lanterns lined the long steeped lane. Electric lights were a wondrous sight for us as well as many of the people in the rural areas. In those days of the early 1940's, not many people could afford to have lines strung to their homes, and even if they could, there was always the cost of the electricity to worry about.

Rose said, "The Ashers have so many lights. Look! You can see them shinin' though the trees. Imagine having all them lights burnin', and here we are sittin' in the dark."

Granny Lee settled back into the porch swing, closed her eyes and said, "Honey, that place needs all the light it can get. As purty as it is in the daylight, at nighttime, things creep. I believe there is some kind of curse on that house!"

Rose said, "Granny, just because the house is big and fancy, don't make it no evil place."

Granny Lee answered, "I know that, child, but homes carry the history of their owners inside their little cracks and crevices. If people was happy in a house, then the house has a happy air about it. If bad things happen in a place, then the ugliness of it all stays right there in the air forever." Suddenly interested, I scooted over next to Granny's feet and begged her to tell us about the big house.

Granny said, "I outta not tell you all about it, but I reckon you both are old enough to hear it."

Like many of the older folks in Appalachia, Granny Lee had a penchant for storytelling. And like most, she loved a good ghost story – especially when there was more than just a grain of truth to it. Since Granny Lee detested a lie, she sincerely believed the story she was telling, which made it sound even more credible. That night, I listened intently as she told of how a man had brought his family up from Frankfort, and then began building Creekstone House on Wilder Point. She said, "I was about ten years old then, but remember when they came like it was yesterday. I had heard Mommy say that the buyer of the land was a rich lawyer whose daddy had some fancy government job in Frankfort. I recollect that the man's rich daddy was originally from around Harlan and had deeded the land on Wilder Point to his son. From what I understand, his daddy helped him start a law practice in Cumberland where there was more people. We lived on Sam's Creek. Our place was a mile or so down the road from Wilder Point. Your Granddaddy Lee was a miner over in Bell County, and some Sundays when he was off, he would take us buggy ridin'. Men were buildin' the house then, and Daddy liked to see how the construction was comin' along. We'd stop along the creek and just sit and watch men haul rock right out of the creek bed. Dad said they were usin' them rocks to build the outside walls of the house. The man was particular, I reckon, and had a big blueprint for them builders to go by. He stood right over them builders and watched them beat and grind the creek rock into smaller blocks. A lot of work went into that part, and if I remember right, it took over two years or better to finish it. After it was done, it was really something. I was smitten with it too, just like you girls are now, but thought it was too fancy for Harlan. Back then, there was nothin' like it. Still ain't nothin' like it around close. People all around the valley and even from town came to look at it after it was finished. Anyway, that man and his family lived there about three years. I guess they kept purty much to their selves. I heard tell that the man stayed in Cumberland a lot because that's where his law office was. Mama said he hired people to do their tradin' and yard work and such. One night a stablemen went to the barn to check on the horses before going to bed. He'd shined a light around and seen the owner hanging from the rafters. He was still wearin' his fancy lawyer's suit. Nobody knows why he done this. Some people claimed he was depressed because his oldest daughter had come down with polio and would never walk again. People were guessin' though because nobody knowed much about 'em. After her man died, the woman and her children moved back to Frankfort."

Granny Lee took a long breath and asked for a cold dipper of water. After Rose got her the water, she drank, then wiped her brow and proceeded on with the story. "About a year or so later, a young doctor and his pretty wife moved up here from Pennsylvania to start a practice. I reckon the wife fell in love with the Creekstone house, so her husband bought it for her as a wedding present. It took the doctor a year or so to get his practice goin'. I don't see how he made much money, being that people here was even poorer then as they are now. A lot of his patients paid him with a sack of ground meal or a crock of homemade butter. When the vegetable gardens come in, some people paid him with vegetables. From what I understand, he was a nice fellow and he took the goods as payment without turning a word." Granny Lee's eyebrows knitted together in remembrance. "The doctor's wife was a tiny little woman, fragile I guess you could call her. Of course, everybody wondered what she was like. Mama said she thought she was kind of bashful, 'cause she wadn't real friendly. About a year or so after they bought the house, word got around that she was with child. Agg Skeen's cousin Bella worked as a receptionist in the doctor's office and told everybody how excited the doctor was about being a father. Some of the women from the church where the doctor and his wife worshipped made the doctor's wife a baby quilt and some other little things." Granny Lee drew a long breath before saying, " I don't know how far along she was when she lost the baby, but things started to go wrong up there at the big house after that. Some said losin' that baby drove her mad. I remember the night Dad came home late after workin' at the mine and told Mommy how he had seen the doctor's wife walking along the road in her nightgown. I could hear what he was telling Mommy because my bed was right off the kitchen. Anyway, he felt sorry for the poor thing, so he tied his horse to a tree by the river and helped her get up the hill to the house. Dad said the doctor's wife never said a word about where she was goin'. The woman that took care of her told him that it was almost impossible to keep up with the poor woman. If I remember right, she'd wandered about like that for a year or better before she finally killed herself."

"She killed herself?" I gasped. Granny Lee nodded grievously. "It was summertime and a big rainstorm had blown in. Sometime during the night, she jumped out one of them third-story widows. It was the poor doctor who found her all twisted up in one of them Formosa trees underneath the window."

Granny Lee's story of Creekstone House would cause me many sleepless nights. I had a good view of the house from my bed, and sometimes at night I'd look at it all lit up and picture a little blonde haired woman plummeting through the rainy darkness and then landing in the pink feathery Formosa tree below.

Granny Lee was quiet for a few minutes. I can still hear the creak of the porch swing as she shifted her weight. Rose was the first to break the silence. She asked, "So the Ashers bought the Creekstone House after the doctor's wife died?"

Granny Lee answered, "The poor doctor couldn't live there no more after his wife done that. A few months after the funeral, he put it up for sale and moved back to Pennsylvania. It stayed empty for years before old Britton Asher finally bought it as a wedding present for his only son, Brock. Now I don't know much about the Ashers except that Britton Asher was big in the coal business and could well afford that house. I'm guessin' Big Brock ain't too far from my age. I remember his daddy and his wife Armanda, but not real good. All I know is that neither of them lived very long after they bought their son the house. Big Brock had inherited his daddy's coal business of course, but accordin' to some, knew next to nothin' about it. I doubt he regretted sellin' the mine near Flackie after that explosion killed your all's Granddaddy and them other men. I've heard tell that he bought Creekstone House mainly for the coal on Wilder Point. People said he could sniff out mineral like a huntin' dog. But you can hear anything," she was quick to add.

"Old Britton died at that house. People say that he'd gone out to the smokehouse to get a ham for dinner and when he didn't come back, Big Brock went out and found his daddy with his face against the patio floor. I guess he'd had a stroke or heart attack."

"Oh, God!" I gasped in disbelief.

Rose was equally stunned. "What about his wife? What happened to her?"

"She died in one of the upstairs bedrooms not even a year after her husband. Nobody ever said what killed her; likely, she just faded away from missin' him."

I recall that night of Granny Lee's storytelling with such clarity. I can almost feel that warm wind caressing my face and bare arms and that smell of soured earth mingled with the stench of the coal--always the coal.

2 DEATH IN NO. 5 MINE

Maybe it was just a coincidence, but it seems to me that the worst things always happened to our family in the sweltering dog days of summer. It was the sixteenth day of August, and Mama was in the hot kitchen cooking supper while Rose and I were sitting on the porch swing talking and trying to fan away the heat and mosquitoes with homemade cardboard fans. I was about to get up and go into the kitchen for a glass of water when I heard the shrill blast of a siren directly behind us. Bolting off the swing, I ran out into the front yard followed by a wide-eyed Rose who asked, "What was that?" Her strange blue eyes had turned almost white in fear.

"Somethin' must be going on at the mine," I said in a shaky voice.
The screen door flew open and Mama came running out onto the porch with a dishrag in her hand. Under her breath, she whispered "God almighty! That was the alarm from the coalmine. Somethin' bad's happened up there." Throwing down the dishrag, she started running in the direction of the dirt road adjacent to our home leading up to the gates of No. 5 Mine.

The roar of engines sounded in the distance and then grew closer and closer. A string of trucks came racing up the dirt road and heading in the direction of Asher mine. A few minutes later, two ambulances with their screaming sirens stirred up clouds of dust as they passed.

"Where did Mama go?" Rose asked in a quivering voice and then wailed, "Oh God, Daddy!" Just as she said it, our redbone hound, Buster, came charging toward Rose barking furiously at the passing ambulances.

Unnerved by the shrill scream of their sirens and Buster's agitated barking, I commanded Buster to "sit!" Although Buster was usually obedient, the strange noise and the constant movement from the hillside had gotten him stirred up. Walking nervously to the west side of the porch, I looked beyond the creek and the bridge to where Creekstone house stood lording over everything below it. The wide uneven landscape was a flurry of movement. Alby Dennison's old green flatbed pick-up was the first one down the hill, followed by what looked like a newer model truck. I recognized Mr. Dennison's truck because he often drove it when he picked Mama up and took her to work at the Asher Funeral Home in cold weather. As they passed us, I spied a woman on the seat beside him. I recognized Joelyn Asher, the wife of Little Brock Asher, the owner of No. 5 Mine.

"There's Miss Joelyn!" Rose cried.

"I wonder how many got hurt up there," I mumbled, more to myself than Rose.

"I hope it wadn't Daddy," Rose cried.

Fear slowly blossomed inside my chest, making it hard for me to breathe. I thought of Floyd Wilkes' ghost and knew he would somehow show me the truth if I called on him. In an effort to comfort my weeping sister, I touched her arm while trying to reassure her that things would be all right. Although I was three years younger than Rose, whose birth given name was Rosaline, I felt older and more responsible. Rose could be very emotional and often fell apart over the smallest of things. Maybe it was because Mama was so rough on her. Rose was what she called "naturally willful." Although Mama wouldn't admit it, she was stubborn too and liked things her way. Never one to put herself in someone else's shoes, Mama saw life from her own point of view and never went beyond that. Granny Lee had told me to always look at all sides of things before deciding if something was wrong or right.

Daddy seemed to understand Rose better than anyone else and was perhaps the closest to her. Sometimes when Rose behaved badly, he made a small effort to intervene between her and Mama, but in the end his efforts were futile. Mama usually made whatever Rose had done sound a lot worse than it actually was and defended whatever punishment she dealt her. Mama had a way of wearing Daddy down to the point that he would leave the house so he wouldn't have to deal with the situation anymore.

Looking as pale as a ghost Rose said, "I don't see how Mama could just leave us here! Maybe we should walk up to the mine and see what's going on!"

"No! Mama wouldn't like that," I warned.

Sliding off the swing, Rose nervously paced the length of the porch. Buster paced alongside her, wagging his tail. "We can't just sit here and do nothin! How do you know they ain't all dead? What if there was an explosion like the one that killed Granddaddy Wilkes Haley?"

"We would have heard it," I stated.

It seemed like hours before we heard or saw anything. Finally Rose cried, "Look, there's one ambulance comin' and its light is off. That means whoever's in there is dead," she sobbed.

"Stop it Rose!" I snapped. "You're makin' us both nervous!"

I knew Rose was right. Whoever was in that ambulance was dead. Just as I thought it, I heard the shrill scream of one siren and then another. "More are comin'," I said. "Somebody must be alive."

"I hope nothing's happened to Daddy or any of our kin. I can't stand waitin' much longer," Rose moaned in a voice filled with anguish and pain.

I stood up just as a screaming ambulance appeared, followed by another. I watched their red lights flash the color of blood and heard their tires spinning through the dirt leaving behind a cloud of dust. "Maybe we'll see somebody we know and they'll tell us what's going on," she offered.

"I'll bet there was a cave-in," I finally said through chattering teeth. Feeling suddenly cold in spite of the hot oppressive air, I was too nervous to sit. Making my way to the west side of the porch, I glimpsed the Asher house through the trees on Wilder Point. It stood beyond the Wilder Creek Bridge on a hill in front of a line of dark pines and fuzzy firs that blended into the ghostly white sycamores like dark bleeding inkblots. I imagined the dark faceless things that might lurk about the uneven hills behind the big three-storied house with its fractured limestone exterior. The split personality of the Asher property made me uncomfortable each time I looked it. In the front, its beauty lay in the rolling lawn, where in the summer every kind of flower imaginable trailed down the hill, enhancing the picturesque scene of lovely red maples and the pink feathery Formosa that dominated almost every corner and rise. As a child, I thought the property looked more like a glossy picture in some fancy magazine than a real place. Near the separating creek, the little stand of woods were alive with clumps of pink Formosa, bushes, and dark green broad leaf cucumber or cowcumber, as some folks called them. Not one raindrop had fallen in well over a month, yet the Asher property was as green and lush as it could be, even in dog days. Several men armed with watering hoses drenched the grass and trees daily, perpetuating most of the unnatural greenness of the foliage. The Ashers spared no expense to keep their world separate from the rest of us--at least that's what Mama said, but not in those exact words.

A large limestone wall separated us from them. Someone had taken great pains in building the three-foot barrier. I couldn't help but wonder how the Ashers felt knowing their mine had hurt or maybe killed people. Deep down inside myself, I knew men had died. I could feel some things with great certainty. According to Mama, the coal had a history of killing people. So many miners in the history of Harlan had lost their lives in mining accidents. Frustrated because Daddy wouldn't live up north where the lands were flat and there were fewer coal mines, Mama often lashed out at him, saying that miners were a dime a dozen and that she deserved something better. Daddy seldom got mad at Mama, but on one occasion, he had lost his temper. With an angry tremor in his voice, he said, "Heddy, when you throw off on the coal miner, you are throwin' off on your own Daddy and me and my brothers as well as your own! It takes some guts to climb into that dark pit ever' day. Miners ain't no dime a dozen, Heddy! We inherited the coal! You and me was born into it and we just can't walk out on what we are!" Nevertheless, Mama had a different opinion and voiced it as often as possible. "We could walk out on it! This is the land of the free and nobody has to live nowhere unless they want to. Why you and your brothers want to slave away in a place that's gonna end up killing you all is beyond me."

As a child, what little I knew of the outside world I had learned in school. Coal was a part of my everyday living as was the ghost of Uncle Floyd Wilkes and the mysterious Creekstone house with its sad haunting past. We were poor and I had accepted that. Mama and Rose never could. Mama said that money brought happiness and that poverty kept people at each other's throats. One day, I would come into the knowledge that she was wrong about the true value of money as well as many other things.

I remember the evening of the cave-in. Time crawled by at a snail's pace. When the inky darkness settled in, the screaming sirens finally ceased and Buster had calmed down. Now the trucks crept by us; no one was in a hurry any more. I could feel the oppression and almost smell death in the dry cracked earth. Somewhere in the distance, a woodpecker pecked away at a hollow tree stump, and the whippoorwills called a mournful, "whippoorwill, whippoorwill." My eyes fell on Daddy's shed that stood in the dark shadows of the willow tree. I remember staring at that shed and picturing him sitting on his little stool, carving and whittling away at a piece of wood. His expression was one of deep concentration. In the corner, there was a pile of half-finished wooden dolls.

"Why don't you fix these pieces Daddy?" I asked, feeling a little sorry for the eyeless faces and those with disjointed limbs that might never dance.

"I don't know June-Bug," he said. "I guess I am waitin' for the initiative to do it."

"But you just started on another without fixin' these first," I said, puzzled.

"I'll get around to it. Don't you worry. One day, all of them little dolls will look perfect and will dance on a string for you."

Fear surged through my chest, making it hard for me to breathe. The thought that Daddy might be lying up there under tons of coal was almost more than I could bear. My eyes fell on the big spreading willow tree in the front yard near the fence that separated our place from the road. Stepping off the porch, I walked over to the tree and parted its long spindly limbs. Taking a seat on the stool Daddy had built, I tried to still my shaking limbs. Squeezing my eyes shut, I prayed to the ghost of Floyd Wilkes. "Show me the truth Floyd Wilkes. Is Daddy all right? Please give me a sign of some kind. Please!" In the past, Floyd Wilkes' ghost had come to me only in dreams, but somehow I knew he would come to me in some other form if I called on him.

Rocking back and forth in an effort to soothe my frazzled nerves, I closed my eyes and pictured Floyd Wilkes' ghost as it looked in my dreams. He was barefoot and blonde with eyes as blue as cornflowers. Soon the world around me ceased to exist. I could no longer hear the pecking of the woodpecker or the ominous sound of roaring engines and sirens. Rose's voice became hollow and far off, like an echo from inside a bucket and then faded away. My mind flashed black and white images of the surroundings No. 5 Mine. Feeling as if I were floating high above the ground, I looked down and saw the rutted, grassless land with long, cutting tracks that ran up the hillside. Hovering above ground, I could plainly see the shaft or the opening of No. 5 Mine. Lit by several bare bulbs the gaping tunnel seemed to go on forever. As I searched the darkness, my sense of hearing seemed heightened. Somewhere a woman wept mournfully, while masculine voices blended, saying things I couldn't quite make out. Faces were blurred and unrecognizable, yet I could smell the distinctive scent of coal mingled with that of the dry dust.

No one looked my way or even noticed me. Faceless miners dressed in well-worn jackets, overalls, and brogan shoes milled around the large gaping hole, each one covered with black dust. The ghost of Floyd Wilkes dressed in clean overalls with threadbare galluses stood above the crowd. His hair was as light as pale straw. Although I couldn't see them in the distance, I already knew that his eyes were of the brightest blue--like cornflowers. I smiled in his direction and followed his gaze to the crowd of miners. There, amidst the bleak surroundings, stood people I instantly recognized. Daddy and Uncles Corbin, Harlan Ray, and Harvey James were all alive. When I turned to look for the ghost of Floyd Wilkes, it was gone. As quick as a blink, I snapped awake. In front of me, the tiny leaves of the spindly willow branches blew lightly in the hot wind. Just as I stepped out from underneath the willow tree, a panting Buster came charging towards me. His long pink tongue quivered from the heat. After reaching down and absently patting his head, I stepped up onto the porch and made an effort to comfort my weeping sister. "It's not Daddy or the uncles. Men are dead, though."

"Are you sure it ain't none of our people?" Rose cried anxiously.

"I'm sure." I answered.

"How can you know all this?" Rose asked.

"I just know," I answered.

"What if you're wrong this time?"

"I'm not. Don't worry!"

"You scare me, Junie Mae. There's somethin' wrong with a person who has visions like these. If you can really see the future, why don't you conjure up a vision to see if I'm gonna marry Bart Asher?"

Strangely relieved by a subject other than No. 5 mine, I answered, "I don't need to see a vision to tell you that marryin' Bart Asher is out of the question."

"That's all you know," she pouted.

"I don't think there's nothin' queer about me seein' and knowin' things," I said in defense. "Granny Lee told me that she had a little sister named Etta who had visions just like me. She died when she was real young. Maybe I'm like her."

"What are the visions like?" Rose questioned, with curiosity spilling out of her strange gray-blue eyes.

I mumbled something in a guarded tone, not willing to share the ghost of Floyd Wilkes with anyone other than Granny Lee.

More time passed and evening had fallen gray. The air remained still and hot. While Rose continued to pace nervously the length of the porch, I sat on the steps wishing someone would come and tell us something. What if Floyd Wilkes was wrong? My mind raced as I recalled past dreams or visions. It seemed that I had developed the knack of finding lost things after my first encounter with Floyd Wilkes' ghost. I thought of the time Buster was missing for two days. Daddy said he had just gone off hunting but I had known better. On the second night, I dreamed of Buster. I saw Floyd Wilkes' ghost standing on top of Chimney Rock. Down below the big three-tier rock, he showed me a vision of the dog with his leg caught in the jaws of a steel trap. The next morning, I told Daddy where to find him. He'd gone out looking, not so much because he believed me, but because he knew how much I loved Buster. Daddy found the dog in the very spot I had told him to look. Buster was bleeding badly from where the jaws of the steel trap had torn his leg and right foot, but he was alive. Mama treated the wound with black salve. It wasn't long before he was as good as new.

As I grew older, I began to develop a kind of sixth sense concerning places. Both the Wilder Creek Bridge and the Creekstone House on Wilder Point stirred a kind of unease deep within me. However, when it came to the people I was close to, I was sometimes at a loss, especially where Rose and my Mother were concerned. Still, a part of me believes that if I'd taken a closer look, maybe I could have prevented a lot of what would happen to us later. But after all was said and done, Granny Lee assured me that I wasn't at fault and that only God could have stepped in and changed things. I don't know. Maybe I will never know. Blinking back the tears, I turned to Rose and said, "It's getting dark. We'd better light the lamps."

"I wish Mama and Daddy would come home," Rose whimpered.

I was too tired and full of anxiety to soothe her with comforting words. My legs felt as heavy as the heat-laden air as I stumbled through the house lighting the lamps, first in the living room and then the two in the kitchen. Daddy always referred to the house as "the lodge" because Big Brock Asher had built it and once used it as a kind of hunting lodge and a place where the hunters could gather to drink and talk. Although far from being modern with its aging wallpaper, leaks, and cracks, the lodge was far nicer than the houses in the Asher mining camp. But Mama hated the lodge and the coal, and had dreams of moving up north where the land was flat and green. Rose had dreams of marrying Bart Asher and living in Creekstone House. To me, her hopes were nothing more than fairytales that she had conjured up in order to escape Mama's constant belittling of her. Unfortunately, I was the only person who was privy to Rose's lofty hopes and dreams. If Mama had known that she had so much as looked at an Asher, there would have been hell to pay. My knowing and not telling Mama would become a source of guilt and an ever-present burden throughout my early childhood.

Like Daddy and Granny Lee, I naturally accepted my surroundings, good or bad, without question. However, I'd had dreams, too -- dreams of becoming a teacher, but they stopped there. It was hard to see beyond the coal, or the summer heat, or the dead smell of the river.

Once I lit the lamps, I put away the supper and the food Mama had hastily left on the table. Afterwards, I went into the living room in order to get away from Rose's predictions of gloom and doom concerning the mine.

In the living room, I peered out the window at the darkness and beyond the dirt road where the stand of woods blocked the view of the middle fork of the Cumberland River. My mind conjured a picture of waters that lay still and stagnant with the ugly white film on its surface. In the daylight, you could see its silvery waters through the bare spots in the trees. In the winter, when the trees were naked, the river was no longer a mystery.

Rose's constant whimpering tore at my nerves. I finally told her to go about heating some of the rinse water left over from the day's washing, so Daddy could have a bath when he got home.

"There might be snakes out there! Daddy says they're blind in dog days and will strike at anything that moves!" she shuddered. Feeling my agitation rise, I decided to do it myself. "At least grab a lantern so I can see what I'm doing," I snapped. Once out in the back yard, I dipped the soapy rinse water out of the tubs and into copper kettles, which I placed on the hot burners of the cook stove in the kitchen. Everything is ready for them when they come home, I thought. Rose was never much good for chores and got out of them when she could. Nevertheless, she somehow always found the energy to sneak out off to the coal camp and talk to the Mattingly sisters.

Mama had almost stripped the sad little peach tree in the back yard bare of its limbs, which she used on Rose. The whippings, though, did nothing to cure my sister of her laziness or her willful streak. Although Rose hated the switches and the razor strap, she remained faithful to her lazy streak and continued her rebellion by sneaking up the road to the Asher camp every time she got a chance. Mama said when it came to Rose's willfulness there weren't enough trees to cure her. She also predicted that Rose would have a baby on her hip before she reached her sixteenth birthday. Mama had a habit of bringing up Daddy's youngest half-sister Marie, who bore her first child when she was only fourteen years old. Marie was the result of the brief marriage between Granny Lee and a man she had met a few years after Grandpa Chester Raymond Lee died. Unfortunately, Marie would never see her daddy except in a faded photograph that Granny kept on her dusty mantle. He'd died of a heart attack four months before she was born.

By the time Marie was twenty, she had already bore three children out of wedlock. Mama called her a disgrace and rarely missed a chance to warn Rose that she was shaping up to become a whore just like her aunt. Although Daddy rarely said anything, I could tell he was hurt. Daddy, like Granny Lee, usually made excuses for family members who had gone astray, and their excuses infuriated Mama. She would say to Daddy, "You're just like your mother! You both think that forgiveness is the answer to everything. Did forgiveness save Marie from having two more children after the first one? Don't you think it would have been better to tell or at least punish her for the wrong she done instead of forgivin' her and allowin' her to do it again?"

When Mama brought up Marie's illegitimate children, Daddy usually said nothing and walked away. His silence on the matter infuriated Mama worse than if he had argued with her.

"It's nine o'clock," Rose whimpered. "Where are they? If Daddy ain't dead, then why are they not here?"

"They'll be here soon. A lot's goin' on up there and Daddy wouldn't leave until it's all over," I said a little impatiently. My heart lurched with the sharp bang of the front screen door behind me. "Mama?" I asked expectantly. Daddy's second youngest brother Harvey James and Granny Martha Lee stood in the dark doorway. "God love you all! I'll bet the two of you are scared to death," Granny Lee cried.

Harvey James, still in his mining clothes that were never quite as dusty or black as Daddy's, took a gentle hold on Granny Lee's pudgy arm. "You sit down here, Ma," he said, steering her to Daddy's chair in the corner.

"Rose, please get your Granny a dipper of water," Harvey James gently commanded. Harvey James was an educated man whose speech lacked the long vowels typical of the native Kentucky speakers. There was a certain sophistication and quiet dignity in the way he spoke. When he finished high school, Daddy and Granny Lee had both pitched in and sent him to a trade school up in Ohio. Harvey James became a mechanical engineer but took a job with Little Brock Asher. His pay was better than that of the rest of his brothers but still not great considering what he might make in a bigger city. Granny Lee often bragged that two of her four boys graduated college. In Appalachia, having an education was a true achievement.

"Is Daddy alright?" Rose cried.

"He wasn't hurt. Your Uncle Corbin and Harlan Ray are okay too. The four of us were in another section of the mine when it caved in."

"Praise God!" Granny Lee proclaimed with pudgy outstretched arms; her hands waved upwards in praise.

"Who got killed?" I asked, dreading the answer.

Harvey James sighed tiredly and answered, "Five dead and two are buried under the coal. Men are up there trying to dig them out right now. Big Wayne Lewis got crushed, and so did the Wilson brothers. Tant Brock and Paul Winley are gone too."

"Dear God, look out for their families." Granny murmured in a prayerful voice. She was calm and stoic, but in an instant entered a rapturous, trance-like state starting with a nodding of her head. "Sha na na! Sha la la na!" Granny chanted out incoherently with her eyes squeezed shut and her pudgy arms still outstretched to heaven and flailing about wildly. Granny Lee often spoke in tongues, even when there wasn't a tragedy.

Granny Lee was of medium height and was very heavyset. Her legs were huge, reminding me of tree trunks. Her breasts were large too, and sagged down pendulously almost to her belly button. Like most Pentecostal women, she wore her dark gray-streaked hair long and fashioned into a ponytail or a braid. As in many religions, short hair was considered a sin. Mama claimed the faith, too, but stubbornly wore her dark hair shoulder length. She and Daddy belonged to the First Pentecostal Church in Evarts, but weren't regular churchgoers, and only attended in spurts. Sometimes, though, the spirit of God washed over Mama, and we would attend several Sundays in a row. Then some member of the congregation would make her mad or the preacher would preach directly at her, and we would stop going.

Harvey James said, "Now Ma, I'm going back up to the mine to see what's going on. You stay here with the girls and if you get tired, I'm sure one of them will share their bed with you."

Rose let out an audible gasp. Her big blue eyes looked almost white in the flickering lamplight. Later in the kitchen, she grabbed my sleeve and said, "I ain't sleepin' with Granny! You are! She's too fat and snores too much! If she rolled on me, I would smother to death before anyone found me!"

"Just dry the dishes," I said disgustedly. In truth, I had not wanted to share a bed with Granny Lee either, but I would, if need be.

"Ain't it a little late for you girls to be up?" Granny Lee hollered from the living room.

"I'm going to bed soon. This kitchen is too hot and it's makin' me sick," Rose whined. After drying my hands on a towel and throwing it on the sink, I walked into the living room and asked Granny Lee about Mama's brother, Purl, who was a supervisor at the mines.

"I reckon he's fine," she said, while dabbing at her sweaty face with a worn white handkerchief.

"Maybe it shoulda been him that died instead of the others!" Rose yelled from the kitchen.

A horrified look came over Granny Lee's face. She said, "Lord! Honey, you ought not say somethin' like that about your close kin."

Appearing in the living room, Rose sniffed. "He ain't no uncle of mine! Look what he did to Grandma Haley. He took her house after he married Edith and put her in a little shack across the creek. He takes her social security check every month and tells her how she can spend it! How much money do you think Grandma Haley, Mama, and her brothers have seen after he sold the mineral rights off Grandpa's land? He won't share a dime of that money with nobody. That's the reason Uncle Coy and Uncle Noah shot up his house last fall! The courts won't do a thing either. That's because Purl bought off the judge!"

Granny Lee nodded her head sadly and said, "If he wronged all them people, then he'll get his rightful punishment from God above. It's not your place to condemn him!" I stayed out of the conversation, but secretly I hated Purl too and thought he was a loathsome greedy creature for cheating Mama and her brothers out of what was rightfully theirs.

Rose laughed a harsh bitter laugh. In the lamplight, she favored Mama so much. Both had dark black hair and heart-shaped faces. Each were of medium height but had long slim arms and legs. When Rose was angry, she had Mama's pout. Only the eyes were different; where Mama's were dark brown, Rose's were a kind of gray-blue, but sometimes in a certain light they appeared almost white. Grandma Haley called them "peculiar," while Uncle Coy Haley described them as "wild." Mama seemed very uncomfortable when someone commented on the color and the strangeness of Rose's eyes, and usually changed the subject.

I didn't often agree with Rose, but this time I felt she was right and spoke up. "Why not blame Little Brock for the men's deaths? After all, it was the roof of his mine that gave out, wadn't it?"

Granny Lee said, "Now we ain't gonna blame nobody for this tragedy. Let's just pray for ever'body concerned. The Lord will take care of what he's supposed to. It's in his loving hands now."

"Mama will have plenty to say about the Ashers when she gets home. She never cared for Joelyn Asher anyhow," I stated plainly.

Granny Lee frowned in disagreement. "It seems like Mrs. Asher has been mighty good to your Mama lettin' her work up there at the big house. I know workin' at the funeral parlor pays the rent, but I do believe Miss Joelyn gives your Mama money or food for what she does up there. Your daddy told me she regularly sends you girls down clothes that her daughters can't wear no more." Pausing long enough to dab her sweaty face with the handkerchief, Granny Lee puzzled. "How long is it now that your Mama's been workin' in Big Brock Asher's funeral parlor? Seems I remember her sayin' that she was barely a teenager when she started workin' up there. I think the Ashers have been charitable to your Mama and Daddy."

I opened my mouth to speak but decided against it. I wanted to remind Granny Lee that Big Brock Asher's mine had killed Granddaddy Wilkes Haley, but I knew if I had, Granny Lee would have insisted we pray for Big Brock Asher and I wasn't in the mood for that.

Mama talked very little about her Daddy's death. I knew it hurt her too much to relive it. Mama was a person who buried hurtful things inside. She also hated the show of grief and rarely ever cried, but I knew how much she loved and missed her Daddy. Over the years, I had caught bits and pieces of her memories of the two of them wading in the creek and planting onions in the spring of each year. Mama wouldn't talk much about her little brother Floyd Wilkes, either. Once, when I asked her how he died, she raised her hand in defense and said, "You couldn't take it if I told you! You would break apart." I knew that what Mama was really saying was that she would break apart if she had to relive it, so I left her alone and eventually got the sad details from Grandma Haley who was more forthcoming.

When Mama talked about her Daddy in life, her voice became almost child-like. Her change in demeanor had both surprised and frightened me a little, because I was accustomed to seeing a woman who rarely cried and used anger as a tool to deal with whatever obstacle came her way. This was a different Mama, one with a softer, gentler side. Seeing that was like watching the sun peep out of the clouds. Sometimes when Mama was angry and rigid, I yearned for that softer side of her.

Sadly, I am not sure Rose ever saw Mama's softer, gentler side. When I told her how Mama became a different person when she talked about her Daddy, Rose laughed harshly and said, "Mama is like all them wooden dolls Daddy starts and never finishes. They just lay there in the shed missin' parts. Some of 'em's got only one eye or one leg. Mama is missin' something in her head!"

"Well, Mama's missin' parts are her own business, Rose. We all got missin' parts." I said in her defense.

Rose's voice sounded low and vindictive. "Mama is not who you think she is, Junie Mae. I learned about her long ago. You will too. It's not my place to tell you about her. I'll let you find out for yourself. You ain't ever seen her like she really is, but then you never raise the cream. Mama likes that about you! That's why you don't get the beatin's. Well, Junie Mae, I ain't like you! I can't just accept everything she says and does! Mama's not the saint you believe her to be. You've made her up in your head. If you only knowed..." her voice trailed off.

As usual, anger rose up in my throat and all I wanted to do was defend my mother. "You do things on purpose to aggravate her, Rose. You sneak off to the camp and won't do chores, and you sass her. She's your mother and you know that's wrong!" My objections sounded weak even to my own ears, for somewhere in me I knew Rose was right on some level. Mama had never shown her the kindness that she had shown me. I believe she saw Rose as more of an adversary and often tried to compete with her. For example, if the color red looked good on Rose, Mama found a blouse or sweater of the same color and wore it. If Rose curled or tinted her hair, Mama did the same with hers. I could have cut mine, colored it, and tied a purple polka-dotted bow in it and Mama would have paid me no mind. Her attention was on what Rose wore and how she fixed her hair. Mama's blatant competition with Rose was not lost on her. Once when the three of us were walking the sidewalks in Harlan, some men working on a store roof nearby whistled appreciatively in our direction. Mama giggled and said, "I'll bet they think you and me are sisters, Rose." Later, Rose made a sour face and told me, "Mama makes me sick trying to pass me off as her sister!"

"Why?" I asked puzzled. "Mama's a pretty woman, and she ain't old, Rose."

"Well, she ain't young enough to be my sister, either. Mama thinks more of herself than anyone else in the world. You'd see that if you paid attention."

In retrospect, maybe I was naive, or maybe I didn't want to see Mama as self-centered, vindictive, or hurtful. To me, she was a hard worker, a deep scrubber, and a hater of the coal. As a child, I had watched her fight against the coal with all she had. She would scrub and bleach the floors and take the clothes off the line the moment they dried in order to keep the black dust from settling on them. However, the coal was king and it always won in the end. No matter how hard Mama fought it, it came back in some form.

I heard Mama and Daddy come in sometime late that night. Rose woke too, jumped off the bed, ran to the doorway, and called out for Daddy. Mama came to the doorway instead, holding the coal oil lamp. Sitting up in bed, I squinted sleepily, while searching the hollow points of Mama's face in the dancing flicker of the lamp. I wanted to reach out to Mama, but you didn't just reach out for Mama. You let her come to you.

"Go back to sleep girls. Daddy and your uncles are all right." Mama's voice sounded deep and tired.

Rose pouted, "I want to see Daddy!"

"You can see him in the mornin'. Go back to bed."

Daddy's tired hollow face appeared in the doorway. Black with coal dust, he called to us. "Come here Rosie. You too, June-Bug." Hugging us tightly to him, he said, "I'm all right. You two get some sleep."

After he and Mama left the room, Rose said of Mama, "I could ask her to lend me her hairbrush and she'd say no! No is the only word she ever says to me!"

"Let's go to sleep," I said, fearful that Mama would hear her.

It took a long time for me to fall asleep there in the dark, with only the light of the moon shining on the tree branches outside my window. I thought of Daddy and how brave he acted on most occasions, but knew the cave-in must have frightened him. In a way, Daddy was like Mama and had his secrets. Sometimes, standing near the door of his shed when he was whittling on parts of the eyeless dolls, I would see him looking beyond the wood into a world that was far out of my reach. Maybe his withdrawal from the present was the reason for what I called "the doll graveyard."

In retrospect, Daddy was not much out of the ordinary in some ways, but in others, he was the deepest well. Like Mama, he carefully hoarded his secrets as a frightened little old woman might hoard money in a jar. To the best of my recollection, I was sure that neither he nor Mama took the time to learn each other's secrets. The coal had stolen away their attention. The coal was good for stealing attention and splitting people apart. It had done so for centuries.

In those days of the 1940's, children who grew up in Eastern Kentucky hardly saw anything outside of the mountains, rivers, creeks, and coal. Their parents talked about the conditions of the mine every night. The people who lived in the poverty-stricken mining camps had grown accustomed to poverty and thought little of the hardship. In those days, many families pulled together in solidarity, shared, and made do with what little they had. Looking back, I realize that our family was not as disadvantaged as most. The rooms of the lodge were much bigger than the rooms in the camp. The kitchen, for instance, was long and wide so Mama had lots of room to prepare meals. We also had grass in the summer at least in the front yard, and our outdoor toilet was reasonably clean and used only by us. In some camps, several families had to share one outhouse. The common bond that we shared with the people in the camp was our dependence on the Asher Coal Company. Mama didn't like the idea that we were indebted to them or anyone else for that matter; in reality, without the Ashers we might have been in much worse shape. Daddy was accustomed to the coal and hard work. Like most of the miners in our community, he accepted our situation for what it was. Like many other men, he went off to work, earned his wage, and then came home hoping to find some peace, but finding peace with Mama was almost impossible. She was like the river current that often shifted in different directions. One never knew where she was going or what she would do.

The next morning after the cave-in, I awoke to the rattle of pots and pans in the kitchen. I could smell Mama's biscuits baking in the oven and hear Uncle Corbin's keen stuttering voice. When Uncle Corbin was upset, his stuttering grew worse. The thought of a union coming in had rattled him badly.

"Th- th la-a-bor u-u-nion will be -be -be all o -o -o over th that place to da -day -day and ev -ev -er day fr-fr-from now on!"

Daddy said, "They probably will, and it's gonna start something, all right."

Uncle Corbin said, "I wo-won't join no-no-no u-u-union! Th--they don-don't do-do- noth-noth in but cau-cause kill-kill-killings."

Daddy chuckled and warned, "You gotta go with what the majority decides on, Corbin. It's as simple as that!"

"The- ther-there is-is dea-death-in ev-ev-every mi-mi-mine, Ralph! You-you-you-can-can can't mak-make a mi-mi-mine much sa-safer! Har-Harvey-Ja-ja-James tri-tri-tried to-to-to el-tell Ash-Ash-Asher tha-that som-som-som of-of-of the woo-woo-wood tim-tim-timber be-be-beams hol-hol-holding- up-up the roo-roof was -was rot-rot-rotten; he-he-he would-would-wouldn't lis-lis-listen! He-he-he wa-wa-was prob-probably dr-dr-drunk like-like al-al-always."

Daddy nodded and said, "He drinks whiskey like water and has since I've known him. Poor fellar's just getting worse every day."

"Poor fellar!" Mama laughed bitterly. "Ralph Lee, you take the cake! How can you make excuses for a man whose carelessness took miners away from their wives and children? He's a ragin' drunk! Joelyn Asher tries her best to hide his whiskey problem from everybody, but people know how many times she's sneaked him off hospitals to dry him out. Don't do no good. One time he escaped out a hospital window on a bed sheet." Mama laughed. Daddy and Uncle Corbin soon joined in.

Daddy asked, "How did you find out a thing like this, Heddy?"

"I heard her and her Mama talking one day while I was cuttin' up chicken in their kitchen. They just prattled on like I wadn't there. Joelyn was boo-hooing about how the hospital way up north had called to tell her that Little Brock had escaped through a window on a bed sheet. She whined to her mother about how she'd got two of the stable men to go up there and find him and bring him home."

In the other bed, Rose slept soundly. Her naturally curly dark hair partially obscured her lovely face. I studied her long dark eyelashes and her full lips in the morning light and wondered what it was like to be this beautiful. Unfortunately, I didn't have Mama's tiny frame or exotic looks. I was more like Grandma Haley's lighter haired bunch, but a little stocky and shorter in stature like the Lee women. I considered myself with my blunt cut hair as being simple in appearance, and I certainly wouldn't stand out in any crowd. However, the passing of time would teach me a valuable lesson about beauty and how having it didn't always guarantee women happy lives. Mama had obviously learned that lesson too, and warned Rose repeatedly that her looks could either save or ruin her. She would tell Rose, "You be a good girl and save yourself for someone who will love you. Don't do like your Aunt Marie and give yourself to any man who looks at you." Mama had never given me the "beauty speech." I guess she didn't think I had the kind of exotic features that could either save or ruin me. I was well aware that I wasn't much out of the ordinary when it came to looks. Thankfully, Granny Lee had taught me that true beauty comes from the inside. She said, "A person can be as old as the hills and still be beautiful."

Outside the bedroom widow, the sun hovered over the trees a light touch of yellow. Padding to the kitchen, I saw Daddy at the head of the table drinking coffee; his plate of food remained untouched. Uncle Corbin forked into his gravy, then looked up at me, smiled, and stuttered "Goo goo good mor mor-ning young'in."

Daddy rose from his chair and embraced me. "I'm so glad you are alright Daddy," I said, feeling his big strong hands on my back. Daddy's dark eyes looked wearily into mine. "You doing alright, June-Bug?" His voice sounded low and tired. I nodded and then took a chair beside Uncle Corbin.

"Is Granny Lee still here?" I asked.

Daddy said, "No. Harvey James took her home with him. She was plenty tired."

"Your sister gettin' up?" Mama asked, placing a hot biscuit onto my plate.

"I reckon she's tired from last night," I said, not touching the biscuit or the greasy fried eggs in the bowl.

Mama said, "We are all tired. You go on to school. Rose can stay here and put on a pot of beans and ham. She don't do nothin' there anyways and ain't made a passin' grade in years."

Daddy shook his head sadly and said, "I thought she was doin' better this year. Nobody showed me a grade card."

Mama laughed sourly and said, "You ain't never asked! Rose is wastin' her time in that school. She could be here helpin' me instead!"

. "No Heddy! She is to stay in that school. Learnin' is the only thing that I can give my girls. I'll have a talk with her when this thing at the mine has settled," he said stubbornly.

Mama tossed back her shoulder-length black hair, then reached for a few sticks of wood out of the wood box and then stoked the woodstove. "If you think Rose is interested in readin' and writin', then you don't know her very well." Fixing her dark eyes on Daddy she said, "Rose ain't school material, Ralph. She would rather run the roads or hang out at the camp. I've caught her there three times in the last month. God only knows how many times her and the Mattingly girls have left school without me knowin' about it."

Daddy was quiet for a few minutes before saying, "Today's not the day for us to go into this."

Uncle Corbin said, "You-you wa-wait! They-they- wi-ill be wa, wantin' to u-u-unionize us, th--th-then ther-ther-there-wi--will be st-st-strikes li-li-like the-there was at Ev- Eva-arts mine! No-nobody ca-ca-can live off-off the str-strike pay-pay."

Pouring coffee into Daddy's cup Mama stated, "Little Brock Asher would rather shut down that mine than let a union come in and tell him how to run things."

Daddy remarked of Little Brock Asher, "He's got contracts to fill. He'd lose his hind end if he closed down."

Mama started to relate, "Old Brock Sr. was a smaller operator than his son and got all his men to sign a yellow dog contract. Daddy never believed in the union and signed. That's how he got that house on Sutter's Creek. Out of Big Brock Asher! Big Brock knew about Daddy's influence with the other miners so he allowed him to pay the smallest amount he could afford for the house and land. The other miners went along with Daddy, but a lot of 'em held it against him because he got a house and some land out of Big Brock. Most forgave him eventually, though, because they knowed he would have signed the contract without Big Brock tellin' him to do it. Nobody could afford to stir the cream with Asher. People were just too poor."

Mama continued on, "When Big Brock's mine exploded and killed Daddy and all them other miners, he sold his troubles to someone else and got out of it free as the breeze. He didn't need the mines no more, 'cause he'd already made a fortune at the Company Store stealin' off the miners. The prices of his food was two times as high as anywhere else, and he'd get mad if he found out people went somewheres else to buy groceries. Them widows of them miners was mad when they heard he'd sold out, so a bunch of them got together and threw rocks through his windows. He finally settled with the women just to keep the peace. He couldn't have people thinkin' bad of him. I'm guessin' the sum was small, but back then a bird in the hand was better than two in the bush." Her voice sounded vindictive in remembrance. "Things got worse, though. When the new mine owner heard that the miners was tryin' to organize a union, he sent them eviction notices. All them families was out in the cold within a week. I remember how people went about beggin' the city officials for food, but couldn't get nothin'. The Red Cross didn't help much either. All they gave out was a few pitiful bags of flour. We was better off than most, because we had a home but still didn't have much to eat. Mama never complained about a thing," she said bitterly. "Old Brock Asher rewarded her by giving her the house that Daddy had been payin' on and twenty acres free and clear. The truth is greedy old' Purl is the only one who has ever profited off it. He sold them mineral rights off the land and bragged to anybody who would listen how much he got. He never offered the rest of us a dime. Of course, Mama never said a word to him about it."

After a few minutes of silence, Mama looked at me and commanded, "You get Rose up and tell her to come on in here before breakfast gets cold."

3 THE DEATH OF FLOYD WILKES

The morning after the mining disaster remains vivid in my mind. I recall walking down the dirt road beyond our home with all its ruts and sinkholes with Buster by my side, as always. Hugging my schoolbooks to my chest, I listened to all the early morning sounds. Birds chirped in the trees and no wind rustled through the leaves. I remember how everything seemed to have stopped all at once. The river stunk but its waters seen through the branches remained still and unmoving. When I reached the main highway, I saw little traffic. There was a small rudimentary shelter built by the county for the schoolchildren to stand underneath during cold weather, as well as two long roadside benches for them to sit on while waiting for the school bus. I looked for the Mattingly sisters and children from the camp but not one child showed up. I must have stood waiting for over an hour before Amity Smith came by in his Daddy's truck, stopped, and informed me that there would be no school because of the cave-in. I had seen him and his sister a few times at school but had never talked to them before that morning. The Smiths weren't from the camps, so none of the camp children associated with them mainly because they lived on a farm instead of a shack in a muddy coal camp. The older boys, especially, were green with envy because Amity had access to his father's truck and often drove to school. Many of the miners in the camp didn't own a truck and the ones who did seldom allowed their teenage sons the privilege of driving it to school. In those days, a good running truck or car was considered a luxury that not many could afford on a poor miner's salary.

Billy Ray Wilkins, who was often called "Bully," and Tommy Roberts were among the tough boys who often booed, hissed, and threatened to whoop Amity Smith. However, he paid them no mind and drove past as if he hadn't heard one thing out of them. The Smiths were neighbors of ours, but we'd never associated with them. I knew Mr. Smith farmed and owned a small but thriving lumber mill, while his Daddy taught agriculture at the Harlan High School. Not even a mile from us, I could see the Smith place from the road. I had always thought the big white farmhouse was pretty, standing there sandwiched between two long green fields.

Now, a blue-eyed and dimpled Amity Smith stood staring at me from behind the wheel of his daddy's truck. "Why don't you hop up in here and I'll give you a lift back to your place, Junie Mae?" he suggested as easily as one might ask for change on a dollar.

Feeling the blood rush to my face, I hugged my books closer to my chest and stammered, "I'll just walk back. It ain't far."

"It's gonna get hot. Hop on in here and let me take you back to your lane, at least."

"I don't know you," I said, and began walking back in the direction of the lane.

"Suit yourself," he yelled. "I didn't aim to scare you."

"You didn't scare me. Nothin' scares me much," I yelled over my shoulder.

I remember the sound of his laughter to this very day. His spontaneous guffaws seemed to go on forever. His laughter both embarrassed and irked me, yet a part of me had somehow known that this wouldn't be the last time that I would hear it.

I was sorry that there would be no school. The fall session had just started. School was important to me; I rarely missed a day, sometimes attending when I was sick. Learning was an outlet for me. I loved reading, and had taken it up upon myself to read Charles Dickens's classic Great Expectations. As a young girl, I struggled with the complicated language but I could understand most of it. I especially enjoyed the main character Pip's adventurous nature, as well as the mysterious Miss Havisham whose fiancé jilted her at the altar. Left with only a wedding cake, Miss Havisham had stopped all her clocks but never changed out of her wedding dress. To me, this aspect of the story was very interesting and thought-worthy. I had finally concluded that he must have hurt her beyond belief to cause her to stop time and stay in a wedding dress that was sure to rot off of her eventually.

Sometimes I would stare out the window at Creekstone and imagine it was Satif House. There were many similarities between the two places in my opinion. The darkness of the woods behind Creekstone House paralleled the dark atmosphere surrounding Satif House. The dryness and dust associated with Satif House reminded me of the lingering coal dust that settled on Mama's white bed sheets if left out on the clothesline. In further comparison, rich people owned both homes, and, like Pip, I often found myself daydreaming about what it would be like to live in a place of such wealth. Pip understood that he was poor and had nothing in common with Miss Havisham or her rich niece Estella. Like Pip, I was well aware of the class system early on and the differences in them and us. To my mind's eye, the Ashers with their big fancy house seemed unreal and completely unrelated to us in any way, or so I thought then. But as time passed, I would come to the realization that our family was connected to the Ashers in more ways than one.

. Miss Joelyn Asher was the only Asher who seemed real to me. I had seen her often but usually from a distance. Sometimes, though, I would catch a peak of her through a crack in the front door when she paid a call on Mama. Miss Joelyn sometimes sent Rose and me boxes of various catalogs and movie star magazines. One or two of them had featured Roy Rogers and Gene Autry on their covers. Rose was stuck on Gene Autry. Secretly, I was too, but settled for Roy Rogers to placate her for a little while. Rose had fantasies of meeting and marrying Gene Autry, but her fascination for him fizzled out as soon as she caught a glimpse of Bart Asher on the bridge or across the creek. I knew at a very young age that Rose would never give up on the idea of marrying Bart. Even if she had her pick of the richest, most handsome men on earth, Bart Asher would stand far above the rest. She had wanted him as a husband and thought doing so would be as simple as skimming water into a bucket from the spring. Rose's lofty dreams irritated the realistic aspects of my own personality. My dreams were more humble and lacked the luster of a big fairytale wedding and living in a big house with servants. The things I wanted out of life had little to do with movie stars or a rich boy who was clearly out of my reach. My mind had sketched out a little house in some quiet corner of Harlan, where children played on the sidewalks and wore shoes instead of going barefoot. I would have some nice cream-colored shades over my windows and a little shade lamp that cast a circle of light on whatever book I was reading. I'd get up every morning and walk to the big gray school building on the outskirts of Harlan where I would teach a reading class to small interested children.

According to Mama, my dreams of being a teacher were just as unrealistic as Rose's dream of marrying Gene Autry. She'd scoff every time I mentioned going to college. "Junie Mae, you've got to have money to go to college. Where do you think you're goin' to get it? We can barely afford a sack of meal!"

If in hearing distance, Daddy often intervened and told her that it was wrong of her to destroy and shoot down my hopes and dreams. He would say, "Heddy, you can't take away her dreams. How do you know she won't make it to college?"

Mama's favorite saying was "Unless a big sack of money falls from out of the sky into her lap there's no hope for college. Why should I get her hopes up for nothin'? It's better to tell it straight, that way no one's disappointed!"

Daddy would heave a sigh, "She's a little girl, Heddy! All little girls have dreams, don't they -- didn't you?"

"What chance do my girls have here in this place? The best they'll get is a coal miner and live in a coal camp. If we lived up north, there might be a chance for them to marry somebody different, but you can't see past the damned coal!" Although Mama could be persuasive, the one thing she couldn't do was persuade Daddy to move up north; it wasn't from lack of trying. She would create a picture of miles of flat land dotted with quaint little farmhouses with livestock and indoor plumbing. Mama had never been up north or for that matter away from Harlan County, and what she knew of Indiana came mostly from Granny Lee who got her information from her oldest son, Larkin, who had settled there years before.

Walking the lane leading home, I searched for the small slice of river showing through the trees and decided that I would rather sit on the big rock and stare at the slimy river than go home and listen to Mama and Rose fight. The two of them could not be in the same room together very long without arguing. Sometimes the reasons for their fights were so petty, it was hard to tell just what had started it.

Walking to the edge of the road and parting back the tree limbs, I stooped to dodge the wide cow-cumber leaves. As children, Rose and I had twisted the broad, limber leaves into drinking cups. Sometimes when it rained hard we would sit under the trees, bend back the leaves, and let the cold rainwater run onto our tongues.

When the tide was high, the waters rushed, swirled, and gurgled at the base of the rock, but now the river was low and calm. I so missed the gurgling and the frothy bubbles. Rose and I had decided unanimously to name the rock "The Play Place." For some reason, it seemed to suit it so well. Placing my books protectively beneath a bush, I carefully climbed upon the rock. Once on its flat top, I sat down and hugged my knees. In the distance, the sun looked almost orange in the light blue sky. Its bright rays hugged the treetops and made the water sparkle like tiny beads of glass. My eyes sought the small island that forked the river. I studied the stand of crooked water birch and the sand and thought of Floyd Wilkes. Somehow, I had known that as a child he had played on the rock where I sat and had run barefoot through the wind and sands, dodging the low hanging limbs of the trees in the islands. Floyd Wilkes' presence was everywhere in the little warm wind that blew its breath across my face, bare arms, and legs. The hairs on my arms stood up and there was a prickle about my neck. I recall turning my head apprehensively, thinking that he was behind me, then in front of me. At one point, I thought I saw his pale blonde hair and then his face playfully peeping at me from a little gap in the stand of trees. I could have sworn that I heard a boyish laugh above the wind. I was not exactly scared -- just curious. Later, I asked Grandma Haley if Floyd Wilkes had ever played near the rock or on the island. She told me that both he and Mama used to sit on that rock and fish. Grandpa Haley had a little boat and every so often, Mama and Floyd Wilkes took it out and banked it on the sandy island where they played for hours.

Somehow, I had known things about Mama and Floyd Wilkes. No one had told me much but I knew the two were close as children. Mama was three years older than he was but acted as his mother by cooking special meals and endlessly catering to his needs. Grandma Haley said Floyd Wilkes had called Mama "Eddy" instead of "Heddy" because he couldn't pronounce the H. He had still called her Eddy even after he had grown older. Mama had loved Floyd Wilkes like no other, and couldn't hear his name without blinking back tears. I believe that when he died he had taken the best part of her with him. I had kept this presumption to myself, though. I had reasoned that Mama was hard and something had made her this way. I was sure that people were not born hard and unyielding, and that it was the twists and turns in life that molded them to think and act in certain ways.

Through the years I found out how Floyd Wilkes had died through bits and pieces I had heard from various family members. Floyd Wilkes' death happened just a little beyond two years after the mine explosion that killed Grandpa Wilkes Haley. He had just turned thirteen that summer when he was killed on the old plank bridge on the backside of Harlan. A drunken college student had ran him over with his car and left him to die. According to Grandma Haley, he was killed mid-July when the blackberries had ripened to their peak. She had recounted how he had gotten up early that morning and had caught a ride to the Daisy Camp, where he'd picked blackberries as a child. Before he had left the house, he'd told Mama that he'd planned to sell his berries to a fruit vendor in town. He also promised to share his berry money with her, so that she could order the butterfly print material she had wanted out of the Sears and Roebucks catalog.

After several hours passed and Floyd Wilkes had not returned home, Grandma Haley and Mama finally set out looking for him. Walking in the direction of the plank bridge that eventually led off to main highway, they had spied a line of traffic. Grandma Haley said, "I knowed all them cars lined up had something to do with Floyd Wilkes. It was the most awful feeling. I got sick to my stomach. I remember a man finally got out of his car and told us that a young man had been killed on the bridge. I knowed it was Floyd Wilkes. When we finally walked around all them cars, I seen the bridge and a crowd of people gathered around something. I remember hollering, 'Let me see Floyd Wilkes. I know it's him. I'm his mother!' When the people moved aside, I saw a little colored boy cradling Floyd Wilkes little blonde head in his arms. Poor little barefooted boy had blood all over his arms and clothes. He was crying and wouldn't let go of Floyd Wilkes. A police officer kept saying, 'Now boy, you let go of him! He's gone You can't help him now! Let his mother say goodbye to him.' I felt sorry for the little colored boy and asked him to let me see my boy. I remember pulling Floyd Wilkes from his arms. I held his bloody body as long as I could before I had to let them put him on the stretcher. What else could I do? My poor boy was gone and I knowed it! His body was as limber as a rag. Your Mama just stood there lookin' shocked out of her mind. I wished she hadn't seen what she seen. Maybe she would have been different today. It's no telling what seein' him like that done to her. No tellin'!"

Grandma Haley could tell the story of Floyd Wilkes' death without shedding a tear, but I could see the tremble of her lips and feel the tide of her emotion. Maybe she had somehow made peace with his death, whereas Mama never could. I instinctively knew that Mama carried with her the horrible picture of Floyd Wilkes lying there covered in blood and in the arms of the little colored boy.

Several times during the course of my childhood, I had dreamed of Floyd Wilkes. Blood matted his light hair and ran in streams down the planks mingling with that of the purple juice from the smashed berries. Poor little Floyd Wilkes; all he was trying to do was sell his berries so he would have money to give to his sister for some butterfly print material. Grandma Haley said the young man who had killed Floyd Wilkes never spent a day in jail because his Daddy was wealthy and owned a string of hardware stores. Grandma Haley's voice always quivered when she spoke of the young man who had killed Floyd Wilkes. "A man on the bridge told me that he'd heard that drunkard say that my boy was just a little pauper. I guess he thought he shouldn't be punished for killing a poor boy."

After sitting on the rock for what seemed like hours, I finally walked home, and found Rose in the kitchen chopping up ham pieces to put into the big pot of pintos soaking in water. Her pretty face was screwed up in a frown. "There was no school, I'm guessin'! Could have told you that."

I shrugged, putting my schoolbooks on the chair and laughed. "What do you know about school? You can barely spell cat! Where's Mama?"

"She's up at the funeral home probably helpin' get them miners' bodies ready for the funeral. The two miners that was buried in the cave-in are dead," Rose said flatly. "They dug 'em out early this mornin'. Uncle Corbin was here a little while ago lookin' for Mama to let her know."

"Who was they?" I asked.

Rose answered, "That new man, Todd Worley, and Eddie Singleton. Todd supposedly just got engaged to Widow Hattabaugh's only daughter, Sarah Sue. Eddie wadn't even twenty-one yet," she said, plopping big pieces of ham in the kettle.

"Let me do that," I offered. I knew the ham pieces were too large. Mama liked small chunks in beans. Rose handed me the knife and I went about chopping the ham in smaller pieces. Rose said, "How is it you are always concerned with how Mama does things? You know there is other ways to do things! Don't mean her way is always right!"

Sighing, I said, "It's better to do things her way than to have to hear her go on and on about it. She'll no doubt be tired and ill before the day is over."

"I won't marry a coalminer," Rose said out of the blue. "I ain't goin' through what Sarah Sue is right now." Pursing her lips, her unsettling eyes regarded me mysteriously. "I could have been Sarah Sue."

"What do you mean?" I asked.

"I mean I was seeing Todd Worley for a while. He was sweet on me and used to sneak over to the Mattingly's just to see me. He only started seeing Sarah Sue because I wouldn't give him a chance. He told me this not long before he got killed. It was me he wanted to marry -- not her."

"I never knowed this," I said in surprise. "You never told me."

She shrugged. "It didn't amount to much. He was a coalminer and talked about nothing else but the mine. I got sick of hearin' about it from both him and Daddy. I told you, Junie Mae, I ain't marryin' no coalminer. I got better things in mind."

"There ain't any men around here that don't work in the mines, Rose! Being picky will just make you an old maid. I ain't getting married," I said, dumping shaved ham in the large kettle. "I don't want to be nobody's wife!"

Rose laughed and said, "You'll change your mind!"

As usual, her thoughts were on Bart Asher. Smiling, she said, "I've knowed I wanted to marry Bart Asher since I was five years old. Todd Worley was nice, but he wadn't no Bart Asher."

"Sure, you and the camp girls are all going to marry men with money. It's just another one of your fairytales," I laughed.

"You're Mama made over! You think you're above it all and know more than anybody else. Well, Mama ain't nothin' but a hypocrite. She's always telling us how we can't cross over the Asher fence when she's done it herself." Licking her lips decidedly, Rose went on, "Mama had her heart broke by Little Brock Asher. Grandma Haley told me all about it that summer she had us pickin' beans in her garden. Why do you think she hates Miss Joelyn so much?"

"It ain't true," I said weakly, though knowing there was something to it.

"You know Grandma Haley don't lie, Junie Mae Lee. Look up here and listen to me! Mama lies! Mama lies!"

I turned my back to Rose. I needed time to think about Mama and Little Brock Asher. Rose grabbed my arm but I shrugged her off and screamed, "Leave me alone!"

"Don't act like this, Junie Mae! You ain't some little child no more. You're growin' up! You need to act like a grownup!"

I wanted to laugh in her face and tell her that some part of me realized Mama wasn't perfect, and that I had always known she had feelings for Little Brock Asher. Maybe my gift of knowing had something to do with it, or maybe I sensed that Mama's deep hatred of Joelyn Asher went far beyond simple envy of what she had. Whatever the case, watching her throughout the years would teach me some things I never wanted to learn.

Rose had gone to the kitchen window and pulled back the curtain. Following her gaze, I saw parts of Creekstone house through the naked spaces in the trees. It had so many arched windows, and the shutters, black in color, favored thick eyebrows. My eyes studied the multiple chimneys that jutted out of the steep angular roof. Granny Lee was right: there was not another house like it around Harlan. It was a beautiful place, but there had been too many deaths there for it to be serene and happy. I recalled Granny Lee's potent words: Homes carry the history of their owners inside their little cracks and crevices. I had sensed a presence of darkness hovering about the trees surrounding the house, especially in the early mornings after a scorching hot night. Little jets of steam would rise eerily up from out of the trees and crags reminding me of restless little ghosts.

With a sigh, Rose mused, "I wonder what happened to Little Brock and Mama?" When I didn't answer, Rose pursed her lips in concentration, finally referring to a summer evening two years earlier. As she recounted that evening I remembered it all too well. It was near dark and the frogs croaked in the distant woods. Rose and I were walking in the direction of Wilder Creek Bridge as we often did in the summer evenings. Still wearing her yellow sundress, I thought Rose always looked older then her age. Having just spent a whole day at the Harlan County Fair, we were still excited from having ridden our first Ferris wheel. I was telling Rose how the Ferris wheel had tickled my stomach when I first heard something like a moan coming from the vicinity of the creek. After hearing the groan for the second time, I walked to the edge of the woods and cautiously parted some tree limbs. There on the rocky creek bank sat Little Brock Asher looking disheveled in a white dress shirt that was only half-tucked in his rumpled slacks. In his right hand was a whiskey bottle. Fearful, Rose grabbed my sleeve cowering behind me. "That's Little Brock Asher and he's drunk as a skunk," she frantically whispered.

Upon seeing Rose and me, Little Brock stood up unsteadily then staggered toward us; he stared hard at Rose and spoke to her. "Heddy Mae?" It was a muddled question. Staring harder at Rose, he shook his head in confusion. "Heddy, come here and talk to me. I've been waiting for so long."

Finally speaking, I said, "This is not Heddy Mae, Mr. Asher. It's Rose, and I'm Junie Mae Lee."

Narrowing his eyes in bewilderment, he slurred, "Oh, of course. I thought..." His voice trailed off. With bottle still in hand, he staggered sideways before landing on the rocks, luckily in a sitting position.

"Let's go get Daddy. He's liable to fall and hurt himself bad on them rocks," Rose urged.

Back at the house, Daddy was just sitting down to supper when we told him about Little Brock. Rose said, "Daddy, I think he's too drunk to get up the hill by hisself. He was staggerin' all over the place with that whiskey bottle."

Shoving back his plate Daddy said in a weary voice, "I'll go."

Mama looked perturbed. "Why not just let him stay where he is? A good dunk in the cold creek might sober him up."

Daddy said, "I've seen him like that before. Believe me; he would drown if he was to stumble in the water. I'll be back directly."

Mama pushed her own plate back, rose, went to the window, peered out, and whispered, "Damned drunken fool."

In a low, cautious tone, Rose said, "He thought I was you, Mama. He called me Heddy Mae, and said he had been waiting a long time to talk to you! Why would he want to talk to you, Mama?"

Mama spun around and glared at Rose. "How would I know why he'd want to talk to me? You can't pay no mind to a drunkard. He was talking out of his head. Now you and Junie Mae sit down and eat your supper."

The sound of Rose's voice had drawn me out of the past. "Well? What do you think of him mistakin' me for Mama? Surely you ain't forgot how Daddy had to go fetch one of the hired farm hands to help get him back up the hill and to the house. Little Brock Asher was soused and I think it had something to do with Mama. Maybe he still loves her."

Rolling my eyes upwards in disgust, I told Rose for the hundredth time how she was living in a fairy tale. "If he loved her so much then why is he with somebody else?"

Rose shrugged and said, "Maybe Big Brock put a stop to it with Mama bein' poor and all that. She'll never say why, anyway. The truth ain't in Mama."

"It's none of our business," I said, though I was also curious as to what the two of them had meant to each other.

Twirling a strand of her hair Rose laughed mischievously and said, "I don't guess Mama was as smart as Miss Joelyn. If I get a good hold on Bart Asher I won't be as stupid as Mama and allow some old man to run me off."

"Sure, Rose," I said sarcastically. "You'll out-do Mama, God, and everybody."

"You'll see," she said smugly. "I'll have Bart Asher!"

Mama constantly warned Rose and me to stay away from the stone wall, and never go onto the Asher property unless she gave us permission. I obeyed out of fear of her wrath, but Rose disobeyed and often caught the attention of Bart Asher. He'd sometimes scale the wall and the two of them would talk or sometimes play in the circle of woods around the property. Why they were never caught is a wonder. Maybe it was because they hadn't spent large chunks of times together. Even as a small child, Rose was smitten with Bart and had informed me of all the things he had told her during their stolen playtimes. She'd brag about how far he could throw a stick or how well he rode a horse. On lookout, I'd watch her and Bart from the Wilder Creek Bridge. Since a little thatch of woods obscured much of the bridge and the Asher land from Mama's view, I could watch the two of them without much worry of what Mama might see. It was only when she worked at the Asher house that I worried about her seeing them.

Once in awhile, I'd catch a glimpse of Bart's sisters, Bitsy and Charlene, playing down by the creek. Sometimes their father would set them on their ponies and I'd see him leading them down to the bridge and back. When the girls saw me standing in the yard they usually waved in a friendly manner; I would return the wave but hadn't made strides to talk to them. Mama would have never allowed for that. She'd called them spoiled brats and said that they wasted more food in a week than we ate in a year. Because of Rose's fascination for Bart, watching the Ashers had become a kind of pastime activity for me. Although I was curious about the Ashers, they would never become an obsession to me as they would with Rose.

One summer when I was nine years old, Daddy took Rose and me to the Asher General Store. Neither of us had ever been in the store. Mama wouldn't allow us to go with her when she traded. I vividly recall the layout of the store with its dark wood counter where people sat on stools sipping sodas and talking about everyday life. Along the wall behind the counter, there were dozens of jars of assorted candies and cookies, as well as a long meat case filled with different types of sandwich meats and cold cuts. I remember holding on tight to Daddy's big hand, while at the same time worrying about what Mama would say when she found out that he'd bought us there. Miss Joelyn was very kind to Rose and me. She had made us root beer floats and then gave each of us a sack of candy. Mama somehow found out about our trip to Asher's General Store. She was livid and started screaming at Daddy, "I told you not to take them girls to that store!"

Daddy looked crestfallen and completely surprised by Mama's hateful outburst. "I don't understand you, Heddy! Joelyn Asher treated our girls well and gave them treats they never get at home! What's so wrong about that?"

"What's wrong is that we can't give them these kinds of things! I don't want my girls grievin' over things we can't afford to buy on a coalminer's pay! You know that store ain't nothin' more than a glorified company store!"

Looking confused, Daddy said, "I don't believe it is, Heddy. Their prices ain't no higher than Big Jack's or Buster Holmes' stores. Besides, our girls know what poor is. You remind them every day. They know where they live, Heddy! They know we can't live like the Ashers! What should we do, keep them from the candy aisles in all the stores?"

As usual, Mama reminded Daddy of the Daisy Coal Camp she'd lived in before her own Daddy went to work for Big Brock Asher. Up until that day, I had known next to nothing about her early childhood, Daisy Camp, or her friendship with Joelyn Asher. With the passing of time, I would learn much more. Mama told people what she wanted them to know. She did it in small spurts leaving them to guess the rest. I can still hear her voice recounting those hard childhood days in Daisy Camp and how she and Joelyn Asher were like sisters. "Her people lived right beside us in a worse lookin' shack than ours. I can remember Joelyn being so hungry that once she ate too many green apples and had the runs for weeks. Them green apples gave her worms that nearly killed her. People in Daisy Camp used to say old Vilene Roll, Joelyn's mother, could make ten meals out of one soup bone! I'll tell you what, if a piece of shale hadn't fell on Ivan's head and killed him, they would still be living in some mining shack, and Joelyn would have married a poor miner like I did! Do you know that as soon as the mine owner settled with Vilene she bought a big house in Harlan, and when the children was old enough she sent Jimmy Lee and Joelyn to fancy business schools up north? When Joelyn came back to Harlan, she went straight to the Asher mines and got that secretarial job. She got herself a rich man all right, but inside she's still that dirty, scraggly, little-green-apple eatin' girl from Daisy Camp!" Sometimes Mama's voice sounded sharp and bitter when talking the Daisy Mining Camp.

On the day she'd found out Daddy had taken us to Asher's store she'd brought up the story of Joelyn Asher and how seeing her gave me and Rose false hope for our future. Again, Daddy's face wore a baffled expression. When he reached out to soothe her, Mama angrily shrugged his hand off her shoulder, and said in a vicious voice, "Our girls ain't goin' to marry rich! When they see her, they see hope when there ain't none! Can't you see what I mean?" Her dark eyes pleaded into his.

Shaking his head sadly, Daddy said, "No, Heddy, I'm afraid I'm lost on this one. But I'll respect your wishes, anyway, and not take them to

Asher's store no more."

Thinking back in retrospect, I had never seen Mama socialize with Miss Joelyn or invite her into the lodge even when she graciously brought us her daughter's hand-me-downs or leftover goodies from one of their social gatherings. Not that Mama was outwardly rude; her usual excuses were that the house was messy or the floors were freshly mopped and still wet. On those occasions, Rose never failed to comment on Mama's obvious hypocrisy. "Mama might hate Joelyn Asher, but she never turns down all the goodies she brings here."

After one of her visits, I'd peep out a window and watch Miss Joelyn walk back up the path to her home. I thought her looks were average with her dark hair and large saucer shaped eyes that bore a natural look of sadness, even when she smiled. Her body was bone thin. I remembered while in her store studying the thick blue veins in her hands and arms. I found myself feeling a bit sorry for her, knowing how Mama and some of the women at the camp made fun of what they called her "bird legs" and "long snout." I had learned at an early age what it was like to be plain and simply blend into the scenery.

On the night after the cave-in, Mama didn't come home until two o'clock in the morning. After the beans were cooked and placed into the cold house to keep them cool, Rose and me took turns bathing in the big number ten washtub, and then went to bed. The night was silent and dark. Through the little round window beside my bed, I looked out onto the dark porch where Daddy's bent silhouette sat smoking in the darkness. I watched the red tip of his cigarette grow brighter each time he took a drag off it. Somehow, I could feel the turmoil within his soul and knew he was deeply saddened by the death of his fellow miners. A part of me wanted to throw my arms around his neck and whisper to him that it was going to be all right. However, a bigger part of me feared Mama might come through the screen door any second. She had strict bedtime rules for Rose and me. Once you were in bed, you didn't get up unless nature called.

For what seemed like hours, I lay awake staring into the darkness. The room was hot and humid and my sweaty body tossed and turned continuously in an effort to find a cool spot on the sheet. In the next bed, Rose slept economically, without even the hint of a snore. I had decided that my sister wasn't as troubled as I was by the deaths of the miners and probably didn't think twice about the women and children left behind. Had it been Daddy then she would have been a mess, but since it wasn't she had somehow reconciled herself to what had happened. She was so like Mama, always rearranging life in ways that she could bear up.

But I couldn't forget and had trouble reconciling myself to the fact that these men would never again kiss their wives and children goodnight. I kept picturing crying women and pitiful little children calling out for their daddies. When sleep finally came it brought with it dark visions of the woods and a large bright campfire. I was walking by the rancid smelling river and wondering who had built the fire when suddenly I spied several shadows hunched over the flames. A closer look caused me to scream out in the night. Theirs were the faces of the dead miners I had known in life and had seen often. The leaping flames distorted their facial expressions, causing their skin to appear bright yellow and their eyes dark and hollow. Just as they looked in my direction their faces began dripping like candles and melting in the fire. I tried to run but my feet wouldn't move. And then I felt hands on me shaking me awake.

There in the dim light of the lamp, Mama stood over me, asking, "What on earth is wrong with you? Your Daddy is fast asleep and needs his rest!"

Trembling, I reached out for Mama, wanting to feel her comforting arms around me. "Mama, I'm scared," I hiccupped.

"Now you stop this cryin'!" she scolded, wrenching my desperate arms from around her neck. "I'm bone tired and sore. We've got a full day ahead of us tomorrow and need to rest. Go back to sleep!"

After Mama left and took the light with her, I lay trembling beneath the cumbersome quilt. I thought of climbing into the bed with Rose, but knew Mama would somehow know and accuse me of trying to disturb everyone in the house, so I lay there shaking, while trying in vain to wipe out the frightful images of the nightmare. Turning in the dark to the little round window that looked out onto the front porch, I spied a pale moon through the spaces in the trees. Daddy had called the window the "porthole" because he said it favored a porthole on a ship. For a long time I stared blankly into the dark, trying to forget the faces of the dead miners melting in the fire. Suddenly there was movement; something white flitted through the hot darkness, followed by the unmistakable squeak of the porch swing. I watched in fascination as it rocked back and forth, gaining momentum. Rising from beneath the covers, I got on my knees and peered through the darkness hoping for a better look, and then came the slow etching of a figure in the swing. I knew immediately that it was the ghost of Floyd Wilkes. I could make out his light blonde hair. My eyes grew large but not from fear, for I had never connected fear with Floyd Wilkes ghost -- at least not at first. Raising my hand, I lightly pecked on the window in an effort to get his attention. Floyd Wilkes ghost slowly turned his head and looked in my direction. Although I could not make out his facial features, I felt strangely comforted just knowing he was near me. Smiling to myself, I lay back on the pillow. Closing my eyes, I felt my body slowly relax, thinking that the ghost of Floyd Wilkes had somehow stepped out of my dream world just as he had the day I visited the Play Place. I was lulled to sleep by the soothing squeak of the porch swing.

The men got to the caskets right away. For two days, they worked steadily to get them built in time for the wake and then the funeral. For two days, the women in the camp had been cooking and preparing their houses for the upcoming wakes. When Mama wasn't at the funeral home, she was cooking, baking and getting our clothes ready for the day of the wake.

Daddy wasn't saying much about the No. 5 mine or what was taking place there. Like the other men in the camp, he and his brothers were preoccupied with the making of the coffins. Mama went silently about her chores. I saw that she was tired and irritable, so I did not test her mood with questions.

Around dark, Uncles Coy and Noah brought Mama four jars of Grandma Haley's peaches and a ten pound sack of flour that she would later use for baking pies that would be included in the next day's dinner. Mama was always glad to see her younger brothers who were identical in appearance. I was certain that they reminded her of Floyd Wilkes, with their light blonde hair and dimples. Although they looked innocent, in reality they were anything but. The Haley twins had a name for trouble and had been in and out of jail since they were sixteen years old. Grandma Haley loved her boys unconditionally and had bailed them out of jail on a regular basis until Uncle Purl got wind of it and put a stop to it. He had told Grandma Haley that he wouldn't allow her to waste another dime on getting them out of trouble.

A year or so before the mining cave in, the twins had gone over to a place called "nigger town" in Harlan, and according to an eyewitness had beaten a young Negro man unconscious with a homemade club. The young Negro man recovered but couldn't remember one thing about the night he was beaten. Because there was an eyewitness to the crime, the boys were looking at a prison term. Luckily, Grandma Haley had grown up with the judge and begged him to set a bond. In a show of empathy, he had finally agreed to set a bond for the twins. Since Uncle Purl was the trustee of her money, he was well within his rights to refuse her the amount needed to bond her boys out. Desperate to free her sons from jail, Grandma Haley had gone to Granny Lee for a loan. Granny Lee hadn't thought twice about giving her friend and family member the money. When Uncle Purl found out about the loan, he had gone to straight Granny Lee and promptly paid her back. Mama always laughed when she told the story. She said, "Mama knowed what she was doin' when she borrowed the money from Granny Lee. She knowed Purl would pay her back in a hurry once he found out about the loan. Purl couldn't have people talkin' about how Mama owed money. He wasn't going to be shamed."

As it turned out, the black man that had supposedly witnessed the beating was murdered while the twins were still in jail. Without the eyewitness testimony in court, the case against the boys eventually collapsed. Once again, they were free as a breeze, to the chagrin of Uncle Purl.

Mama welcomed the boys into the house and offered them seats at the table. Coy smiled, showing his perfectly white teeth, and said, "It's been awhile, Heddy." He then turned to me and said jokingly, "I think you just might turn out to be tall yet, June Bug!" Beside me Rose linked arms with Noah and said coyly, "I thought you was gonna to give me a ride in your new Buick,"

Noah laughed and said, "She's used, Rosaline. I couldn't buy nothin' new, but she runs real good!"

Looking irritated, Mama snapped, "Rose you take your sister in the bedroom and pin curl her hair!"

I started to protest but Mama's hateful facial expression caused me to close my mouth. "Come on, Rose," I urged.

In the bedroom, Rose angrily grabbed the box of bobby pins and commanded me to sit on the edge of the bed.

"Mama is such a nasty thing," she said, yanking my head downwards. I said nothing back and was relieved to hear the light banter return to the kitchen. Noah and Coy were both talking to Mama at the same time, telling her stories about the McKinley Coal company where they worked. Noah said, "McKinley's ain't no safer than Asher's but we've got a labor union behind us tryin'. Our wages ain't much better than they was at Asher's, though. If either of us should marry, we couldn't afford a decent place to live on what we make! If it wadn't for Miss Delia Brown letting us do repairs around her boardin' house we couldn't afford a car on what we make. You can't beat free rent in change for labor," Noah declared. It was sometimes hard for me to tell their voices apart; however, I had noticed that Noah's sounded a little deeper than Coy's.

Coy said, "Ole Purl watched us like a hawk while ago! He come over to Ma's as soon as he seen my car pull up to the creek. He stood near the porch and never said a word to us. Guess he just wanted to see what we was up too."

"Maybe he was afraid his house would get shot up again," Noah joked.

"Now you boys ought to be ashamed! " Mama laughed mischievously.

Rose said, "Listen to her giggle. She never does that unless the twins come here. She just ran us out of the kitchen, so she could have them all to herself. Hold you head still, now!"

I said, "Mama sounds happy at least."

"Mama is only happy when someone is makin' over her," Rose said, pinning a curl near my temple.

"I hate pin curls! My hair just turns frizzy when it's done up in bobby pins," I scowled.

"You could have just told Mama how much you hated havin' your hair curled," she snapped, and then said, "Hey, I think the Uncles are leavin'. Let's go and at least tell them bye."

Before I could protest, Rose grabbed my arm and pushed me toward the kitchen.

Coy and Noah were already out of their chairs and were hugging Mama goodbye.

Coy said, "I sure am sorry all them men had to die up there. It was a real bad deal."

Noah nodded his blonde head in agreement and said, "It's a damned shame what a man has to go through to earn a livin' in this hell hole!" Studying the handsome blonde twins with their sky blue eyes and chin dimples, I had decided they had inherited Grandma Haley's light complexion and blue green eyes. Mama must have favored her father with her darkness. In looking at the twins, I could only imagine what Floyd Wilkes might have looked like had he reached their age. He would have been equally as tall and wiry. No doubt, he would have become a coalminer and might have even been among those who died in the cave-in. Maybe it is better that he died young. At least he escaped having to work in the coal.

Rose walked over and took turns hugging the twins. "Now Noah, you remember that you owe me a ride in the Buick, soon!"

Noah laughed, tousled her hair playfully and said, "Lovely Rose Red, I'd be glad to drive you around town. I'll come for you soon. Promise!"

Rose beamed.

Mama smiled at her brothers and walked them to the door. "You boys stay out of trouble, you hear! I worry about you all."

Noah said, "Gee, Heddy, we only get into trouble when we go courtin' the wrong women!"

Once the twins were gone, Rose and I went back into our bedroom. Rose was about to douse my head in a pan of water in order to set the curls when Mama stormed into the bedroom and grabbed her by her hair, then slapped her hard across the face. "How dare you get right up in your Uncle's faces and act like some little tramp!"

Rose covered her hurt cheek with her hand. Looking stunned, she asked, "What did I do?"

"Don't act like you don't know, Rosaline Lee! You know exactly what you was doin' and it better never happen again or I'll send you to stay with your whore-hoppin' Aunt Marie!"

I noticed Mama's twisted facial expression. Her dark eyes looked as if they might pop out of her head. She continued to scream at Rose. "Don't you know that them are your Uncles -- your own kin? Here you are flirtin' with them and rubbin' your body all over Noah! How could you shame me like this?"

"I did no such thing!" Rose screamed, and then stamped her foot angrily on the floor. "Have you lost your mind accusin' me of somethin like that?"

Mama raised her hand threatening to hit Rose again.

"No, Mama!" I screamed. "Don't hit her no more!"

Suddenly Mama whirled around to face me. "You shut up Junie Mae! Your sister acted like a tramp while ago and I won't have none of it! Do you hear me? Now wet that hair and go to bed!"

After Mama stomped out of the bedroom, I turned to look at Rose who sat silently still nursing her cheek. Her blue eyes had turned angry and appeared almost white in the flickering light. "I feel like walkin' to the kitchen and grabbin' a butcher knife and jabbin' it straight into her for accusin' me of that!" Rose said vehemently.

For once, I kept quiet. I could find no justification for what Mama did to Rose. Sitting down beside Rose I pulled her to me and held her close. At first, she let out a little whimper that soon turned to low sobs. "It's okay," I cooed. "I know you didn't do nothin' wrong."

4 THE WAKES

On the morning of the wakes, Mama prepared a small breakfast, but neither Rose nor I took more than a few of bites of the salty bacon. Daddy pushed back his plate and sat smoking while staring wearily out the kitchen window. Mama had been up since dawn pressing the outfits we were to wear to the wake.

    I dreaded having to don the gray skirt, white blouse, and worse, the bobby socks and heavy dress shoes. Rose frowned in horror when Mama came into the kitchen holding a freshly ironed white blouse and black skirt.

    "That's so drab," she whispered.

    Mama heard her and snapped. "You're not goin' to a barn dance! I want you girls to mind your manners today!"

    While getting dressed, Rose mentioned her cheek and said, "Guess Mama's forgot how she slapped my face and accused me of actin' like a whore! What if my bruise had turned big and purple? I wonder what she would have told the women at the camp when they asked how I got it?"

    "You're not going to tell Daddy, are you?" I asked. Rose laughed harshly while slipping on her white blouse. "He won't notice, and even if he did what would he do? He knows she beats me and just acts like he don't see it! He never sees nothin'! Poor Daddy, he's as blind as them snakes in dog days."

    "That's not true!" I said defensively. "Daddy's got a lot on his mind."

    "Junie Mae, you're too good to be true," she said incredulously. "You and Daddy and Granny Lee make excuses for everybody even when they're wrong! Are you all wearing horse blinders? One day you'll have to pull off them blinders!"

    "Look at me! I look awful in this skirt," I scowled, my attention centered on the plump little girl in the mirror, uncomfortably squeezed into a skirt that made her favor a short adult. I grimaced at my reflection and said, "I look like an overstuffed sausage in this get-up."

Rose said, "You look just as good as me! Now hold still while I undo the pin curls."

"It's a frizzy mess! Mama knows it's too straight to hold a thick curl," I moaned.

"I'll fix it," Rose assured me. In the mirror, I studied my sister's striking features and thought she looked beautiful with her naturally wavy black hair that stood out against the white blouse. In the summer, the sunlight bleached my naturally cinnamon colored hair. Lighter in complexion than the rest of my family, I stuck out a like a sore thumb amongst them.

Uncle Harvey James came into the house and loaded the food Mama had prepared the night before into his truck. He and Daddy were set to drive up to the camp early in order to help put up the canopies which would shelter the long wooden tables to help keep the flies at bay. Daddy looked uncomfortable in the starched white shirt and black dress pants. Mama handed him his suit jacket.

"Today's goin' to be a scorcher, Heddy. I can't handle that jacket."

Mama looked irritated but said nothing. Shortly thereafter, Uncle Corbin arrived in his shiny Buick to pick up Mama, Rose, and me. Daddy jokingly said that Uncle Corbin's car speedometer had never registered more than twenty miles an hour. It was a well-known fact that Uncle Corbin was tightfisted with his money. Mama once said that he probably still had the first dollar he'd ever made, but quickly admitted he had freely given her money when she was in a pinch. Uncle Corbin and Mama had a fondness for each other. Patience was not one of Mama's strongest points, but ironically she showed a kind of special tolerance for Uncle Corbin's bad habits of swearing, belching, and stuttering, even at the dinner table. Had anyone else shown such rudeness she would have run him or her out of her kitchen. Her acceptance of him was totally out of character for her, and I never understood it. However, with the passing of time Mama would do other things I didn't understand as well.

Uncle Corbin was what some called a loud mouth and was outspoken when it came to politics. Some thought he was too outspoken when it came to his hatred of the labor unions and any other party save for the Republican Party. Although the people of Appalachia are mainly conservatives with a majority of Republicans, Uncle Corbin's radical rants and raves left many cold. Once at a political rally in Harlan, he'd shot off his mouth one too many times about a local Democratic candidate and was badly beaten by a drunk man who was twice his size. Mama dressed his wounds and took care of him for a week. She had said, "I ought to send Noah and Coy to find the man who did this. Once they got a hold of him, he'd wish he was never born!" Of course, she never told her brothers, but was angry about it. Uncle Corbin seemed to relish in Mama's deep affection for him. She had often jokingly told him that she was looking for him a wife. He'd become upset and would start stuttering so incoherently that you could make out only a few words that he was saying: "Na-na-na Hed-Hed-Heddy, I-I-I-I don-don-don-don't nee-nee-need no-no-no- wo-wo-wo-man! You hush that up!"

Uncle Corbin got out of his shiny black Buick and opened the doors for each of us. He'd said that he didn't want us riding up to the camp in the truck when he had a nice, clean, newly polished car. Sliding in the back seat, I noticed the scent of polish. The car was truly immaculate. "You-you-gir-gir-girls sit-sit-ti-ti-tight, now-now!" Uncle Corbin was well dressed in a pair of creased blue dress pants and starched white shirt. He wore his dark felt hat with its light gray band. He stood only about five feet, five inches tall; Daddy, Harvey James, and Harlan Ray towered above Uncle Corbin. The brothers affectionately called him the "little banty rooster."

By midday, the sun was at its peak of brightness. No wind stirred and the sky had turned an indigo blue mingled with streaks of dark pink. Out of the car window, I stared at the scarred landscape with its ruts and chugholes. On either side of the dirt road, the trees were thick and thirsty for water. Many of the leaves were brown and curled around the edges from the lack of water. Uncle Corbin stuttered, "I-I-I'm dr-dr-dreading- th-th-this da-da-day."

Mama nodded and once again warned, "You girls better be on your best behavior today."

Made up of four long rows of identical houses, the Asher mining camp always appeared stark and desolate. On any other day, the women would have had their wash hung out on clotheslines strung across their front porches. Today, however, the clotheslines were bare and the porches swept clean and neat. The exteriors of the houses were crude and cheaply built and all had chimneys. In the rutted grassless yards, people stood dressed in their best clothes. Women wore dark clothing and huddled in groups talking. Many of the men wore dark suits, and some wore suspenders and plain white shirts. Mama wore black and white very well. She had appeared polished and radiantly beautiful, even amidst the grievous atmosphere. Now sandwiched between her and Uncle Corbin, I felt deeply uncomfortable in my tight fitting skirt and white blouse. I thought I probably looked ridiculous. Like Mama, Rose looked beautiful in her knee length black skirt and crisp white shirt with its black collar and sleeves. A talented seamstress, Mama used bits of material to make even plain outfits look extraordinary. Although we were poor when it came to most material things, Mama made sure we had nice clothes and shoes to wear.

In those days of the late 1940's in Eastern Kentucky it was customary for people to bring their dead into their homes and have the wake there.

Big Brock Asher saw to the arrangements and did the embalming free of charge. I can only imagine how traumatizing it must have been for Mama having to work on the bodies of the men she had known all her life. I suddenly felt sorry for her. If Rose felt any kind sadness in the wake of the tragedy, she kept it well-hidden. If anything, she acted as restless as a cat after a ball of yarn. Her and the Mattingly sisters flitted through the crowd like butterflies. Never mind that it was somber occasion. While watching them I was glad Mama's attention was on Uncle Corbin.

Mama and I followed Uncle Corbin to the canopied food tables. My eyes scanned the many covered dishes and the wide assortment of breads and desserts. Food was served at almost every occasion and was an intrinsic part of the Appalachian culture. Women were skilled at cooking and had learned in lean times to make even the cheapest cuts of meats delicious.

A short distance from the food tables, rows of chairs were lined up. The sitters consisted of mostly women; some of them fanned their faces while others stood near the food tables with cardboard fans in hopes of keeping the flies at bay. Uncle Corbin pointed to the front row of chairs and said," Look-look, Hed-Hed-Heddy! Th-th-there's your Ma Ma, sit-sitting be-beside bi-bi-big Ma-Ma-Maude St-St-Stewart."

Mama's face appeared strained but she managed a half smile and motioned to me and Rose to follow her over to where Grandma Haley was sitting. Uncle Corbin said, "I-I- I'm go-go-going to-to jo-jo-join th-th-the me-men in-in-in th-th-th- ba-ba-barn."

I had been to several wakes and knew what to expect. Men usually paid their respects to the dead and then later congregated in a shed or barn on the property where they drank homemade moonshine or homebrew, smoked, and reminisced about better times with the deceased. In a way, a wake was a kind of celebration of the dead person's life. Women usually took turns consoling the widow or widower. Later many of them served food and doled out kind words.

Grandma Haley was dressed in a dark blue dress with cream-colored lace about the neck and sleeves. Her face looked older than her fifty-two years. Her hair was fixed in a bun about the nape of her neck; once blonde, time had turned it the color of pale straw, especially near her temples. Her eyes were almond-shaped like Mama's, only sharper looking. Grandma Haley was a wizened woman who missed nothing. Her alert eyes studied everyone and everything. "Hello, Heddy -- maybe we can go in the houses together and pay our respects," she offered.

Mama nodded affirmatively and said, "I am ready when you are. Hello, Maude, how are you?"

"I am still going, if that's anything," Maude said, while shifting her ample weight.

"Maybe I will go with you all. I've been putting off going in them houses as long as I can."

Maude reminded me of the pictures of Humpty-Dumpty in my book of nursery rhymes. She was as round as an egg all over save for her legs, which were much thinner than the rest of her. She wore her hair in a crude beehive, and her loud voice rang out like a shot. Her husband, Dan, was Daddy's foreman, and because of his position, Maude was privy to all the latest news and gossip concerning the mine. "There's Bonzelle Creech. I hope she don't come over here," Mama said under her breath. I turned to look at Miss Bonzelle, who always wore loud colors and a big hairstyle. She was a tiny little thing in stature but had large breasts that made her appear top heavy. I had wondered how someone that small could carry breasts so large.

"Hello, Heddy Mae," she greeted. Her voice had a distinct country twang but was soft in tenor. Many of the women at the camp ignored her and called her fast because she was divorced and lived off her daddy. Bonzelle Creech giggled a lot and spoke her mind. She was also the subject of countless scandalous rumors, and Mama believed all of them. I had guessed that she was few years younger than Mama, and I thought she was pretty in an overly made up way. Secretly, I had always had my doubts that all the things Mama and the other women said about her were true.

"This is a terrible day for all of us, Heddy. My Daddy's just heartbroken over losin' friends he's worked with for years. I thank God he wadn't one of them that died, but my heart goes out to the women who lost their men."

"Well, I'm glad that Levi wadn't hurt, too, Bonzelle. You give him our best," Mama said, and then quickly turned in the direction of Big Maude and Grandma Haley. After Miss Bonzelle moved on, Mama whispered, "When Levi finally dies that woman will be in trouble. He's spoiled her to death giving her his paycheck so she can dress up like a tramp. Even in that black get-up she still manages to look cheap."

Grandma Haley scowled and reprimanded Mama. "Heddy, you ought not talk about people you know nothing about, especially on a day like this."

Big Maude rolled her eyes in disgust and said, "Well, it's the truth, Ivy! I've knowed that girl since she was a baby and she ain't never done nothin' but run back to daddy every time some man don't give her everything she wants. Levi works his poor old fingers to the bone to give her everything. She might live in the camp but she ain't never done without nothin'!"

Life was hard in the mountains of Harlan County Kentucky, and most women wore the results of that hardness on their faces. Maude and Grandma Haley were just two of the many women that I'd known who looked older than their years. Some women, though, had managed to hold up well in spite of the coal and the poverty. Mama was a good example; her face was fresh as a flower in bloom and her skin looked even younger than her thirty-two years. Mama had taken good care of herself and always managed to afford cold creams and beauty products. She carried herself well and her exotic dark looks stood out in any crowd. That day was no different; men stared at her appreciatively while some women shot her hateful or envious glances. Watching her, I decided that she must know what she was and the power she had over the men. While one part of me was busy admiring her beauty, the other part felt confused. Mama would have that effect over me for the rest of her life. Even when some of her hidden parts came into the light, I still didn't know who she was.

Grandma Haley said, "We'll go see the Wilson brothers first, I reckon, since theirs is the closest house. Poor old Ella -- I hear is having a hard time dealing with it all." Mama nodded in agreement. It wasn't often that Mama agreed with Grandma Haley. The two had never got on well. Part of it might have been Uncle Purl's fault, though I grew to suspect that their troubles with each other far went deeper than Uncle Pearl's greed and his need to hover over Grandma Haley.

"Do I have to go in?" I asked timidly, already knowing the answer.

Mama hesitated and then said, "Yes, I want you to come. Ella Wilson thinks a lot of you and your sister. You all might be of some comfort." As her eyes searched the crowd Mama said, "Lord knows where Rose has sneaked off to."

Grandma Haley laughed and said, "I seen her earlier and thought it was you, Heddy. She's you made over."

"She's as stubborn as an ox," Mama said with contempt.

Grandma Haley laughed and said, "I wonder who she gets that from?"

Saying nothing in return, Mama proceeded up the rickety wooden steps of the Wilson house. Mourners crowded the porch, whispering among themselves. Mama and Grandma Haley stopped and spoke briefly with a few. Once inside the house the hot air hit me. The room was barely big enough to fit two homemade wooden coffins and there was hardly space to walk. The widows of the brothers sat lovingly guarding their husband's coffins. Ella Wilson, the widow of William, rested her hand protectively on the side of the coffin while gazing sorrowfully down into the still, alabaster face of her husband. While Mama and the others took turns at the caskets, I chose to concentrate instead on the contents of the living room. My eyes roamed over the treasured antique clock above the mantel, and I studied the aging wallpaper, yellowed in places from the smoke from the fireplace. After only a few minutes, the heat in the house became stifling. Like most around Harlan and the rural areas, the Wilsons couldn't afford the extra ten dollars a month to have the electricity turned on, so there were no fans to cool the air.

I thought Ella Wilson's living room was every bit as drab as most of the others we would see before the day was over. It was even drabber than the one at the lodge. Mama was a good decorator but could never quite make our home look pretty. Our furnishings were like those of Ella Wilson's: dreary, well-worn, and no amount of wild flowers, colorful slipcovers, or doilies could make them look otherwise.

Big Maude embraced Ella Wilson to her ample bosom and said, "God be with you honey. I know how you must feel."

Ella nodded and said, "Over in the corner is his baby brother -- two of them killed and only one's face can be showed. His face was too messed up. Oh God! Poor Mabel! This is so unfair, you know!"

My eyes strayed to the corner where Mabel sat dry eyed, her face drawn and forlorn. Her hand also rested lovingly on the lid of the closed coffin. I felt a rush of intense sorrow fill my insides. I wanted to cry but quickly mastered the need. Mama's eyes remained dry but appeared sad and hollow. Mama had taught Rose and me that tears were shameful and for the meek at heart. She said, "Your Granny Lee can cry at the drop of the hat and it's an embarrassment. You girls will stay strong no matter what! Being strong can keep out a lot of the hurt!"

My eyes fell on the two mining caps resting on separate tables near the coffins. The women had tried to clean up the caps, but their yellow surfaces remained scarred from years of having scraped up against the shale and flint walls of the mines. The caps with their carbide lamps appeared ominous to me. Daddy had a cap just like the ones sitting there on the tables. The caps brought about a kind of bleak reality to me. Daddy could be lying in one of those homemade coffins. At any time the mine could fall in on top of him!

Big Wayne Lewis's house was at the end of the first row of crude houses. He and Bonnie Faye had five children -- three girls and two boys -- and the youngest girl was three years old. Audrey, the oldest girl, met us at the door and asked in a trembling voice, "You all here to see Deddy?"

Grandma Haley nodded and said, "Yes. How's your Mama holding up?"

Audrey said, "She ain't doing no good! She's in there with Deddy, 'cept he ain't really in there."

Mama looked uncomfortable and said nothing, while Grandma Haley smiled reassuringly and said, "Don't you worry none. He's with God now."

Several people crowded around the casket of Big Wayne Lewis. Like Daddy, he'd had many friends. Saddened miners stood over him looking grave, while women cried unashamedly. Mama stood behind Grandma Haley looking stiff and uncomfortable, but Grandma Haley seemed to know just what to say in times like these. Bonnie Faye was a big, hearty woman whose complexion was as naturally pink as a peach. Had she not been so fleshy, she might have been beautiful. Sitting next to her husband's casket, and with tears streaming down her face she said, "What will I do now? I ain't never knowed nothin' but this life. I ain't worked a day outside of this house." Her heavy shoulders shook as her sobs grew louder.

Grandma Haley eyed the two sad looking little girls in Bonnie Faye's ample lap and said a little sternly, "Don't go on like this in front of these children. I know what you're feeling, Bonnie Faye. I raised four children and lost one. You'll find a way to bear up. When something like this happens you don't have a choice."

Grandma Haley's words seemed to sober Bonnie Faye. Wiping her eyes with a well-worn handkerchief, she said, "I know I can't give up. I'll lose this place of course…" Her words trailed off.

Seeing Big Wayne Lewis in his casket frightened and made real the possibility that I could lose Daddy. I felt an urge to run out the front door, but knew better. I was afraid of what Mama would do to me once she got me home. Grandma Haley whispered, "I think we should go on over to the German woman's house soon and pay our respects."

Mama nodded.

The Winley house was identical to the others save for the color. One or both of the Winleys had painted the house a bright white and the window frames black. Outside in the grassless yard several round wooden barrels overflowed with a variety of brightly colored flowers. Wind chimes dangled from the trees, and any time the slightest breeze came about one could hear the clinking of the chimes.

Mr. Winley's wife, Olga, was from Germany and most of the women in the camp avoided her, claiming she had the "big head" and thought she was better than everyone else was because they had put out the extra ten dollars for electricity. The other miners couldn't afford the extra ten dollars to have their lights turned on. Olga had told Mama that her German grandmother had left her a bit of money and that she was the one who paid for the electricity. Although some of the other women planted gardens and had grown flowers, none looked so well placed as Olga's; she apparently had a way with growing things

Olga was a quiet- natured woman who held herself well and associated very little with the other women in the camp. Part of the reason she wasn't outgoing may have been because her English skills were bad. Ironically, Mama liked her and defended her when the other women said cruel things about her. Anyone could see that Olga Winley was a woman of strength who didn't seem to need the hen-clucking or a meeting around the coffee pot to be happy. In ways, Mama was similar to Olga in strength and didn't really need the company of other women at the camp, either. In reality, Mama despised the camp with its rows of shabby houses that had poverty written all over them. She had vehemently refused to live in one, and had told Daddy that she would rather put up stakes in the woods than to spend one winter in one of the camp houses. I think Asher's Camp reminded Mama of the Daisy Mining Camp. I'd heard her tell Daddy stories of how when she was six years old she and Floyd Wilkes had to share a bed while the twins slept on the cold floors. She related how large river rats would sometimes come in through the cracks in the floors and crawl all over them. She described in great detail how one had once bitten Noah on the ear and it had become so badly infected that he'd almost lost it. Mama had credited an old Negro woman who also lived in the camp for saving his life when she applied fat back and black salve to the wound.

Although equally as poor as the people in the Asher Camp, I believe Mama thought herself as being a cut above the other women. Never mind that like them she was indebted to the Ashers for her livelihood. Even so, Mama had nothing for the camp and only visited it when she wanted to know what was going on inside No. 5 mine. A few times, during those rare visits, Mrs. Winley saw us and invited over for coffee and cookies. Mama would sit for hours listening to her talk about Germany in her broken English. Olga's house was always neat as a pin and her dresses were a little fancier than any of the other women in the camp -- save for Mama, who was herself a snazzy dresser.

Olga Winley's was a handsome, intense face, but even when she smiled her dark eyes appeared anxious. During our visits, she would pile a saucer full of homemade ginger snaps and pour coffee for Mama and milk for me. The cookies were delicious and, like Mama, I was fascinated with her stories of war and her childhood growing up in Germany. In the summers, Olga Winley's house remained cooler than the other homes because she had a big window fan. I remember standing in front of it and cooling my sweaty face. The fan was a novelty to me, for I had only seen electric fans in the grocery stores.

On the day of the wake, Olga Winley appeared lifeless. Her eyes were red from crying but she greeted Mama, Grandma Haley, and me warmly. "Please come in."

Rarely affectionate, Mama reached out, hugged her tightly, and said, "Olga, I am so sorry. I have been where you have and it is awful. Nothin' can describe it!"

Grandma Haley nodded. "I am so sorry, Olga. Time will help you get through it."

Olga half-smiled and said, "It vasan't supposed to be dis vay. I vought it vould be better here zan in Germany. Zee first vorld var took my fader and all his brothers. It vas a terrible time zen, and now zis! I don't know vat I will do or vere I vill go now!"

Following Mama over to the casket, I looked down on Mr. Winley and thought he looked peaceful, almost like he was sleeping. Olga Winley's voice broke, "God, look at his poor hands vould you? Zat greasy coal dust is still in his vingernails and in zee little cuts on his hand. He has to take zat to heaven with him. Not even death could rid him of zee coal."

My eyes fell on his big hands and square shaped fingernails. I could easily imagine Daddy lying there in the casket. Mr. Winley also had many other features like Daddy. Both men had very dark hair that was thinning near the top. His cheekbones were high and hollow, and in life, Mr. Winley was tall, like Daddy, and bowed in the back from having spent years on his knees, shoveling coal into coal cars. Seeing these poor men in death had filled me with such grief and sadness. Mama must have sensed my inner turmoil and sympathized a little because she bent down and told me in a gentle voice to go outside and play for a while. A kind of relief filled my insides, and I couldn't wait to get out the door and into the sunlight.

Once outside in the heat, I looked in the direction of Tant Brock's house. The youngest of miners killed, Tant was single and had lived with his widowed mother whose own husband died of lung disease caused by breathing in the coal dust. I was glad I didn't have to see the dead boy who was only a year or two older than my Uncles Coy and Noah. Enough was enough!

My eyes searched the sea of people filing in and out of the houses, many appearing red-eyed from crying, while others meandered stone-faced near the food tables, waiting their turn in line. A few men had unpacked their musical instruments; soon bluegrass music filled the air. I had been to a few wakes in the past; all of them had music, and there was always plenty of food and drinks. Appalachian people had been celebrating wakes the same way for centuries.

Scanning the crowd for Rose and not seeing her, I was sure she was still off somewhere with the Mattingly sisters, Doreen, Dot, and Darlene. Mama didn't like the girls and called them flighty, but this didn't stop Rose from seeing them behind Mama's back. Just as I headed in the direction of the food tables, a hush fell over the crowd. The strains of the fiddles hit an off key and the guitars strumming ceased. Soon I saw why. The Ashers had come to pay their respects and were entering the gates leading to the camp. Miss Joelyn was sandwiched between Big Brock and Little Brock. A handsome young son, Bart, walked alongside Miss Joelyn, while her two daughters followed behind. Miss Joelyn was dressed in a plain black dress, while the two men wore black suits and hats. Big Brock Asher was a tall, thin man with thick lips and bushy eyebrows. His hands and feet seemed too big for his narrow body. The wide brim hat he wore had cast a kind of dark shadow that obscured his eyes. In spite of the heat, I shivered at the dark look of him. However, there was nothing mysterious or threatening about Little Brock Asher. Although he had his father's tall features, he was more muscular about the arms and legs. Even from a distance his black eyes stood out like little shiny pieces of coal; they skittered about the crowd bird-like, looking anxious. Though striking in appearance, I had decided that his nose was too narrow and his eyes too piercing to be called handsome. Although Bart had his father and grandfather's tall features, his face was wider and softer. Appearing hatless, his jet-black hair was slicked smoothly back, revealing eyebrows that were thickly arched above dark almond-shaped eyes. But unlike his father's doll eyes, there was a kind of deliberate sleepy sensuality in Bart's. I'd decided that his facial features were more like those of Miss Joelyn's.

The girls looked almost identical to Little Brock and were close to same ages as me and Rose. They were clad smartly in dresses that were the color of dark blue ink, but they were hardly beautiful. It was the dark piercing eyes that made them appear as doll like, which spoiled their looks.

Rose had told me that she and the Mattingly sisters often giggled and talked about Bart Asher's handsome looks. After studying him up close, I had to agree. I couldn't believe how much he'd matured and grown over such a short period. I remembered him as a little boy chasing after Rose and sneaking over the rock wall to see her. Since Rose was a little girl, all her dreams and hopes seem to revolve around him. For me, the thought of marrying someone like Bart Asher was as remote as the moon. The Asher children were nothing like us. Instead of attending a public school their parents had sent them to a private school in Williamsburg, Kentucky. Mama was among the many who thought the Ashers were being pretentious by sending their children to fancy private schools when the school in Harlan was good enough for everybody else's children.

People parted the way for the Ashers as they made their way past the food tables. Some spoke or nodded to them politely but most stood, stared, and whispered to each other. Even though many people at the wake were furious with Little Brock and his daddy, it was doubtful they would make their anger known -- at least on that day. After all, this was a wake and Asher had embalmed the bodies free, probably believing that he had done his part. The miners and their wives weren't worried. There would be a more suitable time to confront Little Brock Asher.

Suddenly a tall gangly man emerged from the crowd and greeted Little Brock Asher and his father. I recognized Uncle Purl even beneath the wide brimmed hat that shaded most of his face. Seeing him hovering about the Ashers made me think of what Mama said about how he was always nipping at Little Brock's heels like a dog wanting a bone. I was about to turn away in disgust when I saw Bart turn his attention away and look in the direction of the big elm tree in Briscoe Benton's yard. Squinting in the sun, I shaded my eyes and then saw what he was looking at. There underneath the shade of the big elm tree stood Rose and the Mattingly sisters, only I was sure it was not them he was looking at. Rose was looking at him, too, and for the longest time the two didn't take their eyes off one another. My heart sank while my eyes tentatively scanned the crowd for the sight of Mama, all the while hoping she hadn't seen what I had. Rose's brazen appreciation of Bart Asher would have absolutely have infuriated her. Thankfully, she either was still visiting with Olga Winley or had gone to view Tant Brock. Their blatant flirting both angered and fascinated me. I watched as Bart smiled appreciatively and waved to her. Rose made a small gesture with her hand, while still locked in his gaze. Finally, one of his sisters said something in his ear and his attention was then on her, but Rose still stared after him until he was out of sight. My own attention was diverted by a light touch on my right shoulder. Turning around, I saw my Granny Lee sandwiched between Marie and Uncle Harlan Ray. Granny Lee's heavy, bold face glistened with sweat. "Lord, honey, it's a bad day for a wake in this heat. Where are your mama and daddy?"

"I ain't shore," I said, glad to see Granny Lee.

"Why don't you and Marie go sit in the shade and cool off?" Granny Lee suggested, and then added, "Marie, where are the youngins?"

Marie said, "They are over there with old Gertie Fisher near the food tables."

"Well, you'd better high-tail it over there before they get in the creek," she laughed, fanning herself.

I didn't know Marie very well. We were eight years apart in age, and all I knew was that Marie had three children already and had never been married. Mama called her "fast" and "loose" and had cautioned us, especially Rose, not to become friendly with her. She'd warn, "You are the company you keep. If you play in the dirt, you always get a smidgen of it on you." More than once, she had warned Granny Lee that she needed to do something with Marie. She had said, "Martha, how can you allow Marie to run amok, gettin' herself pregnant at the drop of a hat? It's just not fair that she keeps havin' these kids for you to raise and you gettin' on in age."

Granny Lee smiled and said, "You don't know how it really was with Marie. Little Chester Harlan is God sent. She wadn't with no man before she got pregnant with him. I know. She showed me her underpants with the bloodstains in 'em. A woman can't get with child and still have her monthly curse. No, the Lord sent us Chester!"

Looking dumbfounded, Mama said, "I've never heard of such a stupid thing, Martha Lee. You can't really believe this! She probably rubbed Oxblood shoe polish in her panties to make it look like she was havin' her monthly. Besides, God wadn't purposely send Marie a sickly child like little Chester Harlan when she has trouble keepin' up with the two she's already got."

"Now Heddy Mae," she said, patiently, "you don't know why God does the things he does. I believe Marie," Granny Lee said with conviction.

I loved Granny Lee but didn't agree with her. Even though I knew very little about having babies, I was certain a man had to be in the picture.

I followed Marie over to the food tables where five year old Brice Dodd was tugging on the tablecloth in an effort to get to the plate of sliced fresh watermelon. "Brice Dodd, I am going to wear you out in a minute!" Marie whined. Old Mrs. Fisher was sitting in a chair smiling and patiently holding Marie's youngest, two year old Chester Harlan, while Uncle Harlan Ray scooped up the middle child, three year old Brenda Sue. Harlan Ray admonished his sister. "Marie, you had better watch these babies today. Mama will be in the houses payin' her respects and I'll be with the other men over yonder in the barn." His voice sounded harsh. I knew Harlan Ray and his wife Rebekah Ann sometimes looked after Marie's children. They didn't have any of their own for whatever reason. Rebekah Ann loved Marie's children and even offered to adopt Brenda Sue, but Granny Lee decided that this wouldn't be fair to the remaining two children.

Mama told Granny Lee sarcastically, "Marie would give all three of them kids to Harlan Ray and Rebekah Ann if they wanted them. They would probably take them, too, if they could afford to raise 'em. Every time Rebekah Ann takes the children for a spell, Marie goes out trying to make another one for her and everybody else look after. If either of my girls acted like that I would disown them!" she spat hatefully. "I ain't about to raise a house full of children born out of wedlock!"

Granny Lee said patiently, "Heddy Mae, children are a blessin' no matter how they come into the world. God is forgiving of Marie's mistakes."

The rest of the evening was filled with sad bluegrass music and people going in and out of the houses. I stayed with Marie most of the time, helping her chase after her wayward children. I'd had plenty of time to study her. I enjoyed watching people and how they acted. To me, it was better than playing tag behind the trees or peeking in the windows at the caskets and then running away screaming. At one point, little Audrey, the daughter of Big Wayne Lewis, came running up to me and said, "Deddy went to heeven." She couldn't have been over six years old and her little face was screwed up in deep puzzlement.

"I know," I said sorrowfully.

"If God can do anything, why can't he give us Deddy back?" she asked.

Marie who was holding a fussy Chester Harlan said, "Come over here Audrey." Her voice sounded compassionate and soft like that of Granny Lee's.

Little Audrey went over and stood in front of Marie. Marie said, "God only borrowed your Daddy, Audrey. Sometimes he needs certain people to do certain jobs. One day you will see him again. Don't worry!"

The little girl looked skeptical. "Are you shore?" she asked.

Marie nodded and said, "I know it! I'll see my Daddy too, someday. God borrowed him a while back."

Little Audrey smiled with satisfaction.

"Now you run along and play with the other youngins."

"I liked what you told Audrey," I said, meaning every word of praise.

Marie smiled and said, "Shoot, it wadn't nothin' but the truth. God takes care of us all in his own way."

I quickly decided that I liked Marie. She had Granny Lee's simple, humble nature. Maybe she hadn't done right having all those babies out of wedlock, but she seemed sweet and kind. She wasn't so pretty to look at with her boyish haircut, tiny eyes, and petulant mouth, but when she smiled, I thought she looked a bit radiant. Any other time Marie would have been dressed in manly attire of baggy khaki pants, a hat, and boots that looked a lot like what the nurses from the Frontier Nursing Service wore. When Granny Lee admonished her for her choice of manly attire, Marie always said, "If it's good enough for the nurses then it's good enough for me." Granny Lee wouldn't argue with that since many in the community thought of them as being true angels as well as lifesavers. According to Granny Lee, before Mary Breckinridge started her nursing services at Wendover, Kentucky, sometime in the 1920's, many towns in Eastern Kentucky had no hospitals or even a doctor on hand. Breckinridge and her nurses, along with helpful couriers, created outposts all along the rural areas. Before there were roads or even automobiles it was common to see nurses on horseback riding up the steep hollows and mountain trails, splashing through creeks and braving ice and snow in order to either deliver a baby or call on a desperately sick person. Mrs. Breckinridge had a deep love for children, and the community loved and respected her. Granny Lee first encountered the nurses after she'd cut her hand while cutting up cabbage. The wound was deep and she might have bled to death had it not been for the skillful hands of the nurses who stitched up the wound. From that day forward, Granny Lee was indebted to the nurses, and her house was usually on their agenda. They often ate meals with her and sometimes after a long day of rounds, one or two might even spend the night. The Breckinridge midwives delivered all three of Marie's babies and stopped in often to check on them. Rose and I were also Breckinridge babies, as were most children born during our time. Granny Lee said that without the Frontier Nursing Service, many babies and small children would have died from common childhood diseases.

As the evening wore on the sun grew more intense. At nightfall, a little wind stirred and cooled things down. By nine o'clock, the music was over and many of the men staggered out of the barn drunk and ready to go home to bed. Uncle Corbin found Mama, who had me find Rose. Neither of us had seen her much all day. Harvey James would bring Daddy home later. Uncle Corbin had not drunk alcohol and never touched the stuff; he was probably the only sober man on the place. Finally, I helped Mama gather up the dishes we had brought. Mama also wrapped up some of the leftover food that would go in the cold house at home.

Once inside Uncle Corbin's car, I rested my head on the back of the seat. My eyelids felt heavy and were dangerously close to closing in sleep. Rose nudged me anxiously and giggled. I was too tired to be curious as to why she was giggling. Once on the road and away from the camp, Uncle Corbin said, "I ha-ha-heard som-som- trou-trou-troublesome thin-thin-things to-to-tonight. Me-me-men are ma-mad- as ha-hell over-over the ca-ca-cave-in. They-they'll vo-vo vote in-in-in a u-u-union, you-you-you wa-wa-wait an-an-and see-see! We-we-we-don't nee-nee-need no u-u-union, that's-that's that's for-for sh-shore."

In a tired voice Mama said, "Corbin, you will have to go with what the majority of the men do. God knows I am so sick of the subject of the coal and seein' men die. I've wanted to run from this place since I was fifteen years old."

Uncle Corbin stuttered, "Now, now, Hedd-Hedd, Heddy, that, that, a-a-ain't no way to-to-to-talk! You, you, ca-ca-can't ru-ru-run from your, your, roo-roo-roots!"

"Who says I can't?" She snapped. "What law is on the books that say I have to stay here in this damned place?"

"You- you- mar-mar-married a co-co coal-mi-min-miner Hedd, Heddy!"

"Who else would I marry but a coalminer? That's all a woman can marry round here -- the kind of men who work their guts out for low wages in a place that most likely will end up killin' em, one way or another!" Mama's loud voice woke me up.

Uncle Corbin's stutter sounded more pronounced. "Hed, Hed-Hed-Heddy, co-co-co-coal-mi-mi-mining is-is-is all-all all we kn-kn-know. Ou-ou-ou-our fam-fam-fam-fam-families are-are-are here-here. We-we-we-ca--ca-ca-can't wa-wal-walk out-on-on-on-em! Aft-aft-after Da-da-daddy di-di-di-died of lun-lung dis-ease, us-us- old-old-old -old-er boy-boys ha-ha-ha-had to-to-to wor-work-to-to-kee-kee-keep foo-foo-foo-foo-food on-the-the the tab-tab-tab-le. Work-wor- workin all-all the -the time wad-wad-wadn't -ou-our-our cho-choice."

In a calmer voice, Mama said. "I know Corbin. I'm sorry for gettin' so worked up. I'm just tired."

Once we reached home, Mama had Uncle Corbin shine his bright headlights into the house so she could see to light the coal oil lamp. She said, "Rose, you hold the light while I put the food in the cold house. Junie Mae, you go on to bed, honey."

Rose whined, "I'm scared of snakes. Let Uncle Corbin hold the light!"

Mama snapped, "I told you to do it! Now go!"

Once in bed and underneath the comfort of the heavy quilt I fell into a deep sleep. Sometime in the night, I felt hands on my shoulder shaking me. I then heard what sounded like Rose's voice saying, "I'm so in love with Bart Asher."

"Go to sleep!" I ordered thickly.

5 BART ASHER

I remember the day after the wakes as if it was yesterday; it was Sunday and Mama let Rose and me sleep late. When we finally got up, we found our breakfast on the table along with a note written in Mama's neat handwriting telling us that she and Daddy were going up to camp to attend the wakes of the two miners who were buried in the coal, as well as funerals of the Wilson brothers and Paul Winley.

I guess Mama thought that Rose and I had seen enough death. I was glad she hadn't made us go to the funerals. I couldn't imagine wearing the tight skirt around another day. Rose looked radiant that morning. Her eyes had transformed to a darker blue and shined with certain intensity that I'd never seen before. I was afraid to ask what had put this sparkle in her eyes. I knew she would get around to telling me, so I braced myself for what I knew was coming.

Neither Rose nor I had an appetite for the cold fried potatoes and gravy left over from breakfast, so I stuck I the leftovers inside the warmer. The fire had long since died in the grate and had only a few hot coals left.

"Don't stoke that fire," Rose warned. "We'll die if you do. I can already feel the heat in here. Besides, Mama won't be cookin' no more today, anyway. We have the whole day to ourselves," she said happily.

"We had better go to the spring for water sometime today," I reminded her, while eyeing the empty water buckets on the water table.

Rose gushed, "I'm goin' for a walk," and then added, "I'm just waitin' for the right time." Tilting her pretty head sideways, she eyed me mischievously.

"I hope you are goin' by yourself," I said knowingly.

"Oh Junie Mae, Bart Asher is the best looking man up close. His eyes are as dark as a block of coal. He's changed so much since I seen him last summer. He's a man now." Her voice quivered with emotion. Eying me with her queer gray eyes she whispered, "He asked me if I would meet him at the wall today so we can take a little walk."

Shaking my head in disgust, I told her what I thought about her sneaking out to see him. "Rose, you all ain't children no more. You don't even know him now. Besides, if Mama finds out you've been seein him she's liable to kill you!"

Rose's eyes flashed anger. "No girl I know would turn down the chance to be with Bart Asher. I've waited all my life for a chance like this!"

"Sounds like you're makin' too much of it," I said scornfully. Reaching for the dishrag, I proceeded to wipe the breadcrumbs from the table.

Shaking her head in protest she said, "He wants to see me. He didn't ask the Mattingly sisters or no other girl to meet him. He asked me!"

"You're too poor for him, Rose! You don't think the Ashers would allow him ever to have you, do you? Did Mama get Little Brock? You said Grandma Haley told you that Mama once thought she could have him. Is she with him now?"

"You're just a little girl, Junie Mae. I don't expect you to understand what I feel right now! A woman knows how a man feels about her. I know Bart Asher is interested in me! I could see it in his eyes. Even when we was little I knowed he was interested."

Rolling my eyes heavenward I asked, "How do you know he ain't asked other girls to meet him places?"

Either Rose hadn't heard me or she had chosen to ignore me. She finally said, "Bart made me forget where I was yesterday. Seein' him and havin' him so close to me was like some kind of magic dream…" Her voice trailed off.

"You wouldn't have forgot if Daddy had been one of the men in the caskets!"

"You can't tell Mama about me and Bart Asher," she pleaded desperately.

"Why would you tell me something like this? It's hard for me to lie to Mama."

"I'm not askin' you to lie to her. Just don't go blabbin' about what I told you today. That's all."

"If you keep meetin' him she's bound to find out sooner or later," I said disgustedly.

"Let me worry about that," she said, and then added, "Maybe you can use that power you have to look into the future and see what will happen to me and Bart."

"It don't work that way," I said in disgust, but secretly wondered if Floyd Wilkes' ghost would come and show me something if I conjured him up. Handing Rose the scraps from breakfast, I commanded, "Go feed and water Buster." Rose scowled but took the scraps out onto the front porch. I could hear her whistling for Buster.

Mama and Daddy didn't come home until almost dark. I had noticed that both of them looked bone tired and Daddy had dark circles around his eyes and was coughing more than usual. Lately he had developed a cough that concerned us all. Instead of going to bed, the two of them sat down at the table and discussed the wake and the two funerals they had attended. I could hear them plainly from my bedroom. Mama said, "I hope Tant Brock's mother don't hold it against us for not goin to Bear Creek for his burial. Bear Creek is a long way off."

Daddy said, "I'm shore she don't. I wonder why they buried him so far away. I thought the Bear Creek Cemetery was closer than twenty miles. I was there as a boy…" His voice trailed off.

In our room, Rose sat at the dressing table in front of the mirror brushing her hair. She wasn't listening to Mama and Daddy's funeral talk. Her thoughts seemed miles away. She had gone on her walk and made it home just a few minutes before they walked in the front door. It made me angry to see how casually she had strolled in, and couldn't help but wonder what Bart Asher had said to her to make her so careless. Had Mama not been so tired she might have asked questions concerning what Rose and me had done that day. The only chore I had finished was filling two water buckets from the spring. Other chores like laundry required Rose's help.

In our bedroom, I whispered in a frustrated voice, "Why did you come home so late, and what if Mama and Daddy had come home before you got back? You're not thinking right! You missed them by a hair," I snapped.

With her face all alight with happiness, Rose described her evening with Bart Asher in vivid detail. "Bart took me to their private pond. It's just on the edge of the woods behind the barn. You wouldn't believe how pretty and fancy it is. There's even a building where you can change clothes. Bart says we can swim there as soon as I bring a bathing suit. He said if I didn't have one I could borrow one of his sister's." Grabbing my arm, she said in a feverish voice, "I've never felt so happy in all my life. The whole place up there looks like something out of a book."

"I'll bet the Ashers don't know he was with you. They would probably be as mad as Mama if they did!"

"Why? Look, June Mae, you are forgettin' that Joelyn Asher was a poor girl. Mama said her family didn't have two sticks to rub together to make a fire. Why would she judge me?"

"Mama hates the Ashers, Rose. She will never agree to you seein' Little Brock Asher's son. If she catches you seein' him she might hurt you bad!"

"She won't catch me unless you tell her! Besides, if things go right it won't matter what she finds out later on!"

Reaching for the hairbrush on the dressing table, Rose ran it through her mussed hair. "God, I am still pinching myself to make sure I ain't dreaming."

"You're dreaming, Rose. I don't know much about men and women and whatnot, but I do know Mama and what she'll do if she ever gets wind of what you're doing. It ain't right, Rose!"

Slamming down the hairbrush on the dressing table, Rose whispered, "If you want to know who ain't right it's Mama. One day you're gonna see it! You're fourteen years old now, and it is time you know the real Mama! I found her out long ago!" On an impulse, Rose walked over and grasped my hands in hers. Her strange blue eyes searched mine. "Junie Mae, Mama hates me. She always has -- and you, you might as well be that rug on the floor. She don't even see you! I been watchin' her since I was a little girl -- been watchin' her when she wadn't lookin. I know how she thinks and I know she'll leave Daddy one day just as soon as she finds a way to do it. And I know somethin' else, too -- the minute you start seein her for what she is, she'll treat you just like she's been treatin' me all my life. The minute you speak up for yourself or against somethin she's done she'll turn on you too, Junie Mae!"

Lowering her voice Rose went on, "I could never suit Mama. No matter what I done it wadn't enough. Daddy don't suit her, either. She hates this place and us too. If you think that you're anything special, you'd do well to rethink it. One day you'll see how right I am. I ain't about to let her ruin my chances of gettin' away from her and this place. I don't care what I have to do."

I turned away from Rose and looked through the little round window and out into the dark night. I decided I'd had enough conversation and was too tired to argue with her. "Turn down the wick on the lamp and go to bed before Mama comes in here," I warned her.

Even after Rose turned down the wick and put out the light I had trouble sleeping. Mama and Daddy had moved to the porch. I could only make out a little of their conversation but knew it was about the mine. Their talks were always about the mine. Before sleep found me, the last thing I pictured was the black gaping hole leading into the bowels of No. 5 Mine.

6 RUMBLINGS OF TROUBLE

The month of August seemed to last forever, and the rainless days made us all miserable. Rose had developed dry chapped spots on her ankles and feet, while my lips dried and cracked. Mama tried to keep the air in the house damp and moist by putting pans of water on the stove and in our bedrooms. Still we suffered because of the hot, dry air. Daddy continued to work the long, hard days in the mine and would come home in the late evening dead tired. At night, his deep wracking cough was enough to wake the dead and left him gasping for air. Mama would tell him he needed to see a doctor but he would just shake his head and go on with whatever he had to do. After Daddy's bath and supper, he and Mama would go out onto the porch and talk about the day's events. Rose and me could hear them if we opened the round window in our bedroom. It opened up just like a porthole on a ship, with its hatch and a rusted hinge that made noise when cracked. Usually I would open it just enough to hear them talking.

After the burial of miners Todd Worley and Eddie Singleton, things started to fall apart up at No. 5 mine. I remember listening to Mama and Daddy talk, and paying close attention to what they said. In those days, families sat at the table and had dinner together. Television and the media were new and as distant and forlorn to us as the moon. We had no computers to take us away from the often grim realities of life. And unlike the children of today who escape into a world of video games or lose themselves in one of the many programs offered on cable television we could only look at our surroundings, family, and culture and evaluate what we saw. I suppose one could say that children grew up too fast then. Maybe this is true. Times were hard, but ours was such that we could not hide from the realities that often banish childhood innocence. How can a child hide from poverty or the dismal look of his surroundings when there is no place else to go? It's not that we didn't try. My escape was the ghost of Floyd Wilkes, while Mama nursed and honed her dreams of leaving Harlan. Rose also had dreams of marrying rich Bart Asher and living in his world of plenty. If Daddy had dreams of a better life, he had kept them to himself. I suspect that like him they were simple and uncomplicated.

After all the dead were laid to rest, hardly a night passed when some a miner didn't show up at the lodge in order to talk to Daddy and usually ended up taking supper with us. Pretty soon we had a half a dozen men or more sitting at the supper table, discussing the United Mine Workers of America and the possibility of a forming a union. Like many of the other miners, Daddy didn't warm to the idea of a union right away even though most of the coal mining companies, including the smaller ones, were under union contract and were paid better wages and had healthcare plans. Daddy talked bitterly of the bloody outcomes of the past one hundred years and how unions had often stirred the pot, causing injury and death. Named "Bloody Harlan" because of all the violence and death associated with coalmining strikes, the people of Harlan County seemed to have done little over the years to change the name. On the contrary, history will bear up to the fact that unionized miners and the opposing scabs have kept violent uprisings going throughout the years. It is a fact that eastern Kentucky is one the richest sources of coal in the world and many men have died in various ways trying to mine it. In retrospect, it is no wonder Daddy and some of the other miners were not quick to accept the idea of a unionized mine. Besides, many of the miners and their families genuinely liked the Ashers in spite of the fact Little Brock Asher didn't pay great wages and offered no health benefits. However, the Ashers were good about helping both the miners and their families when there was sickness or a financial need. Once, when coalminer Sal Watkins's wife, Wilma, stepped on a rusty nail and contracted blood poisoning, Little Brock Asher paid to have her foot treated, and just in time too; had she waited much longer, it might have been too late to save it. When Ben Morgan's old truck gave out, Little Brock had paid a mechanic to fix it. The Ashers were especially charitable on Christmas and saw that all the families in the camp had turkeys, and the children each received a stocking of candy. Miss Joelyn always sent our stockings by Mama. We couldn't wait to get into them on Christmas morning. Of course, Big Brock Asher allowed Mama to work a few nights at the funeral home, which paid the rent on the lodge. Miss Joelyn was kind to Mama and often paid her for her work with last year's beef and pork when they butchered fresh meat, not to mention the clothes and magazines she sent to Rose and me. Perhaps the Ashers thought their bond or connection with the mining community was so strong that men wouldn't vote in a labor union. They might have been right. Had the disastrous cave-in not happened it is doubtful anyone would have complained or tried to take action against the Ashers. One of the main reasons was because much of Appalachia had become inured to poverty. I'd heard Granny Lee say many times that when the Great Depression hit, no one suffered it too badly, because everyone was already just about as poor as they could be without starving.

I'd learned in time that the people of Appalachia came from strong bloodlines, and were accustomed to poverty and hard work. Their mixed bag of ancestors had immigrated to Kentucky from as far away as England, Germany, and Poland. Made up of strong stock, these pioneers fought off Indian attacks and saw their homes burned to the ground by bands of guerilla soldiers during the Civil War. The First and Second World Wars had robbed many families of their sons and brothers, but still they remained resilient, quietly and respectfully burying their dead and then faithfully tending their graves -- and not just on Memorial Day. It is my contention that Appalachia has some of the best-tended graves in the world because people never forgot their dead. The Kentuckian believed that love and family loyalty did not end with death. Storytellers kept their ancestors alive by passing information on to the next generation, and so on. No matter how far back the bloodline stretched, you knew your great-great-grandmothers and grandfathers and somehow loved them. I recall the "graveyard days" which took place in the summer. A week before the event, Mama, Granny Lee, and a host of female relatives would get together and make homemade wreaths and flowers to take to the family cemetery. During the flower making process, the women would decide who would bring what dish to the graveyard. On the day before the dinner, men folk would set up a few tables on the flattest part of the land. The next day those tables were piled with a variety of delicious food, from fried chicken to a pot of steaming dumplings. After the meal was over, people congregated around the graves and lovingly placed colorful wreaths and wildflowers near the headstones. Graveyard days were a well-kept tradition and a way of honoring the dead.

Mountain people are and always have been proud of the kinships they formed with their neighbors and are very loyal to the social bonds. This came from their early interdependence, which is still a large part of the culture. Families in the mountains and rural areas are clannish, and often find homes close to each other. In many cases, two families share one dwelling. During the turn of the century, an average couple raised more than five children. In many cases, it was rare to see a couple with less than ten. Granny Lee had six children but one died in infancy while the other choked to death on a marble at age three. I recall that one family in the Asher mining camp was raising nine children in a four-room house, and had it not been for Miss Joelyn Asher's charitable nature the children may have become malnourished. Several times a year, Miss Joelyn would load up the Asher truck with large boxes of breads and canned goods which she would deliver to family of nine. Mama once complained that the family of nine ate better than the four of us. The coalminers were well aware of all the help the Ashers had given them, and that was the reason for their hesitance to join a labor union. One night over discussions at the dinner table in late August, Daddy cautioned the group of miners, "We can't overlook how much the Ashers have done for the families in the camp. But we also can't shut our eyes to the low wages and bad conditions we are workin' under." Slim Bagshaw, a toothless old miner up in his early sixties complained, "Asher knows about the union leaders talkin' to us, so why ain't he contacted us and tried to negotiate a deal of some kind? Surely he don't think we can just overlook what happened up there?"

He went on, "The other day Purl Haley seen them union representatives talkin' to some men near the shaft and ran them off."

Uncle Corbin said, "A u-u-union would-would on-on-only comp-li-complicate mat-mat-matters! You-you-you all-all will be sorr-sorr-sorry if - if-if-if you-you-you ge-ge-get them-them in-in-in!"

Slim said, "Damn it, Corbin, we can't go on workin' for nothin'. It's bad enough that Asher refuses to replace roof beams," Slim pointed to Harvey James. He turned to Corbin, "Your brother over there inspected them beams. He's took a lot of heat 'cause of what happened with them braces. It weren't his fault! He told Asher the timber was rotten and wouldn't hold the roof up much longer in Shaft B. Asher didn't do nary a thing! People want to blame somebody. Why don't they put the blame where it lies?"

Daddy said, "The union people want to meet with us at the American Legion this Friday. I'm gonna go see what they're offerin'."

All eight miners looked at each other, mumbling low and looking uncertain. Mama stood at the window with the curtain pulled back looking off in the direction of Creekstone House. She said, "I ain't worked a day at the funeral parlor or at the Asher house, since the funerals. How are we gonna pay the rent or buy food to feed us? If you all vote in the union and there's a strike, how are we gonna live on strike pay? When Daddy worked the Daisy Mines, miners everywhere went on strike and families almost starved to death. The Daisy Camp was a bad place but nobody was out of work."

Uncle Corbin looked anxious and stuttered, "I-I-I- rem-rem-remember o-other strikes go-go-goin on then. Gun-gun-gun-tot-toting-thug-thugs desig-designated- from-from the off-off-office of-of the-hi-high she-sheriff was-was hi-hi-hired-by the-the- min-min-mining comp-comp-anies to-to-shoot any-anybody-seen-seen picket-picket-picketing. Two-two-two peop-people got-got shot and kill-killed in-in-in one day."

Mama nodded. Letting the curtain fall back she said to Daddy, "Ralph, You better think real hard before you meet with them union people! The Ashers will fight back. I know!"

Daddy nodded critically before taking a sip of his coffee. "I'm gonna see what the union people's got to say."

Uncle Corbin jumped up from his chair and glared at Daddy. "I wa-wa-want-no-no part-of tha-that meet-meet-meeting!"

Daddy winced and said, "Corbin, I'd hate to see you get hurt! You start takin' that stand against the union and you'll have more trouble than you can handle!"

Harvey James nodded in agreement and warned, "Corbin, just go home and stew about it but keep your mouth shut for now."

Uncle Corbin snatched up his light jacket from off the chair and said, "I-I-I- kno- know-wha-wha-what's com-comin. You-you-you -all-will will-be sorr-sorry!"

I had been standing in the kitchen doorway since the beginning of the conversations but no one had noticed me. Even Uncle Corbin pushed past me, slamming the screen door shut in the front room. As I entered the kitchen, the other men were getting up out of their chairs to leave. Most of them acknowledged me before they went out through the front room. After they were gone, Mama turned to me and said, "You and your sister clear this table. Me and your Daddy are going to the porch for a while. After you all are done with the kitchen, go on to bed."

Rose came into the kitchen after Mama and Daddy had gone to the back porch. She wore a petulant look as she went about stacking the dishes. Speaking in a hushed voice she said, "Daddy and the miners are out to get Little Brock Asher. If they go union this might fix things between Bart and me."

I couldn't believe what I was hearing. Pouring the teakettle of hot water into the dishpan, I said, "I can't believe you're worried about somethin like this when Mama ain't seen a day's work from the Ashers since the wakes."

Rose said, "Bart Asher is my way out of being poor like this. I wish you could understand! If Daddy and the others vote that union in, Little Brock Asher will never let his son near me!"

I laughed, not because what she said was funny, but because it sounded ridiculous. She was willing to sell Daddy out after a few walks in the woods with Bart Asher. I turned on my sister, slamming the teakettle down hard on the table. "It looks like it's them against us, Rose! You can't choose a stranger over your own Mama and Daddy. You're thinkin' wrong if you believe that he's gonna marry you anyway."

Rose's light blue eyes flashed darker. Her voice was cautious. "Hush up! They'll hear you!"

"Maybe I'll just tell them! You've lost your mind, Rose! Eventually that boy will go away to college, and then where will you be?"

Rose's face flushed angrily. "He won't forget me when he goes away. I'll make shore of that!"

You must be planning to jump in his suitcase. Look, a walk or two in the woods don't mean he's gonna marry you. It don't make sense for you to start plannin' a weddin'."

Rose looked unperturbed and in a voice filled with fierce determination she said, "As long as he'll look my way I've got a chance with him. Nobody's gonna take that from me -- not you, Mama, or Daddy! If you just knowed what's passed between Bart and me, you might understand. I got hope, Junie Mae. Daddy says we all gotta keep hopin' for better things. Hope is what keeps us alive."

Wiping the last dish and putting it on the stack, I shut the cabinet door. Pulling the kitchen curtains back, Rose stared longingly in the direction of the Creekstone House. Feeling perturbed, I said, "Daddy's thinkin' about you, me, and Mama, Rose. He wants to make shore we have food on the table. It seems to me that the Ashers ain't too concerned about that! Daddy said Big Brock ain't made a move to talk things out with the miners."

Once again, Rose flashed her strange blue eyes at me but said nothing. I left her in the kitchen and went to the front porch to cool off. Outside the air was hot and still. My eyes scanned the heavens for stars but saw nothing but darkness. I thought of Floyd Wilkes and wondered if his ghost was about. Needing his presence, I squeezed my eyes shut and pictured him standing in a field dressed in his ragged overalls with his pale hair blowing in the breeze. I saw myself with my hand outstretched beckoning toward him, but my vision was fuzzy. I found it hard to concentrate when my thoughts kept drifting back to the earlier conversation between Daddy and the other miners. I thought of how Rose was putting her love for Bart before the welfare of her own family. I thought of Mama too, and worried that she would find out about Bart and hurt Rose badly. I was about to give up on Floyd Wilkes when a little wind stirred the leaves. At first there came softness, barely a tickle to the skin, but then it started gaining momentum, finally sending a coal bucket spiraling off the porch and into the barbwire fence with a clang. The wind now had a power and ferocity to it that was frightening. Visibly agitated, Buster came running at me in leaps and bounds, nearly knocking me down. The trees leaned backwards and the very eaves of the house shook. The pleated dress I wore blew up around my face. I was certain that the ghost of Floyd Wilkes had caused the weather to change. I could feel him all around me. His spirit was as alive as the forceful wind. Buster felt him too. I could tell by the way he raised his hackles and snarled into the black nothingness as if he was looking at something that I couldn't see.

Rising out of my chair, I heard the low rumbling thunder and saw streaks of blue lighting pierce the sky. The sound of raindrops pelting the tin roof caused me to cry out in joy. Like a small child, I jumped off the porch and onto the yard. The feel of the wind mingled with that of the cooling needles of rain in my hair and face invigorated me. Frightened by the sudden howl of the wind, Buster ran for shelter underneath the porch. Turning in his direction, I saw his eyes shining in the dark.

Mama's voice sounded far off as she called to me from the porch, but I ignored her and remained outside with the spirit of Floyd Wilkes. "It's raining, Mama!" I yelled overtop the roar of the wind. The gusting rain hit the house and blew up on the porch, causing Mama to hug herself. "Get in here Junie Mae, that lighting's bad."

"It feels so good out here!" I cried. "Now the river will rise back up and its waters will be clean again!"

Daddy yelled above the wind gusts, "We need this good old rain."

Once inside and in the kitchen Mama grabbed a towel and threw it to me. "Get dry and get to bed!"

That night I lay underneath the heavy quilt Grandma Haley had made for me long ago and listened to the rain which had turned to a gentle patter on the tin roof. The scent of lye touched my nostrils. Mama always washed her clothes in lye soap that Granny Lee had made from the hog fat and guts that Harlan Ray had given her after the yearly hog killing. Harlan Ray had a nice house in the country where he raised pigs and chickens. In the fall when the weather was cool, he, Daddy, and Harvey James butchered the fattened hog and then smoked the meat. Afterwards, they hung the meat to cure in the smokehouse. Harvey James usually gave Mama a big smoked ham for Christmas. I can still remember the delicious aroma of the baking ham wafting through the house on Christmas Eve.

The people and places that made up my everyday life flashed inside my thoughts that night. Daddy sitting on a stool in his shed carving away at the wood but looking far beyond it was the most lasting memory. The river, with its little islands and stands of water birch bent down toward the water, etched its way into my thoughts. Rose standing on the front porch wearing her white shirt and black skirt, with her shiny dark hair teasingly covering one eye entered my thoughts like a sad little sigh. Rose had her beauty -- there was no doubt that -- but was lacking in so many other attributes. I thought of educated Bart Asher and Miss Joelyn, and couldn't imagine Rose generously giving Christmas turkeys out to the families in the camps, or showing concern for a poor family of nine children. No matter what Mama said, I believed Miss Joelyn was naturally generous. I doubted Rose would ever have these qualities -- not that she was a bad person, just self-centered. I thought of Mama the same way -- not overly generous and preoccupied with what mattered the most to her rather than what was best for others. Somehow, I knew that Rose would end up disappointed if she continued to depend on Bart Asher for her happiness.

I was tired of thinking and trying to figure out why people acted the way they did. Thankfully, darkness finally came pulling its curtain of silence over my thoughts.

7 A VISIT FROM BIG BROCK ASHER

I awoke the following morning to the familiar smell of bacon frying in the kitchen. Outside my bedroom window, the grey morning light spilled in. Pulling back the curtain, I noted how green and polished the leaves looked after the night's heavy rains. Daddy had already gone off to the mine. I had heard Uncle Harlan Ray's old truck pull up around six thirty and saw the headlights shining through the window. Sometime in the night I woke up long enough to see Rose standing in front of the window with the curtain pulled back, staring out into the darkness. I had told her to go back to bed. She'd looked at me and said nothing. I knew she still worried about Bart Asher finding out that Daddy and the Uncles were encouraging the other miners to attend the union meeting at the American Legion Hall. One part of me felt sorry for her while the other part felt anger at her for choosing the side of strangers over her own.

Deciding not to wake her, I padded barefoot to the kitchen in time to see Mama standing over the cook stove turning the bacon. Mama was dressed a white sleeveless gown. A few loose strands of her hair had strayed from the little twist atop her head. I thought she was so pretty and fragile with her thin features. Upon seeing me, she asked, "Junie Mae, can you come here and finish up the bacon? I need to go outside and check the rain barrels. I'll start the wash if they're full enough."

In the dry weather, Mama had us help her carry her wash and the tubs down to the river or to the creek under the bridge until Dog Days turned the waters nasty and filmy. If this happened then we had to carry the wash water down in buckets from the spring up in the woods. The spring was a good five minute walk, and it took Rose and me about six trips just to fill one number ten tub. The rain had been a godsend all right. It not only provided us with water to wash our clothes but for bathing as well.

Mama was gone only a minute or two when I thought I heard a knock on the front room screen door. Pausing over the bacon, I strained my ears and heard the rap again. Pulling the bacon over to the cooler side of the stove, I walked gingerly to the front door, opened it, and instantly recognized Big Brock Asher standing there behind the screen, well over six feet tall and dressed in a smooth gray suit. Respectfully holding a matching hat, his peculiar blue gray eyes regarded me in question. "Is your mother about?" His voice was very deep and a little unnerving. Something about him had made me shiver involuntarily. Nodding yes, my eyes fell on the thickness of his lips and then to the oddity of his eyes which stirred up some kind of strange recognition that I would mull over later. Mama was just coming through the back door when I entered the kitchen. "Big Brock Asher is in the living room," I whispered.

Mama's eyes grew large and suspicious. "You go in your room and stay there. Tell your sister to do the same."

In our room, Rose was wide awake and sitting on the edge of her bed shaking all over. Her big blue-gray eyes reminded me of what a calf might look like when caught in a barbed wire fence. Grabbing my arm so hard she pinched the skin, Rose whispered, "Big Brock knows about me and Bart. Oh, God -- I'll bet he's here to tell Mama!"

"Shhh," I cautioned, edging as close to the doorway as I could without being seen. I strained my ears to listen. Big Brock spoke first. "Morning, Heddy, I won't take up too much time here. I reckon you already know why I've come."

"How would I know?" Mama asked coldly.

"Word has it that your husband and his brothers are trying to recruit men into going to hear that union agitator speak tonight."

"I don't know nothin' about that. You'd have to ask Ralph."

Big Brock Asher laughed deeply and said, "I know how these things go; the wives stand behind their husbands on these matters. Why, Heddy? Your daddy wadn't no union sympathizer and went up against the petition when it came around."

Mama laughed harshly and replied, "Daddy was killed when your mine exploded, so I don't know what he was thinking. Guess I'll never know!"

Big Brock Asher said, "That was bad business, Heddy, but coalmining is dangerous and always has been. Your daddy knew this and so did the miners who died in the Number Five mine. I'll tell you one thing, Heddy: if you think being a union member is a guarantee against a man dying in a mining accident, then you have another think coming."

Mama said, "It don't matter what I think. The men will do what they want, anyways."

"Look, Heddy, I heard from a trustworthy source that your husband and his brothers are the main ones pushing for a union. Now this surprised me about Ralph, because he's never rippled the pool in all the years he's worked for us."

"I can't help you," Mama said stubbornly.

Big Brock sighed. "Heddy, I know you hold me responsible for your Daddy's death and all this has brought it back for you. But can't you see that I did the best I could when the mine exploded? I settled with the widows, and seen to it that your mama had a home for you all. I've given you and your Mama work all these years. When you told me you didn't want to raise your girls in the coal camp, I rented you this place, cheap. Our family has been nothing but charitable to you and the camp families, and this is how you all repay us!"

"Charitable?" Mama laughed, and said, "Would you really raise a child of yours in a house with no electricity or indoor plumbin'?"

"Now, that's not fair Heddy! Baring your claws and hissing at me is getting us nowhere! I came here hoping to convince you to talk some sense into your husband."

Mama said in a raised voice, "I don't work in the coal. I know it's bad, though. I've seen the knees of my daddy's britches worn clean to the skin. I can't imagine bein' on my knees all day shovelin' coal in some dark hole. How can I tell my husband what's best when I don't know what doin' somethin like that feels like?"

Big Brock said, "Heddy, you can dance around the truth if you want to, but how much blood has been spilled here in Harlan County because men chose to strike? Just remember, Heddy -- there will always be men willing to cross a picket line in order to feed their families. Men say they want safer conditions, but what's safe about a gun-toting scab taking aim at a picketer?"

After a short uncomfortable silence, Big Brock said, "Heddy, I miss having you at the funeral home, but I can't have you working for me while your husband is out trying to stab my son in the back. Can't he and the others see that they are biting the hand that feeds them? My family has been generous…"

Mama cut him off by saying, "All you people have ever done is dangle enough of somethin' in front of us to make us want more! If your son is so generous then why ain't his miners gettin' paid the same wages that miners are making at other places? You know, my brothers get at least two dollars more on the hour at the McKinley mines!"

"I can't speak for my son about that, Heddy, but I can assure you that his wages are fair considering the area and demographics."

Mama's voice sounded bitter. "Spare me your fancy business talk, Brock! It all amounts up to nothing in the end, anyways. I've lived in coal all my life. You can't tell me nothin' that I don't already know. There's no gettin' away from it. When Daddy died, I heard you tell Mama how there wadn't enough left of him to put in a casket. I won't forget you sayin' that. What's fair about that? Them children up there will never know their daddies, so how can your son make that right? The coal has taken away more than it ever gave anybody – well, the big men like you and your son profit, and that's really all that counts, ain't it?"

"Heddy, we go back a long way. Don't that mean something to you?" Big Brock asked in a gentle voice. I could feel Rose's hot breath on my neck. Her fingers continued to dig painfully into my arm.

Mama laughed harshly. "Do you really want me to remember that far backwards?"

"Now Heddy, I can't go back and change things. I would if I could, but time doesn't go backwards, so it might be best that we forget about things that happened way back. All I'm asking you to do is talk Ralph out of this union thing. You don't want the striking and the possibility of more men dying. I know you don't! Do you want to see your family and the families of the miners thrown out on the street? When a union comes in the first thing they want the miners to do is strike. This could be bad business for the people living in the camps."

Mama spat, "Miners strike because they get paid chicken feed. Greedy owners ain't interested in nothin' but makin' a profit and they don't care who or what they have to sacrifice to make it, do they?"

I knew Mama was furious. Although I couldn't see her face, I remembered how twisted and dark it could become when something didn't set right with her. Big Brock had pushed a button when he'd mentioned the possibility of her and the miner's families losing their homes. Hovering behind me Rose was beside herself with panic, pulling and squeezing my skin and whispering things into my ear, irritating me. "Stop it, Rose!" I demanded, shrugging off her persistent hands. Mama spoke again, "Brock, there ain't no union yet, just some talk and already you are threatenin' to evict people. I'd think twice about doin' that! You mentioned the past and how far we go back. I remember meaning somethin' to you all right! I think you've forgot a lot of things about them days. Maybe I can drag somethin' out to make you remember"

"Now, Heddy, I have no idea what you are getting at but whatever it is it don't have nothing to do with why I came here."

"This place may not be much but it is my children's home. I don't want to see no eviction notice, Brock Asher. If a server comes here, there will be hell to pay! Now you take that out the door with you and pass it along to your son! I've got work to do."

I heard the creak of the floorboards and knew Big Brock Asher was leaving.

"You think about what I said, Heddy!"

"You do the same!" Mama shot right back.

"Oh God," Rose said, slumping on the bed. "How could Mama talk like that to Big Brock Asher?"

Gently closing the bedroom door I said, "Rose, you know she holds a grudge against him for Granddaddy's death."

Shaking her head vigorously, Rose whispered, "There's more to it than that. I got a feelin' that Big Brock probably made Little Brock stop seein' Mama." Turning to me with a tortured look, she said in a tone of defeat, "Either him or his son will put a stop to me and Bart if it ever comes out. I just know it!"

"This ain't about you, Rose," I cried. "It's about minin' and strikin' and people bein' out of work and losin' their places. It's about men gettin' killed because the mine owners don't fix what's wrong. Ain't you ever heard Daddy and Granny Lee talk about how bad it is when coalminers strike? Men get killed for marchin' the picket or even crossin' the picket line."

"Oh yes. I have heard the stories 'til I'm blue in the face. Why do you think I want Bart Asher? Havin' him would mean I'd never have to see that! If we was to marry and have children, they wouldn't have to worry about their Daddy getting blowed up in an explosion or buried underneath the coal. He wouldn't be a coalminer, Junie Mae, he'd own it."

A laugh rose in my throat. I felt near hysterics. How could she miss the obvious? It was right there like a big gray elephant in the room. "The Ashers own Number Five mine, Rose. He would just inherit his Daddy's troubles. Little Brock ain't gonna just give Bart a bunch of money to do nothing. He'll earn it. I've heard Mama talk about how Little Brock didn't want no part in the coal business, either, and how his Daddy bought him the business and made him run it, anyway. It'll be the same way for Bart. It won't matter whether he wants it or not. You'll see."

"Is that what the spirits told you?" she mocked, and then added, "You don't know what you're talkin' about Junie Mae. You can't know everything and that's the truth!"

Walking slowly over to the window, she breathed a long sigh, and after a few minutes whispered, "When I was real little, I used to look out this window and think Creekstone was a castle like in them fairy books. It never looked real to me even when I stood close to it. One day when Bart and me was playing in the woods, I told him how his house didn't look real. I remember that he laughed and said, 'What do you mean? It's a house.' Do you know what he done? He took me right up to the front door and let me touch the wall. He wadn't scared who might see us. Me, well I was scared to death Mama might see us through the window, but she didn't. After that day I knowed it was real 'cause I felt it. It wadn't a picture to me no more." Turning toward me, she asked in a little girl's voice, "Don't you ever wonder what it would like to be an Asher? Them people never havin' to worry about money. They have so much. When I was a little girl, I wanted a charm bracelet just like the one Bitsy Asher wore on her wrist. I saw it on her one day when she was playin' on the bridge. I remember how it sparkled ever' time the sun hit it. I spoke to her for the first time that day, and she was real nice to me. I remember that she was dressed up like she was goin' to a party and had on a frilly blue dress and matchin' lacy anklets. When she seen me lookin' at the bracelet, she asked me if I wanted to see it. I told her I did, so she took it off and just handed to me like it was nothin'. I remember that the bracelet was gold and had little flowers and bells hangin' on separate little chains. I'd wanted one just like it so bad. I told her how much I liked it, and she just shrugged uncarin' like, and told me how she had prettier ones in her jewelry box up at the house. Then she started talkin' about her pony named Teddy after Teddy Roosevelt, and forgot I even had that bracelet. I thought about just runnin' away with it. She said she had prettier ones, so why would she miss it? But I didn't because I knew Mama would beat me if Bitsy ever told." After a minute of silence, she said, "I thought she might give it to me. I had hoped, anyway, but she didn't. When I handed the bracelet back she just stuck it in her dress pocket. She wadn't even careful with it or nothin'. If it had been mine, I would have handled it like an egg. I can't understand why some people have so much and others have nothin."

"Granny Lee says it's a sin to want for things you can't have. She says that the Lord gives us what we need and not what we want!"

Rose regarded me hatefully and said, "Granny Lee just learned to settle for nothin'. I can't do that. I want things and I'll get them some way."

"Maybe the only reason you want Bart Asher's because he's rich," I said triumphantly.

"What's wrong with wantin' somethin' besides a coalminer? Daddy's a coal- miner, and look what we got! Nothin'! You think Miss Joelyn married Little Brock for somethin' besides money? I don't!" she sneered. Her voice had grown louder and within Mama's keen hearing range.

"We best get dressed for school," I said, quickly changing the subject.

Leaving Rose to simmer in her anger, I went into the kitchen and found Mama sitting at the table with pencil in hand scribbling furiously on a writing tablet. Looking up at me with red- rimmed eyes she said in a choked voice. "I'm writing to your Uncle Larkin in Indianapolis. Maybe he can talk some sense into your Daddy, and convince him to move us out there. I've had enough of this place! You don't tell Daddy what you seen here today. Do you hear me? You make sure Rose don't mention it either. I will tell Daddy in my own way. No use upsettin' him anymore."

I nodded.

"Is your sister going to school today?"

"I don't know."

"It's just as well. She can stay here today and help me with the wash."

Just as Mama said it, Rose came into the kitchen dressed for school. "I'm going to school, Mama." Rose frowned down at the half-finished letter and asked her who she was writing to. Looking cornered, Mama self-consciously covered the paper like a naughty schoolgirl.

"Who's that letter to?" Rose persisted.

Mama sighed and said, "If you must know, it's to your Uncle Larkin out in Indianapolis. Granny Lee says he goes all over the place building bridges. I ain't never met him but Daddy talks good about him. "

"Why are you writin' Daddy's brother for?"

Looking irritated, Mama said, "Well, you girls may as well know the truth. If a union comes in here there's gonna be trouble. Unions want to strike and when there is a strike, there's a lot of danger. I don't want us to have to go through all that. I got to thinkin' that maybe your Uncle Larkin might help us find a place and a safer job out there in Indianapolis."

Looking disgusted, Rose said. "Daddy won't like you writin' his brother like that. You know he'll never leave Granny Lee and his brothers here."

A momentary shadow crossed Mama's face. "You let me worry about what your Daddy will or won't do. Just make sure you keep your mouths shut! It's my place to tell him about the letter."

I nodded again in agreement but Rose stood with a look of defiance on her face. Seeing her look of hostility, Mama suddenly reached out, grabbed her shoulders and shook her hard. Through clenched teeth, she said, "I'm so sick of your sassin', Rose. You don't know what's best for you – I do. There's nothin' here for any of us. I just have to make your Daddy see that we'd be better off somewhere else."

"Mama, please!" I begged.

After Mama gave Rose an angry shove, she turned to face the kitchen door, and began sobbing into her hands, quietly at first but then her whole body shook. Rose glared hatefully in her direction then walked apathetically out of the kitchen. Instead of hurrying to embrace her, I simply stood there feeling uncomfortable. Mama didn't cry often and wasn't a hugger. I knew instinctively that if I tried to comfort her she would shrug me off. That was her strong, sometimes unyielding nature.

"You girls go on to school and leave me to work things out," she finally said. Hesitantly she glanced over her shoulder at me and said on a quiet, pleading voice, "You understand, don't you, Junie Mae? I'm only trying to do what's best for us all. You girls don't know what it's like when a union comes in and there's a strike. The strikers get threatened and sometimes even shot, and for what -- a dollar or two more on their paychecks? The strike pay is so low that you can't even afford to eat. I'm tryin' my best to think of ways to keep you girls from havin' to go through this hell."

"I'm trying to understand, Mama," I said truthfully.

Mama sighed and then turned toward me, suddenly looking older than her age. "Your Great-Granddaddy Lewis Haley was killed by a scab in a coal mine over on Black Mountain. He was leadin' a picket when someone shot him in the back of the head. My Daddy was just a boy then but learned to hate the union and wouldn't have no part in any unionized coalmine. I'm afraid of them, too -- afraid for your Daddy and the others because they won't quit until they get a union in. Your Uncle Harvey James has a lot of friends down there at mine. You mark my words -- in a month or two they'll get the majority of the men on the side of the union. Your Granny Lee won't say a thing to stop them, either. Did you know that your Grandpa Lee died when he was only thirty years old? The coal had damaged his lungs so bad that they finally gave out. Is this what you two want to see happen to your Daddy?"

I shook my head no. The thought of Daddy dying and leaving us scared me to death. I couldn't imagine life without him.

Outside the air was cooler than usual. I could see silver streaks of the river through the trees and longed to skip school and go to the rock and sit and maybe conjure up the ghost of Floyd Wilkes. Things were getting complicated at home. Mama was desperate to leave Harlan, while Daddy was desperate to stay and fight for a union. What would he say if he knew Mama was writing a letter to his older brother Larkin, a man none of us had ever seen? I had heard Granny Lee sing his praises many times. She had often bragged about how he'd left Harlan at a young age and made good of his life. He'd found a woman in Indianapolis, married her, and had one daughter named Amy Isabella. Amy Isabella's pictures stood on Granny Lee's end tables and dressing table. She looked to be about eight or nine years old and was dark skinned like the Lees and had an angelic little face. Granny Lee had told us that Uncle Larkin thought the sun rose and set in that child and had spoiled her rotten since the day she was born.

Uncle Larkin's wife Rhodie wrote Granny Lee many letters, and sometimes she would read them to Rose and me. The letters were full of Amy Isabella and how her Daddy had bought her a pony or a swing set. Once he'd even hired a clown to come and juggle pins for her birthday. Uncle Larkin was some kind of engineer that traveled all over the states designing bridges. Granny Lee said Rhodie was lonely in his long absences and wrote many letters to her. She said of Uncle Larkin's visits, "I've only seen my boy three times in ten years. Every time he comes, it's late in the night and he has to leave early the next mornin'. I keep hopin' he will bring his family out so I can finally meet Rhodie and little Amy Isabella. A child needs to know its grandma!"

8 GRANNY LEE'S HOUSE IN PUTNEY

While walking the gravel path leading to the highways and the bus stop, Rose kicked a pebble into the weeds and said, "Old Brock Asher sure got Mama all stirred up."

"She's worried about the union coming in," I said in her defense.

Rose sniffed the air indifferently and said, "She's more concerned with gettin' out of here than she is anything else. She'll go to Indianapolis without Daddy if she finds a way. The union stuff is a good excuse for her to leave. I wouldn't put it past her trying to make Big Brock give her money to shut up and leave!"

"What would she have on him?" I asked incredulously.

"Maybe Miss Joelyn don't know about Little Brock and Mama! You heard what she said and how she said it, a while ago. She's got something on him. I know it!"

Before I could think about what she said, we reached the bus stop and the jeers started immediately. I will never forget the hostile faces of the children I had known all my life. Most of them had stopped talking and stared a hole through us. Rose, suddenly fearful, grabbed my arm and halted my step. Tommy Roberts and Billy Ray Wilkins, who was nicknamed "Bully," started walking in our direction us calling us "union lovers." He said, "Your Deddy's stirring up trouble down there at the mines wantin' a union to come in here. This means war!"

Throwing his books down on the ground, Tommy Roberts came stomping toward me; his face was twisted up in a hateful expression. Rose stepped in front of me and said, "Tommy Roberts, I'll slap you silly if you touch us!" But her threat only enraged him more. With one arm Tommy slung her down on the ground, then turned, and grabbed me by the hair. "Get hold of this'n, Billy!" he yelled. Dropping my books, I felt my face being shoved into the gravel of the path. I could taste the dirt mingled with the taste of my own blood. I couldn't say a word, but my mind screamed, "Why don't somebody help us!" I recognized the voices of the Mattingly sisters begging Billy and Tommy to leave us alone. I heard Rose scream and then there was a struggle. Oh God, what were they going to do to us? I made an effort get up, but every time I moved, I felt my face being shoved deeper into the dirt and gravel. Tommy warned, "Your Deddy and his brothers are gonna get us throwed out of our houses. You go back home and tell 'em all that they're gonna get shot if they don't stay away from them union people! We don't need no union here!"

"Hey cowards, get off them girls!" came a voice I recognized as that of Amity Smith. "What's it to you, Smith? Your Deddy ain't gonna lose his place because of the Deddy of these two bitches. Stay out of it!"

Stepping out of his truck and slamming the door he yelled, "Let 'em go, boys, or I'm gonna beat the stuffin' out of the both of you! I can do it, too! I'm bigger and taller!"

Before Tommy could say a word, I felt him being dragged off me and the weight of his hands on my head lifted. I heard him cry out and there was a thump in the gravel.

I raised myself from the gravel long enough to see Amity walk over to Billy, hitting him hard in the face. The force of the blow sent him staggering backwards, finally hitting the wood of the shelter house with a hard thump. Rose was still sitting on the ground crying and making an effort to pull her dress together where the buttons had been ripped off. Amity rubbed his injured fist with his good hand, looked at the crowd, and said, "Ain't you all ashamed of yourselves, standing here and letting these two bullies beat up on these girls. Not one of you would help 'em. You're all cowards!"

Billy eased himself off the ground and shouted, "This is war, Smith! You'll pay for what you just done!"

Amity laughed and said, "I'll be here every mornin' from now on to see that none of you bother these girls. I'll beat the stuffin' out of anybody who touches them! You hear me?"

Walking over to Rose, Violet Elizabeth, Amity's younger sister, began helping her fix her dress up decently around her, while Amity pulled me off the ground. "I'm sorry, Junie Mae. They won't bother you again -- and that's a promise!"

"You tell your Deddy to stop messin' with the union people or he'll get worse!" Billy yelled.

"You all need to go home," Violet Elizabeth gently suggested. Turning to me she said, "Junie Mae, your face needs some black salve and your lip is bleeding in the corner." Thank goodness Rose hadn't suffered any skin breaks, just a torn dress.

Amity Smith said, "Junie Mae, I'm gonna take you and Rose home. I'll help you all get in the back of the truck. I'm sorry there ain't room for the both of you up front."

Neither Rose nor I objected, not even when Amity took turns lifting us into the truck bed. Even in my nervous state, I noted how tall and muscular he was. Later I would decide it was from all that lifting he did in his daddy's mill. Amity was careful to drive slow and even tried to dodge the chug holes and mud puddles that made up the rough dirt road leading back to the lodge. One mile had seemed like five, but Amity finally got us there. "Will you all be all right?" Violet Elizabeth asked. I nodded and thanked both her and Amity.

Mama was furious when she saw the cut on my lip and how the gravel had left scrapes all over my nose and the left side of my face. When Daddy came home and heard what had happened he cried into his hands. After dinner, Harvey James and Harlan Ray tried to console him, but he was too angry and hurt. Mama warned, "It's already started, Ralph. Can't you see what's coming? "

Daddy nodded silently and finally said, "That meetin' ain't even happened yet, and it's already caused trouble for my girls. I didn't know so many were against us getting' a union."

Harvey James rose from the table and said, "Look, Ralph, we have to make a stand here! Other miners have done it and got whole lot better and safer conditions. If we don't get a union in here, more men are going to die! I will have a talk with the fathers of those boys. Tucker Wilkins is a fair man. I imagine he'll whip the tar out of that boy of his when he finds out what he did to your girls."

Daddy said, "I have a good mind to go up and see them boys' daddies, myself. If it happens again, I will! I'll tell Wilkins one thing: he and that bully son of his better find a steep rock to hide under if this happens again. The same goes for Camm Roberts!" Daddy's dark eyes looked as if they might pop out of his head. Daddy didn't get angry often, but when he did you could see it all over him.

Mama sighed irritably and started clearing the dinner table. "You better hope Little Brock Asher don't take a notion to close down or sell out. I wouldn't put it past him to do what his Daddy done after that explosion killed my Daddy and the others."

Harvey James said, "Well, I doubt Little Brock will close down. There's a lot of money at stake, especially with that new million-dollar contract he just cinched with Kentucky Power. He can't afford to lose one man, let alone a strike."

Harlan Ray chuckled dryly and said, "He can damn sure afford to pay his miners better. He just ain't been made to do it. It seems to me old Big Brock is runnin' the show right now more than his son."

Harvey James said, "I don't give a good gosh damn who's running it. All I care about is getting' a union in to help us -- and I will, if it's the last thing I do."

On the night of the union meeting, Daddy decided to drive Rose and me over to Putney to stay with Granny Martha Lee. He and Mama thought we would be safer there since Granny Lee always had a lot of company, and Mama said that half the time she didn't know or care that was in the house. Marie usually had a suitor or two hidden away on the back porch, and Uncle Corbin often visited, sometimes spending a night or two. Granny Lee's older brother, Hiram, also lived in one of the four bedrooms upstairs. Uncle Harlan Ray called Great Uncle Hiram an idiot and said he was "touched in the head." Granny Lee wouldn't have anyone saying nasty things about her big brother, especially her own sons. In her eyes, Great Uncle Hiram was a hero who wasn't to blame for his nervous condition caused by the horrors he had witnessed while fighting in the First World War. When a storm blew up, he would hit the floor every time a clap of thunder sounded. And when anyone questioned Uncle Hiram's time spent in the Navy, Granny Lee would assure them in her most sincere tone. "Lord, honey, it was the worst war in history and your Uncle Hiram was right in the middle of it all. He was a navy man on a big ship that had big guns like a cannons. When a thunderstorm hits he's right back there in them horrible times. God bless him and men like him for keepin' us all safe."

Uncles Harvey James and Harlan Ray often laughed and made jokes about how Great Uncle Hiram was discharged early from the navy because he suffered from a bad, reoccurring case of hemorrhoids. Uncle Harlan said, "It's doubtful Hiram ever seen combat. I think he was some kind of cook who spent most of the time in the ship's kitchen." But Granny Lee would have none of that, declaring Hiram as a man damaged from the hellacious sights and sounds of war. Deeming herself an expert when it came to both wars, Granny Lee's accounts were so vivid one might have thought she was right there amidst the action.

Granny Lee's two-story house, with its faded red clapboards, was the first one in a row of five other identical houses. Fifteen years before, more houses had stood adjacent to Granny Lee's house and all were part of a mining camp. Across the highway on a steep hill, the winding railroad tracks lead to the now abandoned coalmine. Mama hated Putney because it served as a grim reminder of her early childhood spent in the Daisy Mining Camp.

As soon as Harvey James pulled up to the gate, she sighed drearily and said, "I wouldn't live here if they gave me every house on the block! All I see when I look at this place is coal. I can smell it and taste it. God, I'm so sick of mining towns."

Granny Lee and Uncle Corbin stood on the porch waiting for us to unload. Granny Lee, short and heavy, waved to us, but Uncle Corbin stood rigid and unsmiling. Upon seeing Uncle Corbin, Harvey James groaned miserably. "There's Corbin. That's all we need, and he looks fit to be tied, don't he?"

Daddy said, "Let's try our best not to tweak his nose." Harlan Ray nodded in agreement. Getting out of the car first, Rose was greeted by a smiling Marie who carried a dirty faced Chester Harlan on one hip. Uncle Corbin gave Daddy a fierce look. Shaking his head in disgust he stuttered, "You-you-you-boys, are-are-are-mak-mak-making-a ba-ba-bad-mist-mistake go-go-go-going to-to-to-th-that u-u-union-meet-meetin'. Ash-Asher kno-knows an-an-and will re-re-retaliate again-against-all-all-all of-us-us-fo-fo-for what-what you-you-you all-all are-do-do-doin.'"

Harvey James said, "Don't worry about it, Corbin -- I doubt Asher will do a thing. He's got way too much to lose to start retaliating this early in the game. We want only a decent wage and safer conditions. If we don't fight for these things we'll never get them."

Uncle Corbin stuttered, "You-you-you-all-all are-beg-beg-begging-for-for-trou-trouble. That-that's -all."

Granny Lee said in a patient tone, "Now Corbin, I see nothin' wrong with the boys goin' to that meetin' and hearin' what that union representative has to say."

"The-they-they never-never-never-mean-mean-a th-th-thing they-they say!" Great Uncle Hiram stepped from behind Granny Lee, and with pistol in hand he said in a menacing tone, "Nobody's gonna cause us trouble tonight."

Harlan Ray scowled, while Harvey James moaned in agitation. Uncle Corbin ordered in a loud impatient voice, "Hiram, giv-give-give-Maw-maw-maw that-pis-pis-pistol-ri-ri-right now!"

Harvey James asked, "Hiram, don't you remember how the gun went off upstairs and splintered a window? That could have been somebody you shot. There are little babies here and they could grab that gun while you're not looking. Now hand that thing to Maw!"

Great Uncle Hiram looked dejected and said, "I forgot and left on the safety is all. I'm a clean shot. You'd know that if you was to see me target practice at the range over in Drywell."

Granny Lee said in her gentle tone, "Harvey James is right. There are little babies here, so you might need to let me keep the gun for a little spell. If there's trouble, I'll get it back out for you."

Reluctantly, Uncle Hiram handed Granny Lee the gun while mumbling something I could not make out, and then he sulked back into the doorway of the house.

"You all come in and have some supper if you've got time. Heddy, your Mama's here; she's been helpin' out in the kitchen. Come on in and say hello."

"My Mother is here?" Mama asked suspiciously.

"Yes. She's been here since early this morning," Granny Lee said, smiling.

Mama breezed past Marie. Rose and I followed her into the kitchen where Grandma Haley stood at the sink peeling onions. Putting her hands on her slender hips, Mama said in an accusatory voice, "What are you doing here Mama? Did Purl ask you to come here and spy for Little Brock Asher?" Without waiting for her answer, Mama said, "If Purl asked you to jump off a cliff you would do it to satisfy him."

Looking puzzled, Grandma Haley said, "I don't know what you are talkin' about, Heddy. It's been two days or better since I've seen Purl."

Mama sniffed the air indignantly and said, "I don't believe you, Mama. Purl is like a bloodhound always sniffing at your heels, and you know it."

Granny Lee stepped up behind Mama. Placing a pudgy hand on her shoulder, she said, "Heddy Mae, this mining disaster has got us all on edge, but you can't be taking it out on your precious Mama. We've been plannin' a bakin' day for months. I'm just glad she's here."

Shooting Granny Lee a look of disgust, Mama stomped out of the kitchen. Grandma Haley seemed unfazed by Mama's outburst and continued to peel the onion. Turning to face Grandma Haley, Granny Lee's face was apologetic. She said, "I think we should all gather round the table and have prayer before the boys head off to the meeting."

Harlan Ray shifted uncomfortably then said, "Mama, we need to get on the road soon so we can get a seat. It's no telling how many'll show up."

Uncle Corbin said, "Not-not-not- man-many will-will -will sho-show up! You-you-you-all-will-will see-see!"

Granny Lee's bold face had taken on a somber look. Her light tone had turned serious, "Now, there is no wrong time to pray. Let us join hands. Hiram, will you bring Brice Dodd over to the table? Harlan Ray, grab Brenda Sue before she heads out to the porch!" Just as she said it, Uncle Harlan Ray reached out and swooped up a running Brenda Sue in his arms and began tickling her ribs. Brenda Sue, in turn, squealed loudly. Uncle Harlan Ray made an effort to shush her but it had taken Granny Lee's soft but stern tone to quiet her. Not wanting to draw further ire from Granny Lee, everyone in the kitchen obediently joined hands and bowed heads in prayer, with the exception of Mama, who had gone out and was sitting in the car. Granny Lee's prayers were usually more like long drawn out confessions, and this evening she asked Jesus to forgive us all of our sins. She also told him that some among us "were being pulled by the Devil's strings." I was sure one of the nameless people was Mama because of her suspicions of Grandma Haley. Wrought with passion, Granny Lee's voice gazed heavenward and asked Jesus to lay hands on all the miners who would attend the union meeting at the American Legion that evening. The prayer seemed to last forever. My feet had begun to itch from the strain of standing so long the same place. Always the impatient one, Rose squeezed my hand so hard I almost cried out. Beside me, Harvey James shifted restlessly from one foot to the other while outside, Mama interrupted by firmly honking the car horn.

After the prayer was finally over and everyone customarily squeezed hands, Granny Lee dabbed at her misty eyes with a well-worn handkerchief she had in the pocket of her baggy dress and said to Daddy, "God be with you all, son!"

Harlan Ray kissed squirmy little Brenda Sue on her pink cheek and told her to be good. Daddy hugged me and said, "We won't be gone too long. You and your sister behave."

Granny Lee and Grandma Haley had been cooking all day. The crude flat table in the wide kitchen was piled with good things to eat. On any other occasion my mouth would have watered in anticipation, but having watched Mama go at Grandma Haley had somewhat dampened my appetite. Grandma Haley remained seemingly unfazed by Mama's hateful accusations and went on about the kitchen happily setting the table as if there had never been a confrontation.

Uncle Corbin looked apologetically at Grandma Haley and said, "I-I'll-I'll com-com-come af-af-after-you-you in-in-in the mor-mor-morning. I'm I'm I'm head-head-headed off-off-to-to- the-the-pool-pool-hall to-to-to see-see-see what-som-som-som-of-of them-them-mi-miners-are-are sayin' about-about-this-this-this u-u-union- meet-meet-meetin'."

That evening at Granny Lee's was a happy memory that I have relived during the bad times in my life. Never mind that the big old house was shabby, to say the least. The faded rose patterned wallpaper that covered both the living room and hall was gouged and torn in many places. The window shades had yellowed with age and hung tattered over grimy windowpanes. The linoleum was badly worn, especially in the kitchen and hallways where you could see the bare boards underneath. The rooms were bigger than what I was used to. In the living room, the couch was well-worn, as were the chairs. The end tables were scarred with age and piled with books and old newspapers, all proof that Granny Lee had taught her herself how to read and had kept up with things. She had somehow managed to afford a telephone. The old-fashioned dialer had a ring that could wake the dead. She claimed that the phone was necessary in order for her to up with the business of the Salvation Army, as well as news of Uncle Larkin. Granny Lee's crude bathroom equipped with a water closet rather than a tub was another bone of contention for Mama, but still she was jealous of what she called "Granny Lee's modern conveniences." I'd have all those modern things, too, if I had that many people living with me.

She had her husband and Hiram's army pensions and whatever money Marie could drag out of Brenda Sue's daddy. I doubt very seriously that she'd touched one penny of her husband's life insurance because she said it was bad luck. I recall Granny Lee telling us that after Grandpa Lee had died she had gotten a check through the mail. She said she had opened it and seen that it was an insurance check and dropped it to the floor as if she had touched something hot. "I needed money then, but not death money. The check was nothin' but bad luck 'cause it come from his dyin'. If I'd've cashed it right away it would be like me saying the money was his replacement."

Mama was dumbfounded and couldn't believe Granny Lee's quirky way of thinking. "For cryin' out loud, Martha, he intended for you to have that benefit in case something happened to him. You're crazy for lettin' it sit there in that bank."

Nobody ever said if Granny Lee cashed the insurance check. I can only imagine that she finally did since she always seemed to have cash on hand when someone in the family was in need.

A long stairwell led to four upstairs bedrooms. Downstairs there were four more rooms. Granny Lee's bedroom was beyond the staircase to the left. Mama said many times that if Granny Lee had been able to climb up those stairs she would have gotten a real eye-opener. I was sure she was talking about Marie and her many suitors.

The wide kitchen with its cast iron wood cooking stove smelled delicious. Granny Lee ordered everyone to wash up for supper. Marie grabbed a well-worn rag from out of a sink drawer, grabbed Chester Harlan as he breezed past my feet, and made an effort to clean his dirty face. Chester Harlan, in turn, let out a yelp and began kicking and screaming in defiance. "Now you be still, Chester Harlan, or I'll pull down your pants and give you a reason to scream," Marie snapped. Meanwhile, I had managed to coax Brenda Sue out of the corner, and in a gentle voice, asked her to come get her face and hands cleaned. Brenda Sue dimpled, then shyly but obediently ran over to her mother and waited her turn. Great Uncle Hiram grabbed redheaded Brice Dodd and barked, "Now boy, you get them face and hands clean so's we can eat!" Brice Dodd smiled an impish smile and in a show of deliberate defiance, stuck his little tongue out. Freckled face Brice Dodd was a homely little boy and looked nothing like pretty Brenda Sue or angelic Chester Harlan. Granny Lee called him her "little woodpecker" and gave him extra attention than usual. In a calm voice, she said, "Now Hiram, you give me little Doddy. Granny will clean him up." Little toothless Brice Dodd grabbed onto the hem of Granny Lee's dress and hung on for dear life. Granny Lee had the patience of Job with her grandchildren and anyone looking could tell how much they adored her. I adored her too -- everyone who knew her did. However, as kind and good-natured as Granny Lee was, her housekeeping was less than scrupulous. A dirty house was the last thing Granny Lee worried about, and she made no bones about how important her grandchildren were as opposed to keeping things neat and clean. She had once told Mama that a house would always be there but that little children would grow up and leave. "You have to let them play and be children. Cleaning up after them is a waste of precious time. You can't keep up with 'em anyway."

Mama never understood Granny Lee's bohemian attitude when it came to housekeeping because she was a relentless cleaner who attacked her floors and walls with the fervor of a soldier in battle. It was as if her very life depended on spotlessness.

Granny Lee had set up a little table in the corner where the grandchildren ate. After yet another long prayer, she and Grandma Haley took turns dishing ladles of hot beef stew with big chunks of beef and large squares of sweet yellow cornbread to all of us. The grandchildren made huge messes around their table, scattering the cornbread all over both the table and floor. Little Brice Dodd even slopped his pre-cooled stew all over his little overalls, but Granny Lee paid it no mind.

I had eaten more than I had planned of the stew, which was both hearty and delicious. Rose, on the other hand barely touched her bowl and sat looking miserable. Granny Lee, noticing Rose wasn't eating, teased, "Our skinny little Rosaline is tryin' to keep her figure." Rose forced a smile and said nothing. I could tell her thoughts were somewhere else far away from the supper.

Uncle Hiram scuffed, "Looks like she could use a bowl of stew. She's way yonder too skinny! A person just ain't healthy if he don't eat."

Marie frowned and said, "Leave Rose alone, Hiram! She don't have to eat if she don't want to. Not ever'body gluts theirselves like a pig the way you do!"

"A soldier has to eat quick. I learned that in the war," said Uncle Hiram

"Well, the war's over now, Hiram! Don't you think that you should start eatin' slow like the rest of us?"

"Now, Marie, your uncle can't help how he was trained in that terrible war. It was the worst war in history. Let him be!" Granny Lee's voice was more of a gentle reproach.

Grandma Haley remained quiet throughout the meal, which was her normal behavior. A natural spectator with a keen mind, Grandma Haley was a listener who spoke her mind freely, but only when life upset her enough to do so. And unlike outwardly religious Granny Lee who spoke in tongues and prayed incessantly with fervor, Grandma Haley was less forthcoming in how she felt about religion and God. This is not to say that religion wasn't important to her; it was, and she often quoted scripture in order to get her point across to her children and grandchildren.

I had heard enough family talk to know that life had not always treated Grandma Haley kindly. Death had taken so much that was dear to her. First, a baby died in infancy, then Granddaddy Wilkes, and finally Floyd Wilkes, her precious youngest. How could anyone lose so many dear ones and not become dour and mistrustful when it came to life? Maybe Grandma Haley was hardened to the ways of the world, or perhaps she had simply burned out like an overused wick in an oil lamp. I had loved my Grandma Haley just as I had learned to love Mama -- from a distance; that is all either would allow. When I needed hugs and kisses, I sought Granny Lee's eager arms. Daddy was open and outwardly affectionate, too, when he was home, which was not a great deal, especially during my early childhood. The coalmine had called out to him and had taken what should have been mine. For this, I was sometimes resentful, because the only good night kisses I received were from him -- never from Mama.

Sometimes late at night, when I was desperate from loneliness, I would conjure up the ghost of Floyd Wilkes who never failed to show, though not always in human form. In the starless pitch of those nights, I could feel his spirit hovering around me like a warm blanket. Everyone I knew worshiped God. I worshiped Floyd Wilkes' ghost because to me he seemed more real than a God I had only heard about.

After the supper table was cleared, Marie suggested we all gather around the old Philco radio and listen to The Grand Ole Opry. Granny Lee had bought Daddy a Philco radio just like the one in her living room for his thirty-third birthday. Before the death of the miners in the cave-in, the four of us often gathered around the radio listening to The Opry. Rose and I lay on the floor on blankets near the radio, while Mama and Daddy huddled affectionately together on the saggy old couch. It was a sad fact that drastic changes had occurred in our lives since the cave-in. In the dim light, I studied a sullen Rose, and knew that her thoughts were on Bart Asher, who probably had not given her more than a passing thought. I realized that the collapse of No. 5 mine had reacquainted Rose and Bart and had stoked the fires of her dream of marrying him. I was also sure that Mama would still be working at the Asher house, as well as the funeral home, and that neither Daddy nor his brothers would have considered attending a union meeting down at the American Legion had it not been for the collapse.

I thought of Mama working at the Asher house and wondered how many times she had run into Little Brock Asher. I doubted very much if ever, since Daddy claimed that he often stayed up into the wee hours of the morning in his office tower. According to Uncle Harlan Ray, Little Brock hid his whiskey bottle up there and often got so drunk he couldn't make it down the steps. He told us he'd seen him pass out cold and stay there all night on more than one occasion.

Halfway through the radio program, the delicious spicy scent of ginger biscuits wafted through the house. Great Uncle Hiram, who held a sleeping Brice Dodd, said, "We're fixin' to get a treat from the kitchen. Marie, let's lay these youngins down somewhere so we can eat."

Marie, who held Chester Harlan, motioned Uncle Hiram toward the stairs. After the two sleeping children, save for a very much awake Brenda Sue, were tucked in their beds, Grandma Haley called to us from the kitchen to come get some of the biscuits. "We got thick molasses to go with the sweet biscuits," Granny Lee said happily. I remember sitting in that semi-dark living room listening to some faceless advertiser singing the praises of Clabber Girl Baking Powder and eating the bread that was so light it almost melted on my tongue dipped in the sweet molasses. Little Brenda Sue sat in Granny Lee's lap in the kitchen scattering bread crumbs all over the floor, while Grandma Haley, ever the scrubber, stood at the sink washing up the baking pans and bowls.

When eight o'clock came, Granny Lee suggested that Rose and I take a little nap on the couch. "Your daddy and mama might be late comin' in," she said. Outside, on the front porch, Great Uncle Hiram sat smoking in the dark. I could see his dark profile through the window. Rose, who lay at the foot of the couch, complained, "I hope Mama and Daddy come home soon. I'm getting' leg cramps on this little couch." Feeling tired, I positioned my head on the arm of the couch and soon drifted off in a peaceful sleep. I don't how long I slumbered or what made me snap awake. Sitting up quickly, with heart thumping in my chest, I heard a giggle and then another coming from the direction of Granny Lee's bedroom near the stairs. I saw a crack of light underneath her door. Easing myself up and walking over to the door, I placed my ear to its wood and could plainly hear Grandma Haley laughing and cutting up like a schoolgirl. I wondered what Granny Lee was telling her that made her laugh so much, and it was then I realized that I had made a valuable discovery concerning Grandma Haley -- or maybe it was a gift. In all my fourteen years of life I'd rarely seen Grandma Haley crack smiles, let alone laugh with such abandonment. Hearing her do so now seemed as absurd as the idea of a cat reciting the alphabet. For a long time, I crouched at the door listening as the two of them cut up like teenage girls at a slumber party. For some reason I never wanted to abandon the happy voices. Somewhere inside of me, I must have known that this was the last time I would ever hear Grandma Haley laugh like that.

The union meeting had not turned out as Daddy and my Uncles had hoped. That night, while on our way home, Daddy said in disgust, "Only fifty men come out of nearly three hundred miners. The union man said we needed fifty percent of the men or better to get a union. I don't understand it! I really don't."

Uncle Harvey James said, "Now Ralph, these things take time. We'll just have to work harder. I'll talk to the men on my end and you tell the men on yours what we heard tonight."

Harlan Ray said, "Some of the men I talk to are on the fence, but most of 'em are scared to death of losin' their jobs and homes. I reckon ole Purl has been goin' around puttin' the fear of God in 'em, tellin' 'em that if they sign anything they'll be fired."

Harvey James laughed sarcastically before saying, "Old Asher might just do that, Ralph. He might give us the pink slip tomorrow or any time. He's sure to laugh his ass off as soon as he finds out how few came to the union meeting. We're liable to fall on our faces yet!"

Daddy said, "I don't think Asher has made any move to settle with the widows, though. If he don't give them somethin' people might start thinkin' that he ain't so generous."

"He ain't made 'em move out of their homes, though, so I guess that's smart on his part and good for the widows and their youngins," Harlan Ray said.

Harvey James laughed more to himself and said nothing.

"What are you laughing about?" Harlan Ray snapped.

Harvey James said, "I was just thinking about Corbin and how he's gonna rub that dud of a meeting in our faces saying how he told us so."

"Yeah, tomorrow he'll be struttin' around like a little banty rooster." Harlan Ray laughed.

Throughout the ride home, Mama had kept strangely quiet. Even after we arrived home, she remained self-contained and remote. In the kitchen, she pulled off her light sweater and hung it on the back of a chair. Sighing tiredly, she said to Daddy, "You want a piece of pie or somethin' before we go to bed?"

Shaking his head no, he yawned and said, "I'm too tired to eat."

In our room, Rose lit the lamp and brushed her dark hair before climbing underneath the covers. "You can turn down the wick," she commanded before turning to face the wall. I did so without argument. Once in bed, I stared out the window straight in front of me. Darkness covered every inch of the surroundings. The only visible light came from Wilder Point where the Asher house stood half lit up through the trees. "Wonder what the Ashers are doing up there?" I mused.

Rose answered in a nasty voice, "Why wonder when you can just look into that crystal ball of yours? You're the seer in the family."

"Goodnight Rose," I said, not willing to engage her in an argument this late at night. But Rose kept on talking, her voice a nasty snarl. "If you had any kind of gift at all you could tell me about Bart and if it's gonna work out for us."

"I don't need the gift to tell you that," I said.

"What's that supposed to mean? How can you know what he's thinkin' or how he feels about me?"

"It wouldn't matter much what he thought, if you consider how his Daddy probably dumped Mama when they were young. Mama says that the apple don't fall far from the tree."

Rose sat straight up in bed. I could feel her anger charge the room the way I could always feel the spirit of Floyd Wilkes hovering about.

"Mama said. Mama said! You sound like Uncle Harvey James's parrot, Sodie Cracker, when you repeat Mama's words. I'm not Mama! Just because she didn't get Little Brock Asher don't mean I'm gonna fail with his son. When I was a little girl I knowed someday he would belong to me. Mama don't have nothin' to do with his feelin's for me. I can't help she's all bitter about the way her life turned out!'

Turning on my side, I wanted to shut out the sound of Rose's angry voice. After a few minutes, her voice reached such a loud pitch that it brought Mama to the door. "Rose, I can hear you girls from all the way in my room. You all best stop your bickerin' and go to sleep," she warned.

After a few minutes of silence, Rose said in a playful tone, "I doubt she really heard what I said or she'd be throwin' my things out the door and me behind them."

Knowing she was right, I couldn't help but smile to myself in the darkness.

9 A VISIT FROM UNCLE PURL

The month of October came in with a burst of color. The leaves had changed quickly because of the dry summer. The heavy rains we had had in the middle of September had caused the waters of Wilder Creek to rise considerably. In retrospect, it is hard to describe the wild beauty of Wilder Creek. The land rose and fell like a sorrowful sigh. Houses dotted the riversides and the hills. Most of its residents used boats to cross over to land. The Cumberland River wound through the valley like a snake. Behind it, walls of flint and shale rose straight up out of its waters. The river's surface was shaded in the summer by bent elms, white oak, birch, and sycamore trees. Little islands of sand and small bushes caused the water to fork. In the little shoals behind those islands, spreading moss grew thick and dark green like a carpet. It seemed everywhere you looked a little shoal ran into a freshet, emptying out into a different fork of the river. Long creeks cut into the mountains; their cold waters streamed and trickled off rocks and cliffs and down the dark hollows, where they finally intermingled with the waters of the Cumberland River. As a child, I had learned the name of every island. When it rained the night before, especially during the hot summer nights, a thick fog enveloped the river crawling through the trees like a living thing. On those early mornings, you could barely see the water. In the spring of the year, heavy rains brought high tides. I recall how Daddy used an old bent sycamore tree to measure the depth of the water. Winter often brought heavy snows to the valley. When the sun finally melted the snow, the headwaters would gush out, forming tides or flashfloods. Mama hated the high waters and was grateful that we lived so close to the main highway. She claimed that this was the only good thing about the lodge. Daddy told us numerous stories of how destructive the floodwaters could be. He often recalled how the tide had risen to the front door of their house in Baxter when he was only five years old.

The weather had changed drastically in a few short weeks. Rose and I had started wearing sweaters, and Daddy began chopping and storing the wood boxes with extra kindling for both the cook stove and the hearth. Farmers had begun to gather their sparse vegetables from the field. The drought had stunted many corn crops, but still farmers had to salvage all they could and then burn their fields and stack their fodder into bundles. I recall the sweet scent of the burning fields and sight of men and women gathering their orange pumpkins. Uncle Corbin stopped by the lodge one evening with a bucket full of green beans that he had picked from Granny Lee's garden. "You, you, you tell Hed, Hed, Heddy to string these up," he said. I could tell by the dour look on Uncle Corbin's face that he was still angry with Daddy his other two brothers concerning their efforts to get in a union. Maybe the green beans were just an excuse for him to unburden himself to Mama, who had gone to the store with Marie and Granny Lee.

The mornings were especially chilly, and the walks to the bus stop left me shivering. To my surprise, Amity Smith had kept his word and parked his truck protectively near me until the bus came. Neither Tommy Roberts nor Billy bothered me anymore and I was sure it was because they were afraid of Amity Smith. The subject of the union, however, was still a sore spot with them and others. At school, during recess, I would see Tommy Roberts and Billy Wilkins huddled together with several of the other boys from the camp. I knew they were discussing the union meeting and mimicking the words of their parents concerning how a having a union would ruin their lives. I had seen them looking at me with such fierce hatred, and I just could not understand why. Violet Elizabeth and Amity had become my only real friends. It was sad to realize that many of the other children I had known all my life had turned on me simply because of Daddy's and my uncles' involvement with the United Mineworkers of America. It was either that or they were deeply afraid of Tommy Roberts and Billy Wilkins.

Over the years, Mama had discouraged Rose and me from making friends, claiming we had too many chores to do after school. However, Violet Elizabeth was different from most girls I'd known. She was loving, clever, and very thoughtful, but, more importantly, both of us shared a love for books and literature. She had even loaned me her copy of Louisa Mae Alcott's Little Women, which I'd never read before. Sometimes late at night when Rose was asleep, I would light the lamp and turn down the wick as low as it would go without it burning out completely. Lying underneath the warm comfort of my blanket, I would read Little Women for an hour or so before finally extinguishing the lamp.

Before the weather turned cold, and after my chores were finished, I would take my book down to the Play Place overlooking the river and read for hours, with only the splashing of the beavers to interrupt me. Sometimes Amity's face would flash into thoughts when I least expected it. Often when he stood close to me, I had felt a kind of tenderness creeping up into my throat. It was a strange feeling, and one that I had never felt before. Barley fourteen years old, I wasn't sure what it meant. Violet Elizabeth, though, soon set me straight by letting me know that she thought her brother was stuck on me. Staring at her in disbelief, my face had reddened with just the thought of him liking me in that way. Building up a picture of Amity up in my mind, I thought he favored Floyd Wilkes. Both were tall with thin, wiry builds and had dark blue eyes and pale blonde hair. Amity seemed older than most boys his age. By the time he was sixteen, he had already learned how to saw lumber and could even drive his daddy's log truck. I had seen him drive by our house a few times while on his way up to No. 5 mine. Violet Elizabeth had told me that their daddy sometimes sold 4prop timber to Little Brock Asher. Although I wasn't sure what to make out of my strange new feelings toward Amity, I often found myself looking forward to school days.

Violet Elizabeth was a year ahead of me in school, and Amity was two years past me. However, our difference in ages didn't seem to matter. I thought Amity and Violet looked very much alike. Although her blonde hair was a shade darker than that of her brother's, both had similar faces with blue eyes and pale skin. Each had dimples that were particularly prominent when they smiled or laughed. I remember thinking that Amity was very handsome and Violet Elizabeth was the prettiest girl in the world besides my sister, Rose.

One noon hour in late September, Amity asked me if I would like to accompany him and Violet to their house for a quick lunch. When it rained or the weather was bad, Amity drove his daddy's old panel truck to school, and of course was the envy of the older boys. After all, not many boys had access to their daddy's precious vehicle. At first I had declined Amity's invitations to lunch at his house out of fear that Mama might somehow find out that I'd been in the company of a boy. Soon, though, my curiosity got the better of me and I finally agreed to join them for lunch at the Smith home.

The Smith house was a neat white and two-storied with dark green shutter boards. A long lane led back to it. In the field to the right of the house was a barn and tall silo. Cattle grazed on land that was flat in the front, but behind it, the woods steeped upwards just as they did behind the lodge. A long concrete sidewalk led up to a screened in porch. Timidly, I followed Violet Elizabeth indoors and to the kitchen where Mrs. Smith was setting the table. She wore a nice green dress and a white apron. Mrs. Smith's hair was the reddish blonde, the same color as that of Violet Elizabeth's, and was perfectly coiffed in a stylish way Mama would have appreciated.

"We brought a guest, Mama," Amity said smilingly. "This is Junie Mae Lee. She's a neighbor of ours."

Mrs. Smith said, "You must be Heddy and Ralph Lee's daughter. I met your parents several years back at a funeral -- such nice folks," she said in a genuine tone. "Won't you sit down and join us? I'll just get another place setting." After I sat down, I allowed my eyes to roam over the clean, well-organized kitchen. Everything seemed to shine, from the chrome on the modern gas stove to the grain of the wooden floor. In front of the frilly curtained window, there stood a long counter with a double sink. In the windowsill, a long green potato vine curled and trailed down past the edge of the sink. A fat green fern hung from the ceiling in an empty corner. Behind the table on the wall was a large picture of the Last Supper. My eyes studied the colorful robes of the disciples all crowded at the table in an effort to convince Jesus that none would betray him. "You have a beautiful home," I said with sincerity.

"Well, thank you, honey. You are more than welcome to come here whenever you can."

From across the room Amity's mouth broke into a wide grin and his cheeks dimpled, while Violet put her arm around my shoulders affectionately. I was suddenly overwhelmed by the kindness the Smith family showed me. I and was not accustomed to such an easy atmosphere or such thoughtful declarations. Mrs. Smith said to Amity, "Honey, you and Violet have to come home directly after school. Your daddy's over at the high school helping your granddaddy set up one of his agricultural projects for the 4-H club, so he might not make it back in time to milk the cows."

Amity nodded in agreement.

Violet Elizabeth had told me how her daddy had given up teaching for farming and the mill. I soon learned that Mrs. Smith was from Indiana and had family up there. Violet Elizabeth often talked of her Grandma Parley, and according to her nobody made chocolate gravy like Grandma Parley. I had never heard of chocolate gravy but thought it sounded delicious.

Mrs. Smith ladled large helpings of vegetable beef soup into our bowls, and then gave us each a stack of crackers. Forgetting my shyness, I ate heartily and thought the soup with its little pieces of beef was one of the best things I had ever eaten. Mama didn't like vegetable soup and refused to waste a mess of precious pork or beef to make it, so we seldom had it. Crackers were a bit of a treat, too. Mama rarely bought those, either, and the only time we ate them, or even store-bought light-bread was when we visited Granny Lee, who delighted in the convenience foods.

After we finished the soup, Violet Elizabeth said, "Come on upstairs and I'll show you my room real quick, ok?" I followed her up a winding staircase that led to a big hall that's floor gleamed just like the one downstairs. A big brick chimney centered the room. Violet led me past the chimney near the back and opened the door to her room. Once inside, I stared in disbelief at the sight of the pink flower patterned wallpaper and dainty furniture. A small canopy bed stood in the middle of the floor; its coverlet was a pink ruffled bedspread. It was truly a girl's room with its doll collection and dainty little dressing table. I had never seen anything so beautiful and fancy. I had felt an urge to touch everything. Time was forgotten as I explored the doll collection. Violet Elizabeth seemed pleased that I asked about her vast collection of books. I was thinking of my own stark room with its faded wallpaper and rough wood floors. There was not a picture on the wall or any proof that two girls occupied it, save for the pretty patchwork quilts Grandma Haley made for Rose and me.

Finally, Violet Elizabeth said, "I wish you could come share this room with me. I've always wanted a sister."

"I wish I could, too," I said, meaning it. Later at school, I couldn't stop thinking about the visit to Amity and Violet Elizabeth's home. I thought of Mama, too, and hoped that she never found out that I had gone. In retrospect, I needn't have worried, for both Mama and Daddy's attention was centered on Rose, who had used the bullying incident to quit school. She'd refused to go back even after Daddy begged her to reconsider. He'd pleaded, "Rosie, you're breaking my heart right now. You know how much I want you to get an education. Them boys ain't gonna bother you no more. Your Uncle Harvey James works with them boys' daddies, and Wilkins especially was fit to be tied when he found out his son beat up on you girls -- I reckon young Wilkins got a good thrashin' 'cause of his part."

Rose sat in the kitchen chair looking down at the floor. "I don't like the classroom, Daddy. I can read and write just fine. What else do I need to know?"

Shaking his head in dismay, Daddy said, "I can't make you go to school, Rosie. I wish I could, but I can't. I missed out on an education myself because I had to start workin' in the mines early on. What little I did learn, though, taught me how important a higher education is, and here you are throwin' your chance out the door."

Rose continued to look at the floor. Her eyes refused to meet Daddy's.

"I don't need school, Daddy. I'd rather stay here and help Mama out," she said in a low voice.

Daddy didn't believe her. I could tell by the way that his eyes changed from sad to suspicious. Finally, he said in a tone of futility, "Just go help your Mama gather the wash."

Mama acted indifferent concerning Rose's refusal to return to school and reminded Daddy that she had told him so. "Ralph, Rosie can barely read a primer. She quit tryin' to learn after the third or fourth grade – well, as soon as the Mattinglys moved to the camp. Them girls are dumber than Rose. They rubbed off on her, and now it's too late to change what they put in her head. Neither one of us can make a purse out of a sow's ear."

Daddy remained silent and continued to stare out the kitchen window. I could feel his oppression and walked over to where he sat and embraced him. It wasn't something I did often because for some reason it angered Mama, but on this day, I felt he needed comfort.

Daddy lifted his sad brown eyes and studied me for a minute before saying, "You're a good girl, June bug. You keep them grades up and maybe someday you can go further. Don't give up on your dreams of being a teacher. You never can tell what good might come of it."

His words had brought about a warm rush of love inside me. Daddy was so much like Granny Lee, always kind and generous. He was so different from Mama I'd often wondered how they'd ended up married. Mama had told me that she had met Daddy at a tent revival the church was holding in Harlan. He'd smiled and winked at her while everyone else had their heads bowed in prayer. She must have been about seventeen then. Granny Lee said the two of them hadn't known each other over three weeks before they were married, and that Mama was soon pregnant with Rose. Granny Lee gushed every time she spoke of Daddy's affection for Rose. "You know he named her after a wild red rose he'd seen growin' on the river bank, and after she was born, none of us could stop lookin' at her. She was the prettiest thing you ever seen even as a young baby. Even before she could walk, your Daddy took her everywhere. He would lay her in that old truck seat and haul her everywhere. No Daddy could have been prouder of his little girl."

Daddy's grave disappointment in Rose's decision to quit school had set something off in me. I could barely look at her without becoming angry. What would she do with her time now? More importantly, what had made her decide that she'd rather spend her days with Mama, especially now that Mama was home all the time?

That same evening Mama had sent Rose and me to the spring to get the night's water. On the way there, my anger spilled over. "Mama's gonna be home all the time, Rose! Why would you quit school knowin' that the two of you can't get along for more than ten seconds?"

Rose smiled an impish smile and said, "Mama won't be home much. I heard her tell Uncle Coy this mornin' that she was going to work days for old Arnold Hansley at the Hardware Store."

Halting abruptly in my step, I stared at her in disbelief. "You're makin' that up! Daddy wouldn't let her work for that stingy old goat; besides his old wife Zinnia's jewelry store is in the same buildin'. Mama says she's crazy as a loon. Says she can't even sell a watch or ring because she forgets where she's at most of the time!"

"Daddy don't know yet," Rose said smugly. "I'm shore he'll hit the roof when he finds out, but, like always, Mama will get her way."

Nodding my head in stunned silence, I recalled the stories I had heard about old Hansley's crazy wife, Zinnia. Even before she lost her mind, she accused every woman who came in the store of trying to run off with her husband. I'd thought Mr. Hansley favored a vulture with his skinny veined hands and stick legs. His face was as square as Granny Lee's clock. "Why would Mama work for him?" I asked incredulously.

"Because he asked her too," Rose said, and then added, "Maybe Mama's been eyein' some of the nice rings and watches in his wife's jewelry store. Grace Mattingly took her girls and me in there once. The jewelry store is connected to the hardware part by a door. We just walked right in and looked around. The old biddy's got some fancy stuff in there!"

"So what will you do while Mama's workin'?"

Rose smirked and asked, "What do you think?"

Shaking my head in disgust, I said, "Rose, you are goin' to get caught, and when you do Mama will surely throw you out of the house. This would kill Daddy. Why don't you think of someone besides yourself sometime?"

Rose threw the buckets she was carrying to the ground with a ping. Her strange eyes had turned a shade lighter, reminding me of a streak of gray sky. Her voice was full of indignation as she said, "I am old enough to have a boyfriend! I don't understand why you are makin' such a fuss."

"You know why!" I yelled. My anger was at its peak. "If Bart Asher is really your boyfriend then why don't he take you on that hayride they're havin' at Harmon's Bottom next weekend? Real boyfriends don't hide their girlfriends from other people!"

"He has to hide me, Junie Mae. With Daddy and the Uncles makin' all that trouble down at the mine what other choice does he have right now? Thank God he don't blame me for what they're doin'. He knows I ain't at fault."

It was my turn to feel indignant. "It ain't Daddy or the Uncles' fault, either. You're forgettin' that it was the Asher mine that killed them miners. Daddy says the timbers that held up the roof was rotten and finally broke, causin' the mine to cave in. How can you take Asher's side when you know it was his fault? He knowed about it, Rose, and he didn't do a thing to fix it!"

Rose sighed, shaking her head, "You're just a child, Junie Mae. You don't understand love or what people have to give up just to keep it."

Her voice had taken on a tone of ferocity. "I'll do whatever it takes to get away from Mama. It don't matter whose fault the cave-in was. Don't you know that the mine will stand anyway? Daddy and the Uncles can't stand up against men like Little Brock Asher and his daddy. I love Daddy, but I have to make a life of my own, Junie Mae."

Picking up the buckets she'd thrown down, I shoved them at her and said, "I may not understand love, but I do understand that blood is thicker than water. If I'm such a child, stop tellin' me things about you and Bart. I'm tired of bein' in the middle."

Rose remained quiet as we dipped the water from the spring. I was glad because I wanted to forget the coalmine and Bart Asher, if only for a little while. All around me, the woods seemed on fire with bright orange, deep red, purple, and yellow. On our way back down the path, Rose sloshed water out of the bucket and onto her shoes. Her mind seemed a million miles away. Just as we came up on the side yard, I saw Uncle Purl standing on the porch with his hat in his hand. "Stop!" I whispered to Rose and sank back behind in the shadow of big evergreen tree standing near the corner of the house.

"What's Uncle Purl doin' here?" Rose whispered, setting her half-filled buckets on the ground. Setting my buckets down beside hers, I shushed her and strained my ears to listen. I watched Daddy open the front door and then over the squeak of the screen door heard Uncle Purl say, "Now Ralph, I come here to talk to you, not Heddy Mae. It would be best if she went on back in the house."

"Heddy stays, Purl! Just say what you have to say and be done with it!"

"All right, but Ralph, I'm here to warn you that you and your brothers are makin' a grave mistake by gettin' cozy with that union representative. You're upsettin' a lot of people -- mainly Little Brock Asher, and he's the last one you want to upset. I'm here to tell you that you and your brothers are on the edge off losin' your jobs, and so is every other man you recruited into goin' to them secret meetings you all been havin' at the camp every night."

"All right, Purl -- you've had your say, now go on home!"

"Ralph, I don't think you understand what I'm gettin' at. You live on Asher land and you and your brothers are startin' a little war that's gonna get bigger if you don't give up on the union idea! I'm just here to warn you that Asher could and probably will evict you from your home because of what you're doin'."

"Get off my property, Purl! I still pay rent here, and as long as I do, I have the say on who is welcome! Now get on down the road!"

"Purl Haley, you ain't nothin' but Little Brock Asher's whore! He could turn on you in a second and probably will before it's over," Mama warned.

"You'd know more about the whore part than I would," Purl cracked.

Just as Purl turned to leave, Daddy lunged at him, spinning him around and then punching him in the face with such a force that he staggered backwards off the porch. Rose cried out and turned her head while I stood there, watching it all and unable to move. For a moment Daddy stood with his fist still clenched. Mama finally grabbed hold of him and told him to go inside. Her voice had an urgency to it, but Daddy didn't move from the spot.

After what seemed like an eternity, Uncle Purl raised himself up off the ground; his hand was on his injured cheek. Grabbing his hat lying near the fence and dusting it off, he grunted, "I oughta kill you, Ralph Lee! I oughta go back and get my gun and shoot you for this! You'll pay for this later. I guarantee you'll pay!"

Daddy turned and went through the screen door, slamming it shut.

Rose said, "God Almighty, this thing is gettin' out of hand. Maybe Uncle Purl's right; maybe Daddy and them should give up on tryin' to get a union in."

"Let's just take the buckets in and act like we didn't hear nothin'," I said.

Once inside the kitchen Mama looked down at Rose's half-filled buckets and screamed, "Why is it that you can never manage a full bucket of water?" Before Rose could open her mouth to speak, Mama grabbed one of the half-empty buckets from her hand and then threw its cold contents all over Rose. Rose's scream brought a wide-eyed Daddy into the kitchen. Looking from Rose to Mama, he said, "Heddy, you go get a towel and dry her off right now! You had no business soakin' her like that!"

Mama gave Daddy a baleful look before saying, "You don't have to live with her as much as I do. She can't do nothin' that I ask her to do. She rebels against everything. I ain't drying her off!" she said stubbornly, then crossed her arms.

For once Daddy stood his ground against Mama. "Heddy, you ain't never been fair to Rosie. She is what she is and you ain't gonna make her no different. You can't take out grown-up problems on these girls. It's just not fair to 'em!"

"You don't know your oldest daughter, Ralph. How could you when you're never here? You don't see what I see!"

"No, I don't see!" Daddy said angrily, and then added, "Look at your daughter over there shiverin'! Look at her!"

Mama didn't move. Her dark eyes glittered defiantly like little pieces of wet coal in the light of the oil lamp.

Rose suddenly stepped forward, and what happened next still remains fresh in my memory today. I can see my sister standing in her water soaked dress that clung to her like a second skin. In a fit of rebellion, she grabbed the front of her dress, ripping apart the buttons holding it together. Stepping out of the wet material, she then stood wearing only her bra and panties. Reaching down and picking up the soaked material, Rose proceeded to wad it up in a ball before hurling it at Mama, hitting her squarely in the face.

Mama in turn hurled the wet bundle back at Rose and then lunged at her. Before Mama could reach her, Daddy grabbed Mama around the waist, holding her back. "For God's sake, Heddy, leave her alone," he pleaded.

"Let her go, Daddy!" Rose screamed "She's itchin' to beat on me. But I ain't takin' it no more. No more!"

I don't remember how Rose got hold of the butcher knife, but I can clearly see it in her hands.

"Give me the knife, Rose! " I screamed. Daddy let go of Mama and was suddenly wrestling with Rose in an effort to get the knife. What happened next is a blur. All I remember seeing is the red blood soaking and quickly spreading through Daddy's white shirt sleeve. It was so red, redder than anything I'd ever seen. It was even redder than the images I had of Floyd Wilkes' blood streaming down the planks of the bridge mingling with that of the juice from the smashed blackberries. Oh God! Daddy was stabbed while trying to get the knife away from Rose. I remember feeling light-headed and weak at the knees, and I thought I might die right there in the kitchen. I could hear the distant voices of Rose and Mama. Mama was shouting for Rose to get some towels from the sink, but all Rose could do was fall at Daddy's feet, screaming and begging for his forgiveness. I wanted to move but couldn't. My mind then flashed somewhere else. I was suddenly in a long field near a smokehouse. Everything around me seemed magnified. The grass was greener than any grass I had ever seen. The sky was the bluest of blue. My eyes could barely take in the intense brightness that seemed to engulf me. Suddenly Floyd Wilkes appeared from behind the smokehouse. I narrowed my eyes in hopes that I might see where he was going. For a minute things changed to black and white, but then the bright grass came back and I saw him bending over something. I was afraid to look at what he was bending over. Floyd Wilkes turned his blonde head toward me then moved aside. Gasping, I saw who he was standing over. It was Daddy, and he was bleeding all over the place. Suddenly I was back at home in Mama and Daddy's bedroom and rifling through Mama's trunk in search of bed sheets. Nervously, I found one and then ripped it into thin strips and hurried to where Daddy sat in the chair bleeding. Mama was praying aloud, "Dear God. Please don't let it be a vein or an artery."

Nervously I handed Mama the strips of the white sheets. Mama slowly rolled up Daddy's bloody sleeve, revealing a wide, deep gash near his right elbow. Sighing with relief she said, "Thank God. It's just a gash." Daddy winced occasionally but mostly kept silent while Mama cleaned the wound with soapy water and peroxide. She then instructed him to hold the bloody towel over the gash until the blood clotted.

I looked about the bloody kitchen in disbelief. Rose, still half naked, sat huddled in a corner with her face buried in her hands. Daddy gently spoke, "Rosie, I'm all right. You go ahead into your bedroom and put on your night clothes. You hear?"

Rose got up, trying in vain to cover her half-naked body. I knew she was ashamed of what she had done and regretted the harm it had caused. Rose was by nature impulsive, but this time her actions had gone beyond simple impulse. Rose had tried to kill Mama.

After she'd gone off to our bedroom Daddy said, "I'm taking her to Ma's to stay for a while. I can't have this no more!"

Shaking her head vigorously Mama yelled, "No, Ralph, she's not going there!"

Turning to me he said, "I'll hold the towel, Junie -- you just go on to bed. I'm all right, honey," he assured me. After a minute or two Daddy rose wordlessly from the chair, still holding the blood soaked towel to his elbow. Ignoring Mama, he walked out of the kitchen. A second or two later, I heard him to tell Rose to pack a couple of weeks' worth of clothes.

Getting up from her chair, Mama angrily stomped into the living room where Daddy sat on the edge of the old green overstuffed chair that was a hand-me-down from Granny Lee. "I won't let you do this, Ralph. She'll be ruined if she's anywhere near Marie. I won't have it!"

Daddy said, "You ain't got a choice this time, Heddy. Now leave it be."

In the kitchen I poured some water mixed with lye soap into a dishpan and started cleaning up Daddy's blood. Smears and streaks of it were everywhere. If I hadn't known better I would have thought someone had slaughtered a hog in there.

Later in bed, I lay for a long time in the dark listening to Rose crying softly into her pillow. A big part of me hated her for the injury and hurt she had caused that night, while another part of me wanted to cry along with her. I thought of Floyd Wilkes and wished that he wasn't dead so I could talk with him face to face. I'd needed so badly to tell somebody how my world was falling apart around me. Maybe wherever Floyd Wilkes was he could see what was happening at the lodge with all of us. If so, I wondered what he thought of Mama and how she had treated Rose. Granny Lee believed that when people died they took on other forms. Maybe Floyd Wilkes' ghost could take the form of a tree, or a leaf, or even the wind. Whatever the case, I was happy that he hadn't gone on to the light of heaven.

The following Saturday morning Daddy had gotten Rose up before dawn and had driven her over to Granny Lee's in his old Ford truck. Blinking back tears, I rose from the bed and walked gingerly into the kitchen, where I found Mama sitting at the table, holding onto coffee cup and staring out the kitchen window into the darkness. As soon as she turned and saw me, she said, "Your Daddy just made the biggest mistake of his life takin' Rose over to your Granny Lee's. I warned him, but he done it anyways."

"Is his arm okay?"

"I imagine it's plenty sore by now, but I bandaged it good. He didn't say nothin' this morning…" her voice trailed off.

"Your sister wanted to kill me last night, Junie Mae. She was going to stab me with a butcher knife and your Daddy took her side against mine. I won't forgive that --ever."

Scooting out a chair, I sat down and took a good look at Mama. I allowed my eyes to roam over her arresting face with its high hollow cheekbones and her full lips. Her dark eyes looked weak and tired, and her hair fell about her shoulders like a black curtain. I pictured Rose as merely a younger version of Mama. I then wondered if Mama saw this. She must have, but yet in seeing herself how could she treat Rose so badly?

"Rose will be back soon, Mama. Daddy just thinks the two of you need to be apart for a while. That's all."

Laughing harshly, Mama got up and poured more coffee into her cup.

"Rose's got a man somewhere and you know about it, Junie Mae. Don't bother denying it. I've knowed about it for a while, but kept it to myself. She takes these long walks and don't come in until its near dark. And her face is always blood red from where he's rubbed his beard stubble all over it." Mama eyed me critically and said, "You look like you've just swallowed a fly, Junie Mae. Do you and Rose think that I'm stupid?"

"I've never seen her kissing no man, Mama," I said truthfully. Inside my chest my heart accelerated and fluttered wildly.

Mama said, "That's because he's probably a married man or some worthless bum she's ashamed of. If the man was worth his salt she'd've already had him here, rubbing our noses in it. No, she's following in Marie's foot tracks. You wait and see. She'll get herself pregnant if she's not already there."

"You ought not say stuff like that about Rose, Mama. It's not true."

Mama said in a cryptic tone, "From the time she was born I knowed she was my cross to bear. Rose is a just a reminder of all the sins I committed when I was young and stupid. When you get my age the sins start stackin' up; pretty soon the wall of them is so high you can't see over it."

Walking over to the window, she pulled the curtain further back and stood looking up at the lights of Creekstone house shining through the dark trees. "Someday, I'll never have to look at that house again." she whispered more to herself.

"What sins did you commit?" I dared, quickly regretting it.

"I'll never tell you, Junie Mae. They're not all my sins alone, so I guess that's some comfort."

"Am I a reminder of your sins too?' I asked timidly.

Mama turned toward me. Her face softened and she smiled. "No, Junie Mae. You never gave me the heartaches that Rose has. You couldn't if you wanted to. You're too much like your Daddy and Granny Lee. You're all sinless and think every day's a ray of sunshine. Well it ain't for some of us. Sometimes these sins we done was not all our faults, but we have to pay for 'em just the same."

"Granny Lee says God forgives all sins, and when He does they're washed clean."

Mama laughed again. "Poor Martha Lee. If being simple can get a person into heaven then she is sure to go."

"Granny Lee's not dumb or simple, Mama! She just looks away sometimes. I think it might be good to look away once in a while."

Mama said. "I've tried that, but the truth is everywhere I look. I'd like to go somewhere nice and green where walls ain't so high." Absently pulling back a strand of her hair, I watched as she studied her dark reflection in the windowpane. It was like she was talking to herself and not me. I knew I wasn't part of her thoughts anymore and left the kitchen. Once in the dark living room I sank down in Daddy's saggy old chair. The silence was as thick as molasses, save for the ticking of the tired old clock on the mantle. I thought of Rose and felt a tremor of sadness within my chest. From the kitchen Mama hollered, "I'm making eggs. Your Daddy will be back pretty soon."

10 AMITY SMITH

Rose's absence had left a kind of hole in my heart. I could tell Daddy was miserable, too. Two weeks had turned into almost a month. November came and Daddy still hadn't made a move to bring her back home. Mama was furious at Daddy and had threatened to go over to Granny Lee's house and make Rose come back herself, but Daddy warned Mama to let her be.

The two of them barely spoke to each other on the evenings that he was home. Mama had taken the job at Hansley's store even though Daddy vehemently objected to it, and sometimes she didn't get home from work until five o'clock in the evening. By then, Daddy was usually off with his brothers having private meetings with other miners in an effort to recruit them into meeting with the union representatives.

I thought of Rose and Bart Asher and wondered if she had managed to somehow see him. I was sure she had and would think nothing of telling Marie about him because she knew Marie wouldn't blab it all over. Unlike a lot of women around Harlan and its surrounding counties who didn't drive, Marie had obtained her driver's license and often borrowed Great Uncle Hiram's old pick-up truck. Great Uncle Hiram claimed that the war had made him too nervous to drive it himself anymore, and that he'd taught Marie so she could take him to the bank, stores, and doctor visits.

One day in the middle of November, I came home from school to find Great Uncle Hiram's pick-up sitting in the yard. The passenger door opened and then out stepped Rose. Her pretty face looked drawn and serious but upon seeing me she forced a smile and said, "Me and Marie brought you all some fresh ham from the hog Uncle Harlan Ray and Rebekah butchered yesterday. Me and Marie cut and wrapped most of the meat by ourselves," she finished with pride in her voice.

I laughed picturing Rose doing any kind of work, let alone wrapping bloody pork. Marie was wearing her usual attire -- a man's hat and worn kaki breeches. Rose looked small, wrapped in a long, dark coat. Her hair had grown at least two inches and fell down past her shoulders. "Why don't you all come on into the house? Mama and Daddy won't be home for a while," I offered.

Rose said, "Granny Lee's tending Marie's babies and we've got to get back."

Marie then suggested that maybe me and Rose could take the fresh ham on over to the cold house and talk a little. She said, "Me and Buster will just take a walk down by the creek. A few minutes more won't hurt a thing."

Rose agreed. After I placed my books on the front porch, the two of us made our way around the house, past Daddy's work shed, and then beyond the dying weeping willow tree to where the cold house stood only a few feet away.

The cold house was nothing more than a little underground cellar that Big Brock Asher and his son had built in order to cool and store their the butchered wild game. Daddy told us how he'd buy large blocks of ice every other day in order to keep the game cool. Mama had also bought a few blocks when we'd had a little extra money and they kept real good because the cellar itself stayed cool. Mama stored the perishables like meat, milk, and eggs on the long wide shelves. I wanted to ask Rose all kinds of questions concerning her stay at Granny Lee's house but waited for her to tell me something.

"I've learned to like bein' at Granny's," Rose finally said. "Marie makes it bearable. Me and her go places all the time together. Mama never let me and you go nowhere in town by ourselves."

"What about Bart Asher?" I asked boldly.

Rose shrugged and asked, "What about him? He's the same as always. I see him every other day just like before. Sometimes Marie lets me off at the edge of the woods back there and I wait for him to come. Other times, he meets me in the alley behind Granny Lee's house. One day he didn't show up at all. He said his mama was makin' him spend time with his daddy up at the mine because of all the trouble," her voice faltered. Rose slammed shut the door of the cold house and eyed me critically, "He hates minin', Junie Mae, and can't wait to go to Richmond to that college after the Christmas holidays. He says he don't want no part of the coal and wants to learn about business and maybe one day work in some big office building in the city or start a business of his own." Her pretty face wore a look of defeat. "Sometimes he talks, talk that I can barely understand. He has all these ideas that go way above my head. I listen, but I don't know what he means." Sighing, she went on. "He don't want to get married right away and that's for shore. I understood that part alright, enough. He made it pretty plain to me at the start. I guess I wadn't listenin'."

"I wish things wadn't like they are here and you could just come home."

Rose shook her head negatively. "Mama never will change the way she thinks about me. Nothin' I ever do will suit her – nothin'. Daddy told me to stay with Granny Lee for as long as I needed to. I feel freer there; besides, I don't like Mama much. I'm sorry to say that, Junie Mae, but she's never been a mama to me and you know it."

"Will you keep seein' Bart Asher?"

"What have I got to lose? I gotta try and hopefully he'll change his mind about marriage and miss me a little when he goes off to college. I miss you, Junie Mae." Her voice broke.

Back at the house, Buster and Marie were just coming up from the direction of the creek. When Buster saw us he came running, finally leaping friskily up on Rose. Rose in turn fell to the ground giggling hysterically as Buster licked her whole face. For a minute she looked so much like a little girl. I knew Rose loved and missed Buster. I thought of Mama and how I almost hated her for throwing that bucket of water on Rose and stirring up her anger. She knew Rose was full of rebellion and sometimes showed the gullibility of a child. Her anger toward Mama stemmed from Mama's efforts to make her into someone else. A part of me had always known that no matter what Rose did it wouldn't be right. Daddy had known it too, and that's why he'd sent her to a place where you were accepted no matter how many flaws you had. Granny Lee believed that there was nothing so bad that it couldn't be fixed with a little love.

In retrospect, maybe I had been gullible too in believing in Mama and making excuses for her. Maybe I felt sorry for her having lost her daddy and little brother. I'd known somehow that she was lonely and couldn't turn to her own mama because they didn't get on well, either. In those days I yearned for her attention, but her mind was always somewhere that I couldn't go. I thought of Amity and Violet Elizabeth's affectionate, soft-spoken mother and compared her with my remote mama who never hugged, kissed, or told me she loved me. I'd longed to see her softer side which rarely emerged. I'd wanted to hear her laugh and tell me stories about Granddaddy Wilkes Haley and where she and Floyd Wilkes had played as children. Had she ever skinned her knees or run barefoot through the rock bars? She rarely talked about her childhood days and claimed no pictures existed of her either as a child or a young girl. Somehow, I didn't believe her.

That same day Mama didn't come home until nearly dark. The creak of the screen door caused me to jump up back from the sink where I'd been washing up that morning's coffee cups. Throwing her purse on the table she looked around and asked where Daddy was. "He ain't made it in yet," I answered.

"That figures," Mama said under her breath, then added, "Since he took Rose to Granny Lee's he's hardly spoke a word to me. I fix his supper and it just stays in the warmer, untouched. He don't come to bed until the small hours of the mornin' and all he ever talks about is the mine or that damned union." Walking over to the cabinet Mama took out the grinder and a tin of coffee beans and barked, "You stoke up that fire, Rose," and then she caught herself. Turning to face me, she laughed and said, "Rose could never even build a fire, let alone stoke one. It took her three hours to just light a few sticks of kindlin'." And then in a more spiteful tone she said, "Whatever man she's got stashed away better know she can't even boil water without scorchin' it. The girl can't learn nothin'!"

Mama's usual insults toward Rose had caused my anger to rise like a tide in winter. Unable to hold it in anymore I lashed out at her for the first time in my fourteen years.

"Rose ain't dumb, Mama -- you just made her believe it by tellin' her all the time how she can't do this or that!"

Throwing her hands in the air in a gesture of futility, Mama said, "Well, she ain't got your smarts, Junie Mae! Heaven knows, you're just like prophet Martha Lee -- you know everything!"

"Granny Lee ain't in this, Mama! She didn't have nothin' to do with Rose leavin' here. You were the one that throwed a bucket of cold water on her. Remember? Who does that to somebody?"

Shaking her head in disgust, Mama said, "You don't understand life, Junie Mae. When you have children of your own you'll see how hard it is to raise 'em. I know your sister like the back of my hand. She's livin' in a fairyland. If a man told Rosaline Lee that the moon was made of cheese she'd believe it and ask him to cut her a piece."

Over the sound of the grinder she went on, "You hide and watch! Her belly will be as round as a balloon pretty soon. Marie will show her how it's done. When it happens, Martha, of course, will swear that Rose's baby was God sent." Her laugh was bitter as she reached for the coffee pot, filled it with water, and firmly placed it on the hottest burner lid on the stove.

"You may as well know that I wrote your Uncle Larkin and asked him to come here and talk to Daddy about movin' up north. He sent me a letter last week telling me that his crew would be in Williamsburg come first of the year. He promised that he'd come and stay with us for a few days." Her eyes searched mine for some kind of reassurance. She'd wanted me to tell her that she had done the right thing by asking Uncle Larkin to come, but I kept quiet, knowing anything I said would be wrong.

The next morning Mama cooked breakfast in silence while I dressed for school. I was just about to run a brush through my hair when I heard the squeak of the screen door. Peeping around the door frame, I saw Daddy's hunched figure standing in the middle of the living room. One hand held his dinner bucket, while the other held his mining cap. "They switched me shifts," he told Mama despairingly. Setting his cap down on the end table, he went on in the kitchen. Mama said, "It's plain to me why they put you on night-shift. Little Brock wants to separate you from your brothers -- that way you all can't gather to have your meetin's."

"I'd almost forget this union business, but Harvey and Harlan won't let it go." Sighing heavily he added, "Harvey James told me this mornin' that the German woman is causin' some trouble over at the camp. I guess she's been stirrin' up the other widows and tryin' to get them to sue Little Brock Asher and anyone else involved."

Mama said, "If Big Brock has a say in it, them widows will be out in the street. Mossy Overton came into the store the other day and said she'd heard Little Brock was bringin' in some new hires. If that's true they'll need housing." Mossy Overton's husband was newly retired with a lung ailment but had kept up with the latest news on the mine.

Daddy said, "Heard that too. Truth is he's got every right to put 'em out, too. Them new miners got families and will need a place to live."

Shaking her head in disgust, Mama said, "He can't just put them women and children out in the cold. He's got to give 'em somethin', though no amount of money can give them women and children back what they lost!'

"Don't look like he's offered them nothin' yet. If he had, they would have took it and moved on."

"There was a time when Little Brock Asher was his own man. He didn't care about the coal and done what he wanted to. Somethin' happened to him to make him cruel like his old Daddy." Mama's voice sounded far off.

Daddy said of Big Brock Asher, "He's the power behind his son. I know that much. I see him up there at the mine at least once a day, walking around like he owns it and probably does if you wanna know the truth. I've heard a lot of talk about how he has stock in it."

Mama said, "Of course he owns it. I'll bet you a dollar that he makes most of the decisions concernin' what goes on up there. I guess he finally broke Little Brock's will and that's why he drinks like a fish."

I heard Mama setting the plates and quickly brushed my hair and then went to the table. I wasn't hungry but knew if I didn't eat she might keep me home from school in the morning and dose me with a glass of bitter Epsom salts. Mama thought a good laxative was the answer to all ailments. In the past, it was Rose who got laxed the most. Mama often made flap jacks and drenched them with homemade brown sugar syrup. Not one for eating breakfast, Rose often refused to touch the stack of flapjacks.

"Rose, if you don't eat at least one flapjack you're gettin' a dose of Epson Salts!" Mama warned.

"I can't eat this early, Mama," Rose whined.

"Then go to bed and I'll mix up the salts. You're gonna drink it when I bring it!"

"Please eat just one flapjack, Rose," I'd begged, knowing what was coming if she didn't. But Rose was stubborn and refused to even touch a fork to the flapjack.

When Mama finally realized Rose wasn't going to eat the flapjack, she'd mix the pearly concoction in a glass of water and then stand over her trying to make her drink it. "If you don't drink the salts, I'll pour it down your throat myself," Mama warned.

"You can't make me drink that!" Rose challenged her. The argument would go on for an hour or so. Finally, Mama would sit on Rose, and then pinch her nose with one hand while the other tried to force the bitter liquid down her throat. The violent scene often played out in my thoughts and dreams, and I can still picture Rose wildly kicking the kitchen chair while making an effort to turn her head. I recall how the salts water trickled down the sides of Rose's defiant mouth and how she sometimes vomited up what little Mama managed to force down her throat. I don't believe Rose ever ingested more than a spoonful of the salts, but Mama had tried. I'd hated those episodes that ended up with Rose in bed and Mama daring her to get up all day. Sometimes I'd vomit up my own breakfast on the way to school because my nerves had got the better of me.

That morning and many mornings afterward, I'd ridden to school with Amity and Violet Elizabeth. I knew Mama didn't have to be at the store until eight o'clock in the mornings so I wasn't afraid she'd catch me. One of the Uncles usually picked her up in the mornings, and it was usually Marie who brought her home at night. I wasn't in the habit of disobeying Mama, but sitting close to Amity Smith in the truck was so much nicer than the risk of getting beaten up by the bullies who still held a grudge against me because of Daddy's and my uncles' union efforts.

Throughout the month of November, Daddy, Harvey James, and Harlan Ray continued to hold meetings. Harvey James had drawn in the most support because he'd known what to say and how to say it. On the Saturdays the men didn't work, they usually held the meetings at the home of Granny Lee. Mossy Overton's husband, Van, sometimes allowed the men use his garage for the meetings. Mossy, glad for the company, often baked apple stack cakes or sugar cookies and always had a couple of pots of coffee brewing on the stove for the men to drink. Daddy came home one evening boasting the support of over one hundred men. He said, "If we get sixty more men we can get the mine unionized. I think Mossy's baking did the trick," he joked.

Mama, in no mood for jokes, snidely warned, "You need to be careful what you wish for. The first thing the union will want to do is strike, and you know what trouble that will cause. "

Mama had been working almost until dark at Hanley's store since Daddy had started on the nightshift. Left alone, I sometimes filled the evening hours with long walks in the woods behind the house if the weather wasn't too cold. Buster always tagged along and was good company. A few times, I walked down by the river. It was on one of those evenings that Amity Smith drove up beside me and offered me a ride home. I had just left the banks of the river and was stepping out of the trees into the woods when Amity pulled up and called my name from his rolled down window. "What are you up to?" With my heart fluttering within my chest, I smiled up into his kind blue eyes. Blushing, I said, "I was just walkin' by the river." Buster stood protectively beside me wagging his tale. Upon seeing Amity, he let out a succession of barks in warning.

"Wanna go for a little ride? Violet's up at the house, but you'll be safe without her." He laughed. "Just for a little while," he urged.

I knew Mama wouldn't like me being alone with him but I got in the truck anyway. "Go home, Buster," I gently commanded, knowing he would. Looking dejected, Buster waited a bit before he finally tagging alongside the truck.

"Where are your folks?" Amity asked. I told him how they both worked. He nodded and said, "Mama works two days a week at the Dime Store in town, but it's her day off and she's helping Daddy milk this evening."

"What are you doing out?" I was making small talk, but my heart nearly skipped a beat after he said, 'Lookin' for you. Somethin' told me you'd be out and about."

"Me?" I could barely catch my breath.

Amity looked a bit irritated when he said, "Yes, Junie Mae. Why are you so surprised?"

I didn't know what to say. I hadn't thought a lot about what Amity meant to me because I'd been busy worrying about Rose and how she was getting on with Bart Asher. But now that he'd put the question to me, I didn't know what to say.

"I just need to know if you have the same feelin's for me that I have for you," he asked without compunction.

"Yes," my voice stuttered.

"Yes, what?"

"Yes. I care for you."

"That's better. I was wonderin'," he laughed.

Amity took one hand off the steering wheel and clasped mine warmly. A strange feeling of excitement surged through my chest. It was akin to the tickle I felt when I rode the Ferris wheel during Fair Days in Harlan. I'd only ridden it once but never forgot the feeling of fright mingled with exhilaration. Amity drove down to the low water bridge a mile or two down the road from the lodge. He'd parked on the sandbar and shut off the engine. Turning to me, he smiled and said, "I ain't gonna kiss you, Junie Mae. I just thought we'd sit here and talk awhile before I take you home."

"Why me?" The words seem to pop right out of my mouth.

Once again he looked confused and asked "What do you mean?"

"There's lot of pretty girls at school who look at you. I heard that Charlene Howard has had a case on you since fourth grade."

Smiling broadly, Amity said, "I noticed you right off, Junie Mae Lee. You don't giggle over every little thing and you have a good head on your shoulders. Besides that, you're nice to look at."

Smiling shyly, I turned away from his intense gaze.

"Don't look away Junie Mae. I like lookin' at you. I know you're young but you'll grow older and I want to be here when you're at the right age."

"The right age?" I puzzled.

"The right age to court. I know your folks probably ain't ready to turn you loose yet. I can't blame 'em for that. I'll wait."

We talked a little longer, and then Amity drove me a few feet from the road leading to the lodge and let me out. Now I understood a little of what Rose must be feeling for Bart Asher.

11 STOLEN WATCHES

Darkness came and Mama was still not home. Daddy had gone straight from one of the meetings to work and wouldn't come until the morning when his shift at the mine ended. Alone in the house, I went about lighting the lamps. The lamp in the kitchen wouldn't stay lit, so I brought in the lamp from my room, hoping to shed some light on the problem. Holding the light close to the lamp I noticed its wick had burned up. I knew Mama kept the wicks somewhere in her bedroom. Once in Mama's bedroom, I felt strange and sneaky. Mama never allowed either Rose or me to go in it, but I had to have that wick. Shining the light on the long dresser, I saw Mama's jewelry box and her precious jars of face cream. Walking past the creaseless bed I opened the first dresser drawer and saw only Daddy's neatly folded white handkerchiefs and wool socks. Opening the second drawer I pushed back Mama's slips and underwear, then spied a square flat leather bound case. Puzzled, I lifted out the case and took it into the kitchen where I placed it on the table. Gingerly raising its lid, I saw two rows of dainty women's watches, six in all. Tiny jewels implanted near their faces winked ominously beneath the light. The watches looked like the ones I'd seen in Hansley's store. What was Mama doing with them?

I knew these watches were expensive and that Mr. Hansley wouldn't just let Mama have them. And I also knew that his crazy wife wouldn't give Mama air if she had her in a jug. I doubted she'd even let Mama near the jewelry case. Slamming the case shut, I took it back into the bedroom and carelessly shoved it underneath Mama's carefully folded undergarments. Flushed with anger and uncertainty, I'd forgotten about the wick. Carrying the lamp into my room, I jerked the covers off my bed and made up the ratty old couch where I'd been sleeping since Rose left. Now I had Mama and the watches to think about. It was barely dark, but I wanted to sleep and forget the watches. Trying to seek comfort by imagining Amity's handsome face, I was interrupted by Rose's haunting accusation: Maybe Mama's been eyein' some of the nice rings and watches in his wife's jewelry store. I tried to convince myself that Mama wouldn't steal. All our lives she'd preached to Rose and me on how wrong it was to take something that wasn't ours. There had to be a good reason she had those watches stashed in her dresser drawer.

"Ok, Floyd Wilkes," I said aloud, "If you know everything then come to me and tell me why Mama, your sister, has a case of watches in her dresser drawer." I waited underneath the covers but saw no sign of Floyd Wilkes' ghost. Finally, I'd fallen asleep only to be awakened by the squeak of the screen door. Mama was home and even called out my name, but I kept quiet, pretending I was asleep. I didn't know or particularly care what time it was. For a long time I lay there listening to Mama rattling through the wood box and stoking up the fire in the cook-stove. The fire in the grate where I slept had burned down to hot coals. Eventually Mama came in with a bucket of ashes and covered the hot coals in order to bank the fire so it would keep overnight. I lay very still as she passed the couch.

Sleep was a long time finding me, and when it finally did, morning etched through the windows grey and lifeless. Mama was up early as usual lighting the lamps, stoking the fires, and preparing breakfast for Daddy. When he came through the door, Mama told him she had his bathwater ready. The smell of bacon wafted through the rooms. Instead of triggering my appetite, the aroma made me feel nauseous. For a long time, I lay there on the couch listening to Daddy fill Mama in on the night's events at the mine. Mama complained of how old Mrs. Hansley had followed her about the Hardware store accusing her of flirting with Mr. Hansley and stealing jewelry from the showcases.

Daddy grumbled, "I warned you how it would be before you started working for that skinflint and his ditzy wife. Pert near every person in town knows that the woman needs to be put away. The only reason she's in that store at all is so he can watch her. Mossy Overton said Hansley told her that his crazy wife almost burned the house down when he left her alone a while back."

"We need the money, Ralph. Hard telling how things at the mine will turn out. Besides, it ain't Mr. Hansley's fault; it's that wife of his. She's run off half the customers with her craziness, accusing ever'body of stealin'. He even told me that he's thinking of closing the jewelry store because of her."

So crazy old Mrs. Hansley wasn't so crazy after all and had already missed the case of watches. Why would Mama bother to mention old Mrs. Hansley's accusations of stolen jewelry to Daddy? I didn't want to reason out or find an excuse for what Mama did anymore. It was getting harder and harder to do that lately, with her beating on Rose, writing secret letters to Uncle Larkin behind Daddy's back, and now stealing jewelry from

Hansley' store. One of the things I learned early on was that stealing was considered more of a crime than murder in the backwoods. Folks in my neighborhood considered the taking of someone's property the unspeakable crime. People who stole from their neighbors were permanently ostracized from society. When Old Ben Pickens was caught stealing his neighbors chickens, people turned their backs on him and refused to speak to him. If he was starving to death no one would have given him food because he had committed the unforgivable sin of taking something that didn't belong to him. "No good scum," thief, skunk, and such were names associated with those who stole. Being poor was no sin, but taking someone's property was a killing offense. Had someone shot Ben Pickens for stealing, the shooter would have gotten away with the crime. As far as I was concerned Mama was no better than Ben Pickens. She has taken watches that didn't belong to her.

Maybe Rose was right and I didn't know Mama at all. What other secrets did she have stashed away?

Once out from beneath the covers I realized how cold it was outside. The lodge had always been drafty in cold weather in spite of the fireplace and wood cook stove. I washed and dressed with chattering teeth, making sure my clothes were warm enough to stand up to the cold. The mountains sometimes acted as a barrier against the wind; other times they weren't enough to hold it back, and when it penetrated the mountain barriers there was nothing more powerful and sharp.

Finally, dressed in my heavy gray sweater, long skirt, and heavy Oxfords, I went into the kitchen for my lunchbox. Daddy was sitting at the table drinking coffee and smoking. Upon seeing me his eyes widened and jaw dropped. "Junie Mae you have slimmed down. I had to look twice." His voice held a note of genuine surprise and appreciation. Had I slimmed down? I hadn't thought much about my weight -- especially lately, given what had happened in the past months. But now that Daddy brought it up I noticed that my clothes fitted much looser lately. Later, a look in the mirror confirmed what Daddy had said, for my face appeared slimmer and almost hollow near my cheekbones. My neck seemed longer and my waist seemed inches thinner, even waiflike. My legs that had once been heavy, especially my thighs, now looked longer and more defined. For once in my life I was pleased with what I saw in the mirror and could almost understand what Amity Smith might see in me.

That morning I had taken more pains with my appearance by brushing my hair until it had shone. I had even used a little of Rose's pink lipstick and applied a little rouge to the hollow points of my cheeks. Once out the door and into the rush of the cold wind, I realized my cheeks could have probably done without the rouge. Walking the path leading to the bus stop, I remembered Daddy telling Mama the night before how was planning to meet up with Harvey and Harlan Ray sometime later that day to discuss union business. Amity and Violet were waiting for me in his daddy's truck at the bus stop. Near the shelter house, the Mattingly sisters stood shivering and waved tentatively, while some of the boys simply ignored me. Since Amity insisted on always being there to protect me, neither Billy Wilkins nor Tommy Roberts so much as looked my way. I felt a certain pride in knowing that both Amity and Violet Elizabeth cared for me enough to make sure I was safe. They and school made me temporarily forget the troubles that I was having at home with Mama stealing watches and Daddy seemingly avoiding her as much as possible. As long as I was sitting next to Amity, I could forget how my parents had grown apart. I knew that Daddy's preoccupation with getting a union in was only part of the reason. Mama's inability to treat Rose kindly was in my mind the main reason the two had grown so far apart. At first, I had blamed the cave-in for every bad thing that had happened to us, but in the passing months I would realize that my parents' problems had started long before that. Still, memories of better days always crept into my thoughts and made me wistful. I longed for the days when Mama and Daddy sat close together on the couch listening to the Grand Ole Opry on the old Philco radio. Sometimes Daddy would affectionately drape his arm around Mama's shoulder and she'd rest her head lovingly on his chest. Although she seldom laughed, Daddy sometimes playfully tickled her bare feet in the warm summer evenings, causing her to giggle and like a school girl. Sadly, I realized that it had been years since Daddy had tickled her bare feet and Mama had stopped laughing a long time ago. In retrospect, I knew some kind of caring had existed between them, at least when I was a small child. And even after the lies had finally surfaced, revealing the ugly truth about Mama and her missing parts, I'd consoled myself with the cherished memories.

One evening after school Amity was waiting alone for me in the school parking lot. "Where's Violet Elizabeth?" I asked.

"She rode the bus home," he answered a little sheepishly, then asked, "Do you mind if we take the long way to your house?"

The thought of Mama's possible wrath was lost in the blue of his eyes as they beseeched me. I nodded yes, wanting so badly to forget the union, Mama, and the stolen jewelry. As Amity drove past the school, I studied the gray sky and the lifeless look of the dead landscape. Winter was here, I decided, while wishing for color to match the brightness of my mood. Sitting beside Amity had stirred within me a feeling of safeness that being at home had somehow taken away. Through the rearview mirror the town of Harlan slowly disappeared, giving way to the sight of a few rundown houses to the left and some better looking homes to the right. The Cumberland River meandered to the left of me. In some places its waters stretched out wide, but in others it narrowed. I loved the river and felt an odd kinship to it. I couldn't imagine living anywhere that I couldn't see water. Amity said, "Junie Mae, I'd like to stop by the farm for a few minutes. I got something to show you."

"What do you want me to see?" I asked curiously.

"Just wait 'til we get to the farm," he teased.

A few minutes later we were on the long sandy lane leading back to Amity's father's farm. The big white house with its dark black window shutters stood out against the stark winter landscape behind it. Once out of the truck and onto the property, Amity motioned for me to follow him down the path and across the fence to the stable. Once inside the stable, Violet Elizabeth stepped out of the shadows of a front stall smiling widely. "Junie Mae," she said, "come here and look at what we have." Curious, I followed her into the damp stall where their mare, Chocolate, stood alongside a little brown foal. Taking a few steps forward awkwardly, its spindly legs quivered weakly. "A baby," I giggled in delight. "When was it born?"

"Last night," Violet Elizabeth said, and then added, "It's a girl and we named it after me and you. Her name is Lizzy June." As soon as I saw Amity's wide smile, I wanted to rush to him and fall in his arms. For once, I yearned to forget Mama's rule of keeping it all in and never showing emotion, but I didn't. Mama's rules were so deeply ingrained in me that all I could manage was a smile. As if she had read my mind, Violet put her arms around me and gave me a quick hug.

"Amity and I wanted you to see the foal. It's special, just like you are!" Tears sprung up, blurring my vision. Amity understood and punched me lightly on the arm, "Ah, come on now, it's just a foal. I'd hate to see what you'd do if we'd showed you the three week old calf."

Sandwiched between the people who had become the dearest to me, I followed them a little farther down the paddock to where the little calf ran friskily in the adjacent lot. "I call her Suzy Q. Don't know why," Amity laughed. For a little while I stood beside Amity watching the calf run. I was thinking that I never wanted to go back to the lodge.

An hour or so later Amity and Violet let me off at the path leading to the lodge. "I don't know why you just don't tell your mama you been with us," Amity said.

"I will," I murmured.

Violet hugged me, and then Amity gently squeezed my hand and said "You hurry on down the path, now. It's too cold for you to be out."

Even in the bitter cold of the November wind I felt happier than I'd ever been in my life. Someone loved me and had shown it. I wasn't just thinking about Amity but Violet Elizabeth and the rest of the Smith family. This is not to say I didn't love Rose, because I did, more than anything. It was just that Rose never shared much with me, and hers was a world of make believe that I couldn't understand. Instead of reaching for things around her she sought things that were so far above her head that she couldn't possibly reach them. Obviously Mama had done the same thing when she set out to marry Little Brock Asher and failed to win him. Daddy, no doubt, was seen as a poor substitute since she still seemed unhappy.

As soon as I reached the yard, I saw Daddy's old truck parked around the back of the lodge. Once inside the door, I felt the blessed heat from the blazing fireplace in the front room and could smell supper cooking on the stove but didn't see either Mama or Daddy, at least not at first. My heart squeezed at the thought of Mama being home. She was never home at this time. Then she came into the front room wearing her purple flowered apron that was made by Granny Lee's nimble fingers. It somehow reminded me of a warm summer day and complimented Mama's dark hair. Daddy's tall, gaunt frame came up behind her. "Hello, Junie Mae. You look froze stiff!"

"Where have you been?" Mama snapped.

"I was at school helping Violet Elizabeth Smith with a reading project," I lied.

"Well, how was I to know that? I was worried sick!"

"I'm sorry, Mama."

"Sorry don't cut the mustard around here. I won't have you actin' like Rose, goin' any place you feel like without first askin' me! And don't tell me you walked all the way home in that cold."

"Let it go, Heddy," Daddy said in a tired voice.

Mama turned a baleful look on Daddy and started to speak, but a loud knock on the front door caused her to pause.

"That'd better not be Purl," Daddy scowled.

Walking over to the front window Mama pulled back the curtains and whispered "It ain't Purl. It's the sheriff, and he's got old Arbert Rouse with him." Arbert was Sheriff Joel Baker's little short deputy.

Taking off her apron, Mama handed it to me, demanding that I go into the kitchen and set the table. Taking the apron, I went on into the kitchen. Grabbing the stack of plates out of the cabinet I heard Daddy's deep voice. "Now Joel, we don't know nothin' about no stolen jewelry. That ole woman is crazy as a bedbug and you know it!"

Straining my ears I heard Sheriff Baker's low, apologetic voice. "Now Ralph, we know that but we are duty bound as public servants to come here and at least inquire and maybe look over the house."

"What for?" Mama all but screeched. "Ralph already told you we ain't no thieves. I don't want nobody goin' through my stuff and messin' everything up."

Search the house? Oh, God! If the law finds that jewelry Daddy will be forever shamed. He won't be able to hold his head up in Harlan no more. With a racing heart and quick thought, I grabbed Mama's apron off the chair, put it on, and tied the strings tightly. Mama and Daddy's bedroom was just off to the side of the kitchen, and its entrance couldn't be seen from the front room. Side-stepping the potato bin in the narrow hall, I jerked open the bedroom door and hurried over to the long bureau, gingerly sliding open the second drawer it so it wouldn't squeak. There, underneath a pile of Mama's slips and undergarments, lay the ominous flat box of stolen watches. Sliding it out, I quickly tucked it into the elastic waistband of my skirt, hoping the big apron would hide its sharp edges should the sheriff and his deputy catch a glimpse of me walking through the kitchen in the direction of the back door. But I needn't have worried; Mama was arguing loudly with little deputy Rouse concerning the search, and Daddy was a head taller than both the sheriff and his short deputy. "If you all believe I didn't steal the jewelry then why do you still want to search the house?"

Walking to the kitchen door I carefully opened the screen door and then the main door, closing them both gingerly behind me. Outside, the icy wind whipped about my face as I ran to Daddy's woodshed and turned the wooden latch. Once inside, I searched frantically for a place to hide the long, flat case. Eying all the unfinished pieces among the odds and ends, I quickly settled on the big wooden barrel that held all Daddy's wood scraps. Cramming the case down behind the patterns, I then picked up several scrap pieces and piled them on top of the case. Once I was satisfied that it was well hidden, I picked up a few more scrap pieces so that it would appear I was gathering kindling for the fire, should I be seen.

Once back inside the house, I was aware of the hard hammering of my heart inside my chest. With chattering teeth, I laid the wood scraps in the box behind the stove, thankful that no one saw me to ask me about them. I then slid down into the chair, while making an effort to calm my erratic breathing. What I had done was as bad as Mama's thievery. I was as guilty as she was. I could still hear Mama's argumentative voice above all the others. Finally, over top her strenuous objections, Daddy conceded to the search. He said, "Come on in and search if you have to, but you don't tear nothin' up, you hear? Bunch of nonsense," he muttered under his breath.

"Go on into the kitchen, Heddy, and I'll go with them. Don't you worry none." he soothed. Mama came into the kitchen looking as white as a ghost. Pulling a chair out, she sighed and sat down. Rising from my own chair I began laying the silverware carefully beside each plate, with a clink. I continued to watch Mama, who stared down blankly at the floor. With each creak of a drawer being pulled out her eyes would close as if in silent prayer. The loud squeak of the bureau drawer that had once held the watch case caused Mama to nearly jump out of her chair. Secretly, I was enjoying watching her squirm like a worm on a fishhook.

"There ain't nothin' here," Sheriff Baker finally said, then added, "I don't see no reason for searchin' anyplace else." Daddy and the lawmen came into the kitchen. Deputy Rouse removed his hat and apologized to Mama. "We shore are sorry, Mrs. Lee. I hope we didn't mess nothin' up too bad in there."

Mama could only nod self-consciously. Her eyes remained downcast.

"You all want a cup of coffee or a bite to eat?" Daddy asked politely. Both men declined, and Daddy walked them to the front door. Mama rose and began dipping the food out into bowls. Back in the kitchen Daddy said, "Now do you see why you need to stop working at that store?"

Mama said, "It wadn't Hansley -- it was his crazy wife accusin' me."
Looking disgusted Daddy said, "It's the same thing. He didn't do nothin' to stop her from sendin' the law out here."

"Just sit down and eat," she said in an effort to change the subject.

"I'll eat later. Harvey James and some men on his line are meetin' me over at Levi Creech's place. I heard yesterday that Bonzelle took in the German woman after Little Brock sent her that eviction notice. Don't know where the other women will go. People are mad as heck that he's throwin' them widows and their children out of their homes without a cent to tide 'em over."

Mama's eyes took on a stormy look. I knew she hadn't heard a word he'd said after he spoke Bonzelle Creech's name.

"Why are you goin' to that tramp's home?" She asked.

Daddy looked crestfallen. "Why are you callin' Bonzelle a tramp?"

Laughing bitterly, Mama answered, "Because she is a tramp, and I don't want you nowhere near her! Is this where you've been havin' your meetin's?" she demanded.

Looking angry, Daddy said, "Heddy, this is beneath you. That woman ain't never done a thing to you or anybody else as I know of. You got no right."

"Go, then! I see why you're gone all the time now!" Her voice was at its angriest pitch.

Shaking his head in disgust, Daddy grabbed his coat off of the back of the kitchen chair and started for the door. Turning slightly, he said, "You got no call to accuse me of nothin'."

I stood near the water table shaking all over. I still hadn't recovered from having hidden the watches, and the fight between Mama and Daddy had only made me feel worse. I listened to the loud engine of Daddy's truck die off in the distance. Mama went about slamming pots and pans. "He ain't foolin' me a bit," she spat. "He's been seein' that woman and I know it."

"You don't know that, Mama. I don't believe Daddy would do anything like that," I said with sincerity.

Eying me coldly, Mama said, "What would you know, Junie Mae? He ain't no saint. No man is! Any of them will sleep around if they get the chance. Eat your supper and then clean this kitchen!" she demanded before stomping off toward the bedroom. After a few seconds, I heard her open the bureau drawer. Silently and without much forethought I threw on my coat and went out to Daddy's shed, where I retrieved the square leather box from out of the wood bin. Back in the kitchen, Mama's mouth fell open when she saw the box in my outstretched hands. "Is this what you're looking for?" I asked her flatly.

"How did you know about the watches? When did you hide them?" she asked incredulously.

"The other night I was looking for a wick for the lamp and seen the box. I remembered where it was so I took it out earlier and hid it so the law wouldn't find it."

For a minute she stood staring coldly at me. I thought that she probably hated me for finding the watches. Placing the box on the table I asked, "Why did you take the watches, Mama?"

Mama's eyes quickly averted from my steady gaze. In a defensive voice, she answered, "I didn't take nothin' that I didn't earn."

"Why didn't you tell that to the sheriff, then?"

Mama winced. "Hansley pays niggardly wages. He could afford to pay me right but he don't. I got my pay the best way I could. Don't look at me like that!" she shouted. "You don't understand how things work in this world. Do you think the Hansleys got all their money from being honest? How many poor people do you think they've swindled over the years to get what they got?" Breathing hard, her hands gestured nervously as she talked. "The house they live in is so big they probably get lost every day. Look at our place! Look at it! Do you think it's fair that some folks have so much more than others?"

"You sound just like Rose," I murmured, but she ignored me and went on with her tirade.

Walking to the window she snatched back the curtain and pointed upwards at Creekstone House, which could be seen easily through the bare branches. "Them people up there are the biggest thieves of all. They've stole off poor miners for years. Big Brock Asher robbed my Daddy and the other miners to get what he's got. Never mind what he stole from me, and he's throwin' them widows out of their homes so he can get richer. You think it's a big sin 'cause I took a few watches! Grow up, Junie Mae. It's time you see life as it really is. And don't go preachin' no Martha Lee sermon to me, either!"

Void of any pity for Mama, I reminded her of a time when she thought of stealing differently. "You always told Rose and me that stealing was a great sin, Mama. Licking my lips I continued. "Remember when you thought Rose and me stole the sack of candy from the Christmas box at church? You wouldn't believe that old Mrs. Wright gave it to us, so you took us back in the church and made us prove that we got it honest."

Looking irritated and frazzled Mama said, "It is wrong to steal most of the time, but sometimes a person ain't got no choice. The big people in this world stomp on the little people, and it's up to the little people to do whatever it takes to get out from underneath their heels. I done the only thing I could to get what was rightfully mine."

"What will you do with the watches, Mama?" .

"I'll have Coy get rid of them somewhere. He knows people who'll buy 'em."

"What about the money you get for them? What will you do with it?"

Mama's dark eyes burned into mine as she said "I'll use it to get us all out of this black hell. We'll go where air smells like green fields and flowers instead of river rot and coal."

"Who will you take with you?" I asked, knowing she'd become livid -- and she did.

"My family," she barked, and then added "You, Daddy, and Rose if she wants to go."

Shaking my head, I said "Daddy won't leave here, Mama, and Rose won't go with you neither. Not now, not after everything that has happened with you two." With trembling lips I managed, "I won't leave Rose and Daddy here. It wouldn't be right."

Mama grabbed my left arm; her fingernails dug deep hard into its flesh, causing me to wince. "What's right?" she hissed. "Do you think living here in this shack is right? Your Daddy is dying from the coal right now. Even if it never caves in on top of him or explodes all around him, he is still dying from it. He'll die a young man because the coal dust has filled up his lungs so that he can't draw a decent breath. I've seen this all my life. In one way or another, the coal has took everything I ever cared about -- even Floyd Wilkes. If we'd had a dime to our names my poor little brother would never have gone off to sell his pitiful buckets of blackberries and died on that bridge."

It was the first time she had mentioned Floyd Wilkes in a long time. I could hear the pain in her voice. Slowly, she let go of my arm. I could feel the blood pulsating in my broken skin. Later there would be an ugly bruise to remind me of her unhappiness and desperation. I'd seen her grab Rose countless times and there was always a bruise to remind her of Mama's unhappiness. Self-consciously rubbing my arm, I walked out of the kitchen and into my bedroom. For a while, there was only silence in the house, but then came the familiar rattle of pots and pans as if nothing had taken place earlier. That was Mama; she'd always had a way of forgetting what she didn't want to remember. Looking down at my arm I saw the angry red marks left by her fingers, the little cuts from her nails, and the beginnings of a bruise. I was thinking that I wouldn't forget, and I was glad that it was the winter season. Long coats and sweaters did a good job hiding bruises.

Things between Mama and me took a strange turn after I'd confronted her with the case of stolen watches. Oftentimes, I would catch her looking at me with kind of suspicious wariness in her eyes. I could sense a kind of fearful respect in her for me that had never been there before. Maybe she feared I'd tell Daddy the truth about the watches if she yelled and reprimanded me. Nothing could have been farther from the truth. I would have never hurt Daddy by telling him that Mama was a thief as well as an accomplished a liar. As a matter of fact, I'd planned on taking her guilty secret to the grave with me along with so many other things I would find out about her later.

12 FLOYD WILKES' GHOST

As November dragged on, I'd dreamed of happier times before the cave-in when we were a family, or so I thought. Sometimes when the wind howled through the barren trees in the dead of the night, I'd lay on the couch wide awake wondering if there had ever been happier times. Feeling the loneliness that every child feels after a family unit has been disrupted by tragedy or a loss, I had suffered in silence. In the coming days when Amity or Violet Elizabeth noticed my pensive moods and showed concern, I assured them that I was fine rather than telling them the truth. The art of silence and my ability to keep it all hidden was well ingrained within me. Mama had shaped and honed it since I was a small child. I thought of Rose often and recalled that I'd seen her only once since she and Marie had brought over the fresh hog meat. I was anxious for the upcoming holidays and seeing my sister again.

Three nights before Thanksgiving, I'd awoken in a cold sweat. Sitting up on the couch I could hear the wind screaming through the trees and thought of how it almost sounded like a human being tortured in the distance. Unable to sleep, I lay back on my pillow, staring out the big window into the dark nothingness. At first the noise sounded like the scraping of a tree limb against the house. But the sound had become louder with each passing minute. Throwing back the cover, I rose from the couch only to jump backwards when the front door flew open banging loudly against the wall. The powerful force of the wind caused a wall clock to come crashing to the floor. Suddenly frightened, I waited for Mama or Daddy to come running into the front room, but seconds passed and no one came. Hurriedly, I shut the door and latched it, and then stooped to pick up the clock's glass face that lay shattered on the floor. "Floyd Wilkes?" I whispered, while expectantly eyeing the doorway leading into the kitchen. The hair on back of my neck and on my arms crawled with expectancy, while the air around me seemed strangely charged. Floyd Wilkes was angry at me. I'd known that as surely as I breathed, but why? And why hadn't Mama and Daddy heard the door blow open and the clock splinter apart? After I'd cleaned up the glass from the clock I slid furtively back underneath the covers. With teeth chattering I lay in the darkness wondering what I was supposed to get out of what had just happened. It was a long time before sleep found me.

    As was our yearly tradition, we spent Thanksgiving Day at Granny Lee's house in Putney. Granny Lee and Marie had stayed up half the night before baking the turkey and making the deserts. As usual, Grandma Haley came and brought with her the special oyster and hamburger dressing that Daddy loved so much, as well as her homemade yeast rolls that were always a favorite of Rose. The big house felt warm and inviting in spite of its usual disarray. By twelve noon it was filled with family. Uncles Harlan Ray and Harvey James had brought their wives as well as a deck of cards, much to Granny Lee's dismay. The poker game was a Thanksgiving Day ritual that the men enjoyed. Even though they didn't place bets with money and played for fun, Granny Lee believed that card playing was an abomination. Still, she allowed it -- but not before saying many prayers in order to assure the Lord that she'd had nothing to do with her son's love for the evil game of poker. Rose seemed excited to see us and had even embraced Mama, who in turn patted her absently on the arm, while studying her as closely as a doctor might study a lab specimen under the microscope. I'd studied Rose, too, and couldn't miss the hollowness of her cheeks and the deadness in her eyes. I knew something was terribly wrong with her. When it came Daddy's time to hug her, it was he who held her the longest. His big hand stroked her hair lovingly as he whispered words of endearments in her ears. Tears of emotion flooded my eyes and I quickly wiped them away before Mama saw them. In the kitchen the women gathered to set the table and help with any last minute warming or cooking. Marie's children ran through the house like wild Indians. Often underfoot, especially little Brice Dodd, the children were frequently scolded by Great Uncle Hiram. His scolding, however, was done half-heartedly, and the children paid no attention to him at all. It was Granny Lee's patient, comforting voice along with her natural understanding of little children that eventually tamed their rambunctious actions. "Now Doddy, you need to go sit in your special seat at the children's table so no one else will take it," she gently warned. "Brenda Sue, you are such a big girl I'm going to let you place the silverware beside the plates on the big table. Chester Harlan, you can help Uncle Hiram bring in the wood later on this evening."

    Amazingly, the children calmed down and did as Granny Lee asked them to do. Little Chester Harlan found Great Uncle Hiram and climbed up on his bony knee. As if by habit, Great Uncle Hiram began to absently juggle him up and down while at the same time discussing quail hunting with Uncle Corbin. While the rest of the women cooked and set the table, Rose and I sat on the couch with our arms touching. Rose seemed unusually quiet and introspective. With so many people in the house, I'd found it impossible to get her off by herself. When the food was finally set on the table, everyone gathered around it in a circle linking hands while Granny Lee led us in prayer. As usual, the prayer was long and drawn out. Because there were so many of us, more chairs were brought in from the utility shed outside. Like Daddy, I piled my plate high with the delicious goodies, but Mama and Rose barely touched the food on their plates and both seemed elsewhere in thought. The only time Mama snapped out of her reverie was when Uncle Corbin brought up the No. 5 mine and the secret union meetings that were really not secret at all. Granny Lee, keenly aware of Mama's disdain for the mining talk, said, "Now, Corbin, this is a day to give thanks and not a day to argue over the union. I don't want to hear another word about the coalmine today!" The men obeyed but Uncle Corbin continued to sulk the rest of the day. As far as I knew, Mama hadn't spoken a word to Grandma Haley, which made me feel as if I had to somehow make up for her negligence. After desert was finished, Grandma Haley had begun to gather up plates from the table. Just as she reached for a stack, I gently placed my arms around her boney shoulders. Taken aback by the attention, she stiffened momentarily but then turned to me and smiled. I will not forget the sweetness of that smile.

"How are you Junie Mae?" Grabbing up a pile of silverware, I started rattling off about school and anything else I could think of in order to keep the conversation going. Finally, Grandma Haley bragged about how Fritz, Uncle Purl's new mixed breed dog, had taken up more with her than with him. "He's good company for an old woman like me," she teased. "I told Purl that he might just as well leave the dog with me since he sneaks over to my place every day for breakfast and even hides when he hears Purl's voice." Studying my face, her faded green eyes had grown suddenly serious. "Come on over to the sink, Junie Mae. I have something to tell you," she said, while suspiciously eyeing the doorway. Momentarily puzzled, I followed Grandma Haley to the sink. "I don't want to spoil your holiday, honey, but I think you should know that your Mama paid me visit last week. She asked me to give her enough money to buy a single bus ticket to Indianapolis. I wouldn't give it to her, though and she started screaming at me. I told you just in case you're wonderin' why she ain't speakin' to me today." Lowering her voice, she whispered, "I couldn't give her money to run off from a good man like your Daddy. Besides, she no more knows what she wants than an addled goose." Sighing tiredly, she went on, "Your Mama's been wantin' leave here since she was a little girl. She'll eventually find a way to go, Junie Mae. I just want to prepare you for the day it happens."

I edged closer to Grandma Haley, offering a whispered assurance. "I know she wants to leave. You didn't tell me nothin' that I didn't already know."

Grandma Haley patted my hand. "You're a good girl, Junie Mae. I worry about both you and your sister. You got more goin' on in strength than her, and you're way yonder smarter, too. I ain't maligning her. I just see so much of your Mama's fanciful ways in Rose. That's why the two of them can't get along with each other. They're like two peas in a pod, always wantin' things they'll never get."

Still mindful of the doorway, she went on, "I tried the best I could with your Mama, but she was stubborn and thought the way she thought. Whatever I told her washed off her like water on a duck's back." With eyes downcast she went on, "I've made my mistakes with your Mama, Junie Mae, and I regret so much. But I can't put her back inside me and start over again."

Wrapping my arms around my Grandma Haley's waist, I allowed myself to feel the strange humanness in her. In the past she'd remained reserved, suspicious, and, like Mama, hard to relate to. I recalled the night of the union meeting when I had first heard her laughing like a child in Granny Lee's bedroom. I'd thought her behavior was so strange and out of character, but I had loved that side of her. On that Thanksgiving Day she'd shown me yet another surprise facet of her personality. Like Mama, she could be soft beneath that flint rock façade -- but not often.

Gently moving away from me, she whispered affectionately, "Now you go and visit with your sister and I'll clear the table so the men can start their poker game."

I didn't want to think about what Mama was planning behind all of our backs. Would she sneak off into the night without telling us? Would she even say goodbye to any of us? My stomach suddenly felt sick. Once in the crowded living room, my eyes fell on Harlan Ray's pretty wife Rebekah Ann, who had been chasing Marie's children around the house and giggling and acting just like one herself. I thought how it was incredibly sad that someone who loved children so much would never have any of her own. Beside Rebekah Ann sat Harvey James's well-dressed wife, Ellen, who Mama couldn't stand. Mama claimed Ellen was a snooty woman who thought she was better than anyone else. Harvey James had met her in college. They hadn't been blessed with children, either, but seemed happy anyway. Harvey James was always extremely attentive to his wife, sometimes kissing her for no reason between poker hands. Ellen was a sensible woman who worked as a secretary for the phone company. I'd liked her because she reminded me of my teachers with her intelligent mannerisms. Like Harvey James, she didn't use long vowels and spoke very proper. That day she had greeted me warmly as usual and asked me all about school. I could tell she was genuinely interested.

Mama sought out Rebekah Ann because she'd found her easier to talk to and hung possessively close to her most of the night. Every time Ellen tried to make conversation with Rebekah Ann, Mama would rudely interrupt or drag her off to the kitchen in the pretense of checking on Granny Lee. I knew Mama was acting out of spite, and her rude behavior fueled the anger I already felt in knowing that she was planning to leave Daddy, Rose, and me. How could she look at Daddy -- or any of us, for that matter -- and act as if it was just another day? Rose was right when she said that I didn't know Mama and that I would eventually catch her out. Her missing parts were slowly etching their way in like the grey light of dawn. Making my way past Ellen, I spied Rose sitting alone in a chair underneath the staircase. Her eyes appeared hollow and empty. My heart wrenched as I reached out and took hold of her arm. "Let's go upstairs to your room and talk," I suggested.

"I think Marie's up there tryin' to get the babies to bed. We can go in Granny Lee's bedroom," she offered.

Granny Lee's bed was an antique and had once belonged to her own grandmother. It was made of dark cherry and had an old-fashioned canopy hanging over it. Directly across the room from the bed was a marching dresser with a long mirror. "I'll bet this bed and dresser are worth a fortune," I said, trying to break the silence.

Rose's smile was that of a stranger.

"Oh, Rose," I sighed. "What's the matter?"

Looking down at the floor, Rose shook her head in resignation. Her dark hair no longer shone with life but seemed lackluster. "Things have changed so much, Junie Mae. I don't even know who I am no more."

"It's Bart Asher, ain't it?"

"It's always been Bart Asher. From the time I was old enough to think, he's never been too far away. Ever since I was a little girl I've put all my hopes on him and livin' in that big house, but I'm certain now that it'll never happen for me and him," she finished.

"What do you mean?" I asked with a sinking heart.

"He's for shore goin' to Richmond to college after the Christmas holidays. That's all he talks about when we're alone. It used to be different when we first started meetin'." Turning her anguished, unsettling eyes on me, Rose described her summer days spent with Bart Asher. Until then I could only imagine what the two of them had done together. Her telling of it made it real to me.

"He used to pick me daffodils and I'd carry them around until the sun finally wilted 'em." Lowering her voice she went on, "There's a little house back there in the woods behind the Creekstone House where Bart and his

Daddy and their friends camp when they hunt. It's pretty shabby but it's got an old woodstove, tables, and even a bed in it. He took me there a lot, at first. Some evenin's we'd just sit there at the eatin' table and talk – well, he talked, mostly about things like cars, college, and huntin' and his Daddy's drinkin'. Sometimes he'd pour his heart out about that. I'd listen as close as I could. He told me I was a good listener, but the truth is that I really didn't know what to talk about." Biting her puffy bottom lip, she said in a trembling voice, "He never asked me about me. I just thought about that today. I don't know if he even knows who I am or what my dreams are." A tear slid down her cheek and she quickly wiped it away. "Once when we was down by the creek at the back of the house, Bart showed me a wild rose bush and picked one of the little red roses for me. He said, 'You remind me of this rose, only you're way yonder prettier.' I'll never forget he said that. His words made me feel like the prettiest girl in the world. I remember lookin' right into his dark eyes and just meltin'. So much love was inside of me for him that I thought I might bust." Grabbing my arm, she said in a feverish voice, "It's a mad love, Junie Mae. It's makin' me crazy and I don't know what to do with all these feelin's inside of me." Her fingernails dug sharply into my arm in desperation. I thought of the earlier bruise from Mama's fingernails that had finally healed. Now there would be another to take its place. Suddenly aware of the pain she was causing me, Rose let go of my arm and then fell against me, quietly sobbing. My own heart was breaking for her, but I felt helpless as to what to do or say. In a muffled voice Rose said, "I don't see Bart much lately, and when I do, he don't pay a whole lot of attention to me. Last night I waited in the back alley for hours and he never showed up."

"Come home, Rose," I begged. "You'd be better off there, especially when it's so close to Christmas."

Shaking her head Rose said cryptically, "You don't know what I've done. If you did, you'd never want to see me again. Mama would kill me anyway, and Daddy. Oh, God, poor Daddy don't deserve to have a daughter like me." Turning her strange, unsettling eyes on me, she confessed, "If it is one person I love in this world besides you it's Daddy. No, I'm better off here for the time being, so I can try to work it all out."

The poker game lasted until well after midnight. Granny Lee was tolerant as usual, and acted good-natured about it. Great Uncle Hiram, who had no idea how to play poker, chose to play his harmonica. It sounded awful but kept the women entertained for a while. Rose had gone to bed an hour or two before midnight.

When Mama had finally had enough she'd announced to Daddy that she was tired. I recall the three of us walking in the cold to the truck. The wind was so sharp and fierce that it had blown Daddy's hat off his head. He'd chased it down the dark alley, finally finding it behind a garbage can.

Later, lying on the couch in the living room, I stared into the crackling fire thinking of Rose. Recalling her words, I wondered what she had done that she thought was so terrible that I wouldn't speak to her again. Where are you now, Floyd Wilkes? You could tell me what kind of trouble she's in if you just would. In the darkness I whispered, "Why don't you knock another clock off the wall or even blow a door open? You can do it."

In spite of the blaze in the fireplace the room stayed cold. In the hearth the logs popped and sizzled. As time passed, the flames eventually died down and the low hissing of the logs lulled me into a safe, serene place. With Grandma Haley's quilt pulled high up over my head, I pretended that all was right in my life. I imagined that Rose was lying snug at the foot of the couch while Floyd Wilkes had made himself small enough to fit on my pillow. I pictured Mama and Daddy sleeping peacefully next to each other with no ugly visions of the coal to interrupt their dreams. Sometime in the night, Floyd Wilkes' ghost came to me in a flash of bright light. Standing motionless and dressed in his same faded overalls, he waited in a stand of trees in a part of the woods that was unfamiliar to me. For the first time since I'd seen his ghost, the look of him with his straw pale hair and matching skin filled me with a kind of apprehension. In the past, Floyd Wilkes' ghost had given me comfort by showing proof that things were going to be alright. What was he about to show me now? Whatever it was wasn't going to be right. I knew it. I felt it. But I'd asked for this, hadn't I? Hesitant to follow him, I shrunk back amongst the shadows of the trees. My eyes followed his footsteps until he disappeared deeper into the woods. With unease, I finally trudged forward. Above my head the sun filtered through the naked spaces in the trees. I could no longer see Floyd Wilkes' ghost but sensed that it was somewhere among the dark timbers watching me. Time was of no relevance as I walked beneath the shadowy trees. Finally, I came to a clearing where a little house stood in a bright green field. I looked for Floyd Wilkes' ghost but saw no sign of it. Surrounded by weeds and briar bushes, the house was clearly vacant and its existence a mystery to me. Fragrant honeysuckle vine clung to the side of the chimney. Somewhere close I heard what sounded like a low sob. Pausing in my step, I strained my ears and heard it again. Someone was crying somewhere. Walking gingerly around to the corner of the house I immediately spotted a small dip in the land that was dotted with wild red roses; their color reminded me of dark spots of blood. The sobbing grew closer and louder. Parting some weeds, I saw a girl sitting on what appeared to be a large uneven stone. She was wearing a yellow sundress, just like the one Rose had worn the day of the Harlan fair. Her dark hair fell like a curtain, shielding her whole face from me. In her little white hand was one single red rose. Feeling a pang of familiarity I called out to her, "Rose." At first she didn't respond and continued to sob. Edging closer to where she sat I called her name again. This time she looked up. A scream arose within my throat when I saw that she had no eyes or even a face. It was as if she wore a mask of the blackest black. With eyes wide open in terror, I looked about the darkness of the living room in confusion, but saw only Mama in her long white gown bending over me. "Wake up, Junie Mae!"

"Something bad's gonna happen to Rose, Mama. She didn't have no face!" I cried.

"It was a nightmare," Mama said impatiently. "Go back to sleep!"

Grabbing on to her sleeve, I begged her to listen. "Mama, I know when things are gonna happen. I want Rose to come home!"

Jerking away from my grasp, Mama said, "It's too late in the night for this. You go back to sleep. We'll talk about it tomorrow."

For a long time afterwards, I lay wide awake in the darkness, alone and shivering even beneath the heavy quilt. Why had Floyd Wilkes' ghost shown me this scary vision of Rose with no face? What did it mean? I knew Rose was unhappy, already. For the first time since I'd encountered Floyd Wilkes' ghost I felt frightened. Now I wasn't sure if I wanted him to come to me with anything else.

"Stay away from me for the rest of the night, Floyd Wilkes!" I whispered to the darkness.

13 THE BLIZZARD

The first day of December brought snow. At first the little flakes fell almost timidly through the gray morning hours, but when evening came they'd grown bigger in size and were now accompanied by a sharp wind which caused them to spiral and drift uncontrollably through the air like thousands of feathers. On the second day of December I awoke to the sound of the howling wind thumping against the house and rattling the shutters. Never in my fourteen years of life had I seen a snow blizzard. I wasn't sure if it was beautiful or frightening, or a combination of the two. That morning Daddy had driven me to the bus stop. Only a handful of the camp children stood near the shelter, but of the ones who did most were busy hurling snowballs at each other. Cold and numb, I'd climbed into the cab of Amity's waiting truck. By twelve noon the teachers dismissed classes due to the accumulation of the snow making roadways hazardous. Bracing myself for the cold, I walked the length of the sidewalk and stood wondering if I should wait for Daddy or ride with Amity Smith. Daddy usually picked me up or sent an uncle to get me when school let out early because of the weather.

Just as I thought it, Amity came up behind me gripping my shoulder. "Come on, Junie Mae, and ride with me and Violet Elizabeth. Me and Daddy put chains on my tires last night so we won't slide and end up in the ditch like some of them poor dumb clucks who thought their trucks would make it without 'em," he yelled above the screaming wind. Once inside the cab I huddled up against Violet Elizabeth for warmth. Giggling nervously, we latched on to one another as Amity started what was to become a treacherous ride. "How about some cuddles for the driver?" he teased.

"You just drive, Amity Smith, and make sure you don't kill us!" Violet Elizabeth teased back.

. Outside the truck windows the wind howled, pitching the snow in all directions. I could barely see where we were going. "This is scary," Violet said, clutching on tighter to my arm. Everything was covered in white and the snow kept blowing on the windshield. "Amity, I'm scared," Violet Elizabeth whispered.

"It's all right, Violet. We don't have much farther to go."

My eyes strained to see through the blowing snow. Suddenly I yelled, "Look, Amity, there's a car off near that grade!"

"I see it, honey, but we can't stop to help now. I'll get the tractor and come back and see to them after I get you girls home." The short trip home seemed to take forever. I'd prayed I'd get home before Daddy started looking for me. When we finally arrived at the path leading to the lodge I'd told Amity to stop and let me out. "I can walk the little distance," I assured him. Amity shook his head in protest but I'd already had the door open and was half way outside. "It's too steep for you to drive the rest of the way."

"Anyone in there?" he asked, motioning in the direction of the house

"I'm sure Mama is, but even if she ain't I can make a fire and cook supper If I have to. I'm not helpless, you know," I said over the roar of the wind.

"Just concerned about you is all," he said, and then added, "I almost forgot! You ain't afraid of nothin'!"

"That's right!" I countered back. My own laughter sounded good to my ears. Once outside the truck, the snow spiraled and blew so hard it almost ripped my coat off.

"Get inside," Amity yelled above the roar and hissing of the wind.

Walking through the snow was awkward. I'd nearly slipped three times before reaching the yard. Once inside the house, I saw Mama standing in the kitchen door looking cross. "Daddy's out in this looking for you," she snapped.

"Oh, no! It's so bad out there. I waited for Daddy but thought I'd get home early and save him a trip. I rode home with Violet Elizabeth Smith and her brother."

Mama laughed cynically and said, "Save it! I know why you rode with the Smith boy. You're seein' him, ain't you?"

"He's Violet Elizabeth's brother, Mama. She's my best friend."

"You are seein' that boy and I know it, so stop lyin'. You and your sister must take me for a fool. You think I don't know that she's been sneakin' around seein' some no good. Now you're doin' the same thing.'

"Amity Smith is good, Mama. He's not a low-life." Jerking off my wet coat, I angrily pitched it on the chair.

"He comes from better stock than us, I must say," she smirked, "but why would he look at a girl whose family is as poor as dirt? You better ask yourself why he's payin' attention to you."

"You got it wrong Mama. He ain't like that!"

Placing her hands on her hips Mama said, "Who do you think you're talkin' to? You think I don't know men and how they think? Do you really believe the Smiths would let their boy marry a girl who has never used anything but an outdoor toilet? Them people are well-off and make a good living, and when it comes time for their son to marry they'll make him pick a girl who comes from the same kind of stock as them."

Her cruel words had hit a nerve. Suddenly sick to my stomach, I knew that Mama was right about the Smiths being far better off than us money wise. I pictured their nice two-storied home standing on green acres of flat graceful bottom land where cattle grew fat on the grass and horses ran free on the other side of the fence. Amity's Daddy and Grandfather were both teachers and business owners, and neither had to work their guts out in the coal like my Daddy and uncles were forced to do every day. Although it was less than a mile down the road from the lodge, the Smith place suddenly seemed far out of my reach.

A lump had formed in my throat, but in spite of the pain I made an effort to defend Amity and his wonderful family. "They're nice people, Mama. I've ate at their table and they treated me good."

Mama's face softened. "I'm shore they are decent people, Junie Mae. I'm only lookin' out for you."

"I'm fourteen years old, Mama. I ain't thinkin' of marryin' soon."

"Junie Mae, I don't want you to end up hurt," Mama sighed. She folded her arms across her breasts and said in a defeated voice, "When did you grow up, Junie Mae? It's like I don't know you. It's like I'm seein' my own daughter for the first time."

Looking directly at Mama, I said, "I've always been here, Mama, but you was too busy looking at Rose to see me." I don't know why I said that. The words had just leaped out.

"I guess I deserved that," she finally admitted. "It's just that you and Rose are so different. Rose thinks with her heart and you think with your head. I've never had to worry about you doing somethin' foolish -- but Rose..." She chuckled. "Rose is like that wind out there -- you never know which way she'll blow 'cause she don't know either."

Changing the subject, she instructed, "Go take off your school clothes and bring them into the kitchen to dry. I got water boilin' for the last batch of Mama's orange and chamomile tea. I'll make you a cup. It's almost like a drug in the winter. I guess it's the chamomile."

Changing quickly into my everyday clothes, I wondered what Mama was after. I thought it strange that she had talked to me more like you would talk to a grownup. Once in the kitchen, I found her staring solemnly out the window onto the white landscape where the snowflakes spiraled and the wind screamed loudly through the trees. "It's gettin' bad out there. It's been years since I seen a blizzard like this. I hope your Daddy's all right. He should be comin' in soon." Moving away from the window, she went about fixing the orange tea in silence. I watched as she poured the scalding water over the tea bags in the cups. The sweet aroma of oranges soon scented the kitchen. Handing me a steaming cup, she asked me if I wanted sugar. I nodded as she carefully spooned two teaspoons of the sugar into my cup. "When the Second World War was on this stuff was like gold," she said of the sugar. "You and Rose probably can't remember how it was when ever'thing was rationed. Your Daddy and me was livin' with your Granny Lee then. Times was so bad that we couldn't have made it by ourselves. Wadn't just us, though -- everybody was poor then, and traded foodstuffs. Granny Lee always had a way of getting sugar and coffee." She smiled. I smiled, too, in the shared appreciation that Granny Lee was a resourceful woman.

Mama was silent for a little while before she began to talk again. When she opened up, I realized that this was the first time she had ever told me anything significant about her life and childhood.

"There are things I don't talk about, but if it'll spare you some hurt in the future I'll tell you, so long as you keep it to yourself. Daddy wadn't my first love, Junie Mae; there was somebody else before him. His family was wealthy and had ever'thing ours could only dream about. I growed up with him and learned to love him, but in the end I lost him 'cause his Daddy didn't want my blood mixed with his son's. If I learned one thing in this world it is that the poor class don't mix with the rich. You need to learn that, too. Just go out find yourself a man from a family like yours. It'll save you a lot of heartache in the end, believe you me."

Speaking impulsively, I said, "Amity Smith ain't no Little Brock Asher, Mama. His Daddy don't own a coalmine as I know of, and I know he ain't got a million dollar contract with Kentucky Electric."

Mama's jaw dropped and her face paled. Looking at me through eyes as big as saucers, she whispered, "How do you know that? Who told you?"

"I guessed after that time Little Brock thought Rose was you."

Slumping farther down in her chair, she said, "I had no idea you knowed about me and him." Laughing dryly, she added, "I forget how you can see though walls and such. Does Rose know too?"

"You'd have to ask her, Mama," I said, not wanting to bring Rose into the conversation.

"It don't matter who he was, Junie Mae. All that matters is the lesson I learned all because I loved a man that I could never have. It took a lot to kill what I had for him. The only way I could get him out of my head was to hate both him and his old Daddy. I've tried to bury the memory the way people bury the dead. It's the only way -- just scoop the dirt over the casket and go on. I still think of him sometimes, though," she admitted somberly.

"I wonder what they done with the house back in the woods? After we left the Daisy Camp, the Ashers let us move in their little house back in the woods. It wadn't much but it was far better than what we was used to."

"What did Big Brock do?" I asked.

Without turning to face me she whispered, "He fixed things between Little Brock and me. Let's just leave it at that, Junie Mae."

"That's not good enough," I said, frustrated. "What did he do?"

Mama laughed coarsely and started rambling more to herself than to me. "He said my blood would never mix with his son's. What a laugh I had over that one. If you only knowed how funny this really is," she snorted.

Angry and frustrated I said, "I don't understand any of this, Mama. If Little Brock wanted you what could his Daddy have done to stop it?"

Mama's tone was cryptic. "He knowed what to do, Junie Mae. There's no sense in me goin' into it. I told you this to show you how far rich people will go to keep their own from bein' tainted by the blood of the poor. I'm tryin' to save you the hurt and heartache I got from believin' I could cross over to their side. My dreams wadn't nothin' but puffs of smoke. After I turned twelve years old, Mama thought I was too big to be with Brock anymore so I stayed home and watched over Floyd Wilkes and the twins. Little Brock got lonely for us, though, and sneaked down to our place, but Mama had already warned us not to open the door. I remember hearin' him knockin'. I'll bet he stood out there ten minutes or better. Floyd Wilkes kept wantin' to open the door, but I wouldn't let him. It killed me to shut him out like that."

"He must have found you later," I reasoned

"He did. I was your age when I seen him again. Big Brock had sent him off to some private school in Williamsburg, probably to keep us apart. He had come home on Spring Break and found me at his daddy's funeral home where I was workin'. We was real glad to see each other and met whenever we could. Big Brock finally caught us kissin' in the casket room. He had blood in his eyes that day and I knowed then that he would never let us be together. It took Little Brock longer to face it. He wanted me to run off and marry him. I thought about it but then…"

"You traded a man with money for a coalminer, Mama. That don't make a lick of sense," I said skeptically.

"You write the rest of the story anyway you want it, Junie Mae. I didn't have no choice in doin' what I done."

Shaking my head in frustration, I said, "If you learned to hate Little Brock and his Daddy, why couldn't you give Daddy the love he deserves?"

"Little Brock took all I had inside. There wadn't much left to give your Daddy, but I've done the best I can."

"You ain't told me nothin' that I ain't already figured out, Mama," I said with disgust.

"You're a smart girl, Junie Mae. I don't know who you took them smarts after. I know it wadn't me, and it wadn't your Daddy. He don't see much. I guess he don't want to. You go ahead and fill in the blanks."

I was about to protest when the kitchen door opened and Daddy walked in. A rush of bitter cold came behind him. Stomping the snow off his feet onto the rug in front of the door he said, "It's real bad out there; good thing me and Harvey put chains on the truck tires yesterday evenin'." Turning to me he said, "I've been lookin' all over God's creation for you. How did you get home?"

"I'm sorry, Daddy. Amity Smith and his sister brought me. I was afraid you couldn't make it."

"That's all right. Me and Harvey had to make a run into town to get supplies for Maw, anyhow."

"Ain't nobody workin' the night-shift tonight?" Mama asked, her voice calm as normal. It was as if we had shared nothing.

Daddy nodded affirmatively and said, "Asher ain't gonna lose a dime because of a blizzard."

Peeling off his heavy coat, gloves, and finally his warm flannel shirt, Daddy pulled up a chair and sat down. "Smell's good in here -- like oranges. Got anything to feed me?"

Mama nodded and said, "I brought home a gallon of sweet milk last night. What do you want to bet it's frozen up out there on the back porch?"

"It'll thaw. I'll go bring it in."

"I'll get it, Daddy," I offered, wanting an excuse to get out of the almost overpowering blazing heat of the stove. But Daddy was already putting his coat back on.

Once Daddy was out the door, Mama cast me a stern look, "What I told you is to stay between us, Junie Mae. I don't doubt you, though, because I know how much you love your Daddy, and knowin' the things I told you would only cause trouble between me and him. Lord knows it's not like we don't have enough against us already," she finished in a defeated voice.

Later in my bedroom, a blast of cold sobered me and felt good on my skin. I stared sadly at the made-up beds where the only real color came from the crazy patterns of Grandma Haley's homemade quilts. Rose's empty bed further depressed me. Throwing myself down upon it, I begin to cry. It seemed that all the good feelings I'd had about Amity had trickled out like water from a spigot, leaving me drained of any kind of happiness. Mama and her secrets made me feel like a traitor.

Maybe she should have told Rose the story instead of me, because it was Rose's life that mirrored her own, not mine. It also occurred to me that I was a keeper of both Mama's and Rose's secrets, and the knowledge had left my heart as heavy as a rock. I was young, but it wasn't lost on me that both Mama and Rose had chosen to love hopeless men who could only bring them heartache in the end. I thought of Amity Smith and hoped he wouldn't turn out to be something that I'd have to forget. Suddenly the cold air in the room no longer felt good to my skin. Now huddled beneath the heavy quilt to ward of the wind seeping through the cracks in the wood, I listened to Daddy go on about No. 5 mine and how things were heating up. According to him, Harvey James had convinced the majority of his crew to vote for the union. He said that the turning point came when Little Brock evicted the widows and their children from their homes in order to allow the new workers to come in. "We all know what he's doin'. He's hirin' in a crew that won't go against him. Think about it: who in that bunch of new hires would be foolish enough to come over on the side of a union?"

Mama was in agreement but as usual blamed the detestable move on Big Brock Asher rather than his son. "Old Big Brock's behind it all. Little Brock drinks so much he don't know which end is up."

Daddy was skeptical and pointed out that it was Little Brock and not his daddy who mailed out all the eviction notices, and that it was his name on the dotted line.

Mama's laugh came out more as a snort. "Little Brock ain't never been in charge. I know!"

Daddy's voice soon faded as I drifted off into some dark place where words had no meaning and the pain of life had ceased temporarily, but not for long enough. Soon the wind came blasting through the night, shaking the house and howling like a lost, mournful spirit. Awake, my thoughts were equally desolate and turned to the little house in the woods where Mama said she'd shut the door in the face of Little Brock Asher. Rose's description of the small house where she'd met with Bart Asher sounded a lot like the one Mama had described earlier. I decided that it had to be one and the same. I recalled my own dream or vision of the house, where Floyd Wilkes had shown me a faceless Rose holding the blood red rose. Too young to know of parables or symbolism, I wondered what it all meant.

The blizzard lasted until the third day of December. For three days and nights the wind had howled mournfully through the naked branches, sending snow spiraling through the frosty air like sand blowing across a desert. In the mornings the front porch was packed the white fluff. Paths were snowed over and the main roads were not travelable. Mama spent most of the snow days writing letters to both Uncle Larkin and his wife, while Daddy, when not toiling away in the mines, stayed busy clearing paths to the woodshed and outhouse. It was impossible to get to the spring so Mama melted snow into water. I'd hated the metallic taste of it and drank it only when I was extremely thirsty. The three days' blizzard had felt like years to me. Bored, I'd spent most of those days watching the snow spiral and drift through the window and missing Rose, Amity, and Violet Elizabeth. After a while my thoughts shifted to Mama's letter writing and trying to imagine what she might be telling Uncle Larkin and his wife, Rhodie. I'd heard her inform Daddy that his brother had been staying in Lexington, Kentucky, in hopes that the bid his company had made to a build a major bridge would be accepted. "Your brother has high hopes they'll get it," she said.

Daddy, who had been busy watching the snow from the kitchen window, was only half listening, and this infuriated Mama. "Don't you even care what your brother does for a living?" she snapped.

Daddy said, "I know what Larkin does. He travels all over the place but never finds the time to stop here and see his own Mama or the rest of his family. I know he's busy but more than once that I know of he was less than fifty miles away and couldn't make time to come by here."

"He's coming here the first week of January to visit with the family. He promised me."

"I'll believe it when I see him. Larkin says a lot of things," Daddy said skeptically. "I'm sure he means well…" His words trailed off.

"Rhodie sent me pictures of their place in Indianapolis. It's really something," she said, handing him a packet of pictures. Daddy looked at the envelope and then opened it, spreading out the pictures on the table. My curiosity had gotten the better of me so I edged over to Daddy's chair and looked over his shoulder at a dozen or more pictures of a large white two-storied house surrounded by acres of flatland where cattle grazed in pastures. One picture showed a tall man who I knew was Uncle Larkin standing in a field beside a gigantic pumpkin. Mama bragged how he'd raised it himself. The figure of Uncle Larkin was taken at such a distant angle it was hard to tell anything about his facial features. Another picture showed a pretty little pigtailed girl standing next to a thin, doe-eyed woman who I guessed was Rhodie. Daddy shook his head sadly and commented on how sad Rhodie looked. "She don't look too healthy," he concluded.

"Maybe she's naturally skinny," Mama snapped, raking up the pictures and placing them back in the envelope. After a while she said, "It wouldn't hurt nothin' for us to go spend a week or so with them out there. Rhodie's always invitin' us."

Sighing hopelessly, Daddy said, "Heddy, there is a blizzard outside and here you are talkin' about takin' a vacation. I imagine Indianapolis is havin' bad weather too."

"I meant in the summertime, Ralph," Mama snapped. "Don't you ever get sick and tired of looking at the mountains and the coal?"

Daddy said good-naturedly, "You know I do, Heddy, but we ain't got no money to take a trip. Rhodie don't have to live from paycheck to paycheck. Larkin probably pulls in five times what I make up at the mine. It looks like he's made the best of his education." Daddy's remark was innocent and not said with malice.

Opening up the drawer of the corner cabinet she placed the pictures carefully inside. I could sense her anger at Daddy's nonchalant attitude, but Daddy continued to talk as if he hadn't noticed her change in mood.

After the two of them had brought in extra wood and banked the fires they'd finally had gone to bed. I made up the couch and for a long time lay in the darkness watching the flames leap out of the layer of ash meant to smother them. Outside the wind continued to whip and moan, blowing snow against the roof and window panes. As usual, I thought of Rose and wondered what she was doing at that moment. I also thought of Christmas and how I'd never been without my sister during the holidays. I recalled Thanksgiving Day and how unhappy and sick Rose looked. What had she done that Mama would hate her for?

The three day blizzard had caused a lot of havoc on the landscape. It had taken seven days after the snow stopped for the roads to clear enough so people could travel safely. Daddy was among the men who worked to clear roads and paths leading up to and surrounding No. 5 Mine. Uncle Harlan Ray, who was by trade a heavy equipment operator, worked with Daddy and the crew and was paid a little more, but still his wages were less than what many other heavy equipment operators in other mines made. Daddy said that those who operated the heavy equipment had to know what they were doing, especially the man who ran the coal caterpillar. One wrong move could bring down a whole wall. Daddy often bragged that Harlan Ray could operate the auger with his eyes closed, but he was quick to add that no man, no matter how good he was, could predict a weak wall.

When the winter sun finally came out and melted the snow, the headwaters of the creeks rushed into the river, causing its waters to swell and spill over many of the roads and flood the valleys and lowlands. The weather then turned cold again, refreezing the river, creeks, and mud holes and making parts of the land almost too slick to walk on. On the second day of the cold snap, Daddy had developed a cough that grew worse as the day went on. Hell-bent on going to the mine anyway, he dressed in his work clothes and had started out the door when Mama stopped him. "Ralph Lee, you get yourself back in bed. You're not going to work this sick."

"I have to go, Heddy; there'll be a few that can't get out of their houses because of the high water. If I don't show up there might not be enough for the shift." Daddy's voice sounded low and weak.

"That's too sad! Asher will just have to do without you until that coughing and fever stops. You're a dead man walkin' if you get out in the cold and breathe that dust tonight."

"I wouldn't be the first who's done it," he argued.

"Don't go, Daddy!" I pleaded.

Looking up at me weak eyed, Daddy suddenly slumped down on to the floor. His dinner bucket had fallen bedside him with a clang.

"Ralph!" Mama screamed, and then hollered for me to help her get him off the floor. Still conscious but obviously weak, Daddy tried to pull himself up. "You get one arm and I'll get the other!" Mama commanded. Finally, with one of us on each side of him we managed to get him into a kitchen chair.

"Are you all right, Ralph?" Mama asked in a panicked voice.

Breathing hard, Daddy said between breaths, "I'm just so darned weak and winded."

"You're burnin' up with fever. We gotta get you into bed," Mama said.

With my help, Mama got him to the bedroom and then commanded me to get the coal oil lamp from the living room. I obeyed but was scared Daddy was dying. I'd heard of fast acting pneumonia and wondered if he might have contracted that because of the cold air. I hadn't spoken my fears to Mama but figured she'd already felt them. Mama undressed Daddy and covered him with every quilt in the house. "I'll go for the doctor tomorrow, Junie Mae. You'll have to stay home from school and look after him till I get here with the doctor."

I nodded in agreement. That night I hardly slept at all. My head was full of dreadful images of Daddy lying in a homemade coffin. Outside, the wind blew cold and steadily. With each rattle of the shutter I jumped, praying that it wasn't the ghost of Floyd Wilkes there to show me another frightening image. The faces of the dead miners haunted my thoughts. I kept hearing the pitiful cries of their wives and children. "Please, God, don't take Daddy now -- not with Mama plotting to leave us all," I prayed aloud.

The grey light of morning had come too soon. Still drowsy, I climbed out of bed and padded into the warm kitchen where Mama sat sipping coffee. Her eyes were red and tired and I could tell she'd been watching after Daddy all night without sleep.

"Is he better?" I asked hopefully.

Mama shook her head no and said, "He's bad, Junie Mae. We've got to get Doc Ben Minor up here as soon as Noah gets here." Just as Mama said it, I heard the roar of an engine and knew it was Uncle Noah in the driveway. "Thank God," Mama sighed and grabbed her coat and purse. "I won't be long, Junie Mae. Keep a good eye on him and watch it when you give him water. He can't drink too good and might choke."

With my heart hammering hard in my chest, I grabbed the coal oil lamp and walked gingerly into the dark bedroom where Daddy lay under a mound of quilts. I could hear his labored breathing from the doorway. Swallowing hard I braced myself for the sight of him. Although the lantern was turned down low, its light glared on his pale, sunken face. "Daddy," I whispered.

Daddy's eyes flickered open at the sound of my voice. "Mama's gone to get Doc Minor. He's gonna make you better," my voice quivered.

Daddy closed his eyes and nodded. My heart rushed with fright as I sat there watching him underneath the flickering light. His breathing seemed more labored with each passing minute. Finally, after what seemed like hours, Mama and Noah came back with Dr. Minor, and the sight of him brought a flood of relief inside me. Relaxing a little I told the old doctor about Daddy's labored breathing. Dr. Minor followed Mama back to the bedroom while Uncle Noah and I sat silently at the table waiting to hear news about his condition. Noticing my apparent distress, Uncle Noah reached out and grasped my hand. "The doc will fix him up, Junie Mae. He'll be good as new soon. You'll see." I wanted to believe Uncle Noah, but something inside told me Daddy would never truly recover. Maybe Mama's dire prediction was right. Maybe the coal had finally gotten to him.

Fifteen minutes or so passed before Dr. Minor and Mama came out of the bedroom. Sitting his black bag down by the chair, the doctor sighed and said, "He's got pneumonia, and there's not a lot that can be done to help him. He'll just have to tough it out. If he's strong he'll weather it. Hopefully the coal dust hasn't eaten through his lungs too badly, though I wouldn't get my hopes up."

"You mean he could die?" I asked.

"He could," the doctor said, not mincing words. "I've given your Mama some pills and a bottle of cough syrup that'll help him breathe. It'll knock him out cold so he can rest a little. I can't do much more," he said apologetically. "Now if he gets worse we could put him in the hospital under an oxygen tent. You let me know if you wanna do that," the doctor added.

Mama nodded and said, "I'll keep an eye on him and see how he does." Noah rose out of his chair and reached into his pocket. Withdrawing his wallet, he asked, "How much do we owe you, doc?" The doctor shook his head, "I'm not gonna charge you all for this. I didn't do much as it is. Just take the best care of him you can, and let me know how he's doing"

In those days pneumonia was a terrible sickness that had no real cure. A few antibiotics existed but none were strong enough to fight against the stubborn infection; many people died from it, especially miners whose lungs were already weakened by the coal dust. Others who survived were never healthy again.

During that second week in December when most families were

looking forward to Christmas, our close family members had gathered at the lodge in order to help with Daddy's care while Mama worked. Before my Christmas vacation from school started on the last day of the third week of December, I'd told both Amity and Violet Elizabeth about Daddy's sickness. Saying goodbye to them was hard for me, but they had promised I would see them before Christmas Day. "If we can help anyway with your Daddy you let us know," Amity had said earnestly.

Surprisingly, later on that evening, both Amity and Violet Elizabeth had shown up at the door with a basket of baked goods. I'd felt embarrassed and a little awkward standing there in the doorway with Mama and Granny Lee looking on from the living room. "Don't just stand there, Junie Mae -- invite them in!" Granny Lee gently scolded. Opening the door wider, I asked them to please come in. Mama's eyes studied Amity with interest. "This is Amity and Violet Elizabeth Smith, Mama," I said nervously.

Mama nodded and forced a smile. Violet Elizabeth handed Mama the basket. "There's a fruitcake and some cookies in there. I think Mama made you a loaf of her homemade spice bread that's really delicious," she said easily, seemingly not one bit put off by Mama's obvious scrutiny of her expensive fur collard coat. Mama never missed a chance to inspect people's clothing.

"Well, thank you all so much," Granny Lee said warmly grasping both Amity and Violet Elizabeth's hands. "Won't you all have a glass of warm cider with us?" she asked.

Both Amity and Violet declined, saying they couldn't stay long. "My folks wish you all the best and wanted to let you know they are praying for your husband's health." Violet said sincerely.

Suddenly I felt so proud of them. I was especially pleased that they had thought enough of me to come out in the cold to show some concern for Daddy's sickness. I looked to Rose who stood in the corner regarding us with her strange eyes. It was hard to tell what she might be thinking. When it was time for them to go, I'd walked Violet Elizabeth and Amity to the truck.

"Violet, can you give me just a second with Junie Mae? I won't keep the two of you out in the cold too long," Amity promised.

Violet hugged me and squeezed my hand. "I hope you have a Merry Christmas. I'll be praying for your Daddy," she whispered. I recall the clean smell of her hair and how her fur collar tickled my nose. I remember thinking that the only real hugs I got were from Violet Elizabeth, Amity, and Granny Lee.

Outside, Amity motioned me toward the corner of the house. Following him I glanced up toward the darkening sky in search of a star but there was none. Reaching into his pocket he withdrew a box. Placing it in my hand Amity said, "This is for you. I hope you like it,"

Staring at the box in surprise, I looked up at Amity and in a regretful voice said, "I have nothing for you."

Amity lifted my chin and said, "It don't matter, Junie Mae. I wanted to give you something to make you feel happy."

Trying to hold my emotions back, I opened the box. Gasping, I pulled out a dainty silver chain with a heart-shaped locket. "Oh, Amity -- it's so pretty! I ain't never had nothin' like this before." Not yet dark, I could see the satisfaction in his wide smile while his blue eyes seemed to look deep into me. Suddenly aware of his warm breath on my cheek, I felt him edging closer and then brushing his lips gently against mine. The kiss was quick and had felt like a soft feather brushing against my mouth only to fly away in the wind before I could absorb it. Later, I would recall the moment and experience so many strange feelings of want mingled with a kind of need to be near him.

"Let me see if I can put it on you," he whispered. Pulling back my hair, I allowed him to place it around my neck and then snap the latch into place.

"I'll never take it off," I promised.

"I'm glad you like it. I know you're having it bad, Junie Mae. I wish I could take some of the load off."

Smiling, I said, "You made me so happy tonight. I won't forget it."

After saying goodnight to Amity I walked furtively back into the house. With one hand wrapped protectively around the silver heart-shaped locket, I made my way past both Mama and Rose, who were sitting on opposite ends of the couch. Once in the kitchen where Harvey James and Harlan Ray sat drinking coffee and talking about the coal, I felt safe from prying eyes -- at least momentarily. Busying myself with putting away the food Amity and Violet Elizabeth had brought, I was privy to the argument the brothers were having concerning the influence Olga Winley and Bonzelle Creech were having on the women in the camp.

"I think they're pushing way too hard," Harlan Ray said of the women. "Somehow they've managed to turn pert near every woman in the camp against Little Brock Asher. Trouble is there ain't no union in place to protect 'em. We're getting real close to havin' enough signatures. I'm just afraid Asher will retaliate against us before we get one in and it'll be mostly the women's fault for forcin' his hand."

Harvey James stared thoughtfully into his coffee cup and shook his head in disagreement. "We need the women to wake their men up. Our meetings haven't got us the numbers we hoped they would. Word has it that Asher offered the widows a small settlement, but according to Olga Winley the sum wasn't nearly enough to satisfy them and they turned it down."

"Them women want blood, Harvey! I don't think it's about money no more."

"It's not!" Mama said, suddenly appearing in the doorway. "Don't you know that no amount of money can give them women back the husbands they lost?" Eying the brothers coldly, she spat, "You all eat, breathe, and sleep that damned mine! Don't you all realize your brother is lying back there in that bed so sick he can barely get a breath and it's all because of the coal? But you all still can't get enough of it. You both sit here and plot and plan thinking somehow you're gonna get the better of it. But you won't! In the end the coal will win. It always does. Every man I've known in my life has tried to beat it; none of 'em lived to tell it. I'm sick of hearin' about it! Do you hear me?"

Looking a little sheepish, Harvey James said in an apologetic voice, "Heddy Mae, I understand the grudge you have against the coal because of your Daddy, but you married a coalminer. Somebody has to get the coal out. It's the coal that has fed you and kept a roof over your head."

Mama placed her hands on her small hips and said in a loud, spiteful voice, "Oh, yes, somebody's got to dig out that precious coal. You all act like the coal is all there is in this world and there ain't no other place but Harlan County Kentucky. Your brother Larkin's got more sense than any of you all. He got out of this hell hole and is makin' it good up north!"

Granny Lee appeared in the doorway. "Your all's loud arguin' is upsettin' Ralph."

Mama turned on Granny Lee. Pointing an accusing finger at her she said, "Martha Lee, you are the worst one of 'em. You won't say a bad word against the coal even when you know it's made a widow of you. Never mind that it ate up your husband's lungs and he died a young man, leaving you with all these children to raise by yourself! I don't understand none of you!"

Smiling sympathetically in Mama's direction, Granny Lee turned to Uncles Harvey James and Harlan Ray and said, "Boys, we better go home for a spell and let Heddy rest. She's not herself right now, and who would be?"

Shaking her head in disgust, Mama rolled her eyes heavenward, but neither Granny Lee nor Harvey James seemed to notice. Harvey James walked slowly over to Mama and hugged her, but Mama stood as straight as a stick in his arms and showed no sign of reciprocating his affection. Granny Lee reached over and kissed her left cheek, while whispering words of encouragement in her ear. "God will look after your husband, Heddy. I know this. You've just got to have faith." My eyes sought out Harlan Ray who merely stood looking grim and not making a move to comfort Mama. He can't stand her. Like me, he knows what she is.

On their way out the door, Harvey James assured Mama that he'd come back the next day to chop more wood. Mama nodded begrudgingly, then turning to me she said, "You and Rose need to go to bed early. You all have got to be on your toes tomorrow. Daddy's weak and fightin' for every breath he draws."

14 ROSE

I'd thought having Rose back in our room and in her bed would be like it was before Daddy took her to Granny Lee's house. So many nights I'd yearned to wake up the next morning and see her dark hair spilling across the pillow. But since she'd been back, things had changed drastically between us. Preoccupied with Daddy's illness, Rose had sunk into some kind of silent despair. Some nights I'd hear her sobbing into her pillow. When I'd asked her what was wrong she'd start blaming herself. "I know God's punishing me for all my sins. Why didn't he make me sick instead of Daddy?"

"You didn't give Daddy pneumonia. The cold weather did it."

"You don't know nothin', Junie Mae. God punishes us when we do wrong things. I done wrong and now Daddy has to pay for it."

That night, Rose's mood was more pensive than usual. Moving the lamp over by the window, I handed Rose one of her old nightgowns and began to get ready for bed myself. I was pulling my sweater over my head when I heard Rose gasp, "Good Lord, Junie Mae -- you are as skinny as a stick. You ain't sick are you?" she asked with genuine concern in her voice.

"No," I answered.

"Then you must be in love. I ain't never seen you look this good. You're growin' up, I guess." She sighed, and then in a more somber voice asked, "Why didn't you tell me that things had got this far between you and Amity Smith? We're sisters."

"It just never came up," I answered in a bashful voice

Rose's eyes suddenly fell on the silver chain and heart-shaped locket. Looking up at me in surprise, she asked, "Did he buy you that for Christmas?"

"Yeah, he just gave it to me tonight. I like to died when I opened the box," I giggled.

Pulling her own sweater off, I noticed that Rose appeared thin. Her protruding breast bones reminded me of a pair of plucked chicken wings. I'd guessed Granny Lee's good cooking was lost on her. I'd said nothing to her about her weight loss and started brushing my hair which had grown and was now shoulder length. "You've turned out to be real pretty Junie Mae. It's like I've been gone for years instead of a few months. Do you love the Smith boy?"

"I'm fourteen, Rose. I reckon I 'm still tryin' to figure out what love is. I ain't even had time to think about Amity much with everything goin' on."

Rose laughed and said, "What would you have to think about if you love him? When you love somebody you know it. You beat it all, Junie Mae. Maybe Daddy should have nicknamed you 'Miss Mouse' instead of June bug. You keep everything to yourself. You hide in your little cubbyhole and I never know where you are. When we was little nobody ever noticed you, 'cause you was so quiet and out of things that was happenin'. Everybody noticed me, though. I couldn't find a good enough place to hide where they couldn't find me."

Averting her eyes from mine she said, "I've got a lot to answer for, Junie Mae. I disappointed Daddy 'cause I hated school. I accidentally cut him with a butcher knife when I was aimin' for Mama. I'll never forget the look on his face after I done it. It was like I killed him." Her voice began to tremble. "And there's Mama. I never knowed what she wanted me to be, and she punished me for not knowin'. Sometimes I almost hate you, Junie Mae," her voice hissed.

Now it was my turn to be surprised. "You hate me?" I asked incredulously. "But why?"

"'Cause I'm like my Mama," she spat. "I hate anything I can't understand."

Unshed tears momentarily blinded my vision of Rose. Blinking them away I noticed how cold and unforgiving she looked beneath the nervous flames from the coal oil lamp. She's so much like Mama. Daddy's sickness was taking its toll on her. She's hurt and feeling guilty for cutting Daddy.

"Why don't you say somethin', Miss Mouse? Why don't you tell me how selfish I am and how I'm just like my Mama?"

"Please stop it, Rose," I whispered.

"Please stop it, Rose," she mimicked cruelly. "Why don't you go grab one of them books you've had your head stuck in for years and act like I'm not here. You're real good at ignorin' things, Junie Mae. You're shapin' up to be just like Daddy and Granny Lee."

"Stop it," I sobbed. The lump in my throat felt as big as an apple. Swallowing hard I croaked, "You ain't got nothin' right, Rose! I see more than you think I do. I ain't so blind."

Rose got up from the bed and snatched the hairbrush from off the dresser and started furiously brushing her own hair. Suddenly pausing with hairbrush in mid-air, she turned to me and asked suspiciously, "How is it that Amity Smith can come in here and Mama acts like she don't even see him? If some boy come to see me she'd've had a screaming fit. What have you got on her, Junie Mae?"

"What do you mean?" I whispered.

"You know what I'm talkin' about. You had to come out of that mouse hole after I left, didn't you? You caught her out and she's afraid of you now. What has she done? You owe me this. For years you blamed everything on me. You said I caused Mama to be mad and treat me mean like she did."

Sinking down into my feather pillow, I decided to tell Rose what I knew about Mama. My words streamed out like a flash flood. I began with the stolen watches and how I'd hidden them in Daddy's shed to keep the law from arresting her. I also told her about how Mama had tried to get money out of Grandma Haley before Thanksgiving to buy herself a one way bus ticket to Indianapolis. Lastly, I recounted Mama's story of her childhood and how Big Brock Asher had stopped Mama from seeing Little Brock when they were young. "I don't know what he said to her to keep her away from him. She wouldn't tell me that part," I whispered, adding, "I wouldn't tell Daddy these things for the world. It would kill him to know the truth about her."

Rose said jealously, "You got something that I'll never get from Mama for long as I live, and that's her respect. She's afraid of you 'cause you're good, Junie Mae. You're good like Granny Lee. Mama don't understand goodness. She knows I'm bad like her and she understands that, but she still hates me for it. I might not be the smartest person in the world but it don't take a lot of smarts to figure Mama out. I've had a long time to study her."

"You ain't like Mama, Rose."

Rose laughed bitterly. "I am like her. When she was young she wanted exactly what I want now. Simple dreams won't do for me and Mama. No, we have to dream big. Mama never got what she wanted and I won't either. I see that now, and it hurts so bad, Junie Mae." Tears filled her eyes as she said, "That Smith boy cares about you. I seen it in his eyes when he looked at you tonight. He'll never break your heart like mine and Mama's has been broke. You're lucky. I wish I could've settled but I couldn't. If you only knowed what I've done for love…" Her voice trailed off.

"Tell me," I coaxed, taking her small hand in mine.

"Not tonight, Junie Mae."

Her words tugged at my heart and made me fearful. "You rest, Rose. We got to see to Daddy tomorrow. We can't let nothin' happen to him."

Rose nodded and slipped underneath the covers. Turning down the wick, I silently prayed to God to keep Daddy safe, and not to let Floyd Wilkes' ghost come to me that night.

15 DADDY

Daddy's sickness had marked a drastic turning point in my own life. Having to take care of him had quickly changed me from a child to a woman. Beginning that week before Christmas Day, I was forced to perform tasks that no fourteen-year-old child should ever have to endure. In the early mornings before Granny Lee or Marie showed up I would help Mama change Daddy's soiled bedding. Sometimes almost as soon as the sheets were changed out, they had to be done again. The constant changing out of linens and quilts meant constant washing. In spite of the cold weather, both Rose and Marie spent several hours carrying water from the spring, boiling the sheets on the stove, and then hanging them out to dry on the line. The weather had been so cold that the sheets were frozen stiff and had to be hung on nails behind the woodstove to dry out. Mama and Daddy's bedroom that had once smelled so clean had taken on the stench of vomit and other bodily waste. Though Daddy could take in very little food, whatever he managed to eat would on any given day pass through him almost as soon as he ingested it. I remember cleaning Daddy's naked body. Barely conscious, he'd look at me with such pity and sorrow each time I had to turn him on his side and change out the linen. I'd tried hard to cover him and make the sheet change as decent as I could, but more often than not the covers would slip down, revealing nothing but skin and bone. While I washed his body I tried to make normal conversation about everything I could think of. Sometimes his skin had felt as hot as fire while other times he'd felt cold and clammy. I was always relieved when Granny Lee showed up and took over the sheet changing. Thankfully, neighbors and friends who had heard we needed bedding donated several boxes of used sheets, pillowcases, and quilts. Some of the miners had even taken up a small collection for him at the mines which helped Mama buy food and Daddy's cough medicine. Two days before Christmas Eve, Granny Lee's friends from the Salvation Army brought several large boxes of food, bedding, gauze, and medicated vapor salves. To thank them for their gifts, Granny Lee and Marie cooked a big pot of pinto beans with fat back and baked a big pan of yellow cornbread. After the women left, Granny Lee watered down some of the bean soup for Daddy, who could only take a few spoonfuls before he started coughing and gasping for breath.

After having witnessed Daddy's coughing fit, Rose ran out of the room and threw herself on the couch. "I can't take this no more," she cried. "Daddy looks like he's dead already. You have to tell me if he's gonna die, Junie Mae. You know how to do it. I don't care if you read tea leaves or talk to the trees. I gotta know."

"It's not that easy," I said, recalling the last horrible vision Floyd Wilkes' ghost had shown me of Rose without a face. From that night on I'd purposely pushed Floyd Wilkes' ghost far from my thoughts. Even in sleep I was conscious enough to rebel against any sign of him invading my dreams. A part of me felt guilty for avoiding the ghost that had once made me feel so safe, but with Daddy so sick I couldn't face the possibility of seeing him dead in my dreams.

Two days before Christmas Uncles Coy and Noah took some of the burden off of Rose and Marie by carrying several days' worth of water from the spring. They'd loaded Great Uncle Hiram's old truck with barrels and buckets that they'd found somewhere and filled them to the brim. Afterwards, they lined them all up on the back porch so we would have easy access to the water. Uncle Purl had even dropped Grandma Haley off that morning so she could help with Daddy's care. Rose said, "I'm glad Grandma Haley is here. Marie had to stay home and give Rebekah Ann a rest. Marie tried leaving the babies home with Great Uncle Hiram the other day and he let Chester Harlan burn his arm on the heating stove. It made a big blister and he cried all night."

Folding the last of the towels, I nodded absently. My mind was remembering better days and past Christmases when Daddy, Rose, and I had gone into the woods looking for a Christmas tree. I recalled how Rose would fall backwards in the deep snow while flapping her arms and giggling in the cold sharp wind. "I'm makin' a snow angel," she announced. I can still hear her giggles echoing through the bare trees and bouncing off the mountains. Once Daddy had knocked the snow off the carefully chosen tree, we'd drag it in the house where he would stand it up by the window. He always bragged to Mama that the tree we picked was the best one in the woods. Later, Rose and me would happily pop popcorn and then string it around the tree. Mama eventually dragged out her box of old ornaments and picked through them, seeking the prettiest ones to put on the tree. Daddy always allowed Rose to put the star on last. He'd lift her up so she could she could reach the top of the tree. I don't remember ever having felt angry or jealous of the special attention Daddy gave to Rose, especially on Christmas. In truth she loved the magic of the holiday more than I did. Daddy had given her his patience and love -- the two things Mama showed very little of.

As if she'd read my mind, Rose said, "We ain't gonna have no Christmas this year. Shoot, we ain't even got a tree and Daddy's lyin' in that bed dyin'. I know he is. And where's Mama when he needs her the most?" she asked bitterly.

"Lower your voice, Rose. You want Daddy to hear you? You know that ain't fair," I said in Mama's defense. "Now that Daddy's laid up, someone's got to pay the rent and buy food."

Edging closer to the table Rose whispered, "You think Granny Lee would let us starve or be homeless? Don't you think our Uncles Harlan Ray and Harvey James wouldn't help is if we was in that bad of a shape? Mama don't need to work right now. We have enough food in that kitchen to last us a month or better. People have seen to that." Rose's unsettling eyes stared suspiciously into my own. "What about the money the miners took up for Daddy? Where do you reckon Mama stashed that at?"

"That's enough, Rose," I snapped. "We got two days before Christmas, and I don't want to think about nothin' but Daddy gettin' his strength back so he can see another one."

Rose straightened her shoulders in determination and said, "Daddy don't want us takin' care of him; he wants Mama to do it, Junie Mae. He won't get well unless she stops workin' and stays here with him. I ain't no seer of the future but I know that much! Looks like your seein' powers have dried up!'" she snipped before walking out of the front room.

Rose was right. Daddy needed Mama in order to recover. He didn't want family members changing his soiled sheets and emptying his pee jars. Once a strong, self-sufficient man, Daddy was helpless and at the mercy of others. I knew he hated that and probably decided that he'd become nothing more than a burden. It dawned on me that since he was too weak to speak for himself that I would have to do it for him. Somehow I had to make Mama see that unless she took over Daddy's care he might die. I decided that I'd wait until after Christmas to speak to her, but as it turned out I felt I couldn't wait that long.

Granny Lee wanted our family to have a nice Christmas in spite of Daddy's illness. That same evening that I'd made my decision to talk to Mama about Daddy after Christmas, Great Uncle Hiram and Uncle Noah had brought in a beautiful cedar tree and ordered me and Rose to start decorating it. Uncle Hiram smiled his toothless smile and said, "Some long chains of popcorn would shore pretty it up -- wouldn't it, Noah?"

Uncle Noah agreed and said, "Now Rosie, I reckon you don't need my help to put the star on the top of that tree."

Rose smiled for the first time all day and joked, "I reckon I'm tall enough this year." Since the first of December Uncles Coy and Noah had been working different shifts. Uncle Noah claimed the switch was good because it not only enabled him to pick Mama up from work in the evenings, but also freed him up to help out with the chores at the lodge. During those long weeks of Daddy's sickness the lodge was always filled with family and friends offering to help out in any way they could. Hardly a day went by that someone didn't bring us a homemade pie or some kind of casserole. It occurred to me that although Daddy might have been poor in material things he was definitely rich in friends.

16 THE REVELATION

After Rose and I finished decorating the tree with popcorn chains, gold and silver tinsel, and finally Mama's faded, overused ornaments, Rose placed the gold star on the top of the tree. With tears in her eyes she said, "I've never put the star on without Daddy standing beside me." Granny Lee, who had been looking on, said, "Rose, your Daddy is still very much alive and will be around next year to watch you put the star on the tree. God is merciful and knows how much we all need him."

Granny Lee's words only caused Rose to sob harder. Marie, who had come to watch the decorating of the tree, took Rose by the hand and led her away into our bedroom. Filled with sadness myself, I kept quiet as usual. Although I wanted to cry, too, I reasoned that one of us falling apart was enough, and someone had to keep it together for Daddy's sake. Later, Granny Lee had decided that we should bring Daddy into the living room to see the tree. Great Uncle Hiram, usually not one to question his younger sister's wisdom, looked doubtful and then spoke up, "Are you shore he's strong enough to sit up?"

"He'll be alright," Granny Lee assured him. "Besides, it will do him good to see the tree and Heddy when she walks in the door."

We were all shocked by the sight of Daddy. Out of the harsh lamplight he appeared even whiter and gaunter than ever. The loose shirt he wore made him look like a clothes hanger, and his breastbones protruded through the skin. I noticed that his eyes had sunk even farther back in his head. I didn't want him to see my pity and forced a smile in his direction. Uncle Hiram and Coy had placed him in his favorite chair in the corner. Granny Lee had piled two blankets on top of him to keep him warm. His eyes greeted me weakly and he tried to smile. I noticed how rapidly his chest moved and realized he was having a lot of trouble breathing. Seeing Daddy in the daylight made me realize that he was truly dying. I didn't need Floyd Wilkes' ghost to tell me that. Uncle Corbin had brought Mama home around six. When she saw Daddy sitting up in a chair, she gasped and then asked, "Why is he out of bed, Martha?"

Granny Lee smiled serenely and said, "We wanted him to see the Christmas tree." Mama bent down and kissed Daddy's poor sunken cheek. Daddy seemed to come alive and even had a sparkle in his eye.

"We are all gonna have a little bowl of soup and some warm cider to celebrate God's grace," Granny Lee announced. I recall that night as one of the best night's we'd had since Daddy got pneumonia.

A little dusting of snow fell on Christmas morning. Outside my window the trees were outlined in white and the landscape looked clean and new. The Cumberland River sparkled through the bare limbs and the air had a nip to it. I turned to look at the other bed and saw that Rose was wide awake. Her eyes appeared red and her face was puffy from crying. Not knowing what to say to her, I turned toward the wall and stared out the round window into the porch where I had seen Floyd Wilkes' ghost on the night the miners were killed in the cave-in. It had seemed ages ago. Now my whole world revolved around the lodge and Daddy. My life had changed so much I wasn't even sure who I was, or, for that matter, who anyone was anymore, either. Rose was sad all the time, and Daddy, once strong and vital, had become helpless and dependent. Amity Smith had become more like a dream, and had it not been for the silver heart-shaped locket that encircled my neck I might not have believed that he existed at all. Suddenly I'd felt so cut off from the things I had known and clung to for comfort in the past. Floyd Wilkes' ghost had become almost unreal and seemingly part of the childish blinders Daddy's sickness had forced me to shed like a snake sheds its skin in the summer months. I yearned for the normalcy of school which would begin again soon, but with Daddy the way he was it seemed unlikely that I'd be able to attend – unless, of course, I talked Mama into staying home and caring for him. Granny Lee was slowly tiring out and winding down like an old clock. I could see it in her face and in the way she labored from room to room. Marie had the babies to contend with, and Rose was almost useless at anything besides keeping the water hot for Daddy's steam vapors. Sometimes she wasn't even good at that, though, and let the water boil until there was little or none left in the kettle. I knew she was hurting because she was losing touch with Bart Asher, not that she'd ever really had him, but in her mind there had been a chance; I'd known differently right from the start. It wasn't so hard to figure out. He'd flirted with her because she was truly a beauty. What man could pass her up? But her beauty had not been enough to hold the attention of a boy like him, who could have anything and anyone he wanted. Bart had led her on by making her believe that she was the most beautiful girl in the world to him. He'd probably told her that she was special, and she'd hung on to every word. Now that he was getting ready to start college she was forgotten. Feeling weighted down with troubles that weren't even mine, I longed to pull the covers over my head and shut the world out for a while, but I knew that was impossible. I could hear Mama rattling about in the kitchen. Maybe she was giving Daddy his morning steam with the vapors. If only I could have stayed in bed, but with it being Christmas Day and Daddy needing so much attention I knew the idea was just a wish. Feeling the cold wood floor beneath my bare feet I changed into a simple dress, socks, and a sweater. Rose lay wordlessly looking at the ceiling; her thoughts were clearly far away. "I'm going to help Mama ready the house for Christmas dinner," I said. "You gettin' up?"

She nodded her head yes. I noticed that her face appeared particularly white and pasty looking. Worried, I went on into the kitchen were Mama was filling the kettles for Daddy's vapor steam. "Somethin's wrong with Rose," I said to Mama.

Mama nodded affirmatively and placed a tea kettle of water on the burner lid. "Grab that poker," she ordered.

"I can't take no more sickness," I said tiredly.

"She'll be fine in about six or seven months," Mama said sourly.

'What do you mean?" I asked, puzzled.

"What I mean is that she's gone out and got herself pregnant," she whispered, and then added "Shut the kitchen door and make sure Daddy's door's closed."

Stunned, I went about shutting the doors, and then began to stutter worse than Uncle Corbin. "I-I- how can you say somethin' like that? It's not true!"

"I've been pregnant twice and know all the signs, Junie Mae. I've knowed it since Thanksgivin' day. I was in Granny Lee's kitchen and glanced out the window and seen her throwin' up her dinner in the garden."

Unable to find the words to describe what I was feeling, I slumped down in the kitchen chair and cried.

Mama said, "Are you gonna tell me you didn't know already? I figured she'd told you."

"No, I didn't know," I said from mouth as dry as cotton.

"I warned your Daddy not to take her to your Granny Lee's, but he wouldn't have nothin' else," she said, poking hard at the hot coals and sending orange sparks flying up and out of the open lid.

"What does Granny Lee have to do with Rose getting herself pregnant?" I asked, still in shock.

Mama snorted. "Your sister had way too much freedom to do whatever she wanted there. Marie taught her real good." Mama's face twisted in disgust. "I wonder who the daddy is. Best thing that could ever happen is he'd marry her and get her out of my hair." Mama's voice sounded far off and what she was saying was drowned out by my own thoughts. Surely Mama was wrong; she had to be. But something told me that she was right and that Rose was pregnant. Rose's own words of self-degradation kept coming back: You don't know what I've done for love.

Snapping back to the present I pleaded, "You can't blame Granny Lee for what Rose has done, Mama."

"Who should I blame, then?" she asked in a louder voice. Placing the hot poker in its stand and then closing the burner lid she said, "Your sister didn't get that way here. She got that way there because nobody cares what goes on in your Granny Lee's house, especially her. I'll bet you a dollar Martha Lee don't know who climbs them stairs at night. And even if she did she'd forgive whatever, because Martha Lee believes forgiveness is the answer to everything!"

"You said Rose was seein' a man while she was still livin' here. How do you know she didn't get that way then?" I asked.

Mama's dark eyes flashed like lightning. Her voice was laced with indignation. "Don't you try and lay this at my door, Junie Mae Lee. I've tried my hardest to teach her right from wrong. If your Daddy finds out about this it will kill him," she whispered. "He's already at death's door. I've never seen a sicker man in my life."

Tears of hurt and frustration burned my eyes. One part of me wanted to go in our bedroom and shake Rose until her teeth rattled while the other part mourned for Daddy. It had never bothered me that Daddy felt a kind of special love for Rose. I believe that it was her beauty and her lack of worldly wisdom that had drawn him to her and made him act so protectively toward her. I'd always known that Daddy loved me in a different way. He'd told me many times that I was more responsible and dependable than Rose, and though he'd never said it, I somehow knew he wanted me to look after my sister even though she was older by three years.

"He won't find nothin' out from me, and I'm shore Rose won't tell him, either," I promised.

Laughing sarcastically Mama said, "Oh, I'm shore of that. She'll try to hide it from him for as long as she can."

Momentarily turning my thoughts from Rose I asked, "Do you think Daddy will get better?"

Mama sighed and said, "I really believe he might die, Junie Mae. Last night he was wheezin' so loud I could hear him all the way out on the back porch. He ain't gettin' much air and his color is awful."

In a rush of desperation I pleaded, "He needs you, Mama. He's so much better when you're takin' care of him. I think he feels bad when Granny Lee and the others do things for him. Even Granny Lee says he does better when you're here."

"Well, I have to work, Junie Mae. The rent won't pay for itself and we have to eat."

Placing my hand on Mama's shoulder in an affectionate manner, I said "The rest of the family will help us, Mama. Granny Lee will make sure we keep the house and even Great Uncle Hiram told Marie he'd help us with money to buy food."

"Daddy won't take no charity off his family. Besides -- I can't just up and quit that job. Hanley probably wouldn't hire me back."

"Daddy needs you," I pleaded. "He might die if you ain't here with him, Mama. Could you live with that?"

Mama turned from the stove looking perplexed. Her voice was a sharp whisper. "How dare you blame me for your Daddy's weak lungs! I didn't cause his pneumonia. The coal is mostly to blame. Here I am out there working long hours to keep our heads above water while you and your sainted Granny are here plannin' how I should spend my time."

"I'm looking out for Daddy, Mama. That's all."

"Will you ever look out for me?" she hissed. "I swear sometimes I think you and Rose hate me." Grabbing up a dishrag she began furiously scrubbing the sink. "When will I ever stop havin' to pay for not just my sins but everybody else's too? I didn't cause your Daddy to keep workin' in the coal and I wadn't nowhere around when Rose got herself pregnant, but who do you think they'll blame when it's all said and done?" Throwing the rag in the sink she said, "All right, Junie Mae, I'll stay here and take care of your Daddy till he's well, if he gets well. But I won't take care of Rose's bastard child. You can't guilt me into that! Granny Lee and Marie can have that responsibility."

17 CHRISTMAS AT THE LODGE

Granny Lee, Uncle Corbin, and Uncles Harlan Ray and Harvey James and their wives came to the lodge a little before noon bearing gifts and food. Mama was too busy caring for Daddy to cook Christmas dinner, so Granny Lee, Grandma Haley, and Marie prepared all the food. The long kitchen suddenly felt small, smothering, and hot with so many people gathered around the table. Great Uncle Hiram arrived a few minutes after the others, bringing extra chairs with him. Mama had the uncles bring Daddy into the kitchen where he was helped into the big living room chair that took up a large space at the head of the table. Looking pale, drawn, and weak, Daddy smiled in thanks. After a long, drawn out prayer, Granny Lee made an effort to feed Daddy some extra thin turkey gravy and smashed green beans, of which he ate very little. Mama made small talk with Rebekah Ann but spoke very few words to Grandma Haley. Marie busied herself with trying to round up her children who ran amok in a relatively strange place. "Now Chester Harlan, if you don't eat something you'll be crying hungry on the way home," scolded Marie. Rose, who sat beside Great Uncle Hiram, seemed sad and withdrawn. Harvey James and Harlan Ray, who had been warned earlier by Granny Lee not to mention the coalmine, seemed at a loss as to what to say to Daddy. The coal was all they had talked about for years and was part of the glue that bonded them together.

Granny Lee said, "I am so glad God has granted another Christmas together." With her hands high in the air she began speaking in tongues. "Ah sha-na-na. God bless our family and may the Lord be with Ralph in his time of need."

Later Daddy's chair was moved in the living room where everyone exchanged gifts in front of the tree. Granny Lee had knitted all the women beautiful colorful shawls with matching hats and mittens. With the help of

Marie, who was also a talented seamstress, they had made each man one Sunday shirt and dress pants. Daddy's white shirt matched the color of his pasty, gaunt face. The children each received a stocking of candy and a toy apiece. Had it not been for Daddy's sickness and Rose's pensive mood, Christmas would have been wonderful that year. Not wanting to tire Daddy out, Granny Lee and the rest of the family left around five o'clock that evening. After the dishes where done and the food stored away, Mama gave Daddy his medicine and vapor steam. Afterwards, she'd sat down at the table and started writing letters. I knew she wrote mostly to Uncle Larkin. I'd seen a large stack of his return letters in the little cabinet drawer in the kitchen, but just a few from Rhodie. I'd wondered what Mama and Larkin had found to write each other about. After saying goodnight to Daddy I joined Rose, who was already in bed. Her beautiful red shawl was draped carefully over a chair in the corner. "You always look so pretty in red," I told her, my emotions creeping up.

She said, "Mama's is red too. I guess Granny Lee thought we both looked good in dark red. Ain't yours dark blue?" she asked.

"Yeah, I guess Granny Lee thinks the dark blue goes with my light hair. She must have worked all summer knitting and sewing for all of us."

"She did," Rose said.

Sighing, I pulled my well-worn granny gown over my head and then saw Rose crying in the mirror in front of me. "What are you going to do, Rose?" I asked.

"About what?" she sniffed.

"About the baby you're carryin'," I whispered.

Watching Rose in the mirror I saw her gasp. Her strange eyes grew wide with shock. Sitting up quickly in bed, she asked. "What did you say?"

"You heard me, Rose. I know you're pregnant, and so does Mama."

Rose's face paled and with her blood red lips she appeared unnatural looking in the lamplight -- almost like a ghost. "How do you know that Mama knows?" she asked.

Turning to look at her directly, I said, "Because she told me. How many months are you along?"

Still in shock Rose whispered, "I didn't have my monthly in November and December is almost over. Oh, God -- she's goin' to kill me, Junie Mae."

"Why did you go that far with him, Rose? Didn't you know there could be a baby?" I knew what "too far" meant thanks to Mama, who had made certain that Rose and I knew what went on beyond kissing and touching. Her descriptions of sex between a man and a woman were often so frightening and degrading that I was hesitant about ever committing to it. According to Mama, sexual intercourse was an act meant exclusively for a man's pleasure. To a woman it was a dutiful wifely sacrifice and not an act of pleasure where she was concerned.

Rose moved to sit on the side of the bed. She whispered so low I almost didn't hear her. "He wore this rubber shield over his thing that fit like a second skin. He told me as long as he wore that there couldn't be no baby. But one night it broke; after that he was scared to do anything else with me."

"So you didn't tell him that you might be pregnant?" I asked in disgust.

"God, no. Why would I tell him? He wouldn't want it. I don't even want it. I see Marie chasing after her three and all it does is depress me." She began to cry softly.

"Too bad you couldn't see that picture before you done it with him," I said carelessly.

"You're just too perfect, Junie Mae. You'd never do what I did. Ha! You don't know what's like when a man wants you. What it feels like to have his hands all over you and you're drownin' in the smell and taste of him. I don't think you've been close enough to that Smith boy yet to feel it, but you will someday, and then you'll understand what I'm talkin' about."

Blushing, I thought of the strange want I felt when Amity had brushed his lips against mine the night he'd given me the locket. Recalling the little trill in my throat and the quickening of my pulse when he was near me, I somehow doubted the sexual act was anything unpleasant like Mama claimed.

"Mama don't know about Bart, does she?" Rose asked with desperation both in her eyes and in her voice.

"No. I didn't tell her about you and him."

"You can't ever tell her that Bart Asher is the father of this baby. It's no tellin' what she'd do with that if she knowed. Who's to say she wouldn't go right up there and tell them all? And who's to say Miss Joelyn wouldn't try and take the baby?"

"What would be so bad about that? You said you didn't want it!"

Rose's pretty face suddenly took on an expression of viciousness. "I've thought about goin' up there myself and tellin' them all. I've played it out a thousand times in my head. I can see Bart now denyin' it. 'That baby ain't no blood of mine. I only know her in passin'.'" Her laugh sounded more like a hollow sob.

"Does Granny Lee know you're expectin'?"

"I'm sure she does. I didn't tell her but maybe Marie did. Marie thinks I should let Rebekah and Harlan Ray raise the baby."

"If you don't want it," I mumbled, and then added, "Don't you think you should at least tell Bart? It wouldn't be right not to tell him even if he don't want it."

Rose said, "He won't want it or me. What good is a baby unless it has its Mama and Daddy to raise it? If his folks found out -- especially his granddaddy, Big Brock -- he might disinherit Bart, and then he'd be ruined, wouldn't he? Not that he don't deserve to be ruined. Look at me; I'll never be able to find a good man with a baby on my hip. I'm tainted goods now. Bart, though, will marry someday and never have to go through what's waitin' for me. How unfair is that, Junie Mae -- that I'll be the only one who suffers from the sin we both done?" Licking her puffy lips her wild eyes stared into mine. "You promise me right here, tonight, that you'll never tell Mama or Daddy that Bart is the daddy. If you don't promise, I swear I'll kill myself," she warned.

Out of a real fear that she might truly take her own life, I promised her I wouldn't tell but asked, "What will you say when they ask you who the father is?"

"I'll come up with something," she promised.

Once the lamp was extinguished and darkness filled the room, I thought of Floyd Wilkes' ghost for the first time in weeks and recalled the horrible vision he'd shown me of a faceless Rose. What had it meant? Did it have something to do with Rose being pregnant? I pictured her little white hands cupped around a bunch of red roses and was sure the ghost of Floyd Wilkes had meant for me to figure it out. But I was only fourteen and not that knowledgeable when it came symbolism. I thought of Granny Lee and wondered if she might know. Maybe I would ask her soon when Daddy was well again. In desperation I once again prayed -- not to Floyd Wilkes' ghost but to Granny Lee's Jesus Christ. My trust in Floyd Wilkes' ghost had waned and now I needed something with real healing powers to help Daddy recover.

After my prayer I thought of Amity Smith and pictured his handsome face with his dimpled smile and his cornflower blue eyes and unruly blonde hair. I recalled the feel of his hand warmly cupping mine, and sound of his laughter filled my ears. When Amity was with me, I'd had no cares; everything bad in my life seemed to melt away like the frost when hit by the glare of the sun. Did I love him, though? I wondered. Was I old enough to love a man with a woman's heart? I was so mixed up then. I thought of Mama and for some reason couldn't equate her with any feelings of love. Did I love her? Maybe I had always feared her more than I loved her. Did I still fear her? I didn't think so, not after all the weakness I had seen in her. In retrospect those weaknesses had been her undoing in my eyes. As a child I had seen my mother as bigger than life, someone who was a cut above everything and everyone else below her. Mama had painstakingly drilled life lessons into my head and then disillusioned me by breaking her own rules. Rose had warned me that Mama was bad underneath her mask of prettiness and righteousness. I thought of Daddy and wondered how he could have missed what I was eventually forced to see. How could he not know of her devious nature? As a child I had believed every word she said, simply because she had said them with such conviction, such strength. I had believed in her and had obeyed almost every rule that unruly Rose had broken. But because Rose was like Mama more than she was like me, Daddy, or Granny Lee, she had been the first of us to see the devious things in Mama that we'd missed. I thought of an old saying that I heard all my life: "It takes one to know one." Beneath the covers I had longed for a warm, safe place. I realized that never again could I look at the winter months or snow without being reminded of Daddy's sickness and Rose's pregnancy. Even without a vision from Floyd Wilkes' ghost I'd known that the worst was yet to come. Sometimes when we look at life and think things couldn't be worse, something else comes along that tops that "worst" thing. Life is like that, and it always will be.

18 THE CONFRONTATION

Mama had kept her word by quitting Hanley's Hardware and staying home and caring for Daddy. And, as Rose had predicted, Daddy's health slowly improved enough for Uncle Larkin's visit. He came on the sixth day of January, but this was no surprise to Mama. When not caring for Daddy, she had been preparing for his older brother's visit for a whole week by scrupulously clearing the house and washing up all the dirty laundry. The look of pure radiance on her face caused Rose to remark, "Who's coming -- the King of England? She even sewed new curtains while she was sittin' in there with Daddy."

"Uncle Corbin stopped here this morning and told Mama that Uncle Larkin was in and would pay us a visit sometime this afternoon."

"That stuttering old fool gets on my nerves," Rose said, making a face. "Daddy said Uncle Corbin had enough money to burn a wet cow," she added, throwing Grandma Haley's colorful patchwork quilt on the bed and then placing the pillow at the head of the bed.

"Better make that bed look good. Knowing Mama she might have him sleepin' in here"

"Where would we sleep?" Rose asked in an irritated voice.

Shrugging, I said, "She won't care about where we sleep. She's been waitin' for Uncle Larkin to come for months. Heaven knows they've written enough letters back and forth."

"You mean Aunt Rhodie wrote the letters," Rose interjected.

"No, I mean Uncle Larkin wrote most of them. I seen his name on a whole stack of letters that Mama keeps in the first drawer of the kitchen cabinet. Aunt Rhodie wrote her less than a dozen."

"Did you read 'em?" Rose asked incredulously.

"I couldn't do that. She'd have knowed, because Uncle Larkin's letters was tied together in a special way," I answered grimly.

Rose laughed and said, "But you were goin' to until you seen how she had 'em fixed special." In a more somber voice, Rose asked, "You think Mama's gonna have him try and talk Daddy into movin' out there in Indianapolis with him and Rhodie?"

"That's what she told me," I answered bitterly. "I guess she figures Daddy's too sick to work in the mines now so she's got a better chance of getting him to go out there with her."

Shaking her head in disbelief, Rose said, "Mama don't know Daddy as well as she thinks she does. He'll never leave here, not even for her."

I nodded in agreement, thinking that it was good to have Rose back home even if she was pregnant. But the good feeling wasn't to last, for the minute me and Rose entered the kitchen, Mama handed us the empty buckets and then ordered us to start filling up the big barrels on the porch. She said, "I'm gonna need plenty of water for the weekend. Your Uncle Larkin is coming for supper and I want to make sure there's enough water to cook with and for everyone to wash up."

Averting her eyes away from Mama, Rose grabbed two buckets and quickly started for the front door. Grabbing the two remaining buckets, I followed her to the back porch. The slam of the screen door caused me to jump and look up in time to see Mama pulling her wrap closer to her body. Eying Rose knowingly, she said, "I know you're going to have a baby, Rose. I've knowed since Thanksgivin'. Now who's the daddy?" she asked sharply.

Looking directly at Mama, Rose deliberately dropped her buckets on the planks with a ping. "What difference would it make, Mama? Would knowin' make you any less ashamed of me? "

"You've made your bed, Rose, and now you have to lie in it. I can't take no baby to raise, and Lord knows you don't want it, either. I know you don't. Have you thought for one second what your Daddy will say when he finds out what you've done?" she hissed.

"It ain't your all's worry no more. Remember? I was sent to Granny Lee's to live, and the only reason I'm here is for Daddy." Rose's voice was laced with tempered anger that was sure to come out in full force if Mama kept pushing.

"Oh yes, you'll be fine havin' a baby with no daddy in sight. What, did he do get you pregnant and then go back to his wife?"

"My baby's daddy is dead," she hissed back. "He died in the cave-in." Mama's jaw dropped, and I gasped and was equally surprised, so much so that one of the buckets slipped out of my own hand and onto the planks with a loud clang.

"I don't believe you," Mama said shaking her head.

Rose spat, "I don't care what you believe. It's true. He was in love with me and had asked me to marry him before he died."

Crossing her arms against her breasts, Mama laughed loudly against a cold wind that blew strands of her long hair onto her mouth. Quickly brushing them away she said, "That's the kind of story I might have made up if I'd got pregnant and the man I was seein' left me holdin' the bag."

I wanted to say something but was afraid to open my mouth. Deep down I had known this was coming. Words had to be said, so I would let it play out between them without trying to intervene.

"It's no lie, Mama. The father of my baby was Todd Worley. Me and him was seein' each other long before he met Sarah Sue. The only reason he got engaged to her was because I wouldn't agree to marry him when he first asked me. I couldn't settle for a coal miner. He died before I knowed I was carryin' his baby."

Shaking her head in disbelief Mama said, "How could you give yourself over to a man you knowed you'd never marry? You just throwed yourself away for nothin', and now you're gonna pay dearly for doin' it. I don't guess you thought about what this was gonna do to your daddy," she said in a triumphant voice.

The look of smugness suddenly vanished from Rose's face and was quickly replaced with a look of deep shame. Saying nothing, Mama turned toward the door, opened it and went back into the house.

With her head still bowed, Rose retrieved her buckets and made her way to the back steps. Filled with a deep sorrow, I followed her in silence. When we reached the spring, I asked her how she could make up such a horrible lie about her and Todd Worley.

"I had to," she declared with chattering teeth. "Besides, it wadn't no lie about him wantin' to marry me. He'd have gave up Sarah Sue in a minute if I'd agreed to marry him."

How like Mama she was. Even Mama admitted it with that crack about how she might have made up the same kind of story if she was in Rose's position. Filling my buckets quickly from the cold spring, I started down the hill without Rose. I was thinking how life had become almost unbearable for me after the cave-in. I longed for the normalcy of school and to escape into a good book. I yearned to see Violet Elizabeth and hold the hand of Amity Smith. Things had changed so much at the lodge that I pined for the past with its warm summers and uneven bottoms along the Cumberland River where daisies and black-eyed Susans grew thick and beautiful. I recalled the white sandbar and the feel of gritty, warm sand beneath my bare feet. I pictured a healthier, more vibrant Daddy and me on the river bank holding our cane poles and waiting for the fish to bite.

Rose had never liked to fish but sometimes she'd tag along beside Daddy with Buster in tow, squealing every time she came across a spider web on a bush or when some bug landed on her. When she'd jump or squeal he'd almost keel over in laughter. I'd laughed, too, suddenly wondering where the giggly Rose had gone. I'd had no idea that people could change so much in just a year or two. Now Daddy spent most of his time in bed looking like a sick old man at thirty-eight. He'd aged so much in the past year. Mama blamed the coal and said it made young men look like old ones. I thought of all the miners I knew and ticked off each one in my mind; their bodies and faces marched before me -- a bunch of stick thin men with loose trousers, baggy shirts, and worn out jackets and hats. Most had lost their teeth because they'd had no way of paying for dental work. Their cheekbones were always hollow beneath their dead eyes. I thought of Harlan Ray and pictured how his once boyish face had changed into that of someone much older than his twenty-nine years. These miners all looked like old men, and for what? A few pitiful dollars that never stretched far enough to afford them even the bare necessities of life. I'd lived that life, but before the cave-in I'd never thought it strange. I'd never seen us as poor or lacking in anything. Unlike Rose, I had never wanted anything more. What was more -- a few extra candy sticks in a brown paper bag? A loaf of brought on light bread? A cold soda from the Asher soda fountain? To me, these things were nice when I got them, but they weren't things I had to have. Mama coveted the Asher house and the way they lived. She'd spent most of her life hating Joelyn and Big Brock Asher for stealing her dream of marrying Little Brock. For years, she despised the coal and battled with it as a soldier battles his enemies, but in the end she had accomplished nothing but hate and a need to run from the memories of her loss. Mama wasn't a woman who took losing well. I knew Rose was like that, too, and that one way or another Bart Asher would eventually pay for what he'd done to her, just as Daddy would pay for not doing and being what Mama wanted.

19 A VISIT FROM UNCLE LARKIN

Larkin Alan Lee was perhaps the most handsome man I'd ever laid eyes on. I'll never forget how he sauntered in the door of the lodge behind Granny Lee and Marie just a little past twelve noon that cold January day. Glancing over at Mama, I knew she'd thought it too because she couldn't take her eyes off him -- but neither could any of the rest of his family members. Uncle Harlan Ray, however, seemed to eye his older brother with a look of suspicion. Uncle Corbin also seemed hesitant to warm to him. Mama had placed Daddy's big chair at the head of the table. Dressed in his new white dress shirt that Granny Lee had made him for Christmas, he looked washed out and weak-eyed. When Daddy saw his brother, only two years his senior but appearing much younger, he held out his big hand in a gesture of greeting. Uncle Larkin had gone to him immediately and hugged him for the longest of times. Happy and grateful, Granny Lee raised her hands skyward and began praying aloud, thanking God for his grace in allowing her second oldest son to recover this far, and having her beloved oldest son near enough to hug him. "Blessit Jesus, you are good in allowing most of our family members this precious time under one roof. We are not worthy of your love and goodness but we keep striving to worship you in the way you require of us. Hallelujah, praise God." Granny Lee continued to pray in silence. I watched her lips move and her eyelids flutter as they always did when she was deep in silent prayer. My attention snapped back to Uncle Larkin who energized the kitchen with a strange kind of light. He wore perfectly creased gray khaki pants and a tan shirt which blended nicely with his outdoorsy appearance. His face was perfectly sculptured, his chin nicely squared with a tiny cleft. His hair was very dark, thick, and straight, and I didn't see a gray streak in it. When he looked at you his eyes sparkled like water washing over rocks in a creek bed. And when he laughed, it sounded like Daddy's once did before he'd gotten sick. Regarding him closely throughout dinner, I came to the startling realization that there was a genuine sincerity about Uncle Larkin's manner that naturally drew people to him. In other words, he seemed truly interested in others and what they had to say. I had sensed a kindness about his easy manners that would not allow me to dislike him as I thought I would. Mama, in obvious awe of Uncle Larkin, placed him at the opposite end of the table where she could look directly at him. She'd worked hard preparing her best dishes of fried chicken, biscuits and gravy, and soup beans cooked with little chunks of ham. Granny Lee, Marie, and Rebekah Ann had made an assortment of pies for desert. Although our table wasn't long enough to sit the whole family, we'd managed with extra chairs and benches that Uncles Corbin and Hiram had brought with them. Some of the women had taken their plates in the living room and talked among themselves. Mama, though, stayed in the kitchen throughout dinner, not wanting to miss a minute of Uncle Larkin's visit. That day was the happiest of days and one of the first times I'd seen Daddy laugh so heartily since the sickness. Seeing Uncle Larkin had brightened his mood and for that I was grateful.

Uncle Larkin was also wonderful with Marie's children. He'd held little Brice Dodd on his knee and had listened to his jibber jabber with the same rapt attention he might pay a grown-up. He'd also garnered pretty little Brenda Sue's attention as well as that of fidgety Chester Harlan by showing them wallet sized photos of his daughter and her pony, Apple Blossom. He'd patiently tell little stories concerning the pony and how his nine-year-old daughter, Amy Isabella, had fallen off the horse several times before finally mastering the saddle. His voice was rich and strong but not overly deep, and there was a kind of sensitivity to it that made me want to endlessly listen to him. Glancing over at Rose, who sat woodenly beside Uncle Harlan Ray, I noticed that she seemed to be in her own world as usual and was disconnected to the present. It was only when Uncle Larkin called her by name that she snapped to attention. He said, "Your mother told me you were beautiful," he said easily, then added, "You bear a strong resemblance to her. It's uncanny." Rose forced a little smile and mumbled something unintelligible. Granny Lee interjected, "From a distance you can't tell them apart."

Grandma Haley contributed to the conversation by commenting on Rose's strange eye color. Whether she did it to purposely aggravate Mama is unknown, but I had a suspicion that she did it to garner Mama's attention -- either that or she'd observed something that irked her concerning Mama's overly attentive looks toward Uncle Larkin. "No one knows how Rose ended up with such a queer eye color. She don't take it after our side."

Mama paled and shot Grandma Haley a baleful look.

Uncle Larkin turned to me and said, "Junie Mae, you look a bit like your Granny Ivy Haley. You're very pretty." I thanked him, knowing that he meant it. He'd used the word "beautiful" to describe Rose, and "pretty" to describe me. I appreciated his honesty and the time he spent carefully studying things and people around him. I was like that, too, and hardly missed a thing -- or so I thought. I was to learn that sometimes the truths of life are right there before your eyes, but you fail to see them. More often than not, the things that people omit from their stories are what tell the tale, but people miss the clues. Life is like that -- full of riddles and mazes.

When dinner was over the men were left in the kitchen to talk of manly things like hunting, fishing, and riding horses. The women gathered around the living room and talked of sewing, the weather, and other things women talk about. I sat beside Granny Lee, quietly listening to the conversations. The subject of the coalmine was purposely avoided except in the kitchen, where it crept into the men's conversation. Leave it to Uncle Corbin to bring it up. "Them-them-them- ne-new -men Ash-Ash-Asher-hired was-was-was- talkin' trash ab-ab-about-th-th-that Ger-Ger-German w-wo-wo-woman an-an-and-Bon-Bon-Bonzelle Cr-Cre-Creech. Th-they-sa-sa-said tha-that- th-th-they're st-st-st-stirrin' up-up-up tr-tr-tr-trouble with-with-the-their pro-pro-pro-protests."

Uncle Harvey James said, "Those new men didn't lose family members in the cave-in. Asher probably eggs them on. He sure don't seem to care how much they threaten people. Big Wayne Lewis's widow is going from relative to relative with them little kids, and some of the widows are saying that Asher's settlement offer was more like a bad joke. I don't blame them for turning it down."

Harlan Ray added in a fierce tone, "I heard they hired ten more last week. I'm pretty shore he's gonna get rid of a bunch of us ones that are tryin' to get a union in. Them men he hired are more like thugs than men tryin' to make a livin'. They've been goin' round startin; trouble with some of the men on the line. One new hire they call Butch shoved poor old Levi Creech up against the wall -- all because Bonzelle is giving that German woman a place to stay. Somebody has to! Big Brock's behind most of the trouble if you want my opinion," he said assuredly.

Uncle Corbin argued, "You-you-you-boy-boy-boys are-are mak-mak-makin-it sa-sa sound wor-wor-worse than-than -it-it-it -is. I-I-I-ain't-ain't been-been-been bot-bothered no-none- by-by-by them-them-new-ne-new hires."

Ignoring his older brother, Harlan Ray said, "Levi told me that before the blizzard happened somebody shot holes in his truck bed. I seen the bullet holes myself. That poor ole fellow can hardly tote his dinner bucket. What harm could he do to anybody?"

"He-he-he's hous-housin'- that-that Ger--Ger-German wo-wo-woman. His-his-daught-daughter-ought-ought-ought-to st-st-steer-cle-clear

-of-of her. She-she-she ai-ain't got-got-got no-no- business here in-in-in the U-U-United-St-St-States-any-any-anyhow!"

Uncle Larkin, who had kept quiet during his brothers' conversation about the mine, suddenly spoke up in the German woman's defense. "What does her nationality have to do with anything? Obviously she's here legally. People have a right to come here and work, Corbin. The war is over."

I couldn't see Uncle Corbin's face but could imagine his look of disdain. How dare his older brother who'd never worked a day in his life in the coal mine speak up concerning something he knew nothing about!

Harlan Ray said in an irritated voice, "I don't believe her bein' German has a lot to do with what we're talkin' about here, Larkin. There's a war goin' on inside that mine right now and the underdogs finally stand a chance of gettin' better wages. We got almost all the support we need to get the mine unionized, and Asher knows it." His voice shook with anger as he went on. "That German woman depended on her man for everything. He's gone now, and what has she got? Asher's mine took about all she had to her name, and now he don't want to give her enough money to make up for what she lost. Like he could," his voice sneered.

Harvey James interjected thoughtfully, "I'm afraid Larkin may be partially right. The war hasn't been over long enough for people to forget their hatred of Hitler. A lot of us here lost family in that war, too. Olga Winley is just a reminder of the enemy."

Uncle Larkin agreed, "That's right! The Germans are not too fond of us, either. We killed a lot of their kinfolk, but people here tend to forget that in any war there are always two sides."

Great Uncle Hiram, who up until then had been sitting quietly listening to the men talk, raised his opinion on war by first puffing out his chest and saying, "You boys ain't seen a war. I know what killin' and sufferin' is. I seen men blowed to pieces where there wadn't enough left of 'em to send back home."

"It was the worst war in history," Granny Lee said, shaking her head sadly. "Poor Hiram here is a living piece of history." Granny Lee's fierce belief in her brother and the validity of his war stories had left the uncles bemused -- all save for Uncle Corbin, who considered Hiram a liar simply for the fact that he'd not served long enough in the Navy to have seen much action.

Stuttering in agitation Uncle Corbin said, "Peep-peep-people say-say-say tha-that about-about all wars. When-when-when- the Civ-Civ-Civil War bro-broke out peep-people said-said-said it-it-it was-was the-the war of all-all-all wars. Well, well-well all war-wars we-were bad if-if-if you-you ask-me. They-they-they all took-took-took men-men a-a-away fro-from their fam-fam-families and-and -and thou-thousand-thousands of them di-died."

Uncle Hiram shot back, "What would you know about war, anyhow?

You wadn't in one. You never seen men die the way I have! You don't know what you're talkin' about, Corbin. World War One was the worst war in history."

"Now, Corbin, your uncle's right: World War One was the worst we've ever had as far as I know of, so don't argue with somethin' you didn't have no part in," Granny Lee scolded.

Uncle Corbin looked dejected but said nothing else.

When recalling the conversation that day, I decided that Uncles Harvey James and Larkin were two of the most intelligent family members. In retrospect, they sounded almost like teachers evaluating the reasons behind things, whereas Daddy was more of a listener and less a talker. Not to say that Daddy wasn't intelligent, for he was, but, like most of those men born in the mountains not long after the First World War, he was forced to work in the mines at a young age and never had the opportunity or the money it took to get an education. Granny Lee, who had taught herself how to read by using the Bible, had in turn taught Daddy, Harlan Ray, and Corbin to read simple words. None were great readers, but all three could write their names clearly and could read well enough to make it in life. Daddy, who'd always wanted an education, made sure his youngest brother, Harvey James, got the advantage and worked hard to send him to a trade school. Marie, the youngest of Granny Lee's brood, dropped out of school before she was ten years old, and, like Rose, could barely write her name. Uncle Larkin, according to Granny Lee, was not cut out for the coal and took off at when he was barely fourteen years old in order to escape it. Born with an industrious nature, he'd found work here and there and finally saved up enough for an education. Whatever success he'd achieved, he'd done it all by himself -- and this made him extraordinary in my book.

The best way to describe my Uncle Harlan Ray is to say he was temperamental and always ready for a good fight, while Uncle Corbin was better at starting fights for others to finish. He was also the kind of man who despised any type of change and thought things ought to stay the same all the time. Of all the boys, Daddy was the most like Granny Lee with his understanding and forgiving nature. And like her, his only downfall was that he chose to ignore the distasteful aspects of life rather than deal with them. There was something both doleful and accepting about his nature that had always both delighted and puzzled me.

Looking through the doorway and seeing Daddy at the table I realized that although he looked as weak as a kitten, he remained interested in what was happening with the union and No. 5 mine. Working or not, he would remain a coalminer for the rest of his life -- if not in body, then at least in spirit, regardless of whether the pneumonia might have permanent consequence that wouldn't allow him to ever enter a coalmine again.

By the time it reached seven o'clock in the evening, Marie was ready to take her cranky children home. Brice Dodd acted up the worst by spilling a whole cup of milk on Mama's kitchen floor. Restless Chester Harlan kept wandering in and out of the bedrooms, while Brenda Sue whined loudly on Granny Lee's lap. Granny Lee finally rose from the couch and said, "We better take these youngins home and get them ready for bed." In the kitchen the men were already out of their chairs and saying goodbye to Daddy. Uncle Larkin announced that he wanted to visit a bit longer if Daddy wasn't too tired. Mama quickly spoke up, "He'll be all right for a little while longer. We'd love to have you."

After everyone was gone Mama gently ordered me and Rose to clear the table. Uncle Larkin had helped move Daddy and the big chair into the living room. Meanwhile, Mama flitted about the kitchen like a carefree butterfly. Her voice remained in a strange, sweet, artificial tone that made me feel sick to my stomach. Rose had noticed her change in demeanor and made a face. After the large stack of dishes was done, I went straight to our room and started getting ready for bed. Rose did the same. In the living room Uncle Larkin was telling Daddy about his home in Indianapolis and what his job entailed. Daddy's voice was barely above a whisper, and his coughs were deep rattles that left him gasping for breath.

Mama said. "I'll get his vapors."

"Maybe I should go and come back tomorrow after he gets a good night's rest," Uncle Larkin offered.

I could hear Daddy's weak voice trying to reassure him to stay.

Mama said to Uncle Larkin, "You can help me get him out of the chair and into bed. He's too weak to walk and we'll have to hold him up. "

"All right," Uncle Larkin agreed. Daddy continued to weakly protest, but Mama was adamant that he get his rest. "Now Ralph, you've got to get your rest so you can get your strength back."

Rose, who sat before the mirror brushing her hair, said, "Mama's makin' a play for Uncle Larkin, and don't bother to deny it. She's doin' it, and right under Daddy's nose, too." Using the brush for emphasis, she said, "I swear Junie Mae, she's done some awful things, but this takes the cake."

"She's hopin' Uncle Larkin can talk Daddy into movin' to Indianapolis. That's all," I defended weakly.

Rose's laugh sounded hollow. "You don't believe a word you're sayin'. You can at least tell the truth. You said it yourself that Mama's been writin' more letters to Uncle Larkin than to his wife, and it's no tellin' what she said in them letters. She musta really buttered him up good, 'cause here he is after what -- ten years? I think Granny Lee said she's not seen him herself but two times in ten years. Amazin', ain't it!"

"Yeah, it's amazin'," I answered smartly. "Now put out the light. You're closer to it."

"God, Junie Mae, will you never stop taking up her cause? You know what she's done. Look how she's kept that secret about Little Brock Asher all these years, and Daddy don't have a clue about him and her. She could have at least told him. He'd forgive her of anything. Look how she stole Hanley's crazy wife's watches and hid them, and even went to Grandma Haley for money to buy a bus ticket. She wadn't plannin' on takin' any of us with her, was she? She was gonna leave Daddy here all by hisself, and if he hadn't've got sick she'd be already be gone. Say it, Junie Mae! If nothin else, say it to yourself until you believe it!"

Getting up and turning down the wick myself, I kept quiet, instinctively knowing that Mama was after something from Uncle Larkin, but to believe she was capable of going after him in a romantic way was just too incredible. Even Mama wouldn't stoop so low as to go after her husband's own brother. Once underneath the covers, I tried to shut out the girlish giggles coming from the living room. Surely a bright man like Uncle Larkin wouldn't fall for his brother's wife. How could he? Couldn't he see right through her? But then it occurred to me that he might be like Daddy and Granny Lee and just looked past it all. After a while the voices inside the living room had changed to low murmurs. What was Mama telling him? What was he saying to Mama?

I cannot remember what time Uncle Larkin left that night. I'd had other things to think of, like school, the new year, and seeing Amity Smith for the first time since Christmas.

20 A NEW YEAR'S CELEBRATION

The New Year of 1949 brought just enough flurries to cover the ground. I recall getting up and helping Mama with starting the fires, and then later assisted in helping her get Daddy out of bed. Since Daddy was too sick to travel to Granny Lee's for the traditional New Year's Day dinner, the family had decided to bring food to the lodge. By twelve o'clock noon the house was filled with people. Marie and her children were the only ones missing. Granny Lee said that Chester Harlan had spiked a fever during the night and that Marie thought it best to keep him and her other two children home. Uncles Harlan Ray and Harvey James arrived with their wives shortly after Granny Lee and Uncle Hiram showed up. Uncles Noah and Coy brought Grandma Haley with them while Uncle Corbin brought Uncle Larkin. I helped Mama set the table. She'd brought out her white lace placemats that were given to us by Granny Lee several years before. Mama had Rose polish her best silverware while I laid out our best plate settings. Mama loved pretty, dainty dishes and kept her best set in the corner cabinet for special occasions. Daddy looked as pale as milk that day and hardly touched his plate of food. Mama was too busy listening to Uncle Larkin talk about his life in Indianapolis to notice. His conversation was all about the sights and sounds of the city and how he'd had the best of both worlds because he loved only ten miles out of the city. He talked about how quiet the countryside was and how level and green the rolling fields looked in the summer. It was easy to see that Mama was captivated not only by his good looks but also his lifestyle. I could feel her excitement and her want of a similar lifestyle. He'd also painted an idyllic picture of Rhodie planting beautiful flowers and gardening in the quiet of the evening, and he talked of Amy Isabella's pony and how pretty she looked riding her pony in the green paddocks. It was plain to me that Uncle Larkin was a happy man for the most part, but I sensed his immediate attraction to Mama. I wasn't sure if it was her good looks that charmed him or her attentive listening skills or both. Whatever the case, Daddy didn't seem to notice and sat listening attentively to his brother's stories of his home. I remember feeling not only a vast love for my Daddy but also a great pity for all the things he should have noticed but for some reason ignored -- or so I had thought then. Later I would learn that Daddy had been more intuitive than I'd ever dreamed.

21 SCHOOL AND AMITY SMITH

Three days after the New Year, I climbed enthusiastically out of bed, wondering what I should wear on my first day of school since Christmas. The thought of seeing Amity Smith after all this time made my stomach flutter. Tiptoeing gingerly over to the closet, I turned to see Rose lying twisted up inside Grandma Haley's colorful quilt with only the top of her dark head showing. Intent on choosing just the right outfit, I finally withdrew a dark blue skirt and white blouse that I thought would go well with the dark blue shawl Granny Lee had knitted me for Christmas. I could hear Mama's voice and knew she was in the bedroom taking care of Daddy, and I felt glad that at least she hadn't deserted him in his time of need.

Once in the kitchen I saw Mama standing in front of the stove. Eyeing me in disapproval she asked, "Where are you goin', Junie Mae?"

"To school," I said, grabbing my dinner bucket and opening its lid. "Is there any pie left?"

"It's in the warmer," she answered dryly, then added, "Junie Mae, your Daddy is still an invalid and it's impossible for me to take care for him by myself. I can't believe that you'd even think of goin' back to school and leavin' me."

"Daddy wants me to go to school, Mama."

Waving her hand in dismissal, she said, "Don't give me that! It's that Smith boy that you wanna see, and not so much the school."

"That ain't fair, Mama," I wailed, feeling at a loss. "I love learnin'. You got Rose here today to help. She can carry water from the spring if Great Uncle Hiram and them don't get it." Slicing lines down the pie, I scooped it out of the plate and quickly placed it in Reynolds Wrap. After slipping it in the lunch bucket, I snapped its lid shut. Looking up, I saw Mama's dark eyes burning into mine. "Who do you think you are makin' decisions about who does what here? How much help has Rose ever been to me? You hounded me to quit Hanley's so I could stay here and care for your Daddy. I figured you planned to quit school for at least a little while until he gets well -- if he ever does."

"I can't quit school," I said stubbornly.

Mama's dark eyes bulged. "It would seem that you care more about that boy and that school than you care about your poor sick Daddy."

"That's enough, Mama!" Rose said from the doorway. "You let Junie Mae go on to school. She's gonna be late! I'll start the wash."

Mama stamped her foot angrily on the floor. With hands on her hips she said, "Rose, you stay out of things that don't concern you. You've been gone from here for months. I can see how much you care about what goes on in this house."

"Daddy will hear you, Mama," I begged.

From the bedroom, Daddy began to cough and hack. I could tell he'd heard some of the ruckus and was upset, causing him to struggle to cough up the membrane.

"Do you all see what you've done? He heard you!" Mama hissed, before making her way toward the bedroom to see to him. Slumping in the chair, I closed my eyes and felt tears of frustration trickling down my face.

"I'll stay home," I said in a defeated tone.

"No you won't!" Rose declared. "You go on and get outta here and let me handle her. People are here all day offering to help. She's just being cruel like always!"

Outside the wind was still but the air was bitterly cold. Wiping the tears from my face in fear the cold would chafe it, I proceeded up the path with Buster tagging behind me. I suddenly wondered if Mama was right: maybe I should have foregone school for a little while longer, at least until Daddy was well. Was I really acting selfish by wanting to return to class and be with Amity and Violet Elizabeth? Pulling the heavy shawl closer to me, I walked from the long dirt path and finally up to the highway. Looking in the direction of the pull-off near the shelter, I saw the children from the mining camp standing huddled together. Behind the crowd I spotted Amity's truck. The blast of his horn made me smile and I all but ran in the direction of his truck. My heart beat with joy upon seeing Violet Elizabeth waving energetically at me from behind the glass. My eyes searched for the face of Amity Smith. Buster, accustomed to the morning walk and the sight of Amity's truck, began to happily wag his tail while yapping loudly.

"No, you go back home, Buster!" I commanded. Looking sheepish and dejected, Buster hesitantly obeyed and then trotted back in the direction of the lodge.

"I was afraid your Daddy was still too sick for you to return to school," Violet Elizabeth said, hugging me tightly.

"Me too," Amity whispered. While returning Violet Elizabeth's exuberant hug, my eyes searched Amity's handsome face. Within my chest my heart pounded so hard I was afraid it might stop. Clasping my cold hand in his, he held it for a while. Melting inside like icicles on a sunny day, I never wanted to withdraw from his touch. I recall that day with such happiness. It was the first time I'd felt truly happy since he'd given me the heart-shaped locket at Christmastime. I learned to equate complete joy with Violet Elizabeth and Amity, and without them my life seemed sad and filled with sickness and strife. Floyd Wilkes' ghost had once given me a similar kind of feeling of safety and joy in knowing that I was being looked after by someone. When I'd felt sad I'd turned to him. Sometimes he'd come and other times he wouldn't. Amity and Violet had been there for me when it had counted, and I could reach out and touch them if needed. What was a ghost but a fast glimpse in the window or a laugh behind a bush? Amity and Violet Elizabeth were real, and neither had scared me with strange visions that had no meaning that I could understand.

22 FLOYD WILKES, WHERE HAVE YOU GONE?

I'd finally decided that the trouble with my life was that school didn't last long enough, and rides in the truck to school and home with Amity and Violet were too short. Sadly, it was taking Daddy too long to recover from pneumonia. Four weeks of his sickness had seemed like four years to me. I also thought of Rose constantly. What would she do once the baby was born? She had shamed Mama and Daddy by getting herself pregnant out of wedlock, and Mama had made it plain to Rose that she would have nothing to do with either her or the baby. And what would Daddy say once he discovered that Rose was going to have a baby?

Life inside the lodge continued to be crowded with family on a daily basis. Uncle Larkin stayed on another week and visited daily while Granny Lee continued to help out, but not as often as she once did. Thankfully, Uncles Harlan Ray and Harvey James came every evening after work to chop wood, carry water, and do whatever else they could do to help out. Dr. Minor had told Mama that someone should walk Daddy just as soon as he was strong enough. On the fourth night of Uncle Larkin's visit, it was decided that he and Harlan Ray would help Daddy get out of the chair and to stand on his own feet. I remember watching them raise him up and then stand him on the floor. The episode is almost too painful to recall but still very vivid in my memory. Daddy stood wobbling with bent knees. His breath was coming in gasps as he willed himself to put one foot before the other. I cried sympathetically while watching his chest rise and his lips tremor weakly. Daddy had made only three small steps before finally collapsing weakly against the stronger chest of his oldest brother.

After easing him back into the chair Harlan Ray said to Mama, "He's not ready to walk yet, Heddy. He's still too weak."

Uncle Larkin shook his head in disagreement, saying, "His doctor said he has to keep his muscles exercised or else he'll lose the ability to walk altogether."

Wincing, Harlan Ray scowled, "The man is still as weak as a kitten. He's got to get stronger before he can stand up."

Mama quickly intervened by saying, "Your brother is right, Harlan Ray. The doctor made it plain that Ralph has to work them leg muscles. We'll do it a little at a time." Ignoring them both, Uncle Harlan Ray bent down close to Daddy's ear and told him how he was meeting Harvey James and other miners later at the home of Levi Creech in order to discuss union matters. Daddy, in turn, looked distressed and nodded affirmatively. I knew how badly Daddy had wanted to get up out of that chair and be a part of the meeting, and so did Mama. Looking disgusted, Mama asked the brothers to help get Daddy to bed.

In the bedroom Rose sat crossed legged on the bed looking furious. Her dark hair hung like a curtain around her lovely face. Her eyes favored the ice glaciers I'd seen in my geography book. "What's wrong?" I asked, tossing my books on the bed.

"Shut the door," Rose commanded. After I shut the door she told me what was on her mind. As usual, it had to do with Mama and what she was doing.

Rose whispered, "I swear to God Mama is after Uncle Larkin! I can tell by the way she looks at him. She never takes her eyes off him. Wanna hear what I heard today?" she asked.

Saying nothing, I waited for her to tell me, knowing it would do little to tell her that I didn't want to hear anything about Mama. Never mind that I was happy and looking forward to daydreaming about Amity Smith. Lately it had seemed that happiness was like a flitting butterfly. Sometimes I could almost reach out and touch it, but then it was gone.

Rose said, "This morning, Uncle Larkin told Mama that he planned to go home the day after tomorrow." Mama started begging him not to go, telling him how good he was for Daddy and how leaving him might cause him to have a set-back. Uncle Larkin bought it hook, line, and sinker and agreed to stay till Friday." Shaking her head in amazement, she said, "I didn't think he was that dumb."

"He ain't talked to Daddy yet about movin' to Indianapolis. Mama's waiting for that," I offered weakly.

Rose laughed wryly and shook her head. "He won't talk to Daddy. I heard him tell Mama that this mornin'. He said Daddy had too much of his life vested in the coal and it wouldn't do no good to try and talk him into movin' near a big city."

"Daddy's a coalminer and always will be," I said. "Uncle Larkin's not so dumb. He told Mama the truth."

"He's doin' whatever she wants just like Daddy always does what she wants. Nobody can say no to Mama. Just like Daddy, he's under her thumb. I know -- I seen it! If she told Uncle Larkin to jump off a cliff he'd do it. What's more, I hear them whisperin' all day long. Mama had me washin' and hangin' clothes out in the cold just so she could be alone with him. I like to froze to death out there, but she didn't care!"

"Uncle Larkin's too smart to fall for Mama," I said assuredly, then added that Granny Lee would disown him if he did something like that to Daddy.

Rolling her eyes and scowling Rose said, "Granny Lee never disowned nobody in her life. She'd just pray for Daddy and forgive the rest and say it was the Lord's will."

My first thought was to defend Mama, but somewhere inside a part of me believed what Rose was saying. I too had noticed Mama's interest in Uncle Larkin, beginning with the long letters she written to him. He'd written her, too -- stacks of letters. Their correspondence had bonded them somehow. But to think she might view him as a lover instead of a brother-in-law was too much for my fourteen-year-old mind to bear.

Rising from the bed, Rose went to stand in front of the window. Pulling back the curtain, she stared forlornly in the direction of the Asher house. After a while she turned to me with tears in her eyes and said, "I'm goin' back to Granny Lee's tomorrow. Mama don't want me here. She's never wanted me here."

"I want you here," I whispered

"I know that, but pretty soon I'll start showin' and Daddy will know. I can't stand the thought of him seein' me like this. I'd rather die." Turning back toward the window, she said in voice that was almost a whisper. "Damn him! He said there couldn't be a baby. He said not to worry. I ain't seen or heard from him since before Thanksgivin'. That last time we met, he was all jumpy and restless. I could tell he didn't want to be with me. He didn't take me to any of the little secret places we usually went to. He just rode us around in the dark in his Daddy's old truck and hardly said five words to me. I knowed it was the last time I'd see him, I just knowed it." She sniffed.

"You might be better off to tell him about the baby. You're gonna need some kind of help in raisin' it."

Letting the curtain fall back, Rose eyed me as if I'd said the dumbest thing in the world. "You're such a child, Junie Mae. You ain't thought past your nose on this one. If I told him he'd just deny it. I couldn't bear hearin' him do that."

"When Cora Walker went to court and swore Elijah Williams was her baby's daddy, the judge believed her and made him pay for it," I offered.

Shaking her head in disgust, Rose said, "If I done that and the judge believed me, Miss Joelyn would just take the baby. What court would go against her? Them people's got all the money in the world. What do we have? Nothin'!"

Suddenly her pretty face appeared spiteful. Her strange eyes bulged and her lovely face was twisted in a cruel grimace. "Do you think I'd give the Ashers my baby? Do you think I'd give them the pleasure? They'd probably take it out of spite just because of what Daddy and the Uncles are doin' with the union. No, I don't want it," she spat, "but they ain't gettin' it either. I'd see it dead first!"

She looked so much like Mama when she said that. My stomach turned at the sight of our Mama made over. "That baby ain't got a say in what happens to it. You can't just wish it was dead because things ain't going good between you and Bart Asher," I snapped.

"You don't know what you're talkin' about. You ain't standin' where I am. Try carryin' a baby that you don't even want, don't even need. It wadn't my fault that that rubber on his thing broke. He said there wouldn't be a baby. He promised me. He lied like a dog and now I've got to pay for it!"

"That poor little baby is the only one that's gonna pay," I assured her.

"You girls get in the wood," Mama hollered from the kitchen.

I grabbed my coat and stomped out of the bedroom and through the living room, banging the screen door behind me. Tears flooded my eyes and blurred the look of the dead grass and leafless trees in the distance. Now I could see the tear distorted river with its wavering turns and bends. Let Mama get the wood, let anyone get the wood. I didn't care. I was sick to death of both Mama and Rose and their predicaments. Both had made horrible decisions and all they could think to do was run from the consequences. In retrospect, I had been forced to grow up fast and had learned to think like a grownup. Time, place, and circumstance had stolen my innocence and had forced me to see the darker aspects of human nature. As I walked up the dirt road I thought of Rose and how childish she was acting concerning her pregnancy. How could she wish her baby dead rather than place it with somebody like Miss Joelyn, who most likely would see to it that it had the best of advantages? Another avenue for her would be to give it to Uncle Harlan and Rebekah Ann; they would love it and give it the best home they could manage. But desperate people did desperate things in the days before abortion was commonplace.

In the days of my girlhood, society still deemed a young unmarried pregnant girl as being ruined or spoiled goods. To the young unwed mother a prospective baby was thought of as a burden or a thing of fear or shame. While growing up, I had heard many stories of young women who killed their babies rather than face the consequences of family and the God-fearing community that made up so much of Appalachia. I remembered the story Mama had told me of a young girl named Colleen Couch whose family lived near Mama in Daisy Camp. According to Mama, Colleen was barley thirteen years old when she delivered her baby down by Salt Creek and then threw its little body into the water. A week or so later some trappers had found the newborn washed up in some drift wood. When confronted by her suspicious mother, Colleen finally broke down and confessed to being the mother and drowning the infant. I wondered if Rose felt the kind of desperation that this young girl felt, and, if she did, what would she be willing to do to get rid of her baby? The thought was terrifying and unreal. I thought of Mama and how she'd had turned her back on Rose just as society had always turned their backs on women like her. Rose had committed an immoral act, and neither Mama nor society would forgive her for it. And so she was alone, save for me, Granny Lee, and Marie.

My thoughts turned to Floyd Wilkes and how I didn't need a vision from him to know that nothing having to do with Rose and her baby would turn out right. How could it? Suddenly the wind felt colder and the sky hovered darker. My eyes followed the Cumberland River and stopped where it bended around woods. Where had Floyd Wilkes' ghost gone to? Why hadn't he come to me as he had done when I was sick? Maybe my own fear of him had chased him away. Maybe he would never come back. The thought saddened me somehow. If only he hadn't showed me Rose with no face. The least he could have done was let me know what it meant. Now older, I'd wondered if he'd existed at all. Maybe I'd conjured him up because there was no one else to talk to. Funny, I had always believed that the ghost of Floyd Wilkes was responsible for my ability to sense things about people and places that others couldn't. Maybe it was me that had drawn him and not the other way around. I recalled what Granny Lee had said about people and how everyone was born with some kind of gift. Some, she said, could sing like nightingales while others could carve faces out of the river rock. She claimed that all good gifts were from God, and that He'd given a precious few a light that shined from within that had the power to attract even the dead folks whose souls wandered the earth because of unfinished business. Perhaps I was a carrier of this light, but why me? Maybe Floyd Wilkes' ghost had needed a voice and I was it. I'd suddenly felt within me a quiet respect for myself even though I didn't fully understand what or who I was. Granny Lee had always warned me not to question God and why He did certain things, so I decided it best to accept myself. What else could I do? But I couldn't help but wonder why Floyd Wilkes' ghost couldn't rest but chose instead wander the earth restlessly. What did he want of me? Grandma Haley claimed that Mama never got over Floyd Wilkes' death and refused to accept it. Maybe her grief had kept his spirit from going to the light. A feeling of lethargy had settled on both my mind and body. As I stepped over to the side of the road and parted the bare branches, my legs felt tired and heavy. Walking over to the Play

Place, I stepped up on the boulder. Studying the Cumberland River, I listened to the roar of the white capped shoals washing over rocks. How good it was to see the river deep and running fresh! The blizzard as well as the light winter snows that followed had been good for the river. I thought suddenly of Rose and her need to get rid of her unborn baby that wasn't real to her yet. Maybe it would never be real to her. Maybe she purposely chose to make it unreal just as she'd always chosen to live in a fairytale world where people have only to wish hard for something for it to come true. When Rose and I were children, Rebekah Ann often read to us from a big book of fairytales. I'd enjoyed Hansel and Gretel while Rose preferred love stories like Snow White and the Seven Dwarfs and Sleeping Beauty. She was dazzled by the thought of a prince saving her from the poverty and the coalmine. She talked endlessly of how in the end the prince rode away happily away with the princess on a white horse. She had likened the Asher house to a castle and Bart to the prince who would one day sweep her up and take her far away from it all. Mama had truly loved Little Brock Asher, and it wasn't for the Asher money. The thought came to me as quickly as a blink of an eye. I recalled her voice and how gentle and loving it sounded when describing a childhood spent with an affectionate Little Brock Asher. The two of them had formed a true bond of mutual love that I suspected still existed. And, had it not been for the interference of Big Brock Asher, the two of them might have gotten married and stayed together for the rest of their lives. Rose, on the other hand, hadn't formed that kind of loving bond with Bart. A few stolen days playing across a dividing fence did not constitute the kind of bond Mama and Little Brock had.

23 VISIONS OF DEATH

As I left the Play Place, I noticed that the sky had darkened a little more. Feeling strangely defeated I thought, I will go back to the lodge now -- back to the people I love but cannot help. Back to Daddy who remains sick. Rose will leave. I can feel her absence already. Mama will eventually leave too. I know that as sure as I feel wind blowing cold on my face. Daddy might survive bodily, but his spirit will die a slow, painful death. There isn't a thing I can do about that or anything else. I may have the gift of attracting the dead, but I've held no sway with the living.

As soon as I entered the yard I saw Uncle Larkin's fancy green Ford parked near the front porch. He was there to help Mama walk Daddy. He should have been on his way back home according to his original plans, but Mama's pleading had changed that. Once inside the house, I heard Mama, Daddy, and Uncle Larkin talking in the kitchen. Mama's voice sounded high and sickly sweet, while Daddy's was barely audible. Uncle Larkin's voice was fine and cultured and sounded almost exactly like that of Harvey James.

"Now you put your feet on the floor, Ralph," Mama gently ordered Daddy.

"I've got him, Heddy," Uncle Larkin said assuredly.

In our bedroom Rose had packed her clothes in three brown paper bags. The red shawl Granny Lee had made her for Christmas was laid out on the bed along with the matching gloves and hat.

Flopping down on the bed I asked Rose, "So you're leavin' tonight?"

Rose nodded and threw the hand mirror Grandma Haley had given her as a Christmas gift one year inside one of the paper bags. "No use puttin' it off. I ain't gonna get no smaller. Pretty soon I'll be as big as a house and Daddy will start askin' questions. Junie Mae, he can't know about the baby in the shape he's in. I'll tell him when he can stand it."

"I'll miss you," my voice quivered.

Rising from the bed, she changed the subject. "Well, you missed the excitement."

"The excitement?" I puzzled.

"Right after you stomped outside, Uncle Harlan Ray came and told Daddy that the miners were holding an emergency meetin' with the United Mineworkers of America. I guess they finally got enough men to get in the union. I couldn't hear it all, but from what I could make out, a bunch of the miners got mad because the new men Asher hired have been trying to pick fights with the miners that's worked there for years. I reckon the miners are fed up with the thugs and want protection. I know Daddy's itchin' to get well and get back into it all, now that they got their majority."

"What's Mama sayin'?" I asked.

Shrugging, Rose said, "I don't know. She's too busy moonin' over Uncle Larkin."

I thought of the impact a union would have on Daddy's health. No wonder he was up trying to walk. The prospect of going back to work and earning better wages had given him a fresh new purpose. But he didn't know that all wasn't well with Mama, I thought sadly. "Poor Daddy," I said, "He thinks everything is gonna work out. He's got no idea what Mama's cookin' up."

Rose shook her head in despair and said, "I went to tell him I was goin' back to Granny Lee's so I could help Marie with the babies. I know it's a lie but I had to make up some reason for leavin'. Junie Mae, all his fingernails have slipped off and he's lost almost all his hair from the fever. He looked so much like an old man that I could hardly stand to look at him!"

I nodded and said I had seen it, too -- the poor hands and the thin patches of hair that had once been thick and shiny. "I'll never leave Daddy," I said fiercely.

"Is that what you think I'm doin'?" Rose's face twisted in a look of anger.

"I never said that," I countered.

Shaking her head in frustration she admitted, "I might have made some bad mistakes, but I'll never stop lovin' and tryin' to protect Daddy. I never meant to hurt him, Junie Mae. He'd be the last person I'd hurt."

"I know," I cried. Walking over to her I threw my arms around her neck and held her tightly. "I don't want you to leave," I said in a desperate, muffled voice. Sounds of voices in the kitchen interrupted our intimate parting. Rose stiffened and then turned toward the bedroom door. "It's Marie. She's come for me, I guess. Can you grab a bag?" she asked, wiping a tear off her cheek.

I nodded, reaching for a bag. Once in the kitchen, Marie looked distressed. Beside her stood a fidgety Brenda Sue who tugged continuously at her mama's coattail. Both mother and daughter were dressed in their heaviest clothes as the weather had turned a little colder with the onset of the evening. A strange chill from something besides the cold made me put the bag on the floor and hug myself. Daddy sat behind the table in the living room chair looking pale and winded from the short walk. Uncle Larkin sat adjacent to Daddy while Mama stood in front of the sink looking expectant. Marie addressed Uncle Larkin, "Larkin, Rhodie called and said your daughter is in a bad way. It's somethin' to do with her little tummy, and she's had a fever since last night."

Uncle Larkin smiled genuinely and said, "I talked to Rhodie last night on the telephone and she told me. You see, Izzy does this all the time. If I'm gone for over a week she starts missing me and gets a tummy ache. I'll call her as soon as I get to Ma's," he added without concern.

Marie still looked uncomfortable and said, "I don't know, Larkin. Rhodie sounded purty worried when she called. She said to find you and get you on the telephone as soon as possible."

"You know how youngins are," Mama interjected. "When Rose was little she'd get sick every time her Daddy had to work a double shift. She'd cry and whimper and wouldn't sleep a wink until he said goodnight to her. Do you remember that, Rose?" Mama asked sweetly.

Rose said nothing and her face remained purposely impassive. Daddy, on the other hand, looked distressed and said in a pained voice, "Larkin, you'd probably better call."

"Don't you all worry. I know my little girl. She's spoiled and just missing me. If I thought she was truly ill I'd leave right now. You tell my wife I will call her later, Marie. Would you do that?"

Marie nodded, but her face still looked distressed and uncertain.

After Marie and Rose left I settled in my room watching out the window as night faded in. Something was terribly wrong with Uncle Larkin's little girl; I knew it and had to tell him. Closing my eyes, I saw a flash of light and then came a vision of a little girl with long black braids lying in a four-poster bed covered by a bright pink blanket. Holding her stomach and writhing in pain, she begged, "I want Daddy." I had to tell Uncle Larkin. Please, God -- let him believe me, I silently prayed. Rising from the bed I walked into the kitchen where Mama and Uncle Larkin sat talking over coffee. I'd noticed that Daddy was already in bed. I knew she'd given him his sleeping draught and that he was out cold for the night. "Uncle Larkin," I called in a soft voice.

Looking up with a startle, he answered, "Yes, Junie Mae."

"Your little girl is real sick. You have to start for home as quick as you can."

Uncle Larkin looked stunned and said nothing,

"For pity's sakes, Junie Mae -- what in the world would you know about it? You hush that nonsense!" Mama scolded harshly.

"This don't concern you none, Mama," I said hurriedly. Flashing my eyes on Uncle Larkin I said, "I can sometimes see things other people can't. Granny Lee says it's a gift I have. A while ago I seen your little girl lyin' in a big bed with four posts, and she was covered up in a bright pink blanket. She's bad off, Uncle Larkin, and she's beggin' for you to come."

Uncle Larkin's handsome face paled. Studying my eyes critically he finally said, "I believe you, Junie Mae. I'll be on my way, Heddy. I've got to make sure she's alright. I'll write you. Please give my love to my brother." His tone sounded urgent. "Thank you, Junie Mae," he said before going out the kitchen door.

Looking stunned Mama turned an angry face on me and lashed out. "What in the name of God did you do that for?"

"It wadn't no lie, Mama. The little girl is sick. I saw it!"

Shaking her head in amazement Mama said in an incredulous voice, "You're crazier than your sister. You scared that man to death and for nothin'. Why did you send him out of here, Junie Mae? Was it out of spite? He was good for your Daddy. He got better after seein' Larkin."

"I had to tell him, Mama," I pleaded. "I had to let him know how sick his daughter is."

"You and Rose concocted this up didn't you?" she accused. "This whole thing's got Rose wrote all over it. She just had to take one more swing at me before she left."

Shaking my head in fear, I made a move to turn and leave the room when she grabbed hold of my arm and jerked so hard I thought my shoulder had pulled out of the socket. Wincing in pain, I cried, "Let go of me, Mama!" Mama's eyes blazed as she spoke through her clenched white teeth, "Your Uncle was goin' to talk to Daddy tomorrow about movin' to Indianapolis, but you and your sister ruined that! Your Daddy will die if he gets well enough to go back in that mine. You and Rose just put the first nail in his coffin," she hissed, jerking my arm harder. Before I could protest the door of the cabinet near the stove flew open and hit the wall with a bang, followed by the hard slam of my bedroom door. Stunned, Mama let go of my arm and whispered, "What in the world caused that?"

"Floyd Wilkes' ghost," I whispered back, eyeing her almost smugly. "He's here and he sees what you're doin'."

Mama's eyes grew big in fright and her hands visibly shook as she pushed a strand of hair back from her face. "How could you?" she asked shaking her head in disgust. "What on earth has happened to you, Junie Mae? You've lost your mind!"

"I ain't lost nothin', Mama. I know what you're tryin' to do with Uncle Larkin. He didn't have no plans to talk to Daddy at all about Indianapolis. Shame on you! He's Daddy's brother."

Her eyes suddenly changed and lost all their fire. She slumped into the chair like an old woman, and when she spoke she sounded more like a small child. "Why would you bring up Floyd Wilkes? Why would you use him to hurt me just because you believe a lie about me and your Uncle Larkin?"

"You should have let Uncle Larkin go home when he wanted to, Mama," I said, ignoring her question about Floyd Wilkes. But she wouldn't let it go.

"You had to dig real deep to pull out somethin' like this, didn't you? It's hard to face that my own daughters hate me so much that they would dredge up my dead brother just to hurt me," she said in a pathetic tone.

"Floyd Wilkes wants you to be happy, Mama. His spirit won't rest until you know this," I whispered. "Granny Lee told me how spirits are sometimes restless because they didn't get to do or say somethin' while they was alive."

Mama wasn't listening. She was too angry to listen.

"Granny Lee, Granny Lee," she mocked. "I'm sick to death of her feedin' you and Rose a bunch of lies. No wonder you two think and act like you do; it's her influence! Ghosts and visions and babies that's God-sent! The woman belongs in a mental asylum!"

"Uncle Larkin won't leave his family for you, Mama. No matter how bad you wish he would. You can't steal another woman's life. I might not know much about grown-up things, but I know that!"

Springing up from the chair, Mama's eyes had grown even stormier. Her voice shook, "You don't know nothin', Junie Mae. You and Rose think you got it all figured out. You think just 'cause your Uncle Larkin's got money and an education that he wouldn't have a woman like me. Well, I got a little news for you both. He's just a man, and there's not a speck of difference in any of 'em when it comes to a pretty woman. You're old enough to know the truth about men," she spat, "and you might as well learn it early. The only thing keepin' Larkin from me is Daddy. But that would change real quick if I wanted it to. He wouldn't be able to resist me if I come on to him. Every man wants what he's not supposed to have; it's how they're built. I might be his brother's wife, but I could make him forget about that. It's the animal in him. When it comes to a woman, a man is like a ram in rut. I know!"

Who was this woman? I wondered. Where had my Mama gone? Where was the woman who prayed to God for forgiveness in church and scrubbed the floors until not a speck of dirt could be seen anywhere? What had happened to the Mama who lectured her daughters on stealing and how to do so was a great sin against God? I yearned for the Mama who laughed like a little girl when Daddy tickled her feet in the heat of the summer, and the Mama who made her daughters pretty clothes from scrap cloth given to her by others. Maybe it was the cave-in that had brought about the drastic change in her.

I conveyed my thoughts aloud, "What happened to you, Mama? I don't know you now. I've looked for you but most of you is gone. No matter what you did or said to Rose I always made up excuses for you. I can't take up for you no more."

"I never asked you to take up for me, Junie Mae. Let me tell you somethin', little girl – you're gonna find out that life ain't no bowl of honey," she promised. "All I got to look forward to is your Daddy goin' back to the mine and killin' himself. What will I have then, Junie Mae? Have you and Rose thought of that? What have I got now? I've been with your Daddy for seventeen years and I still live in somebody else's house. I don't have plumbin' or electricity or any of the things that women in the city have got. Your Daddy can't see that we are stuck in the same place that we've always been and always will be if we keep livin' here! "

Sighing in disgust she went on, "It don't take nothin' to satisfy your Daddy. He's always been like that. Just put a plate of food in front of him and he's good with the world. Give him an old piece of wood and he'll whittle on it for hours." Pointing her finger in my face she said, "Do you know that before he got sick he hardly said a word to me? Ever since your sister left this house he's treated Buster better than he's treated me. I need more than this."

24 A DEATH IN THE FAMILY

Feeling strangely old, I decided then that I was tired of life on Wilder Creek. I also felt drained and was sick of Mama, the cold weather, and the uncles' endless talk of the coalmine. Not even loving thoughts of Amity Smith could eradicate the present situation. And no matter how long he held my hand, he had to let go sometime. I'd felt suddenly alone in my thoughts and wasn't sure who I was or what I was supposed to do anymore. For the first time in my life a grey kind of depression had settled upon me that I couldn't shake. That night I'd slept fitfully. Frightful images loomed inside a hollow darkness. When I awoke the next morning I was aware of the pitter patter of rain on the tin roof of the lodge. Little teardrops trickled down the windowpane, and I could hear voices in the kitchen. Sitting up in bed, I strained my ears and recognized the sound of Marie's frantic voice. Inside my chest my heart squeezed with fear. Throwing the covers aside I got out of bed and hurried into the kitchen. There in front of the kitchen door stood a sobbing Marie dressed in a man's heavy green corduroy coat and men's pants that were too long for her short stature. Her little eyes were red from crying and her face was shiny from the raindrops. "What's wrong?" I asked in alarm.

Marie glanced sadly at Mama before whispering "Uncle Larkin's little girl died last night."

I gasped, then finally managed, "Did Uncle Larkin make it to see her before, before she died?"

Marie shook her head sadly and said, "She died not long after he left your all's house. Rhodie's sister told Ma that Rhodie's in shock and ain't spoke one word since the little girl died."

"What killed her?" Mama asked

"Rhodie's sister said that her little appendix burst right there in the hospital," Marie answered, her emotions raw.

"Poor Larkin," Mama said, more to herself than anyone else. "I'll have to tell Ralph. He'll be heartbroken."

Marie choked, "Ma's leaving by bus in the mornin'. She's goin' to Indianapolis to help with the funeral arrangements and to be of whatever comfort she can to Larkin and Rhodie."

Mama's head rose in rapt attention. "Martha's going by herself?"

Marie nodded. "I can't go. Rebekah Ann had some female surgery the other day and ain't able to keep the youngins, and I shore wouldn't trust Uncle Hiram with all three that long. Rose ain't' been feelin' well and I doubt she could do much with 'em even with Uncle Hiram's help."

Mama's dark eyes darted in thought, and I could already tell what she was thinking. "Ralph's a lot better and can walk from his room to the kitchen and back with his cane. I'll talk to him and if he says it's all right I'll go with your Mama. I feel so bad for Larkin and his wife. Maybe I can be of some help."

Marie's little eyes widened skeptically. "Gee, Heddy -- I don't know if you should leave Ralph. He's still purty weak. Mama can get by on her own -- you know, with her havin' God on her side and all," she muttered,

But Mama paid no attention and went with her plan. "Rose and Junie Mae can fix his meals and give him his medicine, and Harlan Ray and Harvey James will see to it that he walks every day."

Marie finally said, "Whatever you think is best, Heddy. I'll tell Ma you want to go if it's ok with Ralph."

After Marie left Mama took on a positively radiant appearance. When thinking about that day even now fresh anger boils up within me. How could Mama have taken advantage of little Amy Isabella's death just to get out of Harlan County and closer to Uncle Larkin Lee? After Marie left, I hurried in getting dressed for school so I could get out of the house. With haste I gathered things for my lunch box. In her bedroom I heard Mama's voice above Daddy's weak one. She was telling Daddy that going with Granny Lee to Indianapolis was the least she could do after Larkin had spent the two extra days helping him with his walks and spending time with him. Finding a few vanilla wafers and a soft apple, I quickly wrapped them in foil and threw them in the lunch box. I was walking out the door when Mama called out to me. Turning around I saw her flushed face and shining eyes. She said, "Daddy wants me to go with your Granny Lee. He won't have it no other way, so this means Rose will have to come home and help you with him until I get back."

I nodded and turned back toward the door. Mama said, "I know what you're thinkin' and it's wrong. Granny Lee don't need to make that trip alone -- even your Daddy agrees with me on that."

"You should have let Uncle Larkin go home to his little girl, Mama. I hope he don't blame you for beggin' him to stay."

Mama's happy face turned suddenly stormy. "You don't know Larkin. He's more apt to blame hisself than anyone else," Mama snapped irritably.

Seething inside, I wondered how Mama could know a man she'd only spent a few days with. How could she presume to understand how he might be feeling after losing something as precious as his little girl? Before I could say anything else, a slight knock on the screen door made me turn. To my surprise Violet Elizabeth was standing there in her rain jacket and boots smiling and showing her dimples. She said, "We didn't want you walkin' in the rain. Amity's out there with the truck running. Hello, Mrs. Lee," she greeted Mama, and then asked "I hope it's ok that Junie Mae rides with us?"

Waving her hand in a carefree manner, Mama said, "It was thoughtful of you and your brother to think of Junie Mae in this rainy weather."

Once outside, the rain pelted down in the grey of the morning. "I want some sun," I yelled, hovering close to Violet Elizabeth.

"Me too," she giggled, while slipping her arm around my shoulder. Just seeing her and Amity had lightened my mood considerably. When piling in beside Amity I had done something that I'd never done before. I'd hugged him quickly, then made room in the seat for Violet. I could tell by his genuine look of surprise that a hug was the last thing he'd expected from me. Smiling from ear to ear he squeezed my hand then said, "If I knew coming to your door to pick you up would get me a hug I would have done it long ago." The three of us laughed in unison as he steered the truck out of the muddy driveway. "Hope we don't get her stuck," Amity chuckled. As the rain turned to a drizzle on the windshield, I told Amity and Violet Elizabeth about the sad death of Uncle Larkin's little girl and that Mama planned to accompany Granny Lee to Indianapolis for the wake.

In a heartfelt tone Violet Elizabeth said, "I'm so sorry, Junie Mae. That's awful. Your Daddy must be a lot better or else your mother wouldn't be making that trip, huh?"

"Yeah -- he's some better, but I have to stay home with him while she's gone. That means I'll have to miss school."

Violet Elizabeth promised she'd get my homework for me so I wouldn't miss anything. "We'll bring it to you every evening if it's ok with your Daddy."

Amity said, "It won't be any trouble for us, so don't say nothin'."

Smiling happily, I nodded while thinking that if it wasn't for the two of them I would have felt lost. Being with the two of them seemed to put my life into focus and had given me a glimpse of what happiness and friendship really were. Even now, I have a warm place in my heart for my beloved friends. Granny Lee once said that God gives us not what we want but what we need. She'd explained how people often wanted things without really knowing if what they desire will serve them well in the long run. She said, "God knows what a person should have. Material things often tarnish on a shelf, but needed things replenish the soul."

When lunchtime came Amity, Violet, and I shared a tall thermos of hot vegetable soup and homemade corn cakes from the Smith kitchen for lunch. The rain had stopped and the air was tolerable enough for us to eat in the truck. Amity drove around back of the school near the ball field. The memory of that day comes back as clear as if it happened yesterday. I can vividly recall what Amity Smith wore: a heavy light brown coat with matching khaki pants. His sandy hair blended in nicely with his clothing, and when he smiled his dimples melted me. The feeling of safety and love seemed to surround me like a warm cocoon. Inside I had felt as light as a feather. After we finished eating, Amity and me took a walk down by the fence overlooking the empty baseball field. Violet Elizabeth had walked back to the school building, purposely leaving us alone. Propping himself up on the fence, he gazed down at the dead grass and the mud. For a few minutes he was thoughtful. Every so often I sneaked a shy peek at his handsome profile as a little wind ruffled the front of his hair. Finally, he spoke. "Sometimes I wish we was older, Junie Mae. If we was we could get married and start a family." He paused for a few seconds, then added, "But I know we're too young. I know people our ages or even younger who got married and now they can barely afford to live and feed their families." Turning to me he said in a serious tone, "I'm willin' to wait until we're old enough to make a good livin'."

Inside my chest my heart pounded with both uncertainty and excitement. Amity must have sensed these things because he took my hand in his and held it very gently. "I'm not tryin' to scare you, Junie Mae. We got all kinds of time to get to know each other." Pausing again as if searching for something to say, he finally spoke: "I wish I was some fancy poet so I could come up with just the right words to say what I mean, but I'm not. I'm just a plain old country boy who only reads when he has to."

Smiling, I said honestly, "All I've ever dreamed about is bein' a teacher someday. There wadn't no marriage plans in that dream."

Amity laughed genuinely, finally saying, "Junie Mae, I never expected you to answer any other way. Your honesty is the thing I like best about you."

What had I said? Blushing, I suddenly realized that what I said had sounded wrong.

"Amity, I meant that since you come along, I – well, I've started to think more about you than anybody else, sometimes."

Amity said, "I know what you meant, Junie Mae. You're a real smart girl, and I want you to do what you want to. I just hope you'll keep me in your life someplace."

Looking up into his pretty blue eyes I started to fall apart inside. I'd wanted to be nothing but honest with him in every way -- not like Mama who'd lied to Daddy from the start. Like Daddy, Amity was so good and deserved the best I had. I thought of all the differences in our family and the Smith's, and it made me feel somehow unworthy. Mama's words continued to haunt me as to what a boy like Amity Smith would want with a poor girl whose family had nothing to speak of. In essence she'd likened Amity and me to her and Little Brock Asher and believed that any relationship we might have was doomed to fail because of our dissimilar backgrounds. But what Amity lacked in sophistication he somehow made up for in manners. Still, my secret doubts came to light and spewed out of my mouth in fragments. Unable to express myself adequately, thanks to my mother's rule of keeping it all in, I felt ashamed. "My family's poor, Amity, and there's things goin' on with Mama and Rose that ain't right, and I feel real helpless. I-I- feel lost sometimes, and I'm different in so many ways from other people." My words trailed off but their echo seemed to linger in the uncomfortable silence between us. Finally turning to me, Amity, with a determined look on his handsome face, said, "Look, Junie Mae, I don't know what you're gettin' at but I can tell you that it's you and not your family that draws my interest. Nobody's family is perfect, and surely not mine. And it might not look like it but in the big city, folks would call our family poor. We ain't rich, Junie Mae -- not by a long stretch. We work hard, though, just like your Daddy works hard, so how are we that different -- you and me?"

Without warning, tears bleared my eyes in spite of my effort to keep them inside, and then like a dam that gave way, they cascaded down my cheek and I sobbed loudly. Without a word, Amity gently took me in his arms. Burying his face in my hair I felt his warm lips near my ear, whispering words of endearments. Even though the wind had picked up and turned colder and the sky drizzled once more, I felt warm and happy. Once back in the truck, Amity said, "I'll never give up on you, Junie Mae. I knowed from the start that you was the only one for me. That day I seen them boys from the camp jumpin' on you and your sister I never was so mad in my life. I could have hurt them really bad for what they done to you all."

Feeling stronger I said, without much difficulty, "Amity, bein' with you makes me forget the lodge and all the sickness. I'm glad you ain't givin' up on me."

Eyeing the heart-shaped locket around my neck, he said, "You wearin' that locket tells me all I need to know, Junie Mae. I don't need no words."

I'd decided after that rainy winter day in front of the ball field that I might be in love with Amity Smith. I wasn't exactly sure what love between a man and woman was supposed to feel like but I knew whatever I felt for him was strong. I'd admitted that day that I needed him, but did that constitute love? I thought of Mama and how losing Little Brock Asher - the love of her life - had destroyed her. Rose was destroyed, too, if you considered that the only things she'd gotten from Bart Asher were a broken heart and an unwanted pregnancy. I'd vowed that day that I would never allow any man to destroy my heart, be it Amity Smith or any other man. Mama and Rose had taught me valuable lessons about love and how loving too much caused people to go away. Hadn't Mama loved Floyd Wilkes too much? And look what Uncle Larkin had gotten for having loved Amy Isabella too much. I thought suddenly of Little Brock Asher and pictured him staggering drunkenly around the creek with a whiskey bottle in his hand. Was he happy? I recalled the dull look in his eyes and how he'd mistaken Rose for Mama. I had felt his loss that day and had known that even with all his money he was nothing more than broken man. In spite of my vow to love cautiously, I admitted that Amity Smith made me happy. I'd almost felt guilty considering that there was so much sorrow back at the lodge. I was sure in the knowledge that Amity truly cared for me just as I cared for him. I was also positive that my feelings for him had little or nothing to do with what his family had, for even if he'd been poor and attentive I would have still cared just as much for him. I told myself that I wasn't like either Rose or Mama and that I was like Daddy and Granny Lee who loved honestly. I'd also vowed to myself never to be dishonest like Mama or materialistic like Rose, because I'd learned that wanting too much only leads to sorrow and unhappiness.

25 INTRODUCTION OF A UNION

After school Amity had driven me back to the lodge. I recall the growing dread inside me as I edged closer to the front door. Somehow I knew Mama would be packing up her suitcase and running about the house like a cat after a mouse. The sight of Uncle Hiram's battered old truck in the backyard told me that Rose was home and Granny Lee was probably with her. Opening the front door I felt the typical rush of hot air caused by the heavily stoked fireplace in the living room and the heat radiating off the kitchen woodstove. To my surprise, Daddy was dressed in his everyday clothes and not his usual pajamas and was sitting in his favorite chair in the corner of the living room. Searching his face, I thought it looked fuller and healthier than it had in months. "Hello June-bug," he said, grinning. I also noticed that his voice sounded a lot stronger than it had weeks before. Rushing over to Daddy, I hugged him tight and said, "I guess Mama's going to Indianapolis with Granny Lee."

"Maw needs her worse than I do right now. Your sister's in here somewhere." His eyes looked soulfully into mine as he said, "I won't be alone as long as I got my girls here with me."

"You ain't alone, Daddy. We'll take good care of you -- don't worry."

Daddy said, "Harlan Ray was here a little while ago. He told me that we got our union in last night. It won't be no time before they start tryin' to negotiate some kind of workable contract out of Asher on our behalf."

"I'm glad for you all, Daddy, but what if the union decides to strike?"

Daddy sighed tiredly and said, "That might be somethin' we'll do if Asher don't meet the terms of the contract. Sometimes people's gotta fight for what they want, and that's the plain truth of it, honey."

Daddy still appeared weak but I knew he was coming back physically, and it wouldn't be long before he'd be down at the mines with the others. I dreaded the thought. I could hear Granny Lee talking in the kitchen. Her voice was more of a sob. "I hope Rhodie snaps out of it soon. Let's pray that God gives her the strength she needs to face this awful ordeal. I talked to poor Larkin this mornin' and you could hear the grief in his voice."

Daddy's eyes were suddenly downcast and once again he favored a tired old man. He said of Uncle Larkin, "I wished he'd've gone home to that sick youngin instead of stayin' here with me. "

"It wadn't your fault, Daddy. You didn't ask him to stay here. He did it because he wanted to," I reasoned, while trying not to think of Mama's influence on his decision to stay.

Before he could speak Mama appeared, saying, "That's right, Ralph. You had nothin' to do with it. If he'd've knowed how sick that child was he would have left, but he didn't. You got nothin' to feel guilty over."

After Granny Lee and Uncle Hiram left, Mama gave me and Rose a list of things we needed to do in the house and for Daddy while she was gone. She'd stood in the kitchen and gone over the list meticulously. Beside me in a chair Rose sat looking tired and a little heavier around her middle. Even in the bulky green sweater I could see the growing bump and it depressed me, but probably not half as much as it weighed on her. Mama's words seemed to blend in with the roar of the fire and the sound of Daddy's radio program in the living room.

Later in our bedroom I'd talked endlessly about Amity and our conversation at the ball field that noonday. Rose seemed nervous and distracted, nodding absently even when I'd finished talking. It was doubtful she'd heard a word I'd said.

"I wrote Bart a letter and told him about the baby," she said nervously, then added, "Marie helped me on it, and even addressed it and sent it to his college dorm. I don't know how she got the address. She probably asked somebody in the post office..." Her voice trailed off.

Startled, I asked her when she'd decided to tell him. For a long time she lay there on the bed saying nothing. Finally in a meek voice that was not hers she replied, "Marie made me do it. She said if I didn't tell him she would. I guess all I can do now is wait to see what he says."

Speechless, I sat listening to Daddy's radio program. It had been a long time since Daddy had listened to the radio. For some reason he always turned the volume way up. I plainly heard a man praising the delicious taste of a steaming cup of JFG coffee on a cold frosty morning. Finally, I asked Rose if she loved Bart Asher. Up went her head and her strange eyes narrowed in agitation. "That's a stupid question, Junie Mae," she spat.

"What did he do to make you love him?" I asked sincerely.

The question seemed to rattle her. "What do you mean askin' a question like that? He's Bart Asher. Every girl I know would give her eye teeth to get close to him." Licking her lips nervously she went on, "I've wanted him since I was a little girl."

"I care for Amity Smith because I know I can count on him. He gave me this locket to let me know that he's always thinkin' about me and he's always talkin' about how we'll eventually marry and start a family. I feel safe with Amity and I trust him because he's always lookin' out for me."

Rose laughed sarcastically and said, "You think you know all about love since that Smith boy paid a little attention to you. Well, Junie Mae, let me whisper you a little secret -- there's more to love than that. Sometimes it can be hard."

Shaking my head in disagreement I said, "I don't think love ought to be so hard. If two people care about each other in the same way then it ought to be easy."

"Leave me alone," she moaned, then seethed, "I didn't want to come back here at all! If that little girl hadn't died I'd still be at Granny Lee's. I hate it here! I've got Mama lookin' at me like I'm a plank in the floor, and poor Daddy -- all he can think of is gettin' back to that mine. You look down on me, too; I can see it every time you look at me."

"That ain't true," I cried. "I'm just trying to understand you is all. I guess me and you think pretty different on things." Walking over to the vanity table which was no more than a tarnished mirror on the wall above a little crude dresser Daddy had made out of wood scraps, I said "I don't like Mama goin' on that trip. I'm thinkin' she might not come back."

Watching Rose's face in the mirror, I saw her anger quickly turn to surprise. She said, "I must be losin' my power to predict what Mama does. I hadn't thought of that, but you're right -- she might not come back. God, what would Daddy do if she decided to stay?"

"I don't know," I answered, feeling distracted and frightened by the thought of Mama abandoning Daddy. Suddenly I could no longer hear the radio and knew Mama had switched it off and was helping Daddy perform his daily walk. I imagined that the uncles were at a union meeting discussing possible ways to get Asher to pay the miners better wages.

"She surely wouldn't be cruel enough to leave Daddy and him so sick," Rose said half-heartedly.

Before I could reply, I heard the opening of the kitchen door and then an unfamiliar voice.

"Who's here?" Rose asked.

"I don't know," I answered. Straining my ears I heard a woman's voice but couldn't make out all she was saying. Rising from the chair, I walked into the living room and peeped around the kitchen door. My mouth dropped open at the sight of Miss Joelyn Asher standing in the doorway holding a basket of what looked like bread and other food stuffs. Daddy was nowhere in sight and I assumed Mama had helped him to bed so he could rest after his walk. Stepping back and leaning against the wall, I stood waiting to hear what they would say to each other. Rose appeared in the doorway, took one look in the kitchen, and then paled, looking as if she might faint.

Moving quickly to stand beside me she whispered, "Why is she here? She couldn't know about the baby already. The letter to Bart was just sent out yesterday."

"Shh," I cautioned, straining my ears to listen to what she Miss Joelyn was saying.

"I've been concerned about Ralph and thought about coming to see him sooner, but with things being the way they are at the mine I thought it would be awkward."

"Ain't things more awkward than ever now with the union coming in?" Mama asked in a matter-of-fact tone.

"I guess it is, Heddy, but I didn't come here to talk about the mine. I came here out of concern for you and Ralph. Would you take this basket of food?" she asked, nervously, then added, "I'm gonna have a seat at your table if you don't mind."

Mama said, "Sit anywhere you want to, Jo. It's your house."

Miss Joelyn laughed uncomfortably and said, "It ain't my house, Heddy. You pay the rent here so it's yours." In a lower voice she added, "Heddy, you might not believe this but I've come in peace. How is Ralph? I heard he's been bad."

"He almost died on us," Mama said. "The pneumonia's done damage to his lungs – well, that and the coal dust. But he'll go right back to the mine when he's better -- that is if he still has a job."

"I don't have a lot of say about what goes on down at No. 5 mine. Brock and his father run the business –well, lately my father-in-law has made most of the decisions. Oh, Heddy," she sighed, and then in a defeated tone said, "The mine accident has all but destroyed my husband. Nobody knows how hard it's preyed on his mind. I don't have a soul to talk to about it, except Mama. Since the cave-in most of the women in the camp avoid me like I had something to do with it."

"I don't think the women blame you, Jo," Mama said in a flat, unfeeling tone.

"They do, Heddy. They're mad and hurt and I can't say that I blame them for hating our whole family. I know how I felt when my Daddy was killed because of the coal. You just don't get over something like that -- at least I never did."

"But your family fared way better than the widows in the camp. At least the mine owner was merciful and gave you all a decent settlement," Mama was quick to inform her.

"You're right, Heddy; the owner was kind, but the money we got couldn't replace Daddy."

"Then you oughta know how the widows feel. It didn't help none when Little Brock throwed them out of their houses only a few months after they lost their husbands."

"It's business, Heddy, and I didn't have nothing to do with them losing their homes. Brock told me that he had no choice but to hire replacements for the men lost. I know it might seem cold to you. . ." Her voice trailed off.

"And it don't seem cold to you?" Mama's tone sounded sarcastic

"Now, Heddy, over the years I've tried my best to help the families. Brock has been generous too, paying some of the miners and their families' medical bills and vehicle repairs. It seems people forgot." Her voice was filled with hurt and dejection

"They'd rather have better wages than gifts and handouts, Jo. I know I would. People like to be able to make their own way."

In listening to Mama I suddenly realized that there was a kind of practical truth to what she was saying. I glanced at Rose who stood biting her nails and looking as if she might throw up at any moment.

Miss Joelyn remained quiet for a few seconds before saying, "Money don't always guarantee happiness, Heddy."

"No, but money puts a roof over your head, and it guarantees that there'll be food in the pot."

"I know that, Heddy. I've not forgot what it was like to live in a coal camp. I have so many bad memories of rotted floors and big ole rats crawling in through the wide floor planks. I've been hungry, too; that's something nobody forgets. I know you've not forgot either, Heddy, and I've tried my best to share a little of what I have with you and yours."

I suddenly braced myself for what Mama would say to that. I could feel her anger just as sure as it was my own.

"A little is right!" Mama snapped. "We could have done with a little of that electricity you have up there but the electric line stopped at your door. The only light we get shines down from your house. Sometimes at night I can almost see how to get the wash off the line. If you and Little Brock want to help the miners then why not make the mine safer and pay the men what they deserve? Our families have as much right to electricity and plumbin' as anyone else in the world!"

"Oh, Heddy -- don't you think I don't know that! You know me. Your family lived right next to mine and we played together as children in that awful Daisy Camp. You know Brock, too, and if you remember anything about him it's that he's a good man." Miss Joelyn's voice pleaded desperately.

Mama said, "I knowed your husband when we were children. I don't know what he growed up like. All I know for sure is that his mine is just as unsafe as his daddy's was when it killed my Daddy. I know too that the widows of them dead miners are livin' from house to house because your husband and his Daddy are refusin' to settle with them."

Mama's words cut like daggers, but I sensed that she was holding back more anger than she was expressing. Miss Joelyn had only scratched the surface and I prayed she'd just turn around and leave. I knew Rose was hoping and praying for the same thing.

Miss Joelyn's voice pleaded, "Heddy, I've always thought you and me were friends. You've worked in my home for years without one complaint. You and me have gardened together and cold packed food -- I don't understand!"

Mama said, "I worked for what you gave me, Jo. It wadn't free -- none of it. You wadn't so free with money so I took what I could get in food and other things you throwed my way. You decided what I should have, just like you decided what the miners' families should have. Well, it's not just up to you or your husband or Big Brock to decide no more. The miners have taken a stand."

Miss Joelyn said, "I shouldn't have come here, I guess. It's plain to me that you have turned against me just like the women in the camp. But I'll tell you one thing, Heddy: the coal has stolen from me too -- first my Daddy and now my husband. I hardly see him these days and when I do he's usually dead drunk, being dragged up that hill by some miner or one of the stablemen. How can I tell him what to do with the mine when he's never home? Even if I did suggest something he'd just forget it! I tried to do right by the coalminers and their families. I done all I knew to do."

I knew Daddy was up as soon as I heard the shuffle and his cane bumping the floor. Rose's strange eyes had grown as big as saucers.

"Now, Heddy, I heard some of the things you said to Miss Joelyn and I don't think you're being fair. She don't run the mines and she's been mighty good to us. If I was you I'd apologize to her."

Mama remained stubbornly quiet, but Daddy spoke to Miss Joelyn in his most patient tone. "You'll have to overlook Heddy, Miss Joelyn; she's had it rough here takin' care of me these last few months." He went on to tell her about the death of Uncle Larkin's little girl. When he was through talking, Miss Joelyn seemed genuinely mortified and apologized for barging in on their grief. "I'm so sorry for you both, Ralph. Heddy, I hope you'll forgive me intruding like this."

After she left, I stood quietly looking at Rose, who remained pale and shaken by her visit. No longer wanting to eavesdrop, I walked over to the couch and sat down. Rose followed. In the kitchen, Daddy told Mama that he couldn't believe she had treated Miss Joelyn so badly. "That woman ain't done us no harm, Heddy."

"You don't need to be so upset over it, Ralph. Just go back to bed!"

"I don't understand you sometimes, Heddy."

"Yeah, well, it's been comin' for a long time. Please just go on back to bed and rest so I can finish packin' for this trip!"

For what seemed like an eternity, Rose and I sat silently in the living room listening to Mama bustling about, making a path from her bedroom to the kitchen. A part of me felt sorry for Miss Joelyn even though Mama had been right about the low wages Little Brock paid the miners. But I thought her concern for Daddy was genuine. Later in the bedroom I told Rose, "I think Miss Joelyn is a good person."

Sitting on her bed and hugging her middle, Rose whispered, "I wonder what she would've said if I went out there and told her that she was gonna be a grandma?" Rose said it like she had just thought of it.

Shrugging, I said, "She seems like the kind of person that would want to help."

Laughing sarcastically, Rose said, "For once Mama's right; Miss Joelyn comes up here with a basket of food and talks about how she's helped all of us out when all she's really done is give away things she don't need. She donates food to them poor people and their youngins in the camp, but if you think of it, what she spent probably wouldn't even make a dent in all they got."

Even though the word "condescending" was not in my vocabulary at the time, I knew what it felt like and what Rose was saying. I didn't agree, however, and told her so.

"Maybe Miss Joelyn is tryin' to make up for her husband and old Big Brock cheatin' the miners."

Rose's face became twisted and her words sounded spiteful, "She's rubbin' what she's got in all our faces, is all. Mama's always knowed it and that's why she hates her. She wouldn't help me with my baby. She'd never even admit that it belonged to her precious son."

I was a little taken aback concerning Rose's change of heart when it came to the Ashers. All her life she'd envied them and wanted to emulate Miss Joelyn by marrying Bart and living at Creekstone. Being deserted by Bart had made her angry and cruel.

"When will he get the letter you sent tellin' him about the baby?"

Shrugging her shoulders, she said, "I don't know, but you can bet he'll find me somehow when he gets it. He'll want to see me then," she added sarcastically.

26 INDIANAPOLIS

Mama left early the following morning so that she and Granny Lee would make the Greyhound bus in time. The house was left so meticulous that it appeared as if no one lived there. The kitchen table was bare and the floor swept clean. With Mama gone the rooms seemed void of life, as if she had taken its sprit with her. Sleepily, I gathered wood from the wood box behind the stove and stoked both the woodstove and the fireplace. Daddy got up a few minutes later and sat at the table with his cane propped up beside him. I made coffee, scrambled eggs, and fried bacon while Rose slept soundly in our room. Outside the window morning etched in gray and silent. Daddy greeted me warmly and took the cup of black coffee I handed to him. Before he drank it I gave him a spoonful of his cough syrup. After he took it he was seized with a coughing spell that caused him to lose his breath several times before it was over. I'd grown accustomed to Daddy's coughing spells, and I didn't need Floyd Wilkes' ghost to tell me that he would probably cough that way for the rest of his life.

"How cold is it out there, June Bug?" Daddy asked, staring out the window into the bleak morning.

"I don't know," I answered. "I'll step out the door and see."

"No, I'll check it out later. It looks pretty cold judging by the ice crystals on the weeds."

Daddy sat bent forward in the kitchen chair. I could tell from the pained expression on his face that his back hurt. It had been two months since he'd had a cigarette and I knew he wanted one badly. I knew he missed Mama, too. I could sense his loneliness. A part of me was always deeply connected to Daddy. It was as if I'd had some deep insight into his soul. On that morning I'd known that something preyed on his mind. While refilling his cup, my eyes met his dark soulful ones that reminded me so much of Granny Lee's. Without looking away he asked, "What's wrong with Rosie? Is she sick?"

I'd almost dropped the coffee pot when he'd asked about Rose. "Sick? No. Why would you think that?"

"She's been actin' peculiar since I left her with her Maw. She hardly says a word to me. Maybe she thinks I still hold that night against her. Do me a favor, June-bug -- you tell your sister that I love her and that what happened was an accident. Would you do that for me?"

Sitting the coffeepot back on the stove I said, "I'll tell her Daddy."

"I was looking at her the other day and I don't think she's well. Her face was as pale as chalk and it looked swollen. I noticed she's put on some weight too. I figure Maw's cooking is doin' that. You sure she ain't sick somewhere?"

"She's not sick nowhere, Daddy. I'd know if she was."

Daddy said, "Junie Mae, I hate that you have to miss school because of me."

"It's ok, Daddy. I'm not really missin' nothin'. Amity and Violet Smith said they would drop my homework by here every evening so I can keep up."

"Amity Smith? That's David and Anna Lee Smith's boy, ain't it?"

I nodded, placing the bacon slices on the plate. On cold mornings like this Mama kept the bacon in a tin on the porch.

"Ain't that Smith boy the one who stopped the Roberts boy from beatin' on you and Rose?"

"He's the one," I said proudly.

"Well, he's got some nice folks, I can tell you that. I've talked to Dave many a time when he sold Asher prop timber. His daddy's a teacher of some kind, ain't he?"

I told Daddy how Mr. Smith's daddy taught agriculture at the high school. I also told him that Amity and his sister Violet had brought a Christmas basket of goodies to the lodge while he was laid up with pneumonia.

"Well ain't that something," he said. I watched his eyes fall to the locket around my neck. "I been meanin' to ask you where that pretty heart-shaped locket come from. I figured it wadn't a gift from family 'cause it looks more like something a boy would give a girl he's stuck on."

Blushing, I admitted that Amity had given me the necklace.

"Does your Mama know about the Smith boy?" he asked.

"She knows, but she ain't warmed too much to the idea that we are goin' steady."

"She knows he's bringin' your lessons in the evening?"

"I told her," I said truthfully.

Shaking his head in disbelief, Daddy remarked, "I can't believe she's lettin' you see that boy without her sharp eye on you. But then you're trustworthy and have got a good head on your shoulders -- always did." Eyeing me critically Daddy went on, "You know, Junie Mae, you look a lot like your Grandma Haley since you've slimmed down. I just now noticed that. Shaking his head incredulously, he chuckled and said, "I guess I know how old Rip Van Winkle felt when he woke up after all them years of sleep. I feel like I've missed years. "

Handing Daddy his plate of food I said, "I'm glad you're better."

Picking up his fork and pointing in emphasis he said, "As sick as I've been, though, I found out somethin' about your mama through all this. I know now that she loves me. That woman's been through a lot. Since I've been laid up, she's waited on me hand and foot. She didn't have to do that with all the family steppin' in, especially Maw."

Inside my chest, my heart sank like a rock. Catching my breath, I looked over at Daddy and saw the most serene look of trust on his face. Blast Mama! She'd quit work to take care of him all right but only because I'd made her. Poor Daddy; he hadn't a clue that she wanted to move away from him. He would never believe that she flirted with his brother -- his own brother. How could anyone hurt a simple, kind man like Daddy? I wanted to cry but knew better. If I cried, Daddy would know that something was wrong.

Wanting desperately to change the subject, I asked about the mine and what the union was up to. At the mention of the No. 5 Mine his eyes lit up as bright as the Asher house after dark, "Harvey James and Harlan Ray are comin' this evening to give me the news on it all. I'm hopin' Asher will accept the terms of the union contract and there won't be no strike, but nothin' ever works out that right when it comes to the coal. Nothin' ever has. My Daddy and the other miners battled and battled years ago, and by the time they got their raise and benefits my Daddy was too sick to work in it anymore. I'll bet he didn't live a year after the strike. It was an awful time then, Junie Mae. I was a young boy then but I knowed what was goin' on. Men was fightin' amongst each other, and the law was always there at the mine tryin' to break up the fights between the union members and the scabs. I never saw such treachery and greed. The coal always brings out the worst in people. The coal's all we ever had here. There's timber, of course, but it don't bring in the same kind of money coal does."

"I dread you havin' to go back, Daddy," I said mournfully.

Looking up at me with a weak, pitiful expression, Daddy put his fork down and said, "Junie Mae, I'll be truthful with you. I had to be truthful with myself first and it was the hardest truth I've ever had to face. I doubt I'll ever lift another shovel. I'll get better, I guess, but it takes a lot of stamina to work in the coal. I ain't got it right now and I don't feel like it's ever comin' back. My daddy done the same thing. He got the lung disease and caught pneumonia and it nearly killed him. After he got over it he was never the same."

"Oh, Daddy -- don't say that," I pleaded. "You'll get better and get back to work."

"I've been prayin' for that but I don't see it happenin'. I'll just have to go on a government pension I guess." He sighed, "Your Mama deserves so much better than me. I knowed that when I first met her." Turning to look out the window, a faraway look came in his eyes. He said, "I've always wondered if she'd've been better off with that man she was pinin' for when I met her. I don't think he was a coalminer, though. She never said nothin' about him but I knowed there was somebody."

Daddy, I breathed, not knowing what to say. He'd known there was another man. I knew my daddy very well, but it hadn't occurred to me that he'd had so much insight on things -- especially when it came to Mama.

"How do you know there was a man?" I asked, realizing that I couldn't deny what Daddy was saying and feeling guilty because I knew he was right.

"A man who really loves a woman knows what's inside her heart. I knowed your Mama had somebody else on her mind, but I loved her anyway and always hoped I could make her love me back. I think she does now." Daddy's eyes critically studied mine before he spoke, but I knew what he was going to say beforehand. He need not have worried. I would never tell Mama what he'd told me.

"Sometimes I forget your age, Junie Mae. You seemed grown-up even when you was five years old. There's something old and wise inside your eyes. It's like you can see right through people. Maw's little sister, Etta, was like you. Seems like she just knowed things and how people worked. Sometimes she'd see things in water. One time she told Maw that she'd looked in a shallow pool and seen a vision of her own death. A week or so later, she come down with some kind of fever and died. She was only thirteen years old. Maw calls her a mystic. Maybe that's what you are, Junie Mae."

I will never forget Daddy's words. There was so much emotion in his voice. No wonder I'd never doubted his love for me. In retrospect, Daddy had a unique way of loving both Rose and me without causing jealous feelings between us.

Mama and Granny Lee's one week in Indianapolis had turned into two. During her absence, either Uncle Harvey James or Harlan Ray would come get Daddy and take him over to Granny Lee's house so he could talk with Mama on the telephone at least twice a week. Afterwards, the uncles would usually take him to the union meetings so he could keep up with what was going on with the contract. Because Rose was depressed over not hearing from Bart Asher during the first week Mama was gone she stayed in bed; therefore, both the inside and outside chores were left to me.

Thankfully, Amity Smith was very happy to help me carry water from the spring and had even chopped kindling for the wood box. Noticing that the woodpile in the backyard was getting low he generously loaded his Daddy's truck with some scrap lumber from the mill and unloaded in in our backyard. During Mama's absence, Amity had become a familiar figure at the lodge.

Because Amity had remained diligent in getting the day's lessons to me I stayed caught up in my studies, though I missed seeing Violet Elizabeth during our morning and evening rides to school.

The month of January had brought enough sun to melt away the snow. Each day was the same for me. I'd get up early to fix breakfast for Daddy and give him a dose of his cough syrup. After lunch I'd help him walk through the house and out onto the porch. If the weather was tolerable, we'd walk across the yard and over to the shed where his doll carvings lay waiting to be finished. Rose stayed in our room most of the time, purposely avoiding Daddy even after I told her that he wanted to see her and was hurt by her avoidance of him.

"What will I say to him?" she asked after I'd lectured her.

"You're gonna have to tell him about the baby, Rose. You're startin' to show and he ain't stupid!"

Shaking her head vigorously, Rose argued, "Not until Granny Lee gets back from Indianapolis."

"Just start talkin' to Daddy and start helpin' me a little around here. I can't do it all and keep up with school," I snapped irritably.

"Well, it ain't like you're doin' all the chores alone. Amity Smith has been here every evening since Mama left," she spat jealously.

"Mama won't be back until the end of the week. Daddy talked to her on the telephone last night and she said things was bad down there. Rhodie, I guess, ain't spoke a word since she found little Amy Isabella dead. She won't eat and she has to be force fed. Mama said that she just sits in a chair and looks out the window like she ain't got a thought in her head – well, that's what Daddy said Mama told him."

"So how's Mama helpin'? I guess she's there force feedin' Rhodie and actin' like she really cares when we know she ain't got it in her to care about anybody but herself!" Rose said bitterly.

"I don't know," I answered, but admitted to myself that Rose had a point. I couldn't see Mama caring about Uncle Larkin's sick wife. More than likely, she was taking advantage of the sad situation in order to get closer to Uncle Larkin and further away from us.

27 MORE DEATH AT THE NO. 5 MINE

It was during the beginning of the second week of Mama's absence that drastic changes came about in our lives, beginning with the rumors of trouble brewing down at No. 5 Mine. According to Uncle Harvey James, the minute Big Brock Asher heard about the induction of the union he'd put out the word that his son wouldn't even look at a union contract and intended rip it to shreds the minute it was presented to him.

I remember how depressed Daddy looked the night he came back with the uncles from the fateful union meeting held at the local community center. Uncles Harlan Ray and Harvey James looked equally unhappy and were unanimous in the belief that a mining strike was inevitable. While sitting at the kitchen table drinking coffee that I had made and served them, they talked freely as if I wasn't even in the room.

Nursing his cup and looking thoughtful, Uncle Harlan Ray said, "We ain't even elected union officers yet and already he's turnin' down a contract that ain't even been made yet. The bastard's actin' purty stupid seein' that he just cinched a million dollar contract with the electric company. What's gonna happen when the miners strike and he can't fulfill his obligation? Even with the scabs, they won't have enough of a crew to get the coal out!"

Harvey James answered, "The scabs will keep coming. Men are desperate to make a dollar these days and as sad as it is, even with the low wages the mining industries pay, it's more than the men would make in a lumber yard."

Daddy nodded thoughtfully and then took a sip of his coffee. I could tell he was exhausted by the weakness in his eyes. "Heddy will be fit to be tied when she hears the news about a possible strike."

"She's probably heard it already. I told Maw last night on the telephone. I probably shouldn't have but with her being so close to God, she would have known anyway. Maw always knows when things are off kilter," Uncle Harvey James said with a chuckle.

"Heddy wouldn't like how Purl is actin', and that's for sure." Harlan Ray noted. "He's as bad as any of them thugs, walkin' around like he's somethin' special. He's liable to get shot by somebody if he don't stand back from this thing."

"Corbin's mad as a wet hen, too. As soon as he got wind of a possible union contract, he came over to the house and before it was over, he was so mad he could hardly get a word out. He's blaming the three of us for all the upheaval in mine number five right now. He swears there'll be a killing or killings," Harvey James said.

Uncle Harlan Ray said, "I ain't seen a sign of Little Brock since the day he got word of the union. He's probably passed out drunk in a field on his property, leaving his Daddy and Purl to deal with the mess."

Nodding in agreement Daddy told his brothers about the visit we had had from Joelyn Asher and how she'd admitted Big Brock was the one making the decisions concerning the mine.

"That's no surprise to anybody. How can Little Brock make decisions when he's on the bottle most of the time? In my opinion neither of those men were cut out for the mining business," Harvey James said critically.

Harlan Ray nodded, "Big Brock should stick to undertakin'. Little Brock used to be a better man but the drinkin's finally got to him."

Harvey James pledged, "We have to see this thing through. I don't know what's going to happen at the onset, but whatever it is we have to go with it."

Daddy said, "I don't agree with no strike, but we knowed that could happen when we inducted the union in to it, so I'll stand by the union until the end."

After the uncles left, Daddy remained in the kitchen deep in study. When I brought his cough syrup to him, he drank it almost begrudgingly. I could tell he wanted to talk but was reluctant. Night had fallen and the air had turned bitter. "I've got to bank the fires," I told him.

He nodded and then said, "Your Mama will be home Saturday. I just dread how she's goin' to take all of this."

"I know," I said, lacking anything else to say.

After banking the fires, I sat down next to Daddy who remained thoughtful. "Junie Mae, I've got to find the strength to walk the picket if the miners strike. It's somethin' I got to do. Your Mama ain't gonna like it, especially since she got a taste of the big city. She always wanted to live in a big city and away from here. It's got me worried," he confessed.

Again, I was at a loss for words. Daddy was right; Mama wouldn't be happy coming home to a strike, and seeing Daddy up and picketing all day would no doubt set something off in her. Walking over to where he sat at the head of the table I reached around his neck, hugging him as tightly as I could. I remember thinking that I wanted to protect this good, vulnerable man who only wanted to do right by his fellow workers. I am convinced that there wasn't a mean bone in Daddy's body. In essence, my Daddy was truly the epitome of a simple, uncomplicated man who had made the tragic mistake of loving a complicated woman.

After Daddy was settled into bed, I tried to find sleep. I could hear Rose tossing restlessly in the next bed as well. This was unusual because by nature Rose could sleep for hours on end. I, on the other hand, am a nocturnal creature who cannot turn off my thoughts so easily at night. Even as a small child, I seemed to come alive as soon as the curtain of darkness fell. As I tossed and turned that night, visions of Mama leaving Daddy continued to haunt me. I thought of Rose's predicament and could hardly stand to imagine what might become of it. Thank goodness Daddy had ordered me to go back to school. Maybe being in class again would take me away from all the burdens I'd been carrying for the last few months

Sleep only came with the thought of Amity Smith. I pictured his handsome face and his tousled hair. Knowing that he cared had comforted me.

Sometime in the wee hours of the morning, I was awakened by the shrill sound of a siren in the distance that kept growing closer. Automatically jumping up out of bed, I raced to the living room and raised back the curtain. I saw lights quickly approaching. Something had happened at the mines. My mind suddenly sharpened. Jerking a jacket off the nail in the kitchen I hastily put it on, then opened the front door and stepped out onto the porch. Once outside, a rush of cold air blasted my face. Behind me, Daddy yelled over the screaming sirens. "Somethin' bad is goin' on up there June-bug. You better come back in!" The urgency of the approaching siren had awakened Rose, who came out on the porch and stood behind me wrapped in a blanket and wanting to know what was going on. Just as she asked it, the revolving red light of the ambulance appeared, casting a flashing red glow on her frightened face. Two sheriffs' cars followed behind flashing their own red lights but had no sirens on. "It's just like it was the night the mine caved in," I whispered.

Rose whimpered and hovered close to Daddy.

Other vehicles followed. At first there were only a few, but then came a barrage of trucks and cars. The beams from their headlights cast a harsh light on the dead trees and the river in the distance. Shielding my eyes from the brightness, I waited for the cars and trucks to pass, but Daddy made his way slowly down the porch steps in hopes of catching someone who might know what had occurred at the mine. The string of traffic had come to a quick standstill. Men were stepping out of their vehicles and talking to one another, all of them dressed in mining clothes. Rushing to help Daddy, I took his arm and guided him across the yard to the cluster of men gathered around an idling truck. "It's too cold for you out here, Daddy," I whispered, but Daddy wasn't listening. Instead, with the help of his cane he made his way to over to the truck. Big Dan Stewart stepped out of the cab. Dressed in clean mining clothes, he was one of the few miners who didn't live in the camp and was just heading off to the mines to start his shift.

"I reckon they ain't lettin' people through the gates," he hollered over the sound of the truck's engine.

Daddy nodded, and asked if he'd heard anything.

"Nah, but I'll bet there's been a fight or a killin' up there. If it was a cave-in there'd be more ambulances and lawmen. That shit boss, Purl, has been rakin' them unionized men over the coals since he heard they was gettin' ready to elect officers. I reckon you'd know about that, wouldn't you, Ralph?"

Coughing raucously and shaking weakly, Daddy steadied himself against me and finally said, "I ain't takin' no officers' position in the union, Dan. They ain't picked no officers as I know of."

Dan said, "I like you, Ralph, but I think you know how I feel about the union -- and I ain't just speakin' for me. There's others who don't want it. The truth is a union never done nothin' for my daddy and his people. It ain't gonna do nothin' for them miners up there, either, but get 'em killed. Mark my words on that, Ralph. If somebody got killed up there tonight then their blood is on the hands of you and your brothers, and every man who's fought tooth and nail for it."

Rose piqued up defensively, "Somebody believes in the union. Mines all over Harlan and other places have brought them in."

"We don't need a union interferin' with Number Five Mine!" A man shouted nastily. I would find out later that his name was John Harvesty and that he was one of the new hires. I could sense his resentment of Daddy, and it prompted me to grab hold of Daddy's shirtsleeve protectively.

John Harvesty affronted Daddy. His angry voice echoed through the cold morning and bounced off the distant cliffs. "I got four kids and a wife to feed. I can't afford to walk no picket. I've been on strike pay before, and my family liked to have starved to death. I've been told that you and your brothers started this union business. I take offense to anybody tryin' to take food out of the mouth of my babies."

Big Dan Stewart turned to the young man whose stance was that of a fighting man. His feet were wide apart and his hands clenched and unclenched at his side.

"You ain't causin' no trouble here, Harvesty. You go get back in your car before you get hurt."

Turning to Daddy he sneered, "He couldn't hurt nobody! Look at him! He can barely get a breath,"

Suddenly I felt something whiz by my head. John Harvesty cried out and then and slumped to the frozen ground clutching at his chest.

Rose stepped forward. Her voice was near hysteria. "You get in that car before I get Daddy's gun and shoot you dead. You better be glad I just hit you with a rock!"

Another miner rushed over, grabbed John Harvesty under the arm, and said, "You ain't hurt that bad. Just get in the car and leave the Lees alone before you get shot!"

Turning to Rose, Daddy asked, "What in the world did you do that for? Junie Mae, take your sister inside. She's all tore up."

"I ain't goin'," Rose protested.

This time Daddy spoke in a stern tone, "Rose, go with your sister right now!"

The last thing I wanted to do was leave Daddy, but I knew he wanted Rose in the house and out of harm's way. Taking her arm I said, "Come on Rose." At first she refused to go but then Daddy urged, in a gentle voice, "You go with your sister, Rosie."

"Daddy's either gonna get shot or die from the cold," Rose sobbed. "He just can't take all this cold air in his lungs."

Once inside the lodge I stood before the grate warming my hands. "You hit that boy right in the gut." I laughed in spite of myself.

"I did, didn't I?" she said, as if she were surprised at her own actions. "I just couldn't let that man make fun of Daddy and him still sick."

Now standing in front of the living room window, I watched cars and trucks spin, turn, and then narrowly pass each other. Men were dead! My intuition so overwhelmed my senses that I stumbled backwards. I won't close my eyes. I won't see who's dead up there. At that moment I felt the most intense fear for Daddy, the uncles, and all the miners who had become union members. Stories I'd heard from various family members about Bloody Harlan came rushing in. Words like death and bloodshed seemed to take on a reality that they hadn't had before. The need to run to Daddy was almost overpowering, but I stayed rooted to the floor, wishing that he would come back out of the cold air that might kill him.

In the next room, Rose lay in bed huddled beneath the covers waiting for Daddy. Full of nervous energy, I went about stoking fires and straightening up. Sleep for me seemed miles away. An hour would pass before Daddy finally came back inside. Appearing pale and cold, he stood before the grate shaking his head in disgust. "I'm goin' to lay down awhile Junie Mae. Harvey James or Harlan Ray will be here early in the mornin'. You go to bed now. You got school tomorrow."

I awoke to daylight streaming through the bedroom window. Groggy,

I hurriedly dressed, stoked the fires, and fixed breakfast for Daddy as usual before dressing for my first day back to school. Uncle Harvey James came after breakfast with the awful news that poor old Levi Creech and a young miner named Donny Calvin were the ones who were murdered near the Bern in the back lot of No. 5. Donny was nineteen years old and newly married. "That boy believed in the union. That belief probably got him killed if you want to know the truth," Harvey James said sadly.

Appearing overworked and stressed, Uncle Harvey James drank his coffee in silence while Daddy bowed his head as if in prayer. When Uncle Harvey James finally spoke, it was with a weary voice. "I knew there'd be some trouble because of the union, but I never imagined somebody would stoop so low as to kill a harmless old man and a young boy who was as green as grass. That boy was just going along with us, Ralph. He believed in the cause because we made him believe. We told him that the union was the right thing!"

"Big Dan Stewart said if there was a killin' up there, that me and you and Harlan Ray had blood on our hands. You reckon that's true?" Daddy asked in a feeble voice. Harvey James had gotten his second wind. Now energized by some kind of silent truth, he shouted, "Hell no! The blood of those men is not on our hands. It's on the hands of Big Brock Asher and his drunken son." Pointing his finger at Daddy in further emphasis, he ventured, "I'll bet you a dollar to a dime that Purl Haley's all over those killings. Heddy was right when she called him a lap dog. He'd do anything Asher told him."

Looking thoughtful, Daddy shook his head in disagreement and said, "Purl's a lap-dog all right, but I don't think he's got it in him to shoot a poor old man and a boy. I ain't even sure the Ashers would be this cold-blooded. It's more like one of them new scabs took it on hisself to kill 'em as a warnin' to the rest of us."

Uncle Harvey James nodded in agreement and said, "'You're right, Ralph, but the Ashers are still responsible anyway. If they'd've just settled with the widows and paid the rest of us what we deserve this would have never happened."

"Where are Bonzelle and that German woman? Somebody better be worried about them," Daddy warned.

Uncle Harvey James answered, "I heard Bonzelle is in a bad way. I don't know if the German woman is with her or not. Maybe I'd better see where she is for her own safety."

28 A NOTE FROM BART ASHER

The remaining week of Mama's absence consisted of Daddy and the other union members attending countless meetings and electing union officers. Uncle Harvey James was the clear winner in the vote for president, while Harlan Ray was chosen to head up a safety committee. Hoyt Right, a line worker, would act as weigher-man, whose job consisted of weighing the coal in order to make sure the miners weren't being cheated. Daddy voted but refused to accept any nomination offered to him, claiming that he wasn't educated or even well enough to act in such a capacity. School had become a kind of refuge for me as were Amity and Violet Elizabeth. Their love for me had helped me to cope with Daddy's sickness and Rose's ongoing depression.

Daddy remained preoccupied with the union and the impending contract. Not long after the election of officers, union leaders began holding meetings with miners at the local VFW in efforts to hammer out a possible contract to present to Little Brock Asher. Daddy didn't talk much about what the contract entailed but assured Rose and me that the changes would be good for the miners. On the following Saturday Uncles Coy and Noah arrived at the lodge early in order to take Daddy down to the bus station to meet Mama and Granny Lee. Daddy had dressed neatly in the white dress shirt Granny Lee had made him for Christmas and his black dress slacks. Looking pale and thin, his hair, some of which had come back in, was slicked back on his head. My recollections of watching him hobble to the kitchen door with his cane as support were painful. I'd wanted to cry when remembering how strong he once was. Earlier that morning Daddy had called both Rose and me into the kitchen and asked us to tidy things up for Mama's arrival. I could tell he was jittery but anxious to see her.

Not long after Daddy and the uncles left for the bus station Marie showed up at the door with a white envelope in her hand. She said, "I gotta hurry. I left the youngins with Uncle Hiram and he can't handle 'em for long. Where's Rose?"

Rose appeared white faced and expectant. Wordlessly, Marie handed her the envelope which she took gingerly. She looked at it and said, "His name ain't nowhere on it, but I know it's from him. Carefully tearing the end off the envelope, she withdrew a small card, scanned it over then looked like she might faint. "He's here, and he wants me to meet him tonight at eight o'clock in the alley behind Granny Lee's house," she whispered.

I felt a deep stab of uncertainty inside my chest. "I don't like to think about you meetin' him alone," I warned her, and then added, "Look what's happenin' down at the mine. Poor old Levi Creech and that boy was shot and nobody knows who done it. How do you know the Ashers didn't have it done?" I asked.

"Well, I got to meet him. He's the baby's daddy and it's too late to turn back now," she said.

"I'll go with you," I offered.

"You can't. I told him nobody knowed he was the daddy. If he seen you hangin' around he'd know."

"That makes it worse!" I said incredulously. Ripping the note from her hand, I read its short contents.

"Rose, I need to talk with you. Meet me behind your Grandmother's house tonight at eight o'clock."

"He didn't even sign his name -- the coward," I said, hurling the note to the floor.

Naturally docile, Marie looked frightened but spoke out in a nervous voice, "He had to know, Junie Mae. He won't meet her if he sees any of us there."

Turning toward my sister, I pleaded with her not to go. "Tell him you'll meet him on Wilder Creek Bridge or somewhere I can keep an eye on you."

"He won't hurt me, Junie Mae. I'm the mama of his baby."

Disgusted, I said nothing else, but inside I seethed. Even after she left out the door, I felt as if I might explode. Why couldn't she see that he wanted nothing to do with her? Hadn't he made that clear by leaving his name off the note? I wanted to feel sorry for her but somehow I couldn't. Sometimes Rose's blatant stupidity killed tender emotions. I knew somewhere inside of her she had not given up on the idea of marrying Bart Asher. Something told me she never would.

29 THERE ARE NO GHOSTS

Daddy, Granny Lee, and Mama arrived back at the lodge a little after one o'clock that afternoon. Uncles Coy and Noah had made plans for the evening and simply dropped them off. As soon as Mama walked through the door of the living room, I had noticed the change in her. It was at that moment I knew we had lost her forever. I can't explain how I'd known, exactly, because there were no visible changes in her appearance save for the loss a pound or two. The faraway look in her eyes told the tale. Oddly, there was something almost peaceful about her demeanor. It was as if she'd found something in Indianapolis that she'd been missing here. I don't know if Daddy had seen it or not. Maybe he had and that is why he would soon agree to let her go back. Once in the kitchen, Granny had hugged me warmly, while Mama patted my head and hugged me almost as it were an afterthought. Looking around the kitchen, she asked about Rose. I told her she was helping Marie with her children, but assured her she'd probably be home either that night or sometime the next day.

Daddy, Granny Lee, and Mama had gathered around the kitchen table discussing Rhodie's sickness. Granny Lee moaned, "That poor woman is off in another world. She hardly blinks her eyes and just sits staring ahead at nothing all day. Heddy had to sit with her on the day of her child's funeral. It was so sad."

"What do them doctors say?" Daddy asked.

"They say she's in shock and may or may not come out of it. I've prayed and prayed for her. I know God will somehow deliver her of this awful pain sooner or later."

Rising from the table, Mama grabbed the teakettle and filled it with water for tea. She said, "Larkin's in a pickle because of her sickness. He's off from work right now and is lookin' for somebody to care for her while he's on the road."

Granny Lee shook her head sadly, and while wringing her fat hands nervously together she said, "He ain't got family out there to help him. If I didn't have Marie and her youngins to look after, I would have stayed there and helped him through this. Lord help him, Jesus." With her arms and hands waving vigorously in the air, she began to speak out in tongues, "Shal la, la na, sha, la na."

Mama said of Rhodie, "It takes an hour or so to feed her. She won't even open her mouth, and when she does, she won't chew and just lets the food lay there on her tongue. I ended up practically pouring soup down her throat, and even then she spit half of it up."

Granny Lee added, "Ain't nobody but her own family has got the patience to feed her like she needs to be fed, Heddy. I feel so guilty not bein' there."

"Maybe she oughta go to a hospital," Daddy offered.

Granny Lee said, "Even with Larkin's insurance plan, he'd still have to pay out of his own pocket. He'd lose everything they got."

After Marie picked up Granny Lee, Uncle Harlan Ray came after Daddy to take him to the union meeting down at the VFW club. Not knowing what to say to Mama, I decided to walk down to Amity and Violet Elizabeth's house. I put on my coat and headed for the door, but Mama stopped me. "I don't guess Rose has said anything to your Daddy about the baby yet?" she asked.

"No. She ain't told him yet," I answered, fighting the urge to run out the door.

"Take your coat off and sit down, Junie Mae," Mama commanded in a strange but gentle voice.

Sighing, I took my coat off reluctantly and then draped it over the back of the chair. Sitting down I waited for Mama to say what was on her mind.

Mama got right to the point, "Daddy has to be told about Rose sooner or later. If she don't do it, I will."

"She was waiting to tell Granny Lee."

"Lord, your Daddy and his mama are just alike; if a skunk prayed either one of them they'd miss it. How can you get through the world missin' everything? As many children as she's had it looks to me like your Granny Lee would have been the first one to notice."

Anger rose within me, and once more the need to protect Daddy was far greater than my fear of her. "Daddy ain't so dumb, Mama, and neither is Granny Lee. Daddy asked me about Rose and wanted to know what was wrong with her. I didn't tell him, but he knows something is." In a lowered voice I added, "He knows more than you think he does, Mama. You just don't give him credit."

Mama's dark eyes flickered like a flame in the wind. "What are you talkin' about Junie Mae? You always talk in riddles, and I never was any good at guessin' riddles."

"You'll be leavin' here for good soon, won't you?" I asked, ignoring her question.

"I don't know about for good, but yes, I'm thinkin' of goin back to Indianapolis and helpin' out your Uncle Larkin."

"I knowed you'd end up goin' back. Daddy probably knows too. Never mind that he needs you worse than anything and Rose needs a mama." Rising from the chair, I looked Mama in the eye, which was something I'd found almost impossible to do in the past. "Daddy won't ever be able to work in the mine again. He knows that, too. If you leave him, I don't know how long he'll live."

Mama's quiet, calm demeanor suddenly disappeared. "You hit it right in the nose, Junie Mae. Your Daddy will never be able to work in the coal again. That damned coal's destroyed him. You'd think he'd want to spend some time with me, seein' as I ain't been home for weeks, but he's at that damned union meetin'." Mama's whole body shook. Gone was the serenity she had first brought with her. But she wasn't through yet -- not by a long shot. In a calmer voice, she went on. "Your Uncle Larkin needs help right now. He wants me and your Daddy to move out there. Your Daddy could work the farm and I could take care of Rhodie while Larkin's gone on the road. It wouldn't cost us a single penny, and he's got this separate little house on his property that's completely furnished. When Rhodie gets well, we could live in that -- a decent place for a change. I'm gonna ask your Daddy to move there with me. I want you girls to go, too." Taking a long shuddering breath, she went on: "Daddy can't make a decent living here no more -- not that he ever could. There he could work at his own speed and I could earn a little, too. We could save up and have somethin' for once. Is that so wrong, Junie Mae?" Her eyes pleaded with mine.

A part of me knew Mama's plan made sense, and I found it hard to argue with her. The offer Uncle Larkin made sounded like something that would be good for all of us. Inside, I felt suddenly confused. By his own admittance, Daddy had known that he would in all probability never be able to work in the mines again, and he had no money coming in save for what family members had given him monthly to pay the rent and buy a few groceries. Mama had found a way for us to survive. How could I argue with her plan when she wanted to include Daddy, Rose, and me in the move? But did she really want us all to make the move with her? The question nagged at me. Maybe the truth lay in her hope that Daddy, Rose, and I would all refuse to go with her.

Finally I said, "The move sounds good, Mama, but Daddy won't never leave his family here. I know he won't, and if he won't go, I can't leave him. Rose won't leave him, either. That's just the way it is."

Laughing bitterly, Mama said, "We are his family! Your Daddy says he loves me more than life but that's a lie, ain't it? If he loved me all that much he'd want to do what's best for me. And what about you girls? Wouldn't he want to do what's best for you all? This wretched place has already got to Rose. She's ruined, just like Marie. I told him that if she went to Putney what would happen. Junie Mae, I've begged your Daddy for years to take us somewhere else."

"He don't know nowhere else, just like me and Rose don't. We've been here all our lives, Mama." My voice pleaded for some understanding.

"He don't think there is no place but here. He's tied to the coal. Even if he never shovels another block, he'll always be a miner. Think about it, the coal's destroyed his health but he still hangs onto it like it's some kind of gold nugget. Don't make no sense to me and it never will." With eyes boring darkly into mine she accused, "You stand here takin' up for him because you don't know no better, either. It's got to be that Smith boy that holds you here."

"Maybe a part of me feels like that, Mama, but you're forgettin' that this is where I was born. I don't want to be nowhere else."

"Men ain't always dependable, Junie Mae. That Smith boy might not feel the same about you in a few years. Where will you be then? Still stuck here waitin' for a miracle to save you. You're so trustin' -- just like your Granny Lee."

Tired of the subject I said, "It's the only place I know."

"Oh, you're going to know more all right," she promised, then warned, "You're in for a rude awakening, little girl. Wait until the strike starts and men pull out their guns and start shooting at this house and maybe even at your Daddy or his brothers -- or worse yet, you or your sister. Things are gonna get dangerous, and there won't be no money comin' in on top of all that! I can't deal with all that no more, Junie Mae. I've seen these kinds of things all my life. The coalmines have taken everything from me. Daddy can't work the mines no more, Junie Mae. We got to have money to live."

"So you're going back Uncle Larkin's soon." It was a presumption more than a question.

"I don't see no other way," she said.

"You could go back to work at Hanley's store," I offered.

Shaking her head, she said, "Your Uncle Larkin would probably pay me three times as much as I'd make there; besides, I'd be helping out family."

"You mean you'd be close to Uncle Larkin," I dared.

"You hush that up, Junie Mae! You don't know what you're talkin' about. I'd better never hear you say somethin' like that to your Daddy."

In a strangely gentle voice I said "It's true though, Mama. I knowed the minute that you first seen him. I watched you. I seen how you couldn't take your eyes off him. You spent hours writin' him letters. There's a big fat bundle of them in that cabinet drawer. There are just some of the things I know, Mama. The truth is in here," I said, touching my heart.

"Yeah, shore! You and them ghosts talk all the time and they tell you things. Your Granny Lee's been talkin' to Jesus and dead people for years. She believes the spirits talk back. I used to think there was ghosts, too. I remember not long after Floyd Wilkes died, I-I thought I seen him in the woods. It was just a little flash of his face. Sometimes when I was out walkin', I'd see somethin' out of the corner of my eye, but when I tried to catch it, it was too quick for me. I finally decided there wadn't nothin' there to begin with, and that it was all in my head. There ain't no dead person gonna come back and tell you things. Why would anybody want to come back to a place like this? So forget your ghosts, Junie Mae. Your sister believed in fairytales, too, and you see where it got her. The only thing that's real is what you can see and touch -- the rest is just in your head."

Grabbing up my coat, I looked Mama in the eye once again and said, "You have to believe in spirits before they'll show. Maybe it really was Floyd Wilkes' ghost and you turned it away. Maybe he was worried about you and...." before I could finish, Mama cut me off. Her tone had turned spiteful. "There ain't no ghosts, Junie Mae! You best stop tryin' to hurt me by usin' my dead brother. What's happened to you, anyhow? You was never any trouble when you was little. You never talked to me like you do now."

"I'm not tryin' to hurt you, Mama. I'm tryin' to make sense out of who you are. I ain't no little girl. I'm almost grown. You can't pull the wool over my eyes no more. I found them stolen watches and listened to you lie to Daddy and the law. I watched you flirt and heard you whisperin' to Uncle Larkin. What was you and him whisperin' about, Mama? It ain't right that you worry more about Uncle Larkin than you do your own flesh and blood!"

"None of this is true," Mama said, stamping her foot angrily. "You stand here tellin' me how I don't love Rose. Since when has Rose showed me any kind of care or respect? Even when she was little, she went against everything I told her to do. She wanted to kill me that night, and might have done it, too, if Daddy hadn't took the cut. What do you reckon I done to deserve that?"

"Oh, Mama," I said looking upward. "Maybe you're the one that's missin' everything."

"Now listen here, Junie Mae! I've had enough of you! Enough of you thinkin' you know everything. You act like the rest of us are idiots -- you always have, you and them smart books. Yeah, you got all the answers Miss Fancy-Pants! You wait and see how much you really know in the end. It'll all amount to nothin'! Get out of my sight!" she seethed angrily.

30 HISTORY REPEATS ITSELF

Outside the wind blew cold as usual, and I was sick of it -- sick of the winter, sick of the mine. But most of all, I was sick of Mama and her inability to understand anyone's pain but her own. Running blindly down by the side of the house, my mind was on getting away from Mama and the lodge. Suddenly aware of my surroundings, I noted how everything around me appeared dead and lifeless. Once on the Wilder Creek Bridge, I stopped and then slumped down on the planks. Down below, the creek was strangely quiet, save for the swishing sound of water washing over the rocks. Breathing steam, I looked upwards at Asher house; behind it the dark firs and pines blotted the hillside and stood starkly full and alive among the tall, skeletal trees. A kind of hatred rose within me as I thought of them. It occurred to me that the Ashers were at the root of all the bad things that had happened to my family thus far, starting with Big Brock Asher's mine explosion that had killed Granddaddy Wilkes Haley, making Grandma Haley a widow and forcing her to raise her children alone. I knew Granddaddy's death had also affected Mama deeply and had poisoned her against coalmining. But the Asher curse proceeded on with Mama falling for Little Brock Asher. It was his fault entirely that Mama couldn't love Daddy, I thought. I somehow knew a big part of Mama never got over him, just as Rose would never recover from her dealings with Bart Asher and would soon have a baby to remind her of him for the rest of her life. At least Mama hadn't gone that far.

    It occurred to me that history was repeating itself with Mama and Rose, and there was no way to escape the Asher curse unless someone took a match and set fire to the big house with all of them in it. I knew this was a terrible thought and God would probably punish me for even thinking about such an evil endeavor, but I couldn't help but wish they would somehow disappear of the face of the earth. For some reason I thought of

Granny Lee and remembered her talk of war and how terrible each battle was. She said that war was history's way of repeating itself, and that each war happened because one country always wanted something the other country had. Suddenly the wind had hushed and the air was as quiet. There amidst the death of winter I felt as if I were standing in a graveyard. A series of thoughts ran through my mind that wouldn't stop -- bad thoughts. "Floyd Wilkes," I whispered, knowing that if I turned my head he would be there among the trees or there perched unnaturally atop one of the deadfalls. History was repeating itself with Mama and Rose. Walking along the line of the limestone wall that separated us from them, I felt a sinking sensation in the pit of my stomach followed by a flash of Rose dressed in her yellow summer sundress. She'd looked just like Mama on the day of the fair; so much so that a drunken Little Brock Asher had mistaken Rose for her. He still loved Mama -- that much I knew. Had Mama slept with him? The voice of Granny Lee echoed in my mind -- or was it in the woods? Your Mama and Daddy hadn't knowed each other more than three weeks before they was married. It wasn't long before your Mama got in the family way. When Rose was born, your Daddy took a shine to her... The unthinkable had reared its ugly head, causing me to stop dead in my tracks. No, it couldn't be. Nothing that awful could have happened. "Floyd Wilkes, you come down out of them woods and talk to me! I gotta know," I yelled, hearing my own voice echo though the stillness. My eyes turned to the Asher barn and beyond where the woods formed a tunnel made up of furs and lofty pines. This place would make a good hiding place for ghosts. My thoughts suddenly flashed an image of a tall thin man in a gray felt hat and dark suit. Beside of him walked a girl dressed in a yellow sundress. Shaken by the unexpected vision, my body swayed uncertainly, nearly pitching forward into the dead leaves and debris left over from a scorching hot summer. The flashes were too strong for me to ignore. I'd had no choice but to see and recognize that the face underneath the wide brimmed hat was that of Big Brock Asher and the girl beside him was Rose. Both stared down at me with their strange gray eyes. Their eyes were identical. Snapping awake, my mind screamed in horrible recognition. History was repeating itself. Little Brock Asher was Rose's father. I had known something was missing from Mama's story. God, this was it -- another horrible part of Mama revealed. Thinking back on our conversation concerning her childhood years spent at the Asher house, I recalled her cryptic words: Big Brock Asher robbed my daddy and the other miners to get what he's got. Never mind what he stole from me. What had he stolen from her? Little Brock, Rose's father? On the mixing of poor and rich blood, Mama had laughed and said, If only you knowed how funny this is. The word "irony" would have been lost on me then, but I'd understood its effects quite well. I'd figured out that Mama's blood had already mixed with the Ashers' in spite of all Big Brock's attempts to keep it separate. Fear and disgust made me cringe inside. Turning back toward the direction of the lodge, I knew I'd have to face Mama and make her tell me the truth for Rose's sake. If this was true then Rose was going to have a baby by her own brother. Nothing could be more awful than that. Nothing!

Mama was putting a skillet of cornbread in the oven when I entered the kitchen. Upon seeing me, her face clouded angrily.

"Mama, I got to know something," I said. Taking a deep breath, I asked her if she had ever slept with Little Brock Asher.

Slamming the oven door shut, she barked, "What made you think of somethin' like that?"

"Mama, please! I have to know!"

"Why don't you ask your spirits? They'll tell you."

"Rose has eyes exactly like Big Brock Asher's, Mama. They don't look nothin' like nobody's in the family. Everybody says that when they see them!"

Mama's face had turned the color of spent ashes. Looking quickly away, she said nothing, and in that moment communicated more than if she'd spoken a thousand words.

"That morning when Big Brock Asher come to see you, I noticed his eyes, Mama. I knowed that there was somethin' familiar about them, but I just couldn't think what. Today I figured it out. His eyes look just like Rose's. They're his eyes Mama -- his eyes!"

"How do you come up with these things, Junie Mae? You're fourteen years old. This beats 'em all. You just won't stop tryin' to torture me, will you?"

"I'm not tryin' to torture you Mama. I just have to know if Rose belongs to Little Brock Asher."

"I never slept with Little Brock Asher. Rose don't belong to him."

Taking a deep breath, I said, "I hope you ain't lyin', Mama, because if you are it's all gonna come back on you. It's history repeatin' itself."

Mama's eyes flicked suspiciously and seemed to see right through me. "What are you sayin', Junie Mae?"

"I'm sayin' that your chickens are about to come home to roost, Mama. If Rose belongs to Little Brock Asher, it will cause more trouble than any of us has ever seen."

"What trouble?" she murmured.

Drawing in a long shuddering breath I said, "It has to do with Rose's baby."

Mama steadied herself against the chair. Her eyes had grown large and wild. "What's Rose's baby got to do with the Ashers?"

"Her baby belongs to Bart Asher, Mama."

"Bart?" She said his name as if she were hearing it for the first time. "How can this be? I kept her away from them Ashers for years. I wouldn't even allow them one peep at her. Rose is lyin'."

"She's not lyin', Mama."

I'd never seen my mother so white and rattled, and her inability to find the right words told me all that I needed to know.

"You couldn't have told me a worse thing. There ain't nothin' worse than this, Junie Mae."

"You mean because Rose belongs to Little Brock Asher."

I saw something terrible in Mama's eyes.

"She don't belong to Little Brock Asher -- she belongs to his daddy, Junie Mae."

I could barely speak. The name Big Brock Asher came out more as a croak. I thought of the vision I had of him and Rose coming over the hill and knew Mama spoke the truth. "How could this happen?" I asked in stunned disbelief.

"He raped me. After he was done, he laughed and said, 'You're ruined now, Heddy. I've fixed it so you can never look at my boy again.' He'd warned me that if I ever told, he'd deny it and nobody would believe me. He said that he'd fix it so that Mama would send me away. He had all the power in the world and could do anything he wanted to anybody. But I told Mama anyway. I told her that he'd took me against my will. Do you know what she said, Junie Mae? She said I'd caused him to act that way. She blamed it all on me! Course I didn't know then there would be a baby, and after I figured it out I couldn't tell nobody. I didn't know what to do. I didn't have no Granny Lee to tell me that children was gifts from God and not some curse. I was scared to death. Then I met your Daddy at a tent revival. He kept lookin' at me and I knowed he was interested. We started seein' each other and, well, you know the rest. I never told him that Rose wadn't his. No one counted months -- except for Mama, who told me she knowed that the baby wadn't Ralph's. I told her the truth, but she wouldn't believe he raped me. She's said that a fine man like Big Brock Asher couldn't do such a thing and that I'd led him on and caused him to do what he done to me," Mama's voice faded away like an echo.

Nervously pacing the length of the kitchen Mama asked, "How long have you knowed this? You should've come to me with it. Don't you see what's come out of it?" Her voice was near hysterics.

"She made me promise not to. She said she'd kill herself," I answered defensively

"She'd be better off dead. You and me both know that baby won't be right. It'll come here all deformed because she mated with her own blood." Talking more to herself, she muttered, "How could she do somethin' like this to me. Who else knows?"

"Marie."

"That figures. Marie will tell her what she done was just fine. What about your Granny Lee -- does she know?"

"Me and Marie are the only ones that know. Even if she told Granny Lee, she wouldn't mention Bart Asher."

"What about Bart Asher? Don't tell me he plans to marry her, because I know better. He won't have no part of no baby born out of wedlock. He'll deny it."

Pulling out a kitchen chair, she sat down, all the while looking as if someone had plunged a knife into her. Her eyes were no longer angry; now they favored the dead branches in the woods. "Old Brock didn't want my blood mixin' with his son's, but look what's happened." Her laugh was cold and harsh and seemed out of place. After a few seconds, she went on in sharp whisper. "I couldn't tell Little Brock what his Daddy done to me. I was too ashamed and scared and wanted to block the whole thing out. I wadn't workin' at the funeral home when Little Brock come home on Spring Break. Big Brock planned it that way and let Mama work instead. He didn't want his son seein' me. But Little Brock found me anyway and I'll never forget that day." Taking in a deep breath, she related the story with pain and regret in her voice. I saw a kind of torture in her face that I had never seen before. "We was livin' in the house Daddy bought from Big Brock on Sutter's Creek. I remember him almost beatin' the door down, but I wouldn't answer it. Floyd Wilkes did, though. He loved him like a brother and couldn't understand why I wouldn't let him in. I remember Little Brock rushin' over to me, and he just kept askin' why I wouldn't let him in or talk to him. I just kept tellin' him to leave. I killed him that day, Junie Mae. I might as well have pulled a gun and shot him right there. A light went out of his eyes. I could almost feel his soul leavin' his body. He really loved me," her voice broke.

"I doubt Bart loves Rose. He stopped seein' her before he left for college. She keeps hopin', though. Hopin' he'll change his mind."

Eying me angrily, Mama said, "You've knowed all this time that she was slippin' off and seein' him and you never said one word to me. I could have put an end to this if you'd just told me!"

Looking Mama straight in the eyes, I said, "You'd have beat her to an inch of her life if you'd've knowed, and that wouldn't have helped none, Mama. She'd've kept on seein' him no matter what you done to her. It started a long time ago with her and him, anyway. They was gettin' to know one another across the fence while you was up there at the Asher house workin'. You missed it all, Mama. She was hell-bent on bein' one of them, just like you was. She done just like you, Mama, so how can you stand here and tell me you could've stopped her?"

Slumping hopelessly, Mama's voice had lost its fire and sounded empty and hopeless. "You've got to bring Rose to me, Junie Mae. We've got to figure out what to do about the baby she's carryin'. I could take her with me to Indianapolis. There's places that would take a baby born all twisted up. Nobody here would even have to know."

"She won't go, Mama," I said quietly. "She's got it in her head that the baby's gonna somehow get her Bart Asher. Marie sent him a letter tellin' him about the baby. He knows."

"She's always been such a foolish girl, believin' anything that sounded good."

"She wanted the same thing you wanted, Mama. How can you put her down for it?"

Mama's eyes flinched as she said, "She's ruined herself and the rest of us to boot. I might have known I'd pay for my sins someday, even if they wadn't mine alone. You're right, Junie Mae: my chickens have come home to roost."

31 MAMA'S MISSING PARTS REVEALED

That night I slept fitfully. My mind was on what Mama had told me earlier. I thought of how she had made a mess for everyone with her secrets and lies. I had exposed her missing parts and suddenly wished that I hadn't figured them out. I thought of Floyd Wilkes' ghost and knew it had been restless in the knowing of our lives and the lies that Mama had hoarded away for years. A part of me had felt that the ghost wanted an end to the lies and secrets and couldn't move on until Mama had settled the debt of truth that she owed her family.

Poor Rose. The next day, she would return to the lodge and Mama would make a mangled effort to explain to her that life as she had known it was built on a stack of lies, starting with Daddy, who wasn't even of her own blood. That part of the lie alone would devastate her because she had loved Ralph Lee with all her heart. What would she do when she learned that the baby she was carrying belonged to her own nephew, and that she existed only because Big Brock Asher had raped Mama? In retrospect, the sorrow and dread I felt then remains unmatched with anything life dealt me after that. Even the death of close family members couldn't top those surreal days when my innocence was stripped away as surely and as crudely as a carpenter strips away old paint from a crumbling wall.

The next morning came with a blast of sun through the bedroom window. Squinting and shielding my eyes, I crawled out of bed and quickly drew the curtains. The look of such a nice, bright sun had seemed absurd considering what was going on inside the lodge. In the kitchen I could hear the low voices of Mama and Daddy talking. Daddy was telling Mama that the union had almost finished drawing up the contract and would soon present it to Asher. Mama was answering him, but I could tell her thoughts were on Rose.

"Will you be seein' Rose today?" Mama finally asked Daddy.

"I expect I will," he answered. "Me and Harlan Ray are goin' over to Maw's to meet Harvey James. Why?"

"Bring her back with you," she said, and then added, "I need to talk to her."

"All right. If she'll come," he said

"Just get her here, Ralph," Mama commanded sternly.

I dressed, hardly taking the pains I usually took to in order look good for Amity Smith. Standing before the mirror, I touched the heart-shaped locket around my neck and wondered if Amity really loved me. Mama had said that in time he might change his mind about me. Maybe he would. The thought scared me a little, but thoughts of Rose had taken precedence over any mulling I might have done concerning the future and Amity's feelings for me. I'd waited until after Daddy left the house to go into the kitchen and face Mama. I found her sitting at the table dressed in a heavy robe holding a coffee cup and staring out the window at the Asher house. Breaking the silence, she said without looking at me, "Rose is gonna hate me when I tell her about Big Brock and what he done to me. She'll never understand what I've had to live with all these years." Laughing sourly she added, "I knowed she would have never settled for that miner she laid the baby off on. Rose wouldn't give herself to nobody like that." In a harsher tone, she said, "You should have come to me with this."

"She told me not to," I answered in defense.

"I guess seein' her big with a baby that belongs to her own kin is a better thing!"

Tired and irritated, I snapped, "It's not my fault, so don't blame it on me. I ain't her keeper." Even though I said it, deep down inside I didn't believe my own words. In truth, I had been my sister's keeper all my life. I'd intervened in the fights between her and Mama for years. Maybe I should have told Mama when I found out she was seeing Bart Asher. Maybe Mama was right and a few beatings would have served her better than this. After all, anything would have been better than this.

That day, school had acted as more of a distraction than a useful place. Later in Amity's truck, sandwiched between him and Violet Elizabeth, I pretended that life was fine. Thank God for Violet Elizabeth's presence. I was glad she spent most of the drive from school to the lodge talking about the fuzzy baby chicks that had just hatched. Listening to her carefree tone, I had wished that I could trade places with her for just a minute or two. It had been so long since I had felt any sort of real happiness. Sure, I'd had a few happy moments, but not enough to stamp out the gloom and strife life had dealt me since the collapse of No. 5 Mine. Occasionally, Amity would glance at me out of the corner of his eye. I knew he was aware that something was wrong with me. I couldn't fool him. When we reached the Smith's lane, Amity suggested to Violet Elizabeth, "Honey, why don't you go see your new chickens while I talk with Junie Mae."

"Ok," she happily agreed. She then reached over, kissed my cheek, and invited me to come up and see the baby chicks the next day. I assured her that I would.

Once we were alone in the truck, Amity turned to me and asked, "What's wrong, Junie Mae? You've been too quiet today."

Shrugging and looking down at my hands in my lap, I said, "I wish I could tell you everything, but I can't. Maybe sometime soon."

Reaching over and grasping my hands in his warm ones, he gently commanded "Look up here, Junie Mae."

Lifting my eyes up, I looked into his blue sympathetic ones.

"That's better," he laughed, showing his dimples "I'm here for you, Junie Mae. I don't aim to pry, but I just want you to know that you can talk to me about anything that's botherin' you."

Before I could answer, his lips were on mine. The kiss had taken me by surprise, and instead of stirring passion inside me, I'd felt a surge of rage and abruptly pulled away. Looking crestfallen, Amity apologized. "I'm sorry, Junie Mae. I didn't mean to scare you."

His soft tone and gentle understanding had brought tears to my eyes. Turning toward the window, I tried to hide them, but he slowly touched my cheek and gently turned my face toward his. Without thinking, I fell into his arms and cried into his jacket. Feeling contented, I'd wanted to stay there forever. His voice whispered words of endearment to me that I rarely heard at home, and I could feel his heart pounding with sincerity against my cheek. "I know your daddy and the rest of the miners are havin' it bad up there at the mine. I heard talk of a contract. If Asher don't accept it, there might be a strike. I know that would be bad business, and that's probably what's eatin' at you Junie Mae. Just try not to worry about it, honey. Things have a way of workin' out," he soothed.

Once back at the lodge, I wanted to stay with Amity. I had felt guilty about pulling away from the kiss that he'd planted on my lips earlier. In retrospect, I realized that a part of me had equated a kiss to more intimate acts that could lead to a pregnancy. The thought of becoming pregnant had frightened me to death. Pausing before opening the truck door, I gazed up at his face that shone with compassion and love for me. The knowledge of that love both touched and overwhelmed me. "I'm sorry Amity, I never meant to hurt you," I whispered.

"I know," he said softly. "It's all gonna be all right, Junie Mae. You'll see."

After I waved goodbye and watched his truck disappear around the bend, I turned to see that Daddy's truck wasn't in the drive and wondered if he had already brought Rose back to the lodge. With my heart racing, I opened the living room door and closed it gingerly, and then walked into the kitchen where Mama sat at the table writing a letter.

"Where's Rose?" I asked in a shaky voice.

Looking up from the paper, she replied, "She's in there. I ain't said nothin' yet. I was waitin' for you."

With my heart in my throat, I walked into our bedroom where Rose was sitting in front of the mirror combing her hair. Upon seeing me she smiled and said, "I've been waitin to tell you the news." Putting the hairbrush down, she closed the bedroom door and then turned to me and said in a tone of secrecy, "I saw Bart yesterday. He was in the alley just like he promised." Looking into her eyes, I saw a kind of merriment in their blue gray depths that I had rarely seen in the past.

"Me and Bart talked about the baby, Junie Mae. He didn't deny it and he promised that he'd help me out with money as soon as it's born. But until then, I have to keep it all quiet. Bart says that his daddy ain't doin' real good right now, and if he found out somethin' like this that it would push him over the edge -- you know, with the union comin' in and all."

I heard my own voice snap, "The Ashers are all evil!"

Rose's face had taken on a woebegone expression, and just as she started to speak, the door opened and Mama said, "The Ashers are evil--the most evil people I know anywhere."

Rose looked from Mama to me. "What did you tell her?" She asked accusingly.

Before I could answer, Mama spoke up. "Rose, I got some things to tell you that's gonna hurt you. I never wanted you to know, but I got no choice now." Inhaling deeply, she spoke calmly. "I know that Bart Asher's the father of your baby. It don't matter how I know; that part ain't even important right now."

Rose's face had turned as white as milk and her voice was full of denial. "That's a lie! Bart Asher ain't my baby's daddy, and whoever told that don't know the truth!" Flashing her strange eyes on me, she asked, "How could you tell her a lie like this? I know it was you!"

"The blame shouldn't be on Junie Mae, Rose. It ain't got nothin' to do with her. You've done like I did, and now you're in a pickle."

"If you're talkin' about you and Little Brock Asher, I know all about that. It ain't got nothin' to do with me and my baby."

Mama moved to where I sat on the bed and eased her small frame down beside me. Looking down at her hands, she began telling Rose how she'd spent her childhood with Little Brock Asher. In a low, reminiscing tone, she spoke of how much Little Brock Asher had once meant to her. "I thought he was everything. We growed up together and had latched on to one another early on. I never felt alone then. It was the only happy times I can remember."

"What's this got to do with me?" Rose snapped impatiently.

Mama sighed and went on with the telling of how she and Little Brock were separated when she turned twelve. "It was like they tore off my arm or leg. I cried every day missin' him. Floyd Wilkes missed him too, and couldn't understand why Mama stopped taking us up to the big house. I didn't understand then, either, but it got plain to me after a while. The Ashers couldn't have their son gettin' close to the daughter of their housemaid. Mama was loyal to them and acted like a colored servant doin' their biddin' all day long. If either one of them had asked her to she would have gladly licked their boots. The Ashers' word was gospel to her."

Mama went on to tell Rose how Little Brock Asher had tried to see her on the sly but that she'd refused to open the door to him. She also told her how Grandma Haley had made her work for Big Brock at the funeral home because they'd just lost Granddaddy Wilkes Haley and were in need of money. She said, "I never liked old Big Brock, even before he done what he done to me. He was always as cold as ice no matter what went on. Nothin' ever bothered him or rattled him. He wadn't even human and could look right at them dead people without so much as a flinch. I remember when Elmira Jordan's little baby girl was brought into the morgue. He'd handled her little body like you'd handle a sack of potatoes. I cried all night seein' it layin' there on that cold table. The next day Big Brock had seen me cryin' and jumped me for it. He told me that death was just a part of livin' and that I might as well get used to seein' it. He made me dress that baby in the little pink dress its mama had made it. I combed its hair…" Her voice trailed off.

After a few seconds, she resumed talking. "Old Asher put his hands on me a few times. Sometimes he'd stand over me even while I was workin' on a corpse. His hands would snake down inside my blouse and he'd try to unbutton it. I never said nothin' 'cause I was embarrassed. I'd just move away from him hopin' and prayin' he'd stop. I finally told Mama what he was doin', and all she done was blame me. She said I'd done somethin' to tempt him, and that I better stop." The next part of Mama's story was new to me and caused me to gasp in dismay.

She said, "When Floyd Wilkes got killed, Mama sent his body over to Asher's." Swallowing hard, she whispered, "Asher never said a word about where he was and took me right into the morgue part where my brother's naked body was laid out on the table. When I seen that it was Floyd Wilkes layin' there I fainted. I couldn't believe what I was seein'. It was too much. He never apologized for takin' me in there. I knowed he done it out of spite."

"Why are you tellin' me this Mama? You never told us nothin' about you and Little Brock before," Rose stated in an irritable tone.

"Because it's time you knowed the truth, Rose. I don't take no pleasure in relivin' this. I've run from it since it happened. I was young and foolish and believed that one day I'd marry Little Brock Asher just like he promised we would. When he told his daddy that he'd wanted to marry me, the old bastard threatened to disinherit him. Little Brock didn't care, though, and told his Daddy so. Back then, Little Brock had dreams of me and him movin' away from here and havin' a business of his own that didn't have nothin' to do with the coal. Big Brock couldn't stomach the thought of losin' his only son to me, so he fixed it so we could never get married and move away. He fixed it real good, Rose."

"What did he do, Mama?" Rose asked in cautious tone.

"It happened the night after old Wesley Mills was shot and killed. I remember standin' in the dressin' room puttin' make-up on him. I'd already put two coats of the pancake powder on him, but his face still looked as white as snow. I was reachin' for a darker powder when I felt two arms go 'round my waist. I twisted around and there was old Big Brock tryin' to kiss me while his hand went down the front my dress. I screamed as loud as I could but nobody come. Rose, he took me right there against my will. He raped me." With tears in her eyes, Mama described the scene. "After he was done with me, there was blood all over the floor. It looked like somebody stuck a pig. I was scared to death and started grabbin' for my clothes and tryin' to hide my nakedness. He just laughed and said, 'Now that you're ruined, you won't be seein' my son no more. You had dealings with me and it wouldn't be right to have no more dealings with my son. It wouldn't be decent. Now put your clothes back on and keep your mouth shut.' He warned me that if I told, nobody would believe me, not even my own Mama. I knowed that what he was sayin' was true." Inhaling a long shuddering breath she went on, "Mama found out later what he'd done, only she wouldn't let me call it rape. She said I'd caused my own situation and that I'd have to just live with it. Well, I have – every day since."

Jumping up from the chair, Rose looked at Mama and said, "I don't believe this, Mama. You're tellin' me that Big Brock Asher raped you to just to keep you from marryin' his son?"

"It's true!"

"Even if he done this awful thing, what has it got to do with me? I don't know any of them Ashers 'cept in passin'."

Mama rose from the bed, walked over, and gently took Rose's arm. Flinching as if Mama had struck her, Rose shrugged her off. Mama said, "After Big Brock raped me I got pregnant with you, Rose. You belong to Big Brock Asher. He's your daddy."

Rose's eyes grew large and disbelieving. Stepping far back away from Mama, she began shaking her head in disbelief. Looking as though she might faint, she said accusingly, "You're lyin'! No. No. That can't be! Why on earth would you tell me a lie like this?" she asked.

"Because you are carryin' Bart Asher's baby, Rose, and it ain't no lie."

Looking wild-eyed Rose muttered, "Daddy will tell me the truth. I'll ask him."

"Daddy don't know this, Rose. I met and married him not long after this happened. He thinks you're his. It would kill him to know the truth!"

Shaking with fear, I watched my sister die that day. I recall the sinking feeling within my chest and the panic that rose like a tide in the winter. The most I could do was sit there and watch her soul crawl out of her body like the morning fog and then dissipate. I can picture her sitting there before the old, scarred mirror protectively holding on to her stomach where her unborn baby lay helpless. Her face was the color of bleached bones and her eyes had become as lifeless, reminding me of the blue marbles boys played with in the schoolyard.

In a strangely gentle voice Mama said, "Rose, that baby you're carryin' won't come out right because its daddy is your close kin. You can't keep it. There's hospitals and places that take deformed babies in Indianapolis. You might want to think about going back with me."

Rose stared emptily at the floor. My heart had gone out to her but I couldn't think of a thing to do or say that would make things right. Deep down inside me, I knew then that things would never be right again for Rose -- or Daddy, for that matter, if he ever found out the truth. When Rose stopped talking to Mama, she left the room but not before reminding her that she needed to start packing for Indianapolis. "You ain't got no choice, Rose. You can't keep that baby knowin' what you do now. I'm tryin' to help you."

Once Mama was out of sight, Rose turned to me and with a grimace on her pretty face said, "I ain't goin' nowhere with her. What's more, I don't believe a single word she just told me." As fast as she had died, a part of her had miraculously come back to life. Watching her was like watching a flame rise up through the ashes.

Taken aback by her refusal to face the truth, I said, "Rose, Mama didn't make none of that up. You have to believe me."

Turning her strange eyes on me she vowed, "I'll not forgive you for tellin' her about me and Bart. Once she found that out, she made up the whole rape story just so I'll get rid of this baby. She hates me, Junie Mae, and will do anything to hurt me."

"No, Rose, it's not like that. She wouldn't have ever told you if I hadn't've guessed the truth myself and told her I knowed."

"You guessed the truth? You guessed that I didn't belong to Daddy? You never once said nothin' like that to me in all the times we talked. How could you guess?"

"I didn't know then. It just came to me today. At first I thought Little Brock Asher was your daddy. I kept askin' her about it and she finally told me the truth. She didn't want to but I had her in a corner."

"You give her the idea to make this whole thing up, and I won't forgive you for it. The baby ain't even here yet and already she wants to put it in some institution."

"You can't keep it if it comes out all twisted and retarded," I pleaded in desperation.

"The baby belongs to Bart Asher; it won't be twisted," she said haughtily.

My pity for Rose had turned to disgust. "Bart Asher's stringin' you along for right now, Rose, because he don't want you tellin' nobody about the baby. For once Mama's right -- the Ashers are dirt! They're evil people who don't care about nobody but themselves. I know that old man Brock raped Mama! He did it so she'd never feel clean or good enough for his son. If they knowed you was carryin' Bart's baby they'd do somethin' to hurt you, too!"

Rose threw back her head and laughed coldly. "You're takin' up for Mama like always. Even though you know that she steals and lies. Oh, she lies real good! Look how she lied to Daddy and the law about them watches. Look how she's goin' behind Daddy's back tryin' to get with his own brother. I hate her," she seethed. "I wouldn't believe nothin' she said if she swore it on a Bible. I'll tell you this -- I'm gettin' out of here as soon as Harvey James brings Daddy home from that union meetin', and I ain't comin back here again. I ain't listening to no more of her dirty lies."

At a loss for words, I watched her go to the corner closet where she began ripping clothes off the hangers and cramming them into a paper sack. "The weather's gettin' warmer and I'll soon need lighter clothes," she said. Her face wore a look of resolution that I'd seen so many times. I had realized then that she'd stubbornly made up her mind to deny the truth. Rose was like that. If the truth hurt too much, she'd revert into the fairytale where everyone lived happily ever after. I couldn't blame her much. Who would want to hear that their whole life had been nothing but a lie? Still, she had to face the truth, no matter how grim and distasteful. Inside of her, she carried a child that might not be right because of blood.

"You can run as far as you want to, but this ain't goin' away, Rose. I know you hate Mama, but what she told you is true," I begged.

Deliberately ignoring me, Rose went about preparing to leave. When Uncle Harvey James finally came, she left with him without saying a word of goodbye. I remember sitting on the bed feeling so helpless inside and wondering how she could rearrange her beliefs so quickly and easily. Somewhere inside her, she had to know that Mama was telling the truth.

32 RUMORS OF MORE TROUBLE

The month of March came in cold with high winds blowing and whistling through the bare branches. The landscape appeared to me deader than I'd ever seen it. Sometimes after school, Amity and I would take long drives through the country. I'd stare out the window at the leafless trees and wonder if they would ever come back to life. Death was all around me, depressing me and reminding me how much things had changed over the course of a year, starting with the mine cave in in back in August. I'd known that Amity sensed my inner turmoil because he was sensitive like that, but he seldom pried. Maybe he was afraid that in mentioning it, he might scare me away, and he might have been right. The last thing I wanted to tell him was that Rose was pregnant out of wedlock by her own kin and that Mama was out in Indianapolis trying to win the attentions of my daddy's own brother.

Things had heated up at the No. 5 mine since Asher had gotten the union contract. It had been a week since it was presented to him and still he hadn't responded. People were enraged by the murders of Levi Creech and Donny Calvin and were demanding some answers from the law. Rumors of who might have killed the men ran rampant throughout the camp. Uncle Harlan Ray swore that it was the first two scabs hired by Asher after the cave-in, Bidge Cornet and Hebert Anson. Someone had told Harlan Ray that the two were seen standing near Levi's truck the morning it was shot up.

One morning at breakfast, Harlan Ray told Daddy, "Them boys ain't nothin' but trouble. I done a little checkin' on 'em and nobody I talked to had one good thing to say about either one of 'em. The Cornet boy is a draft dodger, and Hobart Anson was in on that robbery of that elderly couple's house over on Flackie. You remember that, Ralph? The robbers tied the old couple up and stole everything they had. The old man's heart killed out from the shock and his wife ended up living the rest of her life with her daughter. Anson went to prison for it, but got out early on good behavior."

"Yeah, I remember that," Daddy said thoughtfully, and then asked, "Why in the world would Asher hire thugs like them to work in the coal, especially with all the turmoil goin' on up there? Didn't he know what thugs like that would do in a time of trouble? Hirin' them was like lightin' a fuse to a stick of dynamite."

"Maybe that was Asher's point. He's a coward so he hired men like these to watch his back and do his dirty work," Harvey James suggested.

Daddy argued, "Little Brock Asher ain't no killer, Harvey. I'm tellin' you that he ain't got that in him. I've talked to him plenty of times. I used to go up there to Creekstone when Heddy was housekeepin' for them and he'd invite me into the barn where he had a little workroom. He'd offer me a slug of his whiskey then he'd show me his livestock. I swear that before we got back to the barn he was as drunk as a skunk and talkin' out of his head. I told Heddy that I didn't see how he managed to run the mine drinkin' like that."

Laughing dryly, Harlan Ray said, "It's his old daddy that's runnin' the show. I heard tell that Big Brock got the company that contract with the electric company. Little Brock didn't have nothin' to do with it. Old Brock's been around the block; he's got connections all over the place with the rich. I'll bet you a dollar to your dime that it was his idea to evict them widows. I don't see Little Brock doin' it. He's helped too many of the miners and their families at the camp."

Harvey James replied warily, "You know, Big Dan Stewart told me that Little Brock Asher told him that he couldn't understand why the miners were tuning on him. Dan told me that Little Brock Asher sometimes stayed up there in his office all night drinkin'."

"Well, he needs to sober up long enough to read the contract," Harlan Ray said sourly.

While the men talked I'd gone about the kitchen gathering up plates, pouring second and third cups of coffee all the while listening to the miners' talk that had become a morning ritual. Both Harvey James and Harlan Ray had been moved to third shift and always stopped by the lodge in the mornings when they didn't work over. Daddy got up early in the mornings just to listen and participate in the talks. Since Mama had gone back to Indianapolis he'd had little else to look forward to and gave what little energy he had to the union and getting better pay and working conditions for his fellow miners. Daddy was especially sympathetic to Bonzelle Creech. He'd told Harvey James and Harlan Ray that he'd heard the she and the miners' widows had bonded together and had brought a negligence suit against the Asher Coal Company.

Harlan Ray said, "It was the smart German woman that hissed 'em on. Bonzelle ain't real swift in the head but has more guts than most women."

Harvey James spoke sympathetically, "Well, you can't blame Olga Winley for trying to get something out of Asher. She doesn't speak good English, and even if she did, what kind of work could she get around here? The other widows are hurting for money, too. I imagine their husbands' pensions won't be enough for them to live on."

Shaking his head thoughtfully in agreement, Harlan Ray changed to subject to Uncle Corbin. "The man's an idiot and as hard-headed as they come where money is involved. If you didn't know him better, you'd swear he had a wife and ten children to support. He acts like he ain't got a penny to his name, when I'll betcha he's got thousands of dollars squirreled away in the bank."

Harvey James laughed in agreement and said, "He's still our brother, though, and it worries me because I know for a fact that he'll be the first one to cross the picket line if there's a strike."

Daddy nodded. "Greed will be what gets him killed if he ain't careful. Paw talked bad about the union, and I reckon that's why he hates unions so much."

"Maybe," Harlan Ray speculated, and then added, "It's a damned shame he can't see how havin' the union would benefit us."

33 THE STRIKE BEGINS

Daddy hoped every day for a letter from Mama. Sometimes he'd ask if I could have Amity swing by the post office after school. A week had gone by before he finally got a letter from her. Since he couldn't read very well, I read to him what she had written. Mama was a copious letter writer who had a small, neat script. It was easy to make out what she wrote. Usually her letters consisted of four or five full two-sided pages, and their content full of Rhodie and how hard it was to care for her. According to Mama, Rhodie had become combative and had even blacked one of her eyes while she was trying to bathe her. Mama wrote, "Taking care of Rhodie ain't no picnic. I am so tired by the end of the day I can hardly see straight. She won't talk at all and when I tried to shock her out of it by showing her a picture of Amy Isabella, she just sat there staring at it like she had never seen her before in her life. It was the oddest thing. Larkin told me he'd pay me once a month. As soon as I get the first check I'll send you and Junie Mae some money…"

Daddy always seemed depressed after I read one of Mama's letters to him. He'd say in a guilty voice, "I'm gonna have to sign up for a pension so she won't have to do this job no more. Who knows what that woman might do if she's goin' as far as hittin' your Mama."

Even as a young girl, I was quick to read between the lines. I had learned Mama well and knew that her intention was to guilt Daddy into thinking that she was in Indianapolis more out of necessity than of her own want. Maybe it made her feel better inside to twist the knife further in his heart by leading him to believe that if it wasn't for her working that horrific job we would all have starved to death. I'd hated the sadness that Mama's letters caused Daddy. In the months that followed, I watched Daddy's health decline. Some nights he would cough for hours. On those nights, I made him drink the cough medicine so he could rest. After nearly three weeks of Mama's absence, I noticed that Daddy had lost most of the weight he had gained in spite of the regular meals I prepared for him. One Saturday morning during the first week of April I awoke to find him gone before daylight. I recall the deathly silence of the house and the grayness of the morning. It had rained the night before and I'd noted that the dripping landscape was coming back. The trees were budding and the ground had greened up with the promise of thick grass. The river had a nice clear look to its surface in spite of the creeping morning fog. I stood on the porch that morning shivering in the nippy air, yet feeing a kind of rejuvenation inside me. Amity had promised to take me on a ride by the river that noon, which sent a spreading warmth of happiness inside my chest. With no one to cook for, I settled for a cold biscuit that tasted nothing like Mama's light and fluffy ones. I thought of Rose who couldn't boil water, let alone make a pan of biscuits. I hadn't seen my sister since the day she learned about Big Brock Asher being her Daddy. I wondered how she was coping with the fact that her whole life had been a lie. I also thought of Granny Lee and figured she was bound to know about Rose's pregnancy by now and would soon insist that Rose tell Daddy about it. One thing was certain; Rose would have to tell him soon because she wouldn't be able to hide her expanding belly much longer.

 A little before noon I dressed in a long skirt and donned thick socks. I chose the warmest sweater I could find and then waited by the window in the living room for Amity to show. A few minutes passed before I heard something that sounded like a loud clap of thunder. Stepping back out onto the porch, I heard another sharp crack which sounded like it was coming from the direction of No. 5 Mine. Someone was shooting. Dear God! Daddy was up there! Automatically, I ran down the steps and onto the dirt road leading up to No. 5 mine. My heart felt as if it was in my throat. At first, I didn't see or hear Amity's truck pull up beside me, but then he yelled over the roar of the motor "Where are you goin', Junie Mae?"

 I told him about the shot I'd heard, and that I was going to the mine to check on Daddy. Just as I said it, I heard the familiar screams of sirens in the distance, and they brought about panic within me. "Hurry and park the truck in the yard. If you don't they'll run overtop you," I yelled.

 Amity quickly backed up the truck and steered it to the yard, parking it on the spot in front of Daddy's shed. "We can take the path beside the road and bypass the gate," I said, grabbing his hand even before he stepped out of the truck.

 Shaking his head, Amity said, "Your Daddy will kill me if I take you up there."

 "If you won't go with me I'll go by myself." I said stubbornly.

 "All right, but it might be dangerous to go up there. There's no tellin' what's goin' on. It sounds to me like people might be shootin' at each other. The law might not let us get near the mine."

"We're wastin' time talkin about it, Amity. Come on! "I urged.

As the sirens grew closer, I knew that in just a matter of minutes the law would come barreling past us. Grabbing Amity's hand, I led him across the road and toward the river. A couple of years before, Rose and me had discovered the river path leading up to the No. 5. Once we found it, we sneaked up there often. Neither Mama nor Daddy ever knew about our secret trips. The river path was rough with its deadfalls and briar patches, and in the summer, it was nearly impossible to escape injury from either a thorn bush or poison ivy that grew thick on the hillside.

"Careful, hon," Amity cautioned before reaching down and gently pulling the material of my skirt from the thorn bush.

The screech of the sirens had suddenly stopped, and I could hear cars whizzing by us on the road.

"Why did they turn off the sirens?" Amity asked, and then cocked his head. "Listen! It sounds like somebody's talkin' through a bullhorn."

I could plainly hear a man's voice bouncing off the cliffs, but I couldn't make out what he was saying.

"Somethin' bad is goin' on up there. I can feel it," I said prophetically. Floyd Wilkes' ghost seemed to peep out from the corner of my thoughts, but I pushed it back as I had been doing since he'd showed me the scary image of Rose with no face. My hand was clasped warmly in Amity's bigger one and I felt strangely safe. "We're almost there," I assured him. Once away from the downed tree Amity followed me up the hill where we eventually stepped out onto the road above the gate. There in front of us was the muddy parking lot where a flood of people stood. Some of them held picket signs while others marched back and forth with signs reading, "Better Wages, Safer Conditions." Bonzelle Creech and Olga Winley were among the women who carried picket signs that read "Pro Union: Safer Conditions for Miners." There, just a few feet from the railroad, stood the tall, stilted office tower of Little Brock Asher. Many houses near the river were built high on similar stilts to keep out the water in case of flooding. Daddy said Little Brock had his office built high up in order to see what was going on down below him. Gasping, I pointed upwards to the small terrace or landing where Little Brock stood with a rifle mounted on the railing. One of his hands steadied the rifle while the other held the bullhorn close to his mouth. "He's got a gun!" Amity whispered before leading me farther to the side and out of the line of fire.

The voice of Little Brock Asher rang out and seemed to bounce off every rock. Its tone was slurred and hateful. "You people are worse than Judas with all your signs cursing me and the coal. It wadn't so long ago that you appreciated it. Many of you were glad to be workin' so close to home.

Most of you live in the homes I provided and never complained a bit until the accident. Now you're all out there refusin' to work, knowin' full well there's a big contract with the electric company at stake." Staggering backwards, he caught his balance but nearly tipped the gun he had sighted on the unruly crowd, many of whom were hurling insults right back at him.

My eyes scanned the difficult crowd hoping for the sight of either Daddy or the Uncles, but I didn't see them because there were just too many people milling around, including several law officers who stood down below the high office. One officer pleaded through a bullhorn for Little Brock to come down and surrender his weapon to another officer, but Little Brock refused, saying, "This is my property and the people who ain't workin' are trespassers. If they don't mean to work then they need to get off my property! I ain't signing no contract with the union, so they're wastin' their time picketing."

"Mr. Asher," yelled Joel Baker's short little deputy, Arbert Rouse, "This might be your property but that don't mean you have a right to shoot at people. Now give up that gun and come down from there!"

"A man has every right to protect his property," Little Brock slurred.

I said to Amity of Little Brock Asher, "He's drunk. I've seen him stagger like that before. Daddy says he gets drunk a lot."

"We should get out of here. Them protesters look mighty angry, and you never know. Little Brock might even start shootin' at 'em, Junie Mae," Amity pleaded.

"I am gonna find Daddy! That's why we come up here, and I ain't gonna leave until I see that he ain't hurt!" The anger and resolve in my own voice seemed to convince Amity that I wasn't leaving. Sighing, he grabbed my hand and said, "We're circling around the crowd in case he starts shootin'." Within the wide circle, miners were shouting at Little Brock Asher. Bonzelle Creech appeared out of the crowd and approached the office tower, seemingly without caution, only to be confronted by an officer who warned her to step back. But Bonzelle was in no mood to listen and started screaming up at Little Brock Asher. "You hired thugs to replace the miners that died in your mine, and they killed my daddy right here in this parkin' lot. I ain't heard one word from you about that. I ain't heard one word from the law about it, either. Innocent men died because you was too greedy to pay them poor widows what you owed 'em."

In an equally angry tone Little Brock shot back, "I had nothing to do with your daddy's death. You ain't got no right accusing me of murder."

"You're a murderer! You might as well have shot my daddy and them miners with that gun of yours, 'cause it was your carelessness that caused the mine to cave in, wadn't it? Wadn't it?"

Suddenly two lawmen grabbed Bonzelle and dragged her kicking and screaming out of the crowd. Her screams in turn caused chaos. Two miners I didn't recognize threw down their signs and rapidly approached the deputies, while the rest of the crowd charged forward hurling obscenities. Holding on tightly to Amity's hand, I braced myself in anticipation of trouble. "Get back!" One of the lawmen threatened before pulling his pistol and pointing it directly at the men. Olga Winley approached the lawmen and started screaming at them to let Bonzelle go. "Vat right do you have to grab her like dat?" She yelled.

"Step back!" Sherriff Baker yelled through his bullhorn, then added "Everybody get back or I'll get a hold of the state militia and they'll put a stop to all this. I'm warning you all!"

"I don't believe this," Amity said, while holding me so hard and close to him that I could hardly breathe.

"I do," I whispered. "Mama said it would be like this." While watching the restless angry crowd, I urged Amity to help me find Daddy, but he was uncertain and urged, "We need to get out of the mess, Junie Mae. I don't like the look of things."

Before I could protest, Big Maude Stewart tugged at my arm and said, "Lord, child -- what are you doin' up here? Little Brock Asher has gone off his rocker. Listen at him up there goin' on. He's already fired that gun twice into the air."

Turning to Amity she barked, "Young fellar, you get her home before her daddy sees her. He's over yonder somewhere," she pointed to the right of us.

"Come on, Amity," I urged, pulling on his sleeve, but Amity was still listening to Maude berate Little Brock Asher. "The unions done pushed him over the edge. Look! There comes his daddy and Miss Joelyn, and that son of his," she cried, pointing to the steps leading up to his high office.

"Big Brock's goin' up there to talk him down," I said. Out in the crowd people were shouting insults toward the Ashers. One miner held his pro union sign high in the air and hollered, "You can't get your boy out of this one, Big Brock. You can't get shed of the United Mine Workers of America, either. We're here to stay, and you ain't gonna run us out!"

Cheers went up in the crowd. By now, more lawmen from other counties had shown up as an added measure of protection. I studied the gatherers hoping for a glimpse of Daddy or my uncles, but I saw only Big Maude Stewart and others pushing their way through the crowd in order to get a better look at the office tower where a gray-haired Big Brock Asher stood trying to reason with his drunken son. Down below, Bart Asher hovered protectively next to his mother and tensely watched the scene above them unfold. Suddenly, two deputies appeared and stood next to the Ashers and yelled for the rushers to stand back. I'd never seen such chaos. Seemingly glued to the spot I watched Big Brock mount the steps and then move the gun off the railing. Finally taking his reluctant son by the shoulder, he led him toward the steps. Lawmen had positioned themselves in front of the mob in order to clear the way for Big Brock and his son. "Take him to the river and dunk his head a few times; he'll sober up!" someone yelled. Glancing to the side, I recognized the tall lanky figure of Uncle Purl Haley squeezing through the crowd. Flanked by two deputies, Little Brock was led out of the crowd and over to where Miss Joelyn and Bart stood waiting. Uncle Purl approached Miss Joelyn and whispered something to her. She nodded, and then both she and her son followed him to his waiting truck. "Purl Haley, you can burn in hell alongside the Ashers!" a man's voice yelled.

Feeling a sickness rise in the pit of my stomach, I slumped against Amity who said, "This is enough. We're gettin' out of here Junie Mae." Too sick to reply, I held on tightly to his hand as we pushed our way through the shouting mob. What had they done with Bonzelle Creech and Olga Winley?

I recall that day as if it happened yesterday. The rancid smell of the coal like rotten eggs is still so vivid, as is the charged atmosphere of rebellion. Women screamed in protest while men held up signs and hollered insults at the Ashers. The widows of those dead miners cried out for reparation for their empty beds and fatherless children, but the Ashers seemed deaf to their pleas. I remember standing there in the center of the angry mob, watching the anxious and angry expressions on the faces of some of the people I had known all my life. Olga Winley and Bonzelle Creech were among the many livid protesters who were shouting up at Asher. Once out of the crowd and near the gates leading out, Amity asked me if I was all right. "No," I replied. "I'll never be all right again -- not after what I've seen today." Feeling a sudden rush of adrenalin, I turned to face the crowd in hopes of seeing Daddy. Suddenly, both he and Harvey James appeared near the office tower. "There's Daddy and my uncle," I said, jerking Amity's hand urgently.

"He won't like you bein' here. Let's just go," he urged.

"No! It's too late to turn back. I came here to see him, and that's what I aim to do," I huffed stubbornly.

Amity smiled a lopsided smile and squeezed my hand. "You're as stubborn as Daddy's mule, Charlie." He chuckled. Halfway to the office tower a lawman raised his hand for us to halt. "You all got no business here. You need to move on out the gate."

"My daddy's over there, and I ain't leavin' until I see him. He's sick," I snapped.

"You all better get him over here. She won't leave until she sees him. I won't let anybody put hands on her," Amity warned.

"This ain't no place for a little girl," the big burly lawman warned.

"I don't see no little girl!" I snapped right back.

"There's your daddy," Amity said, pointing in the direction of the office tower.

Looking up, I saw Daddy coming toward us. His face was twisted in anger such as I had never seen before. Harvey James walked beside him looking pale and dawn. "What are you doin' up here, Junie Mae?" he barked. His dark eyes bulged dangerously, which caused me to shrink closer to Amity.

"Answer me!" he demanded

"I heard the shots from the front porch and I got scared and-and wanted to see you," I stammered.

Pointing a finger at Amity he ordered, "You get her back to the house right now, you hear?"

"Yessir. Let's go, Junie Mae."

Turning to the lawman, Daddy said in a calmer voice "I'd appreciate it if you walked them on out of the gate."

Once on the road leading back to the lodge, I couldn't hold back my tears. My heart ached inside my chest while my throat felt as if it might burst.

"I'm sorry I took you up there," Amity said gently.

"I would have went without you," I croaked.

"Oh honey, I know your Daddy didn't mean to get so mad. He was just scared you'd get hurt bad up there. That's all it was."

Nodding my head in affirmation, I used my coat sleeve to wipe away the deluge of tears that cascaded down my cheeks. Placing his arm around my shoulders, Amity whispered, "Hold up, Junie Mae." Stopping in my tracks, I stood looking at the ground and purposely avoiding his gaze, but he wouldn't let me. Tilting my chin upwards, his blue eyes looked sadly into mine. "I'm so sorry you had to see all that back there. The coal is about all a man can do here to make a livin', and that's a damned shame. You know, my daddy never set a foot inside a mine, but his daddy did. I've heard stories about how hard he slaved, shovelin' coal and loadin' it up all day on the pack mules. His back finally gave out on him and he couldn't do it no more. Daddy said that he wadn't that old when he died. The coal ate his lungs out and he couldn't breathe no more. You're the daughter of a coalminer, Junie Mae. It ain't fair that you have to live this way, but it's your lot. You was born into it just like most of the folks around here, and you'll survive it 'cause you're a strong girl. I like that about you."

I nodded, feeling a little stronger inside. Amity knew how to draw out my strengths, and it was the grown-up things in him that I needed and adored so much. Hearing the roar of oncoming cars behind us, Amity quickly steered me toward the little patch of woods leading to the riverbank where we walked hand in hand for about an hour. Very few words passed between us but conversation seemed unnecessary. The remembrance of that quiet walk along the river brings back feelings of sweet innocence. I can see the water so clearly and can hear the rush of its shoals over rocks. The reflection of trees wavering in the green water and the white sands of the islands linger so vividly in my thoughts, as do the tall flinty walls and the hills behind the river.

Once back at the lodge, Amity kissed my cheek and promised, "One day, Junie Mae, I'll get you away from the coal. I'll build you a house back there in the woods where you can raise chickens and play with our babies. I want you to think of that instead of what you seen today."

Amity's sweet promise of a better life had sustained me during what would become some of the most trying days of my life. A part of me coddled memories of Amity the careful way one might guard an egg. I had hung on to his every word and burned his face into my memory because I'd known somewhere in me that someone that good couldn't last.

34 ROSE'S SECRET REVEALED

I found Daddy in the shed whittling on a long piece of wood. Looking up when he saw me, I felt his remorse and knew he'd never meant to shout at me up at the mine. "Junie Mae, I'm sorry," he croaked.

"I'm so glad you're all right. I wadn't thinkin' of myself when I went up there…"

"I know you wadn't, honey, but things have got way out of hand up there. I never…" He sighed, shaking his head in disgust. "I never thought it would be this bad. I figured Asher might study the contract and at least settle with them widows, but it looks like all that contract done was make him crazy. I got a feelin' he'll never agree to negotiate. He's in too bad of shape to decide on anything, so I reckon that means we're back where we started."

Pausing in his whittling, Daddy looked up at me with the saddest of expressions and said, "I seen Rose this mornin'. I stopped over at Ma's for breakfast. I know she's pregnant. Why in God's name didn't somebody tell me before now?"

Unable to look him in the eye, I turned toward the door. "You was too sick. We was afraid if you found out somethin' like that it might kill you".

"It's killin' me now. Maybe your mama was right in warnin' me not to take her around Marie. I feel like it was my fault as much as anybody else's."

"Marie wadn't even around her when she got herself pregnant. Mama likes to blame Marie so she won't be held responsible."

"You knowed and didn't say nothin'?" Daddy asked in disbelief.

"Mama would have killed her if she'd knowed Rose had a man. I didn't know what to do. I was afraid. You know how Mama is."

Daddy returned to his whittling. His face wore the look of deep hurt. "She said the father of her baby was Todd Worley. I can't see it. Todd was a little cross-eyed, and he didn't have a lot goin' on in his head -- not that he was a bad boy or nothin'. He worked like a dog, but I would never have guessed Rose would pick somebody like him. I could see her moonin' over somebody like that Asher boy, but not Todd Worley," he said, shaking his head in disbelief. "From all accounts that boy was engaged to Sarah Sue. It just don't make no sense to me. He was always talkin' about what a good girl Sarah Sue was."

I was glad Daddy couldn't see my face when he'd mentioned Bart Asher. I almost laughed in the realization that he had such a keen perception when it came to Rose and what she liked. I recalled Mama's remark about how Daddy wouldn't know it if a skunk sprayed him. She was so wrong. His insight into Rose made me wonder just what else he had figured out and kept to himself.

Daddy continued talking about Rose and wondering aloud what she would do once the baby was born. "Its daddy's dead and she won't have nobody to help her with it. Your Mama's gone and Marie's got her hands full with her own youngins." Sighing, he threw down the piece of wood and said, "You know yourself that Rose ain't mature enough to have no baby."

Shivering, I said, "Let's go inside, Daddy; it's cold out here." Daddy, however, seemed rooted to the spot and deep in thought. "Why wouldn't your Mama talk to me about somethin' like this? She went off without sayin' a word."

"Mama couldn't deal with Rose gettin' herself pregnant, Daddy. I reckon she dreaded how you'd take it."

"It's more than that, Junie Mae. Your mama never wanted to deal with Rose, not even when she was a little girl. She wadn't never fair to her. God knows I tried to make up for it, but I wadn't enough. Rose needed her Mama. Maybe if she had give Rose the attention she needed she wouldn't have got herself in the family way."

"I don't know, Daddy. Rose is hard-headed like Mama and has always done what she wanted to."

Daddy nodded in agreement and then changed the subject. "Your Mama sent us a check today. I reckon we ought to ride into town and cash it. Our food supply is gotta be gettin' low."

I knew Daddy didn't feel good about taking money off Mama, and what he hated even more was her being gone. I could see his health failing more with each passing day and that worried me. Sadly, I felt that it would take Mama coming home to get Daddy back on the road to wellness, and I wasn't sure that would happen.

35 A BIRTHDAY AND CELEBRATIONS

The mining strike continued, and Daddy had insisted on being up at the mine every day so he could picket with his fellow workers. Little Brock had seemingly recovered from the drunken spell he'd had on the balcony of his office, but he still refused to negotiate with the union or the widows. His stubbornness, though, had made him an enemy with both the widows and the striking miners who could barely make ends meet on the strike pay.

    April slowly faded into May, bringing the warm spring rains and the tides that everyone was accustomed to but dreaded all the same. My fifteenth birthday came and went, but not without some celebrations. Granny Lee had baked me a chocolate cake with fifteen pink candles planted in its center. Grandma Haley had prepared a fried chicken dinner almost single-handedly. For the first time without fear of Mama's retribution, I was able to invite Amity and Violet Elizabeth Smith to the celebration held at Granny Lee's house. Although her house remained shabby and unkempt as usual, I couldn't in good conscience allow myself to feel ashamed of it since my Granny Lee had tried so hard to make my birthday special. Besides, Amity and Violet Elizabeth seemed oblivious to the tattered curtains, faded wallpaper, and the years' worth of clutter. I received gifts of homemade candy, scarves from family, and a fancy hand mirror from Violet Elizabeth. Granny Lee presented me with an antique cameo broach that once belonged to her mother. Afterwards, I gathered her close to me. The feel of her pudgy arms around me gave me a feeling of love and inner peace. For the first time since the mine cave-in, I felt carefree and happy. Once dinner was over, Amity mingled easily with Daddy and the uncles, while Violet Elizabeth talked happily with Rebekah Ann and Granny Lee about knitting and quilting, both of which she had a knack for. Later, after Amity dropped Violet Elizabeth off at their house, he took me on back to the lodge where he killed the truck engine. For a while, we sat watching the evening fade. Finally turning to me and said, "Junie Mae, I have something for you. I better give it you while there's still some daylight left." Withdrawing a small box from his pocket, he placed it in my hand.

"What is this?" I asked, delightfully surprised.

"It matches your necklace, I think," he said softly.

Gasping at its beauty and fragility, I carefully took the dainty bracelet out of its box and inspected it. My eyes marveled at its daintiness.

"You didn't think I would forget about your birthday, did you? Let me put it on for you."

I watched him carefully place it on my wrist and clasp it shut. "It's beautiful," I breathed.

"You are too," he said softly.

Feeling happy but as usual strangely inadequate as to how to act when given such a compliment, I smiled uncomfortably and dropped my head shyly.

"Junie Mae, girl, you need to learn to take a compliment when somebody gives you one." He smile was wicked and knowing.

"Oh Amity," I said, slapping his arm playfully, while feeling a sense of relief that he truly understood me.

"Don't wash your dishes with that on. I had to work two months to afford that," he teased.

"You know I will," I teased right back.

"I liked today a lot. Your family's nice and treated us like they knowed us for years."

Laughing, I said, "I could have told you they would. My Granny Lee's never seen a stranger."

"You're fifteen today, Junie Mae. You're growin' up. I hope you've give some thought to us havin' a future together sometime soon."

Gazing up into Amity's blue eyes, I had not the heart to tell him that my thoughts had been elsewhere. How could I tell him that I worried constantly about Daddy and Rose, and that thoughts of them had kept me so preoccupied that I had hardly had time to think of anyone or anything else?

I need not have worried. He was quick to assure me that he would wait until I was ready. "I'll wait for you, Junie Mae. No matter how long it takes, I'll wait." Even now, I remember those words just as he said them. His sweet, earnest tone will stay with me forever.

36 INJURY ON THE PICKET LINE

School came to its closing at the last part of May, which left me with more time to spend with Amity Smith when he wasn't planting the crops or working in his father's mill. Sometimes in the evenings when Daddy was gone, I would walk over to the Smiths and have supper with them. The lodge was lonely without Mama, Daddy, and Rose. I thought of Rose often and what I knew of her came mostly from Daddy or Uncles Coy and Noah. They visited at least once a week and helped me carry water from the spring. Daddy had become too weak to swing the axe, so Noah cut wood for the cook stove. One evening after I had had supper with the Smiths, I come home to find Daddy pacing the kitchen floor with worry in his dark eyes. "What's wrong, Daddy?" I asked in alarm.

"It's your Uncle Corbin. He crossed the picket line and got hisself beat up pretty bad last night. They broke his jaw and some of his ribs. He's down there in the Harlan Hospital right now. He was so bad they kept him there." Shaking his head in despair, Daddy went on, "The damned fool. Harlan and me warned him not to cross that picket but he done it anyway."

"Who done it?" I asked in astonishment.

"It don't matter, Junie Mae," Daddy whispered. "He was warned not to cross the picket, but he didn't listen. That's what happens when somebody crosses the picket line when a strike's goin' on. He knowed better, so it serves him right."

"Who's with him?" I asked.

"Ma's down there sittin' with him. She'll wear out first before she leaves his side. God, Junie Mae, it's a mess up there. Asher ain't budgin' an inch and men are already complainin' about the skimpy strike pay." Taking in a deep breath, he continued in a weak, defeated voice. "There's talk of Asher evictin' the strikers from their homes. They'll be a killin' if eviction notices go out. The whole thing's got way out of hand."

My heart went out to Daddy. I knew he felt responsible for the upheaval at the mines. Placing my hand gently on his arm, I said, "Daddy, it will all come to a head soon. You and Harvey James and Harlan Ray done the right thing by backin' the union."

"I wonder," he said miserably. "My brother's down there at that hospital with a smashed face and broken ribs and who knows what else. If them miners have to move out of their homes there'll be hell to pay. I don't know, Junie Mae. I reckon I was wrong in thinkin' Asher was human."

Grabbing his coat off the chair Daddy said, "I'm goin' to drive back down to the hospital and see if Corbin's improved any. Don't wait up for me. I might go up to the mine afterwards."

"I wish you wouldn't go back to the mine tonight. Somethin' might happen to you up there. Besides, the nights have been chilly and I'm afraid you'll catch a cold."

"I'll be all right. I have to take my licks, Junie Mae, since I am part of the reason for the strike."

After Daddy left, the house was too quiet. By nightfall, the air had turned dark and a little warmer. Sitting at the kitchen table staring out the window into the darkness, I thought of the Smith house and its happy atmosphere. A part of me yearned for the laughter and Amity's hand on mine. Touching my bracelet for comfort, I told myself that I was lucky to have someone to care for me the way Amity Smith did. I thought of how different the Smiths were from our family. Theirs was an easy closeness that was lacking between Mama and Daddy. Even during their best years, I had sensed a kind of invisible barrier between them that kept them from feeling complete happiness. I had come to realize that the invisible barrier was Little Brock Asher. According to Mama, Little Brock had taken everything she had to give before she even met Daddy.

In retrospect, any true happiness I might have had then with Amity was marred by worry. The mining strike, as well as Rose and Mama's mistakes, constantly hovered like a rain cloud over my thoughts. I sometimes wished that I had had Mama's ability to rearrange life to where I could bear up. Every day I lived with the fear that Daddy or one of his brothers would be shot dead while picketing. As it turned out, poor Uncle Corbin had stayed in the hospital for over two weeks before he finally ended up at Granny Lee's home with her and Marie taking care of him. Daddy said that it might be months before he'd be able to return to the mine. "Maybe by the time he's able the strike will have run its course," Daddy said hopefully, then added, "At least he ain't dead. We can all be grateful for that."

37 A TRIP TO TOWN

Mama sent us a check for thirty dollars on the third day of June. Daddy suggested that I take the check to Buster Holmes' store, cash it, and buy a few groceries. "I'll send Marie over here if she ain't got nothin' planned." His sunken eyes studied me for a minute before adding, "Maybe you ought to ask your sister to come along. You girls could go down at Turner's and get you all an ice-cream float. Bonzelle Creech told me last night that the stores were putting goods out on the sidewalk today. Maybe you all could walk around and look things over."

"Bonzelle Creech?" I raised an eyebrow.

"Yeah, her and the German woman invited me and Harvey up for supper last night. They're livin' in one of Jack Tallon's rentals. Bonzelle told us she got an insurance check from Levi. I reckon they're livin' on that." Averting his eyes he said, "I know what you're thinkin' and it just ain't so."

Smiling I said, "I ain't thinkin' that, Daddy. I ain't like Mama. I think it was nice of Bonzelle and Olga Winley to invite you and Harvey James to supper."

"Don't tell your mama when she comes back. She'll make a big deal out of it. Don't know what she's got against Bonzelle Creech. She's a nice woman."

"I won't tell," I assured him, although I knew Mama wouldn't approve. While one part of me found it almost amusing that Daddy had gone to Bonzelle Creech's house, another part of me was surprised that he did so, knowing how Mama felt about her. For years he had done what Mama wanted. The only time he'd challenged her was over her bad treatment of Rose. Could it be that Daddy was secretly angry with Mama for going away to Indianapolis, and seeing Bonzelle Creech was his way of challenging her? My mind quickly dismissed the idea; Daddy wasn't a vengeful man by nature, and it was doubtful that he'd purposely hurt Mama no matter what she had done. Still, his actions puzzled me and caused me to wonder if I really knew anyone. Later in my bedroom, I went about getting ready to make the trip to Granny Lee's to get Rose. While part of me was anxious with the prospect of seeing her, the other part was busy dreading how she might act upon seeing me. Reaching for the hairbrush, I ran it through my shoulder-length hair. Suddenly a deep sense of dread washed over me, causing me to shiver. Something was wrong. Putting the brush aside, I froze for a moment, thinking that Floyd Wilkes' ghost wanted to show me something. Daddy was at No. 5 mine and there was trouble there every day. "Dear God, don't let nothin' happen to Daddy. He's all I got." I whispered. The toot of a car horn brought me out of my reverie. Pulling back the bedroom curtain, I saw Uncle Noah's black Buick in the yard. Grabbing a light lilac sweater, I ran from the room and shut the front door behind me. Go away, Floyd Wilkes. I don't need to see nothing bad today.

Uncle Noah smiled at me from his rolled down window. "Come on, girl. Let's go get Rosie." Once in the car and on our way, Uncle Noah asked me if I heard from Mama.

"She writes letters and Daddy talks to her on the telephone once a week…" My voice trailed off.

"She ought to be home and not traipsin' all over the country," he said somberly.

"Well, she's takin' care of Uncle Larkin's wife and earnin' a wage."

"She could always earn a wage here if she wanted too. I dunno. Heddy's always been bullheaded. I guess me and Coy are too."

Throughout the ride to Granny Lee's home, I tried to shake the growing dread that had enveloped me earlier. "I hope Daddy's all right," I told Uncle Noah.

"Stop your worryin' Junie Mae. You just get your sister and we'll go on into town. I'll go over to the Billiard Hall for an hour or so and you girls can meet me back there after you're done lookin around."

"Alright," I agreed.

Once at Granny Lee's house, Noah pulled up beside Uncle Hiram's old truck. On the porch, Great Uncle Hiram raised himself from the old cane bottomed chair where he was sitting and greeted us. Turning to me he said, "I ain't seen you in month of Sundays, Junie Mae." Granny Lee then stepped out on the porch and held her pudgy arms out to both Noah and me. Looking down at me, she said, "Lord, child, it's so good to see you. Come on in. Marie and her youngins ain't here. Harlan Ray come and got 'em early this morning. I reckon Rebekah Ann needed some cheerin' up. She still ain't well from her operation, and seein' them children's good medicine for her."

"Is Rose here?" I asked nervously.

Granny Lee's face saddened. Motioning to the back bedroom nearest the kitchen, she said, "Rose has been helpin' me take care of your Uncle Corbin. He's got a long way to go to get better after what them men down there at the mine done to him. They really worked him over, Junie Mae." I noted the look of deep distress in her dark eyes. A few strands of hair had strayed from her long ponytail and hung limply around her tired face. Inside the house, the air had the aroma of stale bacon grease, and the kitchen table and sink were littered with dirty dishes. I remember thinking that Mama would die if she could see the mess in Granny Lee's kitchen. Mama said that the only time Granny Lee cleaned the house was when the nurses or the women from the Salvation Army paid her a visit. Both Noah and I followed Granny Lee into the dimly lit bedroom where Uncle Corbin lay flat on the bed. A shaded lamp cast a dull light on a face that appeared pale and contorted in pain. Rose, sitting in a chair beside the bed, looked up and seemed startled when she saw us. Bending over Uncle Corbin, I told him that I hoped he got better soon. I could not help but feel sorry for him lying there and looking so sick and helpless. "They wired his jaw shut. He can't talk to you all," Rose whispered. I knew Rose wasn't fond of Uncle Corbin and probably hated having to sit with him all day. "Daddy wanted us to come get you and take you to the sidewalk sales in town. He said it would be good for you to get out for a while."

"You look a little pasty. It would be good to get a little of that ole sun on your face, Rose Red," Uncle Noah bantered.

Rose got up from her chair without speaking and left the room. I could hear Granny Lee urging her to go out. "You go with your sister and Uncle Noah, honey. You've done enough today." Rose relented but did so without speaking a word to me. Once in the car she made light conversation with Uncle Noah but continued to ignore me. She said of Uncle Corbin, "He's drinkin' soup from a straw. I don't see how a body can live like that. To be so sick he shore knows how to bang that cane on the floor when he wants somethin'. He bangs it all day long and keeps Granny Lee and the rest of us runnin'. He's wearin' us out, especially Granny Lee. She should have just left him in that hospital."

Uncle Noah burst out in spontaneous laughter. "Why Rosie, hon, that ain't nice. Your uncle's in bad shape."

Rose sniffed indifferently. "Serves him right for crossin' the picket line after Daddy and the others warned him not to."

"He was just tryin' to earn a livin'," Uncle Noah explained, but his voice gave way to mirth.

"He's plain old greedy and you know it, Uncle Noah. Uncle Harvey James said he could sit out ten strikes with the money he's got put away."

"You might not want to hear this, Rosie, but you shore inherited your

Mama's plain talk," Uncle Noah said.

While they bantered back and forth, I studied Rose and realized how unhealthy she looked with her swollen face and blotchy skin. I decided that pregnancy was making her sick rather than making her pretty like it had some women.

Once we reached town Uncle Noah let us off near Walker's Hardware in the center of town. He said, "I'll be in the Billiard Hall down the street. You all meet me back here in an hour or so. That ought to give you time to get a soda and do a little lookin' around."

I was glad the air was warm and the sun was out. All around us, the streets were littered with shoppers and onlookers. My eyes fell on the courthouse lawn where men sat on benches, smoking and swapping knives. "Let's go over to the Soda Fountain and get us a float," I suggested.

"Why didn't Amity Smith bring you to Sidewalk Days?"

"He's workin' at the mill. Besides, Daddy wanted me and you to spend some time together. He thought it would be good for us."

"If Daddy hadn't thought of it I wouldn't be here," she snapped.

"Yes, you would. You'd have went with anybody to get away from Uncle Corbin and his cane," I joked.

Glancing over at Rose, I noted her deep frown had changed into a big smile. The smile was followed by a peel of laughter that broke the barrier between us. "I reckon you're right on that one. He keeps starin' at my belly. When I'm feedin' him through the straw, all he does is give me nasty looks like I done the worst sin in the world. I hate him and wouldn't care if he choked to death on that soup."

While she talked, I studied her bulky wrap and her swollen ankles. Aware that I was looking at her, Rose tossed her head and said, "I know it's warm but the shawl hides my belly better than anything else. I'm wearin' one of Marie's old maternity dresses. I can't wear nothin' else."

"Your ankles are really swollen," I said.

"Yeah, well, Marie said her ankles swelled too when she was pregnant. Granny Lee's called the nurses and one of them's comin' to see me Friday."

After a few minutes of silence Rose asked, "Why did you tell Mama about Bart, Junie Mae?"

"You had to know the truth, Rose."

"I don't want to hear Mama's version of the truth. She ain't told the truth in years and you know it."

Turning the corner of Second and Main, I changed the subject and asked about Bart and if she'd seen him lately. Looking dejected, she answered "No. I know he's back home, but I ain't heard a thing from him. Marie said she seen him coming out of Asher's store the other day."

"Maybe you should have gone with Mama to Indianapolis and had the baby there. Then if it wadn't twisted or retarded you could have brought it back and then decided what to do."

"It ain't gonna be twisted or retarded," she spat. "Them's Mama's words, and as usual you've bought into her lies hook, line, and sinker. Let's just get the float so I can get back to Granny Lee's."

That day is hard for me to think about. Even with so many years gone by I can still hear the little warm wind rattling the leaves and feel the sun's rays kissing my face. I recall with great clarity how absurdly happy people looked as they casually strolled the sidewalks checking out racks of dresses, shoes, and baked goods. I remember wondering how they could act so carefree when only a few miles away miners picketed across muddy, scarred lands where their fellow workers had died just trying to scratch out a living. Happiness to me was almost non-existent. It had been so long since I'd felt young and carefree. Watching the smiling, friendly people go about life as if nothing was wrong had left me dumbfounded. I recall feeling envious and a little angry that they'd somehow found a way to shut out the mining strike and the killings it would surely cause in the future. Glancing over at Rose with her blotchy face and swollen ankles had further depressed me. I'd realized that life was over for her before it had even started. I'd decided that things could get no worse than they already were. But I was wrong. Sometimes I ask myself if I could have changed what happened that day. If only I had allowed Floyd Wilkes' ghost in that morning. If I had waited just a few seconds, I might have seen what was coming and I could have prevented it. Granny Lee had reassured me repeatedly that God willed what happened to Rose and that no voice from the grave or vision could have stopped it. A part of me believed her, and with time I learned to forgive myself.

38 JUST LIKE FLOYD WILKES

The Soda Fountain was directly across the street from Hanley's Hardware. Now approaching the store, I had noted the "Going out of Business" sign in the window. "I reckon after Mama left he couldn't keep it open," I said, breaking the silence.

Grimacing, Rose said, "Maybe Mama taking them expensive watches was the last straw for the crazy old woman."

"Let's take the cross walk," I cautioned, and out of habit protectively grabbed Rose's sleeve as we crossed the street. In front of the Soda Fountain, a trio of pony-tailed girls about our ages laughed among themselves. The sound of their carefree giggles had prompted Rose to say in a wishful voice, "If only I could be like them again. Sometimes I wish I could just call back the time. I wouldn't have done what I done with Bart. Soon I'm gonna be saddled with a baby that might be twisted and retarded--."

Stopping in my tracks, I stared at her in surprise. "You do believe Mama." I gasped

"No, I don't!" she protested. "It's just that it could be that way because I ain't doin' real good with this pregnancy."

"You've got a doubt or two," I said ruthlessly.

Just as we approached the door of the Soda Fountain, Rose froze in her step. Suddenly afraid, I followed her gaze to the bank where I saw Bart Asher with his arm around a skinny brunette. Gasping, Rose grabbed my hand and squeezed it so tightly it hurt. "Bart's with a girl," she breathed. "How could he do somethin' like that with me in the family way? God!" Her face had paled to the point that I thought she might faint dead away.

"Let's just go find Uncle Noah," I suggested breathlessly, while trying to steer her in back in direction of the Billiard Hall. Slinging off my arm she begin to march obliviously across the street and in the direction of the bank where Bart and the girl were waiting to cross. "No, Rose!" I screamed, but she acted as if she hadn't heard me. The dread that had been brewing within me all day had caught fire and was now burning at its peak. Feeling a dryness in my throat, I swallowed hard before yelling "Wait!" but Rose was already halfway across the street. What happened next is a blur. I vaguely remember the truck rounding the corner off the square. I can hear the screech of brakes followed by a sickening thud. For a minute I was unable to move or even scream. I recall the sound of a car door slamming and people rushing the street. A man's voice yelled, "Let's get some help here." I don't remember walking to the scene or how I got through the crowd. The only thing I remember is seeing Rose lying flat on her back with blood gushing out of her mouth. Her strange eyes were wide open in terror. For as long as I live, I will remember how terrified they looked. Just like Floyd Wilkes. For a split second, Rose's face had become that of Floyd Wilkes. Then just as quickly, the face changed back to that of my dying sister. Kneeling down over her I called her name. Instantly a man grabbed hold of my arm and ordered me to step back. "Leave me alone!" I screamed. "She's my sister."

Rose's bloody mouth worked frantically to form words. Through a deluge of tears, I tried to comfort her. "Help's comin', Rose," I assured her.

In a soft whisper she said, "My baby's gone. I know it." Those were her last words. Afterwards, her eyes rolled back showing only the whites, and her head fell limply to the side. Realizing she was gone, my screams were lost in the high-pitched urgency of the approaching sirens.

39 CRY FOR YOUR DAUGHTER

I remember the next few days in a fog of bits and pieces. I vaguely recall Uncle Noah having to pry my arms away from Rose's broken body. The trip back to Granny Lee's house was hazy at best. I remember a room full of faceless people, and all of them crying. At one point Daddy's dear face wavered in front of mine. I recall his arms encircling me, and the sound of his gut-wrenching sobs. Sometime in that same night, Dr. Minor stood over me holding a long needle. "This won't hurt much Junie Mae, just relax." His voice sounded far off. The next thing I remember is bright light streaming through a window and Rose's face swimming above mine. "Rose?" I mumbled thickly. Rose's face continued to waver in and out, reminding me of how a hole of water looks when a pebble is dropped in it. She looks older, I thought, while fighting to keep my eyes open. Someone far off called my name. I heard it again and this time it seemed closer. The face in front of me no longer wavered. I realized in disappointment that it wasn't Rose but Mama. Turning my head toward the wall, I recall studying the faded pink wallpaper with its little rosebuds. Rosebuds. Funny, I'd never really looked at the wallpaper before. For years it had remained unremarkable -- just a covering on a shabby wall in a shabby room. How could I have missed the rosebuds?

"Junie Mae, it's Mama," the voice soothed.

"Rose is dead, Mama."

"I know," she answered, while her hand moved back a lock of my hair. The numbness of the drugs had worn off and now the pain of Rose's death rushed inside me like a flash flood. "You didn't take her body to Asher's did you?" I asked in a panicked voice.

"No. We sent her over to Parks Funeral Home in Hazard. Granny Lee's payin' for it all…" Her voice trailed off.

"Where's Daddy?"

"He took to his bed. Marie's in there with him."

Tears formed in my eyes as I said, "I knowed somethin' bad was gonna happen that day but I ignored the signs. He tried to warn me." I sobbed.

"Who tried to warn you?" Mama asked.

"It don't matter none now," I whispered. "She's gone forever -- her baby too. She was worried about the baby…"

Looking up into Mama's face, I saw a look of silent torture, but her eyes were dry. How can you not cry for your daughter?

The funeral was held at the First Pentecostal Church in Evarts, and all the seats were filled. Our family alone took up four rows on either side, and many neighbors and friends had to stand for the service. The Smith family was among the families that were lucky enough to find a seat near the back row. Throughout the service, Mama remained dry-eyed while Daddy and Granny Lee sobbed unashamedly. Strangely, I had had no tears left and sat there numbly staring at the grieving faces of Uncles Noah and Coy along with Marie and Uncles Harvey James and Harlan Ray. Beside of Mama sat Grandma Haley who looked as if she'd already died and been brought back to life against her will. Her eyes remained dry but her face betrayed a look of deep remorse. No doubt Rose's death reminded her of Floyd Wilkes' death. Uncle Larkin sat somberly in his perfectly creased black suit and tie opposite Daddy. Every so often, he reached over and patted Daddy's shoulder reassuringly.

The sound of the preacher's voice droned a spiritual message of Granny Lee's God and His forgiveness. The meaning was lost on me, though, because I was busy wondering how a caring God could snatch people away at will. How was this love? Granny Lee always said death was inevitable and that it was a natural thing. What had been natural about Rose dying a horrible death in the street? I thought of Floyd Wilkes and how similar his death was to Rose's. I remembered my reoccurring dreams of Floyd Wilkes' blood streaming down the planks and likened it to Rose's pouring out on the pavement. How could I face another day knowing I could have saved my sister? How could I live with myself?

Outside, the sun was warm and the trees were in full bloom at the Lee Family Cemetery. Daddy had chosen a plot next to the edge of the woods where a stand of wild red roses grew and trailed down the separating fence. I thought how appropriate it was that she laid near her namesake roses. After the conclusion of the service, Daddy was the last one to leave the open grave. Mama and Granny Lee stood by his side for a little while trying to persuade him into coming with them, but he had refused. Walking over to where he squatted with head bent, I touched his shoulder and whispered, "Come on, Daddy. They have to cover her up now."

"How can I leave her, Junie Mae?"

"I know, Daddy, but these men have to finish their work."

Daddy rose weakly, and had I not caught him he might have pitched forward into the open grave.

Realizing how sick and weak he was I yelled for Uncle Harlan Ray to come and help me get him into the car. "It's all right, Daddy," I soothed.

Shaking his head in defeat, he sobbed. "It won't never be right again, Junie Mae."

40 "VENGEANCE IS MINE," SAYETH THE LORD

Back at the lodge both Granny Lee and Mama insisted that Daddy go to bed. At first he had balked, but he eventually gave in to Mama. Later, Granny Lee and Grandma Haley made coffee and then busied themselves by putting all the food people had given us away. Mama sat at the table absently tracing the rim of her coffee cup with her finger. Her eyes stared vacantly out the window and in the direction of the Creekstone House. A somber faced Uncle Larkin sat at the other end of the table alongside Uncles Harvey James and Harlan Ray. The silence in the kitchen was as thick as molasses, save for the clinking of cups against the table.

Sitting in the corner opposite the cook stove, I felt strangely divorced from the rest of the family. Inside I felt depleted of life; it was as if some light had gone out in me. Granny Lee finally spoke. "Heddy, I'm worried to death about Ralph. His color is awful and he's as weak as a kitten. Maybe you better not go back to Indianapolis with Larkin tomorrow. Ralph needs you here." Mama's eyes snapped angrily but she said nothing.

"That's right, Heddy. Your husband and family come first. I'll get Carolyn to help me out with Rhodie. You stay here and take care of Ralph," Uncle Larkin assured her.

I could sense anger building in Mama. I had become adept at recognizing her moods. Later, after everyone had gone, I sat in the darkness of the living room in Daddy's old chair remembering Rose. My mind skimmed through memories like one skims the pages of a book. I pictured her splashing in the creek at age five, and later trailing behind Daddy on our way to the river. The memory of Rose flapping her hands in feet in the snow in hopes of making a perfect snow angel brought tears to my eyes. Slowly and lovingly, I'd built her beautiful face up before me and memorized its every dimple and expression.

In the next room, I could hear Daddy sobbing his heart out and Mama murmuring something that I couldn't make out. Closing my eyes, I allowed the tears to rush and slide down my cheeks like rain streaking a windowpane. After a while, my deep loathing for the Ashers had replaced my sadness. Gritting my teeth, I thought of how much I despised and blamed them for Rose's death. I held the whole family responsible for almost every bad thing that had ever happened to our family. They had to pay. What had Granny Lee said about vengeance -- or was it hate? And then it came to me. She'd said that hate was an open sore that grew more infected with each passing day. She had explained vengeance by quoting a passage in the Bible: "Vengeance is mine," sayeth the Lord. Laughing coldly in the stillness, I'd decided that God was sometimes too slow in carrying out his vengeance on those who deserved it. I thought of Mama, too, and how much I'd grown to hate her. She would have to pay, too. I wasn't sure how, but her time of reckoning was coming.

I'd slept in the chair all night and had awoken with a stiff neck and a sick stomach. I could hear Mama in the kitchen moving about preparing breakfast as if nothing had happened. Rising, I padded to the kitchen and saw that Daddy wasn't in his chair at the head of the table. "Where's Daddy?" I snapped.

"He's still sleepin', I reckon. He was awake most of the night moanin' and groanin'. I got a feelin' that this is gonna be the end of him."

"That would be good for you if Daddy up and died -- wouldn't it, Mama?" My mouth seemed to have a will of its own.

Mama spun around and her eyes narrowed. "How could you say somethin' like that, Junie Mae?"

"Because it's true. You've never cared a thing about none of us -- not me, not Daddy, and surely not Rose. You hated her 'cause she was so much like you."

"You keep that voice down, Junie Mae. Your Daddy will come out of that bed if he hears you talkin' to me like that."

"I hope he does!" I challenged. "It's about time somebody here gets the truth. I'm sick to death of all your lies and secrets."

"You wouldn't tell your Daddy about Rose and the Ashers in the shape he's in. I know that, so your bluffs won't work with me."

"Wouldn't I? He might as well know the truth now as later." I challenged her. "Tell me somethin', Mama. Why ain't you asked me about the day Rose died? Don't you even care to know what she talked about or how she got killed?"

"I was just tryin' to spare you, Junie Mae. I knowed you was hurt."

"Daddy wanted to know. Granny Lee and Marie asked me what had happened."

. Turning back toward the stove she busied herself wiping off the warmer.

"Are you gonna stay here with Daddy for good?" I asked.

"I'll go back with Larkin as soon as your Daddy is on his feet."

"You go ahead and leave tomorrow, Mama," I ordered,

Mama paused in her wiping and turned to me with a look of complete surprise on her face. "You want me to leave your Daddy and him sick?" Her voice was barely above a whisper.

"Yes. Just pack your clothes and leave with Uncle Larkin when he comes to see Daddy in the morning."

"Your Daddy might have somethin' to say about how you're orderin' me around."

Letting out a deep, shuddering breath, I said, "Let's see what he says, Mama. I'm gonna go now and get him up."

"You'll do nothin' of the kind."

Rising from the chair, I moved toward Mama's bedroom. Just as I reached for the doorknob, I felt a hand jerk the back of my hair in an effort to pull me back toward the kitchen.

"Don't touch me!" I screamed.

Mama let go of my hair and stood looking at me with fear in her eyes.

"Don't you ever touch me again – ever!" I warned.

At that moment, Daddy stepped through the bedroom door looking disheveled and distressed. "What's goin' on in here, Heddy?" Before Mama could answer, I said, "Mama will be leavin' with Uncle Larkin in the mornin', Daddy."

While running his big hand though his sparse hair, Daddy looked confused and asked, "Is this true, Heddy? Was you plannin' on goin back with Larkin in the mornin'?"

"Junie Mae thinks I should," she said in an accusing voice.

Daddy turned to me with a frown on his face and said, "Junie Mae, why would you tell your Mama to leave us?"

I studied Daddy's poor old hollow face that was as pale as snow and his eyes with their dead expression. I had known what I was about to say might finish killing him inside, but according to Granny Lee sometimes people had to die a little in order to live again.

"Mama's been wantin' to leave us for a long time. That's all she's talked about for years. She don't belong with us no more. Let her go, Daddy. She ain't never been here for us anyhow. Rose died thinkin' Mama hated her."

Visibly crestfallen, Daddy turned to Mama. "If you don't want to stay here with us, you can go back to Indianapolis with Larkin tomorrow."

Looking almost as pale as Daddy, Mama could only stammer "I-I wanted to take you with me, Ralph -- you, Rose, and Junie Mae. I've begged -- but none of you wanted to leave here. Rose is gone, and then there's that strike goin' on. I can't take this place no more, Ralph. I'm sorry." Walking over to Daddy, she bent down and rested her palms on his knees. Her voice pleaded. "We need the money I make, Ralph. You can't work the mines no more. We could live rent-free in Larkin's guesthouse…" Her voice trailed off.

"Daddy will be gettin' his pension soon, Mama. We'll make do 'til then."

"I'm talkin' to your daddy, Junie Mae. Why don't you take a walk down by the river or something?"

"I'm stayin' right here, Mama!"

Daddy said, "I won't ask you to stay against your will, Heddy."

"Come with me, Ralph," she pleaded.

"Daddy ain't goin' nowhere, Mama, and you knowed that before you even asked. He's told you over and over again."

"Listen to her, Ralph! She's talkin' to me like I was a stranger instead of her mama."

Daddy's weak, dark eyes searched Mama's face before he said, in the most ardent tone, "Junie Mae's been right here takin' care of me. She's give up her school just to see to me. You go on to Indianapolis, Heddy. You take care of what you need to. I'll be waitin' for you, when you're ready to come back."

Mama packed up her clothes that night and left with Uncle Larkin before noon the next day, but not before Daddy had a talk with Uncle Larkin. While Mama piled her suitcases in the back of Uncle Larkin's car, Daddy sat drinking coffee with his older brother. And even though I busied myself in the kitchen, the two talked freely as if I weren't there. Over the rim of his coffee cup Uncle Larkin looked puzzled. "Is something wrong here, Ralph -- I mean with you and Heddy?"

"There ain't nothin' wrong with us, Larkin. Heddy just wants to get away for a while. She knows how much Rhodie needs her."

Uncle Larkin shook his head with uncertainty. "I don't want to take Heddy away from you with what's happened to Rose."

"Heddy's havin' a hard time with that, Larkin. Maybe she's better off away from here for a while. Takin' care of Rhodie might be good for her."

I could tell Uncle Larkin was truly upset and believed that he'd somehow contributed to Mama leaving Daddy. I'd decided that he was in essence a good man like Daddy, but he was also just as weak when it came to Mama. After all, he could have refused to take her back with him. Why hadn't he? The answer was an easy one for me to figure out. Uncle Larkin, like Daddy, couldn't say no to her. Mama had somehow managed to sink her claws into him as she had sunk them into Daddy years ago. She was good at leaving permanent scars.

I'd taken a walk down by the river before Mama left, hoping she would be gone by the time I got back. Standing on the rock at the Play

Place where Rose and I had so played so often as children, I felt a kind of deep sadness wash over me. Down below, the water rushed and gurgled beneath the base of the rock, and the islands in front of me were windless and still. I thought of Amity Smith and wondered what he must be thinking. I had quickly decided that seeing him would give me no comfort; like Mama, I preferred suffering alone. I could have saved her, if I had just allowed Floyd Wilkes' ghost to come in. If only I hadn't been in a hurry to go with Uncle Noah. "I'm sorry, Floyd Wilkes," I whispered. I was reminded once again of the vision he'd shown me of Rose sitting there holding that rose with her black face. Why hadn't she had a face? What did it mean when someone's face was gone? As I had done so many times since I'd first seen it, I built up that horrible image before me of Rose sitting there holding the red blooms in her little white hands. A dark gaping hole had erased her beautiful face. I was suddenly reminded of something Granny Lee had once told me when I was a child after I'd admitted to her that I was afraid of the dark.

"You're only afraid of it 'cause you can't see through it without a light. There's nothin' to be afraid of, honey. Darkness is just a coverin' that don't last long before daylight sets in. Everything is still there. You just can't see it."

But everything disappears if it's dark outside. In retrospect, maybe what Floyd Wilkes had shown me was Rose's dying spirit. Bart Asher had killed it after he'd gotten her pregnant and then deserted her for another girl. It occurred to me that Bart had killed more than her spirit; he'd also killed her body as well as that of his own flesh and blood. Had he not been on the street with that girl, Rose would have never walked carelessly out into the traffic. He'd seen the whole thing, too, and had just stood there on that street watching the life drain out of her without moving or saying a word.

41 SOMETIMES GOD DON'T MAKE NO SENSE

I spent the whole month of June grieving for Rose. Daddy and Granny Lee were the only ones who understood my grief, and that was of some comfort. I'd known it was awful to ignore Violet Elizabeth and Amity especially, but I'd felt empty and could find nothing within me to give them. Over the course of the month, Amity came to me and made small talk. Once or twice, we had simply sat in the front porch swing and listened to the sounds of the evening with hardly a word passing between us. During those days it never occurred to me to appreciate Amity's perseverance. How could I when all I could think about was my own loss? But somehow he had understood. In spite of his age, he had thought like a man much older. Had it not been for Daddy's precarious condition I might have given up on everything. But a part of me had known that my withdrawal from reality would have sealed his death. And so I cooked, cleaned, and washed his clothes, all while making sure he took his cough medicine. But Daddy's slow retreat from the world was apparent. Instead of going to the mines every day, he spent his time sitting in the shed carving on the dolls he would never finish. I recall feeling helpless where he was concerned. But thank God for Granny Lee. Her love and belief in God had given her the strength to deal with both Daddy and me with such wisdom. Once a week she would come over to the lodge, cook for us, and sit with us sometimes until late at night. One week in late June after the supper dishes were put away, Granny Lee had insisted Daddy lie down for a while after he had suffered a bad coughing spell. After she had given him his cough syrup, she motioned me to follow her out onto the front porch. Once she had settled her ample weight comfortably on the porch swing she started to speak. "Junie Mae, your daddy's grievin' himself to death. If he keeps on like this much longer, he'll die."

Feeling an intense fear grip my heart, I said, "I know. I feel him slipping away too. I just don't know how to stop it, Granny. I ain't much better than him." My words gushed out like blood from an open wound. "It's all my fault. I could have saved her if I had just listened. Floyd Wilkes' ghost tried to warn me somethin' was wrong that mornin' but I didn't want to listen. I was afraid he was gonna show me somethin' bad about Daddy and I just ignored the signs."

Granny Lee reached over, clasped my hand, and said, "Lord, honey, none of this was your fault. You have to stop thinkin' it was. If you ignored a sign it was because you couldn't handle what it meant, and the Lord knowed that. When God decides to call somebody home nothin' or nobody can stop Him. "

. "Sometimes God don't make no sense, Granny," I said in protest. "He could have chosen not to take Rose, but he didn't."

"Honey, none of us here on earth can understand everything about God and why He does what He does. That's where faith comes into it. We just have to trust that He knows what's best."

"You don't know what I know about Rose and Mama. If you did you'd wonder if God even exists," I snapped. For the first time in my life, I was mad at Granny Lee and her God. I couldn't understand how she could defend something that coldly snatches up people at will, leaving their loved ones alone to grieve. "It looks like your God takes out his vengeance on innocent people instead of the ones that really deserve it, Granny. He let them miners die and watched them little children cry after their daddies and never lifted a finger to help them." Jumping up from the swing, I stood before her full of rage. "Your God looks over them rich Ashers -- ain't nothin' bad happenin' to them, even after what they done to people. You just don't know all the things they have done to us -- done to Mama and Rose. They destroyed Mama, and then Rose -- they--" Suddenly realizing that I was telling too much, I stopped talking.

Granny Lee eased herself up from the swing. Looking anguished, she said, "I don't know what you're talkin' about, Junie Mae, but you do and that's what counts. I just know that you've got to be strong for your Daddy and forget this hate you've got for the Ashers. If they've wronged people then they'll pay for their sins in the end. God has a way of teachin' folks lessons that we don't understated. You can't hate Him, though. He is merciful, and He's your only salvation now. You need Him more than ever. Don't shut him out." Placing a pudgy hand on my nervous shoulder, she said, "Junie Mae, I truly believe that sometimes God takes people home just to spare them from themselves. Poor little Rose was havin' it rough. I know, because I watched her get worse every day. I feared what would happen after she had that little baby. Rose wadn't strong like Marie. I don't think she could have handled bein' a mother." Granny Lee had suddenly grown quiet. Her face looked tense and uncertain. I could tell she was about to say something that I didn't want to hear.

"I want to tell you somethin', honey. I wadn't gonna say nothin', but now I see I have to. A week or two before Rose died, Marie caught her mixin' up a batch of pokeberries in a glass of milk and sugar. She told Marie that she was gonna drink the stuff to kill the baby she was carryin'. If Marie hadn't caught her, she would have died that day. I know that. After she done that we had to watch her like a hawk. We was always afraid she'd find some more berries and try it again. Marie and me was too scared to tell your daddy and mama. We figured if we did she'd surely try it again."

Feeling faint, I slumped woodenly down on the swing, not knowing what to say. Rose had wanted to kill the baby because she knew Mama was telling her the truth. Maybe she wanted to kill herself, too. I recalled the time she had eaten the berries as a child and Mama had forced her throw them up. She must have been so desperate.

"I'm sorry, Junie Mae. I wouldn't have told you but you was blamin' yourself and God. I had to set you straight. God took her home to save her from herself." When I didn't reply, Granny Lee squeezed her hand as it rested on my shoulder. "Honey, she's dead and I know you and your Daddy are grievin', but life has to go on. It can't stop for the livin'. We have to go on and make life as good as we can."

"Mama's not comin' back," I said woodenly. "Daddy was better when she was here. I don't know how to make him better."

"Your poor Mama's lost, Junie Mae. We just have to pray that she'll find herself soon. All you can do is watch after your Daddy, be strong, and trust that God will take over and heal him. That's all you can do."

Since Rose's death, the uncles seemed hesitant to mention No. 5 Mine and what was happening with the strike. When something was mentioned, Daddy seemed far away and uninterested. The uncles, no doubt at a loss as to what to say or do, finally stopped coming to the lodge every morning, and their visits had dwindled to once a week. If Daddy noticed, he didn't say anything. It was as if he was just waiting for death to come and take him away. One morning in late June, I found him sitting at the table staring lifelessly into an empty coffee cup. My heart wrenched at the sight of his bony frame and his sunken eyes. In a gentle voice I said, "Daddy, why don't you go up to the Number Five and see what's goin' on with the strike? Marie told me the other day that Asher was finally reading the contract and there's talk that he's tryin' to settle with the widows." Up went Daddy's head and a spark of interest showed in his hollow eyes. "I don't remember Harvey James sayin' nothing about Asher lookin' at the contract."

"Well, I heard it from Marie, who heard it from somebody that knows," I said.

"I reckon it wouldn't hurt to go up there and see what's goin' on. I thought you didn't want me up there," he added, looking puzzled.

"I don't want you up there, Daddy, but I think you need to go back to what you was doin' before Rose died. You can't just sit here and grieve all day. She's gone and nothin' we do will bring her back," I choked.

"Just like nothin' will bring your Mama back, I guess. Boy I messed up things with her real good, didn't I?" His voice shook.

"Don't worry about her, Daddy. Just go see your friends and brothers at the mines."

"Alright," he finally conceded.

42 LITTLE BROCK ASHER CONCEDES

When thinking back to those days after Rose died, I remember how difficult it was for Daddy and me. Rose's death had set us back miles, but with Granny Lee's help and words of wisdom, life began to slowly fall into a kind of steady routine that had eventually healed us enough that we could carry on. On the last day of June, Little Brock Asher accepted the terms of the union contract and the strike ceased. I recall seeing Daddy after the strike was over. Smiling from ear to ear he said, "It's over. Asher finally gave in and agreed to up the hourly wage by three dollars, plus health benefits. Now we're up with McKinley's and The Black Diamond."

Looking a little forlorn, Daddy went on, "I wish I could go back to work now that the pay is decent, but I can't. I know that."

"It's all right, Daddy. You helped get the pay raise and the health benefits for the others. You can always be proud of that."

"I reckon that's right," he said.

"What about them widows? Is he gonna give them a settlement?"

"Bonzelle Creech told me that he'd made an offer to the women and they was mullin' it over. I reckon Olga Winley's goin' back to Germany as soon as she gets the settlement. Bonzelle is all cut up about it. She's right fond of her."

"When did you see Bonzelle?" I asked curiously.

"Oh, here and there. She was up at Number Five mine this mornin' to hear Asher make the announcement that he'd accepted the terms set up by the union."

"You like her, don't you Daddy?" I teased.

"She's a good woman, Junie Mae. She's had some hard licks but she's a survivor. Now don't you go makin' somethin' out of me and her talkin'," he added.

"I ain't sayin nothin'," I teased. Suddenly life felt so good. It wasn't that Daddy and I weren't still grieving for Rose, it was just that we had learned to cope with our loss better.

43 BONZELLE CREECH AND PEA SALAD

Uncle Corbin had a turn for the worse in mid-July and to be hospitalized again. Daddy said that his jaw wasn't healing right and had to be re-broken. That meant Granny Lee would have to wait on him a little longer. This worried Daddy because Granny Lee had developed bone spurs and could hardly move, let alone wait on his sick brother. Marie had done what she could but her rowdy children kept her busy most of the time. I'd felt sorry for Granny Lee and had offered to help her with Uncle Corbin in the evenings as long as Marie agreed to come and pick me up. I needn't have worried about at ride. After Daddy told Bonzelle Creech that I needed a way to Granny Lee's house in Putney, she offered to pick me up in the old panel truck that had once belonged to her daddy. Although Bonzelle was far from being an adequate driver and could barely manage the clutch, I managed to survive the short trip by keeping my eyes closed tightly until I reached Granny Lee's door.

With the onset of July, Bonzelle began coming to the lodge once or twice a week just to talk to Daddy and me. Olga Winley and the other women had finally settled with Asher for an unknown sum, and Olga returned to Germany after she received the settlement. Bonzelle, though, would never see a dime and talked bitterly of how her daddy's life had meant nothing to Asher -- or even the law, for that matter. "My Daddy worked like a dog up there in that mine. He gave Asher the best part of his life only to end up dead. Asher ain't done one thing to try and find out who the thugs was that killed him and poor Donny Calvin. The law ain't, either. I reckon nobody cares about a worn out old man and a young boy."

Sometimes Bonzelle would surprise us with a basket of food that she'd prepared, and the three of us would eat at the table. Bonzelle was a stupendous cook, and everything she made was like music to your mouth. After a while Daddy begin to put on weight. Sometimes after a visit from

Bonzelle, I would tease Daddy about her. He would just laugh and say, "Now Junie Mae, you're makin' way too much out of her bein' here." Things slowly improved with Amity Smith and me as well. After I'd come to terms with my grief I'd opened up a little to him about Rose. By now the word was out that Rose was pregnant when she died, which scandalized her in the eyes of many, but with the help of Marie and Granny Lee, I had learned to hold my head up high and look people in the face. I'd never told a soul who the baby belonged to, not because people shouldn't know the truth, but because I'd feared what Daddy would do to Bart Asher if he ever found out. Neither Amity nor Violet Elizabeth Smith probed me about Rose or the baby. As usual, they acted as family and showed me the love and patience that I needed to survive the grief. And though Daddy wouldn't admit it, I knew that he'd come to rely on the company of Bonzelle Creech. If he expected her and she was a minute late, he would sit around wondering what happened to her. After having ridden with Bonzelle a few times himself, Daddy had decided that she couldn't drive a lick. He'd say, "I swear if that woman don't learn to put on the brakes at the right times she's liable to end up in a ditch or over a mountain." Bonzelle was the type of person who took chances. I recall how she'd confronted a drunken Little Brock Asher that day he'd stood on the landing of his office tower and shot off his gun. Even now, I cannot help but admire her spunk and the bravery she'd shown during a time when women rarely spoke out in public for any cause. It was apparent to me that Bonzelle and Mama were as different as night and day. Where Mama was quiet-natured and complicated, Bonzelle was an open book with her opinionated personality and her zest for life. She'd try anything new and different. For instance, if a new shade of lipstick came out, Bonzelle would be the first to buy it. And if the hemline of a skirt was raised in the world of fashion, Bonzelle would be the first to raise hers an inch, proudly showing off her legs in public and seemingly oblivious as to what others thought.

Bonzelle was a copious reader of Ladies Home Journal and tried out many of their recipes. Once Bonzelle tested out a recipe for peas she'd found in the magazine and brought the dish to the lodge. I will never forget the look on Daddy's face when he saw the green concoction topped with bacon and sour cream. I'd always known Daddy to be docile and polite, and I couldn't hide my surprise when he began degrading the dish. "Bonzelle, what in the world is this stuff on my plate? It looks like it's already been in somebody's stomach."

Blushing in embarrassment, I said, "Daddy, it's bacon and pea salad. Bonzelle found it in a recipe book."

He turned to Bonzelle and said with a grimace, "If I was you, Bonzelle, I'd throw that recipe book over the hill." Instead of getting angry

Bonzelle started laughing hysterically. She finally managed to say, "Now Ralph, if you're gonna talk like that I'll do the same thing to turnips." Ironically, Bonzelle's bubbly personality had begun to rub off on Daddy and had brought out a side to him that I had never seen before. For as far back as I could remember, Mama had taken center stage and Daddy remained in the background. When he was with her, he'd seldom laughed and had instead taken on her demeanor of misery and seriousness. Suddenly he was laughing, joking, and enjoying life.

44 JUST LIKE ROSE

Mr. Smith hired Daddy part time at his sawmill sometime in early August. Daddy couldn't believe his luck when Amity came to him and told him that his father needed someone to chalk off the length of the logs and make a few short hauls. Daddy couldn't read very well, but he was adept with numbers and measuring and took on the tasks with zeal. The mill job was not only something he could do without much strain, but it also afforded him a small paycheck and gave him a reason to get up in the mornings. I recall those days fondly. I would rise before dawn, pack his lunch, and then fix his breakfast. After breakfast, he'd head out the door with his dinner bucket in hand. Sometimes I'd even catch a little smile in his face, which was something I hadn't seen since Mama left. Although Daddy still suffered from lung disease and continued to cough incessantly at night, he looked healthier than he ever had. I'd credited his good health mostly to Bonzelle, who had remained a diligent caretaker and cook. Her visits once a week had turned into an every night event. She had become familiar with Mama's kitchen and soon started cooking us meals there. Afterwards, she would see to it that Daddy got his medicine before he went to bed. Sometimes I invited Amity to share a meal with us. It had been a long time since things had felt so good.

Since the day Rose had died, Floyd Wilkes' ghost had remained silent. I'd had no visions of any kind -- no inklings of any disasters to come. Still, I felt it and knew that the ghost was merely hiding in the shadows as it had done since as far back as I could remember. In a sense, Floyd Wilkes' ghost had become a part of me, and, good or bad, I never thought about it leaving or me out-growing it. It was just there. Granny Lee once said that sometimes the living wouldn't let go of the dead, and that's why their spirits continued to roam the earth. "If we can't accept that our loved ones are dead, then how can they?"

I thought of Rose and how hard it had been to accept that she was gone, but the acceptance had been forced on me. It stood to reason that if I couldn't accept it, then how could Daddy? One of us had to be strong. Mama, on the other hand, could never let anything go -- not her hatred for the coal or her rage towards the Ashers. She'd held on to that hate for years until it finally consumed her. I believe that she had hung on to Floyd Wilkes the same way, and had loved him too much in life to let his spirit rest. She had to be what held him here -- or was it me? I hadn't considered that I might be the one holding his spirit here. His ghost had saved me from going to the light years ago -- a ghost that already roamed the earth because someone or something held him here.

In the weeks that followed Mama still wrote sporadically. As usual, her letters were all about what a hard time she was having taking care of Rhodie. I would read them to Daddy who listened intently but rarely made comments about what she'd written. Sometimes I felt like burning every letter she sent, because it had seemed to me that Daddy's mood darkened every time a letter came. Occasionally Mama would send us a small check, but as time passed the checks became smaller and finally ceased to come at all.

The month of August was especially hot. I remember how the inside of the lodge felt like an oven. Daddy's cough grew worse in hot weather. At night he would wake up bathed in sweat and would have to go out onto the back porch in order to cool off so that he could breathe better. After I told Bonzelle how much Daddy suffered in the heat, she had suggested we get electricity installed in the house. She said, "If you all can't afford to get it, I'll have it done and that way you all could buy an electric fan for Ralph's bedroom. It would give him some fresh air to breathe." When I told Daddy what she'd said, he'd become angry and barked, "Who does she think she is wantin' to come in here and change things? If I wanted electricity, I'd have it put in myself. Ain't no line strung past the Ashers, and I ain't even shore they'd come this far without costin' a man an arm and a leg." Taken aback by his burst of anger, I explained to him that Bonzelle was only trying to help because she was worried about his cough.

"She needn't worry about me," he said, sounding uncharacteristically crotchety. My eyes shifted to the table where an envelope lay. Without looking at the name on it, I knew it was from Mama and Daddy had managed to read it. "Did you read Mama's letter?" I asked.

"I made most of it out," he snapped.

Mama's letters were all alike. Rhodie was still in shock. Rhodie had bitten Mama's arm while she was feeding her. Rhodie had fallen out of bed, and Mama had no choice but to lift her up off the floor without any help. Disgusted, I threw both the letter and the envelope into the wood box behind the stove. Upon seeing my actions, Daddy's eyes grew big and angry. "Why did you do that, Junie Mae?"

"I throw all her letters away. Why should this one be any different?" I answered defiantly.

"You ought not hate your mama the way you do. It's a sin to hate the one that brought you into the world."

"It's an ever bigger sin to pretend she's coming back, Daddy. You're livin' a lie. Bonzelle Creech really cares for you. Can't you see that? Mama, though, would rather take care of a sick stranger than she would her own family. Think of it! All her letters are full of her whinin' and complainin', but she'd rather be there than here! What does that tell you, Daddy?"

The anger in Daddy's eyes suddenly melted into sadness. "I love your Mama, Junie Mae. I don't care what she's done -- she's still in my heart."

Strangely void of pity, I said, "The best thing you could do for yourself would be to divorce her and then let her go for good. It ain't fair to Bonzelle to have to live in Mama's shadow."

"Nobody asked her to keep comin' here and doin' things to the house. Look in there!" he said, pointing to the bright yellow drapes that Bonzelle had sewn herself and hung on the living room windows. "Them curtains are so bright I can't even look at 'em without goin' nearly blind. Whoever heard of curtains that bright?" My eyes studied the bright yellow curtains for a minute before busting out in spontaneous laughter. Turning to Daddy, I saw his deep frown break out into a wide grin before he cackled aloud. Soon both of us were laughing so hard that our sides ached.

Two weeks before the school session started, I began helping Granny Lee care for Uncle Corbin. Upon seeing his wasted frame and hollow eyes, I realized he wasn't doing well at all. With his jaw newly wired shut for the second time, it was difficult for him to drink even through a straw. I had noticed, too, that Granny Lee's house was more unkempt than usual. In the kitchen, dirty dishes were stacked high on the sink, and even the table was loaded with crusty pots and pans. Marie's children ran screaming barefooted back and forth across the dirty linoleum, seemingly obliviously to the mess, while Marie sat in the corner calmly knitting a shawl for winter. Poor Granny Lee was sprawled out on the couch asleep, while Great Uncle Hiram sat on the porch making an effort to play the harmonica. Tired of hearing the off-key noise, Marie yelled at him at the top of her lungs to put the harmonica away. On the couch, Granny Lee's eyes flew open, and in a thick sleepy tone, she'd reprimanded Marie for hollering at Great Uncle Hiram. "Now Marie, you know how much his music means to him. He's got to fill his time with somethin'."

"What music? It sounds more like two cows in a hailstorm. I've got a headache from hearin' it all day. If he wants somethin' to do, let him go wash them dishes or go wait on Uncle Corbin for a while."

"I ain't doin' no women's work," Uncle Hiram declared.

Uncle Corbin's condition seemed to grow worse with each passing day. He had stopped trying to drink from a straw and he was hardly ever conscious. At the beginning of my second week of caring for him, I'd been wiping his face with a cool washrag when the vision came on me. Staggering backwards, I felt the washrag slide from my hand and hit the floor. Automatically closing my eyes, I saw a wash of bright colors that eventually faded into black. Opening my eyes, I looked over at Uncle Corbin and realized in horror that a black mask had replaced his pasty facial features. Just like Rose! My insides screamed. In a sudden panic I ran to the living room where Granny sat sewing. Grabbing her shoulder I told her what I saw. "Uncle Corbin needs to go to the hospital. Call somebody!" Upon seeing the urgency in my face, Marie ran for the phone, while Granny Lee made her way into the bedroom room where Uncle Corbin lay still and looked as white as a corpse. Granny Lee turned to me and said in a soft whisper, "He's dyin', Junie Mae. I can see it all over him."

45 THE PHOTOGRAPH

Uncle Corbin died not long after he had reached the hospital. The doctors would later inform Granny Lee that he'd developed an infection that had poisoned his system. After learning of his death, Daddy and the uncles gathered in the kitchen at the lodge and talked among themselves. Harlan Ray was bitter and called Uncle Corbin's death "a cold blooded killin'. You know they killed him. If they hadn't beat him to an inch of his life, he'd still be alive today. And it was our own that done it -- not a bunch of scabs, but men we know and have worked with for years."

Shaking his head in in disgust, Daddy said, "I feel like we might have had a hand in him dyin'. If we hadn't got the union in--"
Before Daddy could finish Uncle Harvey James interrupted, "Now wait a minute, Ralph! We can't go blaming ourselves for what happened to Corbin. He was warned not to cross the picket but did it anyway."

"He was our brother, Harvey!" Harlan Ray shouted, pounding the table hard. I don't think I can stand to work side-by-side every day with the men who done this to him." Harvey James shook his head in agreement. "I don't understand why they beat him up so bad. It wasn't like he was a big strapping man. A hard wind could have blown him away."

"I wanna kill 'em myself," said Harlan Ray.

"Killin' them wouldn't solve a thing, Harvey James," Daddy said thoughtfully.

"I don't see how Seth Couch and Les Hensley can live with theirselves after what they done to him." Harlan Ray said, and then added, "They ought to be brought up on murder charges."

Daddy chuckled dryly, and said, "Asher would just buy off the judge. The law ain't made a move to find out who killed poor old Levi Creech and Donny Calvin. Do you think they'd care about Corbin? Asher's got 'em all in his pocket. Anybody will tell you that."

Uncle Corbin's funeral had brought back memories of Rose's death. The casket standing underneath the dim lights inside the mortuary had become Rose's casket, and not that of Uncle Corbin. Once at the Lee family cemetery the sky had opened up and poured rain. Huddled between Daddy and Amity Smith, I studied the left side of the cemetery where Rose's grave lay; its grassless mound of dirt had turned to bright yellow mud. Behind the rusting fence, the wild red roses were dying and had already turned dark around the edges. The deep red of the roses had somehow changed into dark purple pokeberries. Tears flooded my eyes and mixed with the pouring rain. Without bothering to dry them, I allowed myself to realize the horror of what she must have felt knowing that the baby she was carrying would most likely come into the world twisted or retarded. My poor sister. Sensing my grief, Amity squeezed my hand reassuringly. Oddly, as soon as the service was over the rain stopped and the sun peeped out of the clouds. Granny Lee would later tell us that it was a sign from God that Uncle Corbin had passed peacefully to the other side. Walking over to Rose's grave, I stood staring at the muddy mound. Beside me, Amity stood quietly. His hand rested lightly on my shoulder. "I miss her so much," I whispered. My eyes then shifted to the dying roses. Walking over to the fence, I reached over and broke off a few roses and placed the bunch at the base of the newly installed headstone Granny Lee had purchased. Turning around, I saw Daddy's anguished eyes staring down at the grave. "You need to hurry and get home and get them wet clothes off," I said in a mothering tone. Leaving Daddy alone so he could pay respect to Rose in private, Amity and I headed in the direction of the parking lot where Harvey James was helping Granny Lee get into his car. Before Harvey James shut the car door, I wrapped my arms tightly around my precious Granny Lee. Her eyes were red from crying, but they still appeared soft and sympathetic. "It's all gonna be all right, honey. Your Uncle Corbin and little Rose are with God now. He'll look after them."

Later, our family, friends, neighbors, and a few of the miners from No. 5 Mine gathered at Granny Lee's house for a little dinner. Bonzelle and Rebekah Ann had cleaned the house earlier, readying it for company. The women from the Salvation Army gathered in the living room where Granny Lee sat in her big chair. Grandma Haley worked the kitchen, seeing to it that everyone got a clean plate and silverware. As was the custom after the meal, the men folk gathered on the porch and in the front yard talking among themselves. Amity had joined them. Violet Elizabeth and her Mama and Daddy brought food, and they came to the wake out of respect for both Daddy and me. The Smiths had grown fond of Daddy and often invited him to eat lunch in their kitchen on his lunch break from the mill. After everyone was served, Grandma Haley sunk down in a chair at the head of the table. Parting through the crowd, I went to stand by her and noticed that her face appeared strained and tired. "I never woulda thought Corbin would die like he did. Martha said his body was plumb full of infection."

"It's a shame," I said.

"I figured your Mama and Larkin would show up for the funeral. Martha said Heddy couldn't reach him in time. She said he was somewhere way up in Illinois."

"I know. Daddy told me..." My words trailed off.

Sighing, Grandma Haley said, "Your Mama will be wantin' to come back home soon."

Puzzled, I asked why.

Grandma Haley bent forward and in a low voice said, "I don't guess Martha's had time to tell your Daddy about your uncle Corbin's will."

"Uncle Corbin's will?" I asked, feeling more confused than ever.

"Junie Mae, your daddy's about to come into some money. Not just a little money, but a big sum. Martha told me last night that Corbin had left everything he had to her, and that she planned to divide it up between her four livin' children. I'm tellin' you this as a warnin'. If your Mama gets wind that your Daddy's inherited that money she'll be back to claim some of it."

"Are you shore about the money?" I asked, still reeling from what she'd just told me.

"I'm positive! Heddy Mae's acted like a fool runnin' out on you and your Daddy the way she done, and then going to live with his brother. I can barely hold my head up from the shame of it," she added in disgust.

Looking hard at me she went on, "Your mama's after your uncle Larkin and his money, but when she finds out your daddy's got an inheritance she'll break her neck to get back here. Don't let her do it, Junie Mae! You remind your daddy how she didn't give a damn about her own daughter and how she deserted her when she needed her the most." Looking down at her hands, she said ruefully, "I made plenty of mistakes with your mama. I'll admit that! But that don't make what she done right. You and your Daddy are better off without her. You tell him."

"Alright," I promised.

In need of air, I made my way out onto the back porch where there weren't any people. Bracing myself up against the porch railing, I tried to make sense of what Grandma Haley had just told me. Behind me, I heard a shuffle. Turning around, I saw Great Uncle Hiram regarding me shyly. He said, "I got a picture for you, Junie Mae. I took it last summer when Rose first come here. I figured you'd want it." Staring down at his outstretched hand, I reached over and took the picture. Turning it over I saw the close up image of Rose posed on the white fence that separated Granny Lee's yard from her neighbors'. Although the picture was done in black and white, I recognized the yellow sundress as the same one she had worn to the Harlan County Fair. Her exquisite eyes stared solemnly into mine. Unable to contain my grief, I started to cry, and my tears made Great Uncle Hiram shift uncomfortably. "I'm real sorry, Junie Mae," he said, and then walked back through the door and into the kitchen.

    Later, back at the lodge, after I changed out of my damp clothes I sat at the kitchen and waited for Daddy to come home. So many thoughts were running through my head. I recalled Grandma Haley's warning of how Mama would want to come back home after she heard about the money Daddy was getting from Granny Lee. She was bound to find out since Uncle Larkin had money coming, too. I knew for sure that Daddy would take her back in a minute, and the thought scared me. What would come of Bonzelle, the woman who had done everything for him in the last few months? Bonzelle had been good for Daddy in a way that Mama never could be. Staring down at the black and white photo of Rose, I asked it what to do. "You know Mama -- you know how she works." Poor Rose; she never stood a chance with Mama. Every time Mama looked at her, she thought of the rape and how having Rose had killed her dreams of marrying Little Brock Asher. A part of me had felt sorry for Mama and what she had gone through with Big Brock, but still another part hated her for how she'd treated both Rose and Daddy. Granny Lee had told me that people must learn to forgive; otherwise, they cannot enter the kingdom of Heaven. I wasn't sure that I was ready to forgive Mama or the Ashers – unless, of course, God came down suddenly and exacted vengeance on them for all the pain they had caused our family. Only then might I be able to forgive.

46 A VISIT FROM MAMA

I decided not to tell Daddy what Grandma Haley had told me the day of Uncle Corbin's funeral. I would let him come to me after he learned of the will. School was starting soon and I was beginning my sophomore year. Feeling both excited and a little scared, I had spent a good deal of the week after the funeral washing and ironing my fall clothes ahead of time in preparation. When the first day of school finally arrived, Amity and Violet Elizabeth picked me up at the lodge instead of the bus stop. Amity, who seemed less than enthused about the new semester, was preoccupied with the new saw his Daddy had ordered for the mill. "That new saw is gonna make work a whole lot easier for your daddy and me, Junie Mae. It's gonna be a lot harder to operate, but it supposed to cut a lot faster and smoother than the ones we're usin' now."

School as usual had become a respite for me because it gave me something else to think about other than Rose and Mama. But that changed as soon as Daddy learned about Uncle Corbin's will. I had come home from school on Friday of the first week to find Daddy sitting at the table still dressed in his work clothes. After I had changed out of my school clothes, he'd called me into the kitchen and told me to sit down at the table. Once I did, he began telling me about Uncle Corbin's will. "He had a lot saved up. Ma said she wanted to split it four ways. My part is ten thousand dollars." He said it in a tone of disbelief. It was as if he had to say it in order to make it real.

"That's a fortune, Daddy," I said, feeling shock at the staggering amount.

"Do you know what this means, Junie Mae? It means your Mama won't have to work for Larkin any more. When I tell her about the money she'll want to come home," he said happily.

Unable to hide my disgust, I said, "The only reason she'd even think of comin' back is to spend the money.

Daddy's face hardened and his eyes regarded me warily. "Your Mama couldn't take the coalmine or the strikin' -- that's why she left us, Junie Mae. You can't keep blamin' her for not likin' the coal or the killin' associated with the strikes. This place is hard and full of poverty. You know that! Your mama just wanted somethin' better for all of us. With this money, I can give her what she needs. I plan on buyin' her a new home -- one with electricity. We could be happy, the three of us."

Rising quickly from my chair I stared hard at Daddy and said, "Bonzelle Creech loves you, Daddy. Mama loves herself and ain't capable of lovin' nobody else. Once the money is spent, she'll leave again. Bonzelle would stay with you for the rest of her life. You think about that, Daddy!" Stomping off to my bedroom, I knew he was crestfallen. My heart wrenched for him, but at the same time I was angry that he couldn't see Mama for what she was.

The first day of September brought nippiness to the air. The river appeared still and clean, and the trees in the hills had had already started to turn. Daddy celebrated his thirty-ninth birthday at the lodge. Bonzelle had surprised him with a big chocolate cake, and she had sewn him a heavy patchwork quilt that she claimed would help keep him warm. After supper was finished, Daddy went to the woodshed to chop some kindling for the cook stove. Bonzelle and I were clearing the table when she turned to me and said, "I think there's somethin' weighin' on your daddy's mind. He's acted different ever since your Uncle Corbin died."

"Maybe he's just tired," I offered guiltily.

Shaking her head, she said, "It's more than that, Junie Mae. I think it's got somethin' to do with your Mama."

"Why don't you ask him what's on his mind?" I suggested, lacking a better answer.

Placing the dishes in a pan of soap sudsy water, Bonzelle confessed, "I love your daddy, Junie Mae, and I was hopin' he'd grow to love me. But I have a feelin' he'll never get over your Mama." Turning to me with a look of desperation, she went on, "I can't wait forever for him to decide what he wants. I'm goin' to give him a choice, Junie Mae. I have to."

Choosing not to reply, I felt sick inside knowing that Daddy was about to throw away a chance of happiness for a dream or a fantasy. That's all Mama was or ever could be. Daddy, like Rose, had chosen to love an image of his own making rather than something that was real and open to him. I didn't understand any of them, or why they pined for things they could never have. I knew Daddy sensed my anger and was unhappy because I wouldn't take Mama's side. But I couldn't because I'd known what would happen if I indulged his fantasy. Maybe he couldn't see Mama for what she was, but I could. If it were within my power, I would protect him from her.

Uncle Larkin and Mama showed up at Granny Lee's home on the fifteenth day of September in order for Uncle Larkin to receive his portion of Uncle Corbin's money. Granny Lee also summoned the remainder of her children to the house that evening to present them their part. Preferring to stay at the lodge in order to avoid Mama, I nervously waited for the ax to fall. I had fully expected her to walk through the door of the lodge at any time. And she did, later that night. My heart skipped a beat at the sound of her voice in the kitchen. Springing up from my bed, I tiptoed to the living room and peeped around the door in time to hear her laughing at something Daddy had said that I couldn't make out. As if she had eyes in the back of her head, Mama turned to look in my direction. Her dark eyes burned into mine and then with an artificial smile she said, "Come on in here and sit with us, Junie Mae. I was just about to wake you."

Walking wordlessly over to the table, I pulled out a chair and gingerly sat down.

Mama didn't waste any time bringing up Daddy's recent windfall. "Can you believe your Uncle Corbin managed to save that much money over the course of his life?"

"Well, he didn't spend much," Daddy interjected nervously.

Turning to Mama I noticed how her dark eyes danced like moonbeams on a body of water. To look at her you would have never known that she had lost her oldest daughter a little less than three months beforehand. Studying her arresting face, I had decided that she had aged well -- better than any woman I had ever seen. In spite of the coal and its black dust and the hardships she had complained constantly about, she had managed to stay beautiful. I knew that she was conscious of her beauty and had used it often and without compunction to sucker Daddy into doing whatever she wanted.

"Your Mama's come back, Junie Mae," Daddy said cautiously.

"How long will you stay this time?" I asked in a sour voice.

"Well, with Daddy gettin' the money we can finally afford to live without me havin' to work for your Uncle Larkin."

"Mama, you ain't sent us a check in months. It's not like you've been supportin' us. In case you ain't heard Daddy got job workin' at the Smith's sawmill."

"He already told me," Mama said defensively.

"Oh! Have you seen the new living room curtains? Bonzelle Creech made them for us. She made Daddy a quilt for his bed, too!"

Mama's face paled and her full lips had lost their color. Shooting Daddy a baleful look she said, "What was Bonzelle Creech doin' here in my house? Why would you let her take my curtains down?"

Daddy's face had turned whiter than Mama's. Before he could speak, I said, "She was in our house because Daddy needed somebody to help care for him while he was sick. We needed the curtains just like we needed the shelves in the kitchen re-papered, and the wood chopped and stacked---"

"That's enough, Junie Mae!" Daddy yelled. With fire in his eyes, he walked over to my chair and stood over me. "You need to go someplace so your Mama and me can talk."

"This is my house, Daddy. She left it! Remember?"

When I refused to move, Daddy did something that I never thought that he was capable of doing. Grabbing my right arm, he pulled me forcefully off the chair. Dragging me toward the door, her opened it and then slung me hard onto back porch floor. Without looking back at me, he slammed the door behind him. Lying there in a state of shock, I thought that what had just happened had to be a nightmare. The man who was my Daddy had never so much as raised his voice to me. I couldn't remember him even scolding me save for the time he saw me at the No. 5 Mine while the strike was going on. The Daddy I had known loved and protected and had been a gentle, docile man. Sobbing loudly, I raised myself off the floor, but not without wincing from the stabbing pain in my lower back. I was hurt but continued to hobble off the porch and out into the yard where the air was as black as pitch. Feeling completely abandoned, I stumbled over to the willow and parted its spindly branches. Feeling for the stool, I finally found it and sat down. Daddy is all caught up in Mama and could care less what happens to me. Never in all my life had I felt so alone and so betrayed. Even now, after all these years, I cannot think about that night without crying. Sitting there in the dark with the lonely sounds of the whippoorwills calling in the distant hills, it occurred to me that if Mama came back to stay, I would have to move out of the lodge. Maybe I could move in with Grandma Haley or Granny Lee, or maybe I could marry Amity -- but that didn't seem like something I should rush into. I considered my options carefully, but not without feeling a deep remorse that I believed would never go away. "How many people are you gonna take away from me, God?" I screamed out into the night. And then in an angry voice I yelled, "Where are you, Floyd Wilkes? I ain't seen you since you showed me Uncle Corbin dead. Don't you ever have anything good to show me? You don't even slam doors or break clocks no more. And while we're at it why couldn't you save Rose like you saved me?" My anger was at its peak. For a while, my face felt so hot I thought I might catch fire and burn up there underneath that willow tree. It took a while for the anger to dissolve at least temporarily, and in the end all that was left was a dull ache.

Sometime in the night, I had awakened to find myself propped up against the trunk of the willow. Stiff and sore, I noticed that it was still dark outside. I thought either Mama or Daddy might have come out and look for me, but I had seen no one. Raising myself off the stool, I staggered dizzily toward the screen door of the porch, opened it, and then paused before finally opening the kitchen door. A part of me never wanted to go into the lodge again but I knew that wasn't practical. And so I crept inside, then glanced at the clock and saw that that it was five thirty in the morning. Dragging myself over to the couch, I slid down on its ratty cushions and immediately fell into a deep sleep.

The next morning I awoke to bright sunlight streaming through Bonzelle's bright yellow curtains. Startled and confused, I finally realized that it was Saturday and not a school day. The memory of the night before assaulted my senses. Making a huge effort not to cry, I sat up on the couch and quickly decided that I would pack my clothes and go to Bonzelle Creech's house -- if she would have me. The thought of her was spontaneous and not reasoned out, and I prayed that she wouldn't hold what Daddy was doing against me. In truth, I needed her and wanted her support. Since Granny Lee was still mourning for Uncle Corbin, the last thing I wanted to do was visit more pain upon her. Besides, how could I tell her what Daddy had done to me?

In the kitchen, Mama was telling Daddy what a hard time she was having caring for Rhodie. Every word she uttered caused my stomach to lurch, and I thought for a moment that I might vomit right there on the floor. It was plain to me that Mama was all about herself and no one else. Couldn't Daddy see that? Was he blind?

Grabbing the overnight bag that Bonzelle had given me earlier in the summer, I carelessly stuffed a few dresses, sweaters, and pairs of underwear into it. I zipped it up and left it on the bed, then walked on into the kitchen where Daddy sat drinking coffee and Mama stood at the stove cracking eggs into a pan.

Upon seeing me, Daddy dropped his head and said, "Your Mama's cookin' breakfast for us. Why don't you sit down here so we can talk this thing out?"

Eying Daddy warily I said, "I ain't got nothin' to say. I just wanted to let you know that I'm leavin'. I'm gonna go stay with the Smiths or one of the uncles. I ain't shore yet which one."

Daddy's jaw dropped open in surprise, while Mama scowled. "You ain't goin nowhere, Junie Mae. You start out the door and you'll wish you hadn't," she warned.

Feeling my anger once again rise, I said, "I'm goin', Mama, and there ain't much you can do about it. You got what you wanted. You got Daddy and Uncle Corbin's money. You don't need me no more. Rose is dead and you never have to worry with her again, either. It seems like things are lookin' up for you."

"That's enough, Junie Mae! It ain't right you bringin' up Rose into this."

"Sit down, Daddy. I don't want you draggin' me out on the porch and throwin' me down like you done last night."

I watched Daddy flinch and then drop his head shamefully, but I felt void of pity. Walking back to my bedroom and grabbing the overnight case, I stomped out the kitchen door. I was halfway up the dirt road before realizing that Mama was behind me.

"Stop, Junie Mae. Please!" Automatically halting my step, I turned to face her.

Clad in only a thin robe she stood hugging herself. Her dark hair had grown long and cascaded over her shoulders, framing her beautiful face. For a split second, I saw Rose and not Mama.

Catching her breath, she said, "You're thinkin' wrong about me, Junie Mae. I've come back with good intentions. It ain't just because of your Daddy's money."

"You come back because Uncle Larkin didn't fall over you like you thought he would. He's a good man, Mama. I figured that out the first day I met him. And he's smart, too. You couldn't break him like you did Daddy."

"That's a dirty lie, Junie Mae! I've never done nothin' out of the way with Larkin."

"That's because Uncle Larkin's decent and wouldn't sleep with his brother's wife. I knowed from the first minute I seen you with him that you wanted him -- Rose seen it too. Why Daddy couldn't see it is beyond me. Granny Lee says love is blind. I guess it must be. But I'll tell you somethin', Mama: you'd get more money if you stayed with Uncle Larkin. Rhodie's bound to die or end up in the asylum, eventually."

Nervously licking her lips Mama said, "Junie Mae, that sounded just awful. How could you even think like that?" Her voice gave a gentle reproach rather than a harsh scold.

"I'm just bein' truthful," I said

Looking unsteady and unsure, Mama shuffled over to a tall bent elm tree and leaned up against it. After a while, she said in a low voice, "I wish you didn't hate me so much."

"I don't hate you. Maybe you can't help who you are, and what you want. I'm just askin' you not to hurt Daddy anymore."

"I'm not gettin' any younger, Junie Mae. I thought comin' back here would be for the best. Rhodie's real hard to take care of. She's plumb out of her mind. The doctors told Larkin that she already had something wrong with her head before she lost her daughter. I don't think she'll ever get better. More than one doctor told him she'd be better off in an asylum. But he won't put her away. He's loyal to her." Dropping her head, she went on, "Larkin blames himself for her being like she is. Maybe he blames me too. Maybe I was at fault. I don't know."

Changing the subject, I said, "You don't love Daddy like he deserves to be loved. I know that much, Mama. You told me so yourself."

Looking upwards, her eyes found mine. Their dark depths were void of anger and now looked empty and hollow. "I'm sorry for the way I am, Junie Mae. Every day of my life I have to wonder if Rose went to her grave hating my guts -- my own flesh and blood. You don't know how many nights I've laid awake rememberin' her and regrettin' how I done with her. I guess a part of me hated her because she reminded me of what Big Brock done to me. The way I see it, he took everything away from me, Junie Mae -- everything. For years I had to look across that bridge and see that big fine house on that hill. It's been torture knowin' that he's up there with her instead of me. It's like being mocked over and over again." She shuddered. "But Rose wadn't to blame for none of it. I know that now."

For the first time in a long time, I saw humanness in Mama. There beneath her hardness lay a soft fragility that rarely surfaced. She went on, "I was always afraid for Rose. Afraid she'd fall in love with a man that wouldn't love her back. A part of me must have knowed she'd find Bart Asher. Maybe that's why I tried so hard to keep you all away from them people. In my own way, I thought I was protectin' her by tryin' to make her hard. I didn't do right. I know that now"

"You can't change what you done to Rose, Mama. It's too late for that, and if it's any consolation, Rose would have done what she wanted to, anyway. You couldn't have stopped her no more than Grandma Haley stopped you. You can't go on blamin' yourself for that. Granny Lee says that just because people make bad decisions don't mean they're bad."

"Are you sayin' I'm not bad?" she laughed uncomfortably.

"I want you to go back with Uncle Larkin. It would be easier on Daddy in the long run."

Mama sighed and said, "I don't want to hurt your Daddy no more. He deserves a better life…" Her voice trailed off and I could see her mind was somewhere else.

"You think about it, Mama."

"What will I say to your Daddy? I told him I'd stay here and we'd start out new."

"Just tell him that the truth, Mama. Tell him that you hate it here and want a life somewhere else."

"What about Larkin? How do I know he would take me back with him now that he knows I don't need to work for him no more?"

"You can figure that part out, Mama. I imagine it won't be a picnic tryin to find somebody else to deal with her." With that I turned and left her, walking up the road in a cloud of thoughts.

When Amity saw me standing in front of the mill with an overnight bag he looked alarmed. "Your Mama said you were up here," I told him.

"What's wrong? Why are you carryin' that overnight bag?"

"I was wonderin' if you might take me to Granny Lee's house in Putney. I need to see Uncle Larkin before he goes back to Indianapolis. And if you have time, could you take me on to Bonzelle Creech's house? I want to spend a few days with her."

Wiping his hands on a greasy rag he said, "I'll take you to your Granny Lee's, but why are you going to Miss Bonzelle's house?"

"Me and Mama got into it," I answered, hoping he wouldn't ask me anything else. Sensing my trepidation, he told me to wait while he closed up the mill. On the way to Putney, I remained quiet. Amity finally asked, "What's going on, Junie Mae?"

"I told you -- me and Mama are fightin' and I just need to get away for a while."

"I wish you'd tell me a little more about what's goin' on. Sometimes I feel like you're shuttin' me out!" His voice sounded uncharacteristically impatient.

"I'm sorry, Amity. Talkin' about it ain't gonna make it go away. If I thought it would I'd tell you all about it."

"I swear, girl, you're one of the most stubborn people I've ever met. Most girls I know can't keep their mouths shut. You're the other way around."

"Miss Mouse," I mumbled.

"What?"

"Rose used to call me 'Miss Mouse.' I reckon it was because I didn't talk a lot."

"I reckon," he said, then chuckled. "Maybe one day you'll open your mouth long enough to tell me you love me. When you do, I'll believe it. If I'm not close by just holler it on the wind. I'll hear it."

A kind of dread leaped up within my chest at the sight of Uncle Larkin's car still parked in front of Granny Lee's house. What had I come here for? What would I say to Uncle Larkin? Turing to Amity I said, "Will you please go talk to Great Uncle Hiram while I find Uncle Larkin?" Just as I said it, Uncle Larkin came walking out onto the front porch carrying a suitcase. Upon seeing me, his handsome face broke out into a wide grin. He said, "I was just about to go over to the lodge and say goodbye to you all."

Following him over to the door of his car I said, "I need to talk with you." Inside my heart raced so hard, I thought it might jump out of my chest.

Placing his suitcase in the trunk, he shut the lid with a bang and shot me a concerned look. "What's wrong, Junie Mae?"

Swallowing hard, I said, "I think Mama wants to go back to Indianapolis with you.

"What do you mean?" he frowned.

"Mama won't be happy if she stays here with Daddy. She don't belong here no more. If she stays for the money, she'll only cause misery for Daddy. After it's gone, she'll leave him again. That's how she is."

"I don't understand, Junie Mae. Your mama worked for me in order to help support you and your daddy. Why wouldn't she deserve some of the money?"

"She quit sendin' us the checks months ago." I whispered.

"I still don't understand why you've come to me with this."

"Because Mama would be happier with you than she would with Daddy. She hates this place. There's too many bad memories here for her."

"Your daddy loves her, though. I can't ask her to go with me when he needs her with him. He's my brother."

"He don't know her. He only loves what he thinks she is."

Shaking his head in confusion, Uncle Larkin said, "Junie Mae, I won't come between your folks no matter how much I need your mama." After he said it, his face reddened. Looking away, he went on, "I've never said or done anything out of the way when it comes to your mama. I want you to know that."

"I know that. Daddy does too."

It was at that moment that I knew Mama had won Uncle Larkin. I could feel his misery and knew that he had mixed feelings. He'd wanted her but he wouldn't take her away from Daddy.

"If you won't ask her to come, I'll send her to you," I offered.

"I'm going to go on ahead over to the lodge, Junie Mae," he said hastily, acting as if he hadn't heard me even though I knew he had.

Bonzelle Creech lived about a mile out of Harlan on the other side of the railroad tracks. Hers was the first of five houses in a row and the least decrepit looking. Relieved to see her car, I reached over and kissed Amity on the cheek. "You'll pick me up for school on Monday, won't you?"

"You know I will," he answered.

With overnight case in hand I headed for the door, and before I could even knock it opened. "What's wrong, Junie Mae?" she asked.

"I'd like to stay with you a night or two, if that's all right," I said.

"You shore can, honey. Come on in. Here, let me take that bag." The rooms in the house were small and garishly decorated. Bright red throws covered the couch and adjacent chairs. The curtains were solid white and went surprisingly well with the deep shade of reds. The wood floors gleamed beneath round braided rugs, which were the color of an eggshell. "I made us a pot of coffee." Patting the couch cushion she said, "Sit down here and tell me why you left home."

"Mama's back."

"I know. Your daddy told me."

"Did he tell you about the money?"

"He shore did. I'm glad for you all."

The events of the night before came tumbling out of my mouth seemingly against my will. I told her how Daddy had thrown me out onto the porch and how I had stayed outside most of the night. I'd never intended to tell her how Daddy had acted, but there was something comforting and easy about Bonzelle that allowed me to come clean.

Shaking her head in disbelief she said, "I can't believe your Daddy acted like that. It's not like him at all."

"It's Mama," I sobbed.

"He loves her, Junie Mae. I don't think he'll ever quit lovin' her."

"I know things that would make him quit her," I ventured.

"No, you don't. People see only what they want to about somebody they care about."

"You don't understand," I said, then bit my lip, wishing I hadn't said that. In truth, Bonzelle was one of the most understanding people I had ever met.

"But honey, I do understand. Love can be a bad thing for some people, especially when they let their love for somebody rule 'em." Sighing wearily, she scooted down next to me on the couch. With a faraway expression in her eyes she said, "I loved my first husband more than anything in the world. He was such a good-lookin' boy. He had coal black eyes and jet-black hair. He'd slick it back and it shined like a raven's feathers. He always wore these snow-white dress shirts – well, when he wadn't workin' in the mine, that is. I'd have to boil, beat, and soak 'em in lye water to keep 'em that way. But I would've gladly done anything for him. He was tall, too, and just the sight of him comin' toward me made my heart beat in a funny way. We was married for three years. He wadn't a good husband to me. Every Friday and Saturday, he'd go to the honkytonks and stay out jukin' all night long. I didn't like it but I didn't say nothin'. I just went on actin' like everything was good. One Saturday night he come home drunk and for no reason at all, he jerked me outta bed and beat me to an inch of my life. He'd never done nothin' like that before. He never done it again, either. When Daddy seen all them bruises on my face and arms, he threatened to kill my husband. I reckon Daddy scared him real bad 'cause he left and I ain't seen him since," she laughed. "But it took years for me to get over him. I felt pain like I'd never felt before in my life. For a long time, I couldn't even look at a man with black hair or a similar build. I'd just go to pieces. It took me a while to see what I was doin' to myself. I finally decided that cryin' everyday wadn't gonna bring him back. I was young and had my whole life right there in front of me, and I wadn't gonna waste it pinin' away for somebody that didn't care. I love your daddy, Junie Mae, but I ain't gonna let it destroy me."

Placing her hand on top of mine she continued, "A lot of women don't like me 'cause I move on when things don't work out with men. I hear 'em talkin' behind my back, but I don't pay it no mind. I'd rather be happy than be miserable."

47 GHOST PEOPLE

The week I spent with Bonzelle Creech remains poignant in my memory. I recall with great clarity the colors of her home and the delicious food smells permeating out of her kitchen in the evenings. I remember her red bleeding red lipstick, high hairdo, and sweet melodic voice. At night, after supper, she'd pull out a box of quilt scraps, and after I finished my homework, she would show me how to sew the little pieces together to form a quilt block. Bonzelle showed a certain tolerance and patience that Mama never had. When I messed up a block, I'd wait for her to scold me. When she didn't I was amazed. I had slept in the room Olga Winley had stayed in before she finally left for Germany. Bonzelle had made frilly blue curtains for the windows and a matching bedspread for the twin bed. The blue color of the walls reminded me of pictures I'd seen in a book of the ocean. I had never seen anything so pretty.

Bonzelle told me how she missed Olga terribly and that it was nice to have my company. She also talked fondly about her daddy and kept a large framed picture of him in his youth above the mantle. "He was the best Daddy a girl could ever have," she sniffed. "I was his only child. Him and Mama couldn't have no more. She almost died havin' me 'cause it took her hours to push me out. Daddy said she never got well after that. She died when I was barely a year-old. Poor Daddy had a hard time tryin' to work and raise me at the same time. I was always in the home of an aunt or an uncle or a neighbor."

Her voice was suddenly filled with emotion. "There was this big old rock on the bank a little ways from my aunt's house. I used to sit there waitin' for Daddy. I can still hear the sound of his old truck rattlin' down that dirt road. When he seen me sittin' there on that rock he would stop the truck, and the first thing he'd do was put his old dirty carbide-minin' cap on my head." Hearing her talk about her daddy brought back memories of how my Daddy would allow me to spit on the carbide and then tamp it down before he lit the lamp on his mining cap. Our mutual love for our fathers had formed a kind of kinship between us. In seeing her pain and feeling her loss, I'd wanted to reach over and embrace her, but I was afraid she would do like Mama and shrug me off. Soon, though, I would learn Bonzelle wasn't anything like Mama and enjoyed hugs and outward displays of affection.

On the following Friday, Daddy showed up on Bonzelle Creech's doorstep. I could tell by his dull expression that Mama was gone. Opening the door, I stepped back and motioned him to come inside. Still in his work clothes, he walked over to the kitchen table and wearily sat down. Always the pleasant hostess, Bonzelle offered Daddy a cup of coffee. "It's stale and strong, just the way you like it," she said.

Before he could reply, Bonzelle set a cup down in front of him. "I'll just go in there and finish threadin' my sewing machine. You two just talk away," she said with a soft smile.

With a sheepish look Daddy said, "Bonzelle told me you was here. Junie Mae, your mama left for Indianapolis yesterday. I reckon Larkin told Ma that since Heddy left, Rhodie had stopped eatin'. I guess she had a big hissy fit on her sister and throwed herself on the floor and hurt her head bad. She just got out of the hospital yesterday. I told Heddy to go on back and help Larkin. I could tell she wanted to, anyway. I reckon she's growed fond of Rhodie -- even if she won't admit it. You know how she is." After taking a large gulp of the coffee, he went on, "I give her a little money before she left. She didn't wanna take it but I made her. I think she earned it."

"I do too," I agreed.

"Junie Mae, I done wrong the other night. I don't know what got into me. I've been too ashamed to come here and face you. I reckon I was fightin' to keep your Mama with me and you was fightin' to keep her away. I hope you can forgive me."

Daddy's face appeared gaunt and hollow. It was as if something had sucked every drop of energy out of him. I thought of Mama and how lost she had looked the other day, propped up against the tree that had shadowed the road. For as beautiful as she looked outside I knew that time and grief had left her insides empty and hollow. What might she have been had she not seen Floyd Wilkes die on the plank bridge that summer day? Would she have turned out differently if she had never met Little Brock Asher? I thought of Rose and how her longing for Bart Asher had drained her spirit. I realized at that moment that all these years I had been living with ghost people, and I was sick and tired of it. I thought of Mama, Daddy, Rose, and finally Grandma Haley and concluded that there wasn't a bit of difference between them and the ghost of Floyd Wilkes. Granny Lee said that ghosts moved around on earth without knowing they were dead. Mama, Daddy, and Rose had grieved so long for things they could never have that they had eventually lost their energy to live. And, like the ghosts, they moved around on earth without knowing that they had already died.

In the living room, Bonzelle hummed happily off key, which made me smile. Thank God I had finally found a person who hadn't let love suck the life out of her!

I had gone back to the lodge that day with Daddy. Inside, the fires had died in the grate and the wood cook stove was as cold as a grave. "Winter's comin'," said the ghost of Daddy.

October came with its fields of dried fodder, followed by the corn and pumpkin gatherings. I have always loved the smoky scent of fall. I think there is a kind of cold cleanliness about the land, especially after the first frost. By mid-October, nothing was lovelier than Wilder point. In the distant hills, the trees had turned crimson, yellow, orange, and dark brown, reminding me of one of Bonzelle Creech's crazy quilts. I've always found it curiously strange that while in the process of death, nature looks more vibrant and alive than ever. During the month of October, my life once again revolved around school, Amity Smith, and caring for Daddy. One morning in late October, Daddy announced that we might be moving. I had just poured him a second cup of coffee when he said, "Bonzelle got wind of a little place that's for sale that's about four miles this side of Harlan. After I'm done at the mill today, she is going with me to look at it. I thought that maybe you'd want to come too. "

I couldn't help but smile. "I'd be glad to come with you all," I offered.

Eying me mischievously, he scowled and said, "Now don't go makin' a big deal out of Bonzelle findin' that house."

"Don't worry, Daddy. I wouldn't think of it."

Hearing Daddy laugh was like music to my ears. It had been awhile since the walls of the lodge had heard laughter. I decided moving would be good for us -- especially for Daddy, because the lodge would always remind him of Mama. Maybe a new place would cheer him up. Bonzelle hadn't been to the lodge since Mama had left, but Daddy had gone to her. Maybe he'd finally figured out what a special person Bonzelle Creech really was.

That same morning on the way to school, I told Amity and Violet Elizabeth about the possible move. Violet Elizabeth broke out in a dimpled smile and said, "I'm glad you all are getting a better place, but I'll miss having you so close by."

"It ain't that far away," I promised.

"I can still find you," Amity said laughingly, but I sensed somehow that he was tense and holding something back.

Later, after school let out, Amity dropped Violet Elizabeth at the Smith house. On our way to the lodge, I noticed that he was quieter than usual. Glancing at his handsome profile, I saw that his face was fixed in a deep frown as he concentrated on the road.

"You're not sayin much this evenin'."

"I'm just thinkin'," he said obscurely.

"About what?"

"You and me."

"What about us?"

"I was thinkin' about our future. Do you ever wonder what it might be like if we was married?"

"I've thought about it," I said truthfully, suddenly feeling a dark cloud of uncertainty hovering over us.

"I wonder if you love me, Junie Mae. I've told you more than once how I feel, but you never say nothin' back."

"I ain't had time to think about that, Amity. Too much has happened lately," I said cautiously.

"Maybe you should consider it more."

"Alright," I agreed.

"You sound about as enthused as a man goin' to a funeral. I don't know how to take you anymore, Junie Mae! I know you've had it rough. I understand that, but lately you seem miles away from me."

"I'm sorry, Amity. I'm doin' the best I can."

With frustration showing in his handsome face Amity said, "I was up behind the mill the other day. There is a level spot near the poplar grove. It's real pretty and not too far from things. I was thinkin' that maybe we could build our house there someday."

"Maybe someday," I said.

"Damn it, Junie Mae! That's just it! 'Someday, Amity!' 'I'll think about it, Amity!' 'Alright, Amity!' Either you love me or you don't. It's just that simple, girl!"

Suddenly angry, I ordered him to stop the truck. "Just let me out!" I snapped.

Stomping the breaks hard, he spun the truck almost all the way around in the road. Grabbing on to the door latch, I pitched forward, falling hard on the ground.

"Junie Mae. Oh God! Are you ok?"

Unhurt, I raised myself off the ground. Ignoring the anxious look on his face, I said, "Don't you ever think you can force me to do anything, Amity Smith! If you don't want to wait until I'm ready you can just leave me be!"

"I don't think I was askin' for that much," he said, looking crestfallen. "Are you sure you're all right?"

"You're askin' for too much right now. Just leave me alone and go on home!"

Dusting myself off, I picked up my books and stared walking in the direction of lodge that was thankfully just a little ways down the road.

Suddenly beside me, Amity said, "Please stop and talk to me Junie Mae. I'm sorry for the way I acted. I just get impatient and sometimes I don't know what to make of you."

Feeling my anger waning, I said, "I can't be nothin' but who I am. If you want somethin' else -- go find it!"

Placing his hand gently on my shoulder, he begged me to stop walking. "Please stop and listen to me, girl!"

Pausing in my steps, I refused to look at him. Now facing me, his sincere blue eyes searched mine. "I love you, Junie Mae Lee. I'll wait. You just do what you have to, and I'll be here when you're ready."

Feeling the urge to cry, I quickly stifled it. Crying meant showing weakness, and I would not show weakness. It suddenly occurred to me that I was Mama. Mama had stifled her tears so many times that they finally dried up permanently. I couldn't be Mama -- wouldn't be Mama. I would never be a ghost. Tears blurred my vision as I stood looking at the ground, wishing that it would open up and swallow me. I felt so confused. How did I know what I wanted? When had I had time to think about it with so much sickness and dying? Why was Amity Smith rushing me -- demanding that I feel things I didn't yet understand? What was love anyway, but a thing associated with pain and loss? Without knowing why I suddenly pictured a smiling Bonzelle Creech sewing happily on a multi-colored quilt block. Love had eluded her, but it had not taken her happy spirit. If only I could learn to be that happy.

"Don't cry, Junie Mae. I didn't mean to make you cry. I would never hurt you."

The desperation in his voice moved me. Looking at him through my tears, I said, "I believe you. I guess I'm just all mixed up."

When Amity gathered me in his arms, I didn't put up a fight. For the first time since I had known him I let myself feel his love for me. It occurred to me that my own fear of turning into Mama and Rose had kept me from loving him back. Thankfully, Amity wasn't like Bart Asher, who had never intended to love Rose. Amity was good and loved me, and all he was asking from me was to return that love.

"Let's go look at where you plan on building our house," I whispered.

Eying me anxiously he asked, "Are you shore you want to?"

"I do," I said truthfully.

I remember that day as if it were yesterday. I can still smell the smoke drifting from the neighboring chimneys. The air was grey but the colorful leaves livened up the otherwise oppressive landscape. Amity drove the truck past the mill and then turned on a dirt road that led straight up the hill behind the Smith house. Once out of the truck I stood on a little flat looking down at the layout of the Smith farm, including the sawmill and outbuildings. I even had a good view of the Cumberland River winding though the valley. "It's beautiful, Amity!" I gasped. "You never said it was this pretty."

"I guess that means you like it here, then?" He laughed.

"It's the prettiest place I've ever seen. Look at all them evergreens," I said, pointing to the west.

"Figured I would cut a few of them down," he teased.

"You will not!" I gasped.

"I figured we'd put a stable back there," he said, pointing to a level spot. "And we could build a smokehouse over there in front of that sycamore grove. "

I recall Amity standing on the knoll looking happier than I had ever seen him. His handsome face was flushed with excitement, while his blue eyes sparkled like melting icicles. There, against the lovely backdrop of splendid colors, I saw Amity as man instead of a boy. Seeing him as a man had somehow made me see myself as a woman rather than a little girl. This sudden awareness was intoxicating and a little scary. I realized at that moment that time and circumstance had moved me far beyond my fifteen years.

That evening I had gone with Daddy and Bonzelle to see the house Daddy had mentioned that morning. The house was small and stood on seven acres of partial woods. The front yard was not huge but bigger than the one back at the lodge. The backyard, however, was large and met with the woods. Daddy pointed out possible spots for a both a smokehouse and a garden. "We still have a river," I said, happily pointing toward the woods where the silver streaks of the water could be seen through the trees. From that day on, I referred to the new house as "River House," which eventually caught on with Daddy, Bonzelle, and every other member of our family. Like the lodge, the house had both front and back porches. Inside, the living room was larger than the one at the lodge and had a huge fireplace, but the kitchen was smaller. In the back of the house there was one small bedroom, and two larger bedrooms lay off to the side of the kitchen. Surprisingly, the electricity in the house was still on, and I had walked about turning the lights on and off. To me, the whole place was a marvel. I couldn't believe it.

I could tell that both Daddy and Bonzelle liked it, too. After walking the length of the yard and taking a stroll in the sparse woods Daddy had decided that he wanted it. "I'll go talk to seller tomorrow," he promised.

That night I slept more soundly than I had in months. I couldn't have known the heartache that the next day would bring, or why Floyd Wilkes would fail me when I needed him the most.

48 JUST AN ACCIDENT

I awoke the next day to find Daddy already gone to mill. I had heard him tell Bonzelle the night before that something had gone wrong with the new saw and that both Amity and Mr. Smith were working to get it fixed. Since it was Saturday, I decided to laze around the lodge for a while. With no one to cook breakfast for, I settled for an apple and a glass of milk. Sitting in Mama's place at the kitchen table, I had a partial view of the Asher house that looked like nothing more than bulky silhouette. Although it was not yet light outside, I could see the shadow of the trees trailing down the sloping hillside. "I won't miss you," I said to the house. I recalled what Granny Lee said about how the Asher house was cursed. Maybe it was and the curse had somehow followed us. In my mind, the house was nothing more than a haunt for the restless spirits who had died there but had not yet realized it. Shivering in spite of myself, I thought of the doctor's wife who in desperation had thrown herself out of her bedroom window in the pouring rain. And I remembered the rich man who had hung himself from the rafters in the barn because he couldn't face the fact that his daughter had contracted polio. Depressed in life, these people couldn't have found peace at death and no doubt still haunted the halls and hills of Creekstone House. It would be good to get away from Wilder Point and its ghosts, I decided.

    Around twelve o'clock that same day I had decided to walk over to the mill and see Daddy and Amity. Outside the wind was high, but not too cold for walking. I was about to cross over to the highway when I saw Daddy's truck coming from the direction of the Smith home. Smiling and waving, I stood waiting for him to stop. As soon as I saw his face through the truck window, I knew something was wrong. "You need to get in the truck, honey," Daddy said gravely.

    "What's wrong?" I asked, searching his eyes for some kind of clue.

"Just get in the truck," he urged gently.

Once inside the truck and seated, I turned to look at Daddy. His eyes appeared red and his mouth trembled. "Honey, something bad happened a while ago. Amity got into the saw somehow. Maybe he was pushing on it or something... He's gone, Junie Mae."

Amity dead? No! That can't be right. I had heard it wrong. Amity had got into the saw. I tried to scream, but it wouldn't come out. "No," I cried. Somewhere I heard a deep sob. I realized that it came from Daddy.

I don't remember Daddy driving back to the lodge, or what I did or thought the next day. I do recall Granny Lee holding me and praying, and asking her God to look after Amity and Uncle Corbin and Rose, and I have a faint recollection of the Smiths coming to the lodge the next day. Though grief-stricken, they had taken me to the side and told me how much Amity had cared for me. "It was just an accident," said the older version of Amity Smith. Just an accident? People called the cave-in "just an accident." I thought of the drunk driver blindly hitting Floyd Wilkes, but the law had called it "just an accident." Rose had walked out into the street in front of an oncoming car, but it was "just an accident." Uncle Corbin had died from a lingering infection, but that was "just an accident," too.

"There ain't no accidents when it comes to death," I told them. "God takes people whenever he chooses." If I sounded bitter, no one called me on it. Who would?

That evening Violet Elizabeth had shared her grief with me, and had held my hand and cried into my shoulder. I knew she was heartbroken over the loss of her brother. I recalled how close they were and how lovingly he had treated her. "He loved you so much, Junie Mae," she sobbed. Why hadn't I said the words? I do love him, but it is too late to tell him now.

During the wake, I couldn't bear to walk up to Amity's casket. Even from the back of the sitting room in the funeral parlor, I could make out his handsome profile and see his blonde hair, and the slope of his well-shaped nose. Oh Amity, I can't believe you left me. I can't believe that I have to go through the motions of living when I no longer have the heart for it.

Later at the Smith family cemetery, located a mile out of Baxter, I watched the preacher's mouth move but only heard bits and pieces of what he said. "We are dust." You didn't warn me that Amity would die, Floyd Wilkes. Was it because you knew I couldn't take anymore? I don't understand you ghosts. Your warnings always come too late to save anybody. After Amity's funeral service, Bonzelle Creech offered to take me to the Smith home for the funeral dinner. "I can't go," I finally told her.

"All right, sweet pea. We'll go on back to the lodge, then."

In retrospect, I don't know what I would have done had Bonzelle not been beside me during the following weeks. Thankfully, she had done everything she could to keep things normal. Daddy had finally bought the house by the river, and we began moving things out of the lodge on the first day of November. It had taken two days of loading and unloading to empty the lodge completely. On the last day, I remember standing in my hollow bedroom, now void of furnishings, and thought it looked bigger than it had before. Walking over to the portal that looked out onto the front porch, I remembered Floyd Wilkes' ghost and how it had comforted me on that first night when I'd had the horrible dream of the dead miners. I had called out to Mama but had found no comfort in her. Although I couldn't see him, I had felt him that day as I roamed the rooms of the lodge. It was as if his spirit hovered inside me. I couldn't remember when it wasn't like that. Floyd Wilkes' ghost, right or wrong, was mine to guard. Feeling a little lost, I went from one room to another looking at the lighter vacant spots where the furniture had been. Mama and Daddy's bedroom was the coldest of all the rooms. It would be, for Mama had left her imprint on the house. Everything she was still lay here trapped in the cracks and crevices of the tattered walls. Maybe part of me was here, too. For a minute, I was in a state of mourning recalling all that had happened inside the lodge – a house that was never really a home. Granny Lee said a home was a place of happiness, trust, and love. I had known that there wasn't enough of either of those things in the lodge to call it a real home. I had spent the whole of my fifteen years walking across these scarred floors, breathing in the air mingled with the coal dust that permeated from No. 5 Mine. Now in the kitchen I gazed through the naked windows and out to the little bridge where the little boy had fallen off into the creek and drowned so many years ago. His ghost no doubt haunted the dark hills along with rest of them.

Oddly, the sun was bright for November but had done nothing to warm things up outside. Ice crusted the tall barks of the leafless trees that trailed up the hill to the solemn Creekstone house. Their thin bony branches clawed desperately at some invisible thing in the air. The dark furs still favored inkblots, while the ghostly white sycamores towered above them. There were still so many places that the ghosts could hide, even in the winter when the woods were bare and no longer secretive. Maybe I can finally say goodbye to the restless souls of Wilder Point. I thought of Amity and wondered if he had become one of them. Surely, he couldn't be haunting the hills at late at night pining for something he had left behind. Suddenly Granny Lee's prophetic words came to haunt me. Ghosts sometimes stay on earth because of some unfinished business. Their souls can't rest until they fix whatever that's botherin' them. Sometimes the living ones keep the souls of the dead from going toward the light of God. Ghosts don't even know that they're dead. Suddenly I understood. It was as if a light had flipped on inside me. How could Floyd Wilkes go to the light when he didn't even know he was dead? Someone had to tell him. Since Mama would never let go of him, it was up to me to free him from her. And what about Rose? She'd died believing that neither Bart nor any of the Ashers would ever pay for what they had done to her in life. Oh, God! I couldn't allow her spirit to roam these lonely hills at night without ever finding peace and rest! And what of Amity? How could he rest without knowing the truth in me? I would have to tell him that I loved him so that he could go be with the God. Tears stung my eyes as I heard Daddy's truck rattling up the drive. He had come for Buster and his wood scraps in the shed. It wouldn't take long for him to empty out the shed. I would start by setting Rose free, I thought. I would do it tomorrow.

49 RETRIBUTION FOR ROSE

The first morning in River House, I had awoken to the bright sunlight streaming through strange windows. At first I was confused as to where I was. Then my eyes adjusted to the contents of the narrow hallway and I realized that I was in the new house. I rose from the bed and crept through the strange house, feeling almost like an interloper. It would take time to get used to it, I decided. Once in the kitchen where boxes still waited to be unpacked, I realized Daddy had already gone to the mill. Life had to go on. Even though Amity had died on the sawdust floor not even three weeks before, the lumber waited there to be sawed and taken to the places that needed it.

Opening the little door to my small clothes closet, I switched on the light. How nice it was to simply pull a switch and have a closet filled with beautiful bright light! I found my heavy coat easily. Reaching into the pocket, I withdrew the picture of Rose in her yellow sundress that Great Uncle Hiram had given to me on the night after Uncle Corbin's funeral. Holding it to my breast, I promised her that soon she would be free. I forced myself to eat a piece of buttered bread so I wouldn't become weak. I was looking at a four mile walk into Harlan unless someone I knew picked me up and hauled me the rest of the way. I had chosen to wear thick tights and my heavy boots. Foregoing the winter coat, I chose to don the heavy blue shawl that Granny Lee had knitted for me the Christmas before. Pulling the matching blue hat onto my head, I grabbed up the picture of Rose and headed out the door and onto the highway in the direction of Harlan. I was glad that Daddy had tied Buster to the tree in the backyard. The last thing I needed was to have him running at my heels.

I walked less than a mile before old Blue Morgan came along and in his rusty old pickup truck and took me on into Harlan. Blue was a friend of Daddy's and I trusted him. Once in town I thanked him and then proceeded on down Main Street. The Asher Funeral Home was on the east side of town, which meant I'd have to pass the street where Rose had been killed. I vowed that I wouldn't cry -- at least until after I'd completed my task with Asher. The funeral home sat back just a little off Bricked Street. It was windowless in the front save for the yellow stained glass in the double doors. My eyes scanned the parking lot where several cars were lined up. With my heart in my throat, I crossed the street, then walked up to the double doors and entered. Ignoring the scent of fresh flowers and death, I spied the podium where the sympathy book rested. Beyond that lay the chapel where a cluster of mourners stood around a casket. Veering off to the right, I walked a few feet down a wide carpeted hall. Almost immediately, I spied the opened door leading to Big Brock Asher's office. Pausing in the doorway, I saw him sitting behind the desk bent over a ledger. His now snow-white hair stood in contrast with dark blue walls. Sensing I was there, his head went up and his big eyes regarded me quizzically. "Can I help you?" His deep voice boomed.

Taking in a deep breath, I said, "I'm Junie Mae Lee. Can I sit down?"

"Please do," he said.

"Can I shut the door?" I asked. Before he could answer, I reached over and pulled it shut.

Looking perturbed, he asked, "What is it that I can do for you today, Miss Lee?"

"You probably know that my sister, Rose, died a few months ago," I said, forcing my eyes to look into his.

"We didn't handle that service, did we?" he asked in puzzlement.

"No," I answered.

"Then what can I help you with?"

Reaching into the pocket of my shawl, I withdrew the picture of Rose and slid it across his desk. "That was her last summer."

Glancing down at the picture he said, "She's very pretty. She looks a lot like your Mama. How is she?"

"She's gone, Mr. Asher. She couldn't stand livin' here no more. There was too many ghosts hauntin' her."

"Why have you come here?" he asked.

"I wanted you to look at that picture and tell me what it is about her face that don't favor Mama."

"I don't understand."

"Just look at it."

"Miss Lee," he said impatiently, "I'm truly sorry about your sister, but I've got business to attend to so I wish you would just get to the point."

Reaching into the other pocket of my shawl, I withdrew the pretty hand mirror that Violet Elizabeth had given me for my birthday. I turned the mirror toward his face. "I want you to look in this mirror and tell me what you see," I whispered softly.

Looking perplexed, he said, "Miss Lee, what is it that you want?"

"I want you to take a good look at your eyes and then tell me whose eyes Rose has."

His face had instantly turned the color of chalk, and eyes had grown big with fear. "What are you saying?" he asked, his strange eyes narrowing dangerously.

"I'm sayin' that sometimes when Rose was scared she looked just like you do now. Remember that time when you come to the lodge to see Mama and talk to her about the strike? It was then I noticed your eyes, but it took me awhile to put it all together."

"I don't know what you're talking about, Miss Lee. You can put that mirror back in your pocket."

Sighing, I placed the mirror back in the silt of the shawl and then rested my arms on the desk. In a low, shaky voice, I said, "You raped Mama when she was fifteen -- the same age as I am now. Rose come out of that rape. Mama never told you, but I found out."

"Your Mama lied to you! I never touched her. She always had it in for me after my mine exploded and killed her daddy."

"You raped her to keep her away from your son. You didn't want her poor blood mixin' with yours. Well, it happened anyway, didn't it?"

"Young lady, if you go spreading around that dirty lie I will sue your daddy for every penny he's got in his pocket. Now get out!" he ordered.

"You ain't even heard the best part yet," I hissed. "You see, Mama never told Rose about you, and she always thought my daddy was her daddy too. Last year, she started seein' a boy and got herself pregnant. That boy was your grandson, Bart. He just used her and then threw her away, just like you did Mama. You ruined her life just like your grandson ruined Rose."

"You're lying," he croaked. His hand had suddenly gone to his necktie in an effort to loosen it. "What is it that you want? Is it money? I won't let you blackmail me, young lady. You go back and tell your scheming mama to forget it!"

"I don't want your money, Mr. Asher. Mama don't want it, either, and she don't even know I'm here. She wouldn't have told Rose, either, if Rose hadn't've got herself pregnant by your grandson. Looks like you and Mama made a big mess out of everything, don't it?"

Eying him closely I whispered, "Your daughter is dead now, Mr. Asher -- yours and Mama's. Why don't you go see Bart and ask him why he killed my sister, your daughter? He might as well've shot her. He was right there on that corner that day she bled to death on the street!" My voice had viciousness to it that I had never heard before, and even I was frightened by the power of it.

Rising unsteadily from his chair, Big Brock ordered, "Get out!" He looked as though he might keel over on the floor. His thick lips appeared bloodless, and his big eyes bulged dangerously. After allowing myself to study Rose's eyes one last time, I left without feeling any kind of remorse. My keen intuition told me that his time on this earth would be short after he had had time to think about what I told him. What man could live with himself after learning that he'd destroyed several lives by perpetrating one vicious, selfish act?

Bonzelle Creech was the first with the news that Big Brock Asher had suffered a massive stroke. She'd told Daddy the next evening how Big Maude Stewart had told that his secretary found him passed out on the floor of his office. "Nobody knows how long he laid there," Bonzelle said. "I heard he that he's paralyzed on one side and can't speak a word. It sounds like he ain't much better than a vegetable."

Nodding, Daddy confessed that he had already heard the news concerning Big Brock that morning from Mr. Smith.

"Well, if you ask me he deserves everything he's gettin' and more for how he treated them widows."

I was sitting in the living room in Daddy's ratty old chair listening to them talk and serenely looking out the window beyond the yellowed grass and on past the highway where the high hills rose to meet the colorless sky. You're at rest now, Rose. I can feel it. Granny Lee had told me that God had his own way of punishing people. Maybe he had done that through me. According to the Bible, the truth will set you free. I didn't see that happening with Big Brock Asher. Even today, I believe the truth had put an end to him.

50 UNFINISHED BUSINESS

The coming of December brought the first light snow. By this time, Daddy and I had settled nicely in the house by the river. It had taken me a while to get used to catching the school bus instead of riding in the truck with Amity and Violet Elizabeth. I had so missed sitting sandwiched between the two of them and hearing Amity's low, infectious laugh. Violet Elizabeth and I still spent our lunch hour together. Sometimes we would eat in the school cafeteria, and other times we'd sit outside and eat our lunch on the stoop, depending on the weather. During our time together, I had noticed how Amity's death had changed Violet Elizabeth. The changes were subtle; even when she smiled her dimpled smile that was so like that of Amity's, I sensed a somberness about her. I knew she had accepted her brother's death, but with this acceptance came a certain dismal finality that most people cannot come to terms with. I realized that letting go was just too painful, and so they held on to them. After Uncle Corbin died, I had asked Granny Lee how she could bear up through the day without crying. She said, "It would be selfish to hold on to him. Sometimes people can be real selfish when it comes to lettin' go. Some of us keep our dead close to us for our own selfish reasons." I thought of Amity and wondered if a part of me was holding on to him for selfish reasons. But I have unfinished business with him. If only I would have told him that I loved him! What had kept me from saying those words? Selfish or not, I'd decided that I had to say those words to him. I couldn't take the chance that my unfinished business might hold him to the earth. I felt that I had freed Rose by telling Big Brock Asher the truth. Now it was time to free Amity.

One evening in mid-December, I came home to find Bonzelle cooking Daddy's supper. I marveled at how clean the kitchen seemed in spite of all the unpacked boxes. Bonzelle knew how to make a kitchen appear warm and homey, yet still clean and neat. Mama's kitchen at the lodge had appeared cold and sterile in comparison. Turning from the stove to look at me, Bonzelle was quick to notice my pensive mood.

"What's wrong, Sweet Pea?" she asked.

Not accustomed to anyone but Amity asking me how I felt, I could only look at her blankly. At first no words would came out, but Bonzelle's true interest in what I might be feeling made me comfortable enough to tell her about Amity and my guilt.

"He probably knowed you loved him," she said assuredly.

Close to tears, I shook my head no. "I couldn't say it. I was too afraid to say that word," I whispered.

"Oh, Junie Mae, you poor baby," she cooed, while bending down and kissing my head lightly. "Listen, you ain't much more than a little girl -- really. You were just bein' as honest as you could. I know he understood."

"I do love him," I admitted through tears. "I miss him terribly. I just can't have his spirit roamin' the earth waitin' and wonderin'."

"I reckon you could just tell him," she said easily.

"We had a special place behind the sawmill. He took me there the evenin' before he died and showed me where he wanted to build our house. I'd like to go there and tell him," I said.

"Well, I can take you to the sawmill. I reckon you could walk the rest of the way so you could have your special time," she offered.

"All right," I agreed suddenly feeling lighter inside. I couldn't believe that Bonzelle was so understanding and caring. Why couldn't Daddy see this?

The next day during lunch I told Violet Elizabeth that I'd planned to visit the hillside behind the sawmill. I said, "It was the last place I seen him. I just want to say goodbye to him."

Violet Elizabeth nodded and placed her arm around me. "Oh, Junie Mae, how are we gonna make it without him? I know he's gone, but I keep goin' to his bedroom and sittin' on his bed. I feel close to him there." We were walking along the fence line overlooking the ball field. I pointed to a spot near its middle and said, "That's where me and Amity stood last year talking. It was cold just like it is now," I said. My voice broke.

Violet Elizabeth said, "Mama wants to turn Amity's room into a sewing room. I told her no, but she said it was for the best. I reckon she's right about that. I know we have to go on with life."

"We do, I reckon. Bad things come to the dead if we hold on to 'em," I whispered.

"What do you mean?" Violet asked, looking puzzled.

"Granny Lee says they can't go to the light of God if we hold on to 'em."

Violet Elizabeth suddenly sobbed, then threw her arms around me. "You'll always be my sister, won't you?"

"Always," I promised, holding her tightly as I could.

The next day was Saturday. Daddy had promised Mr. Smith that he would haul a load of lumber to a store over in Cumberland, and he was already gone when I woke up. Once in the kitchen I fed the dying fire in the woodstove. Afterwards, I ground some beans for coffee. I'd hated the taste of the bitter stuff, but I figured that Bonzelle would be over soon and I wanted to have some made for her. An early riser, Bonzelle was there with a tin of biscuits before nine o'clock. I fried up some eggs and bacon to go with the biscuits and we had breakfast at the table. While clearing the table Bonzelle brought up Big Brock Asher and said, "I heard tell this morning that Miss Joelyn had to hire a private nurse for Old Brock Asher. I reckon if your Mama was here she could nurse him," she said innocently.

"She'd poison him the first day," I said without thinking.

Bonzelle winced, and asked, "What do you mean?"

"I mean she hates the Ashers," I answered truthfully.

"Well, that's one thing we got in common, I reckon."

I had decided to wait until the afternoon to make the trip to the hillside. It was cold outside and the wind had blown steadily all day. "You'd better dress warmly," Bonzelle said in a motherly fashion, then added, "Junie Mae, this is a bad day for goin' up on that hill. Couldn't you wait for a nice summer day?"

"I know it don't make sense to you, Bonzelle," I said apologetically.

"Well, as long as it makes sense to you," she said.

I wanted badly to explain to her that Amity's spirit needed to rest, but I wasn't sure that she would understand. Only Granny Lee would understand and know why I was doing what I was doing.

I recall feeling sad and unsure as I dressed for the walk. I knew that seeing the hillside where Amity had planned to build our house would break my heart, but I felt I had to go and tell him how I felt inside. I had to take care of unfinished business.

Around one o'clock Bonzelle and me climbed in her daddy's old truck and made the seven mile drive to the Smith home. Seeing the big farmhouse again made my heart wrench, but it also brought back good memories of the three of us walking the paddocks and Amity proudly showing me the foal named for Violet Elizabeth and me. The sight of the long wooden mill shed where Amity was killed had made me bite my lip so hard I drew blood. Vowing not to cry, I knew that if I set one foot in that building, I would have surely seen Amity's death played out just as I had seen Floyd Wilkes die on that bridge.

Bonzelle parked next to Daddy's truck at the back of the sawmill. Opening the truck door, I slid out and held tightly to the heart-shaped locket around my neck. "I don't see a soul back here," she laughed.

"They're all indoors, probably," I said, pulling back a strand of my hair that the wind had blown into my mouth.

"I'll just sit here and wait," she said patiently.

"I won't be long," I promised.

The dirt road behind the hill went straight up into the woods. The climb winded me, causing me stop and rest. When I finally reached the top of the hill the land evened out. Bare of their leaves, the trees swayed and bent in rhythm with the cold, deafening wind. Walking over to the spot where Amity had once stood pointing to the dark fir trees in the distance, I bowed my head and waited for some kind of sign that Amity was there. "Floyd Wilkes," I whispered. I heard nothing but the sound of the wind bending the trees. *Maybe one day you'll open your mouth long enough to tell me you love me. When you do, I'll believe it. If I'm not close by just holler it on the wind. I'll hear it.* Amity's words echoed. It was as if he was standing right next to me speaking them. Taking in a deep breath, I hollered as loud as I could. "Amity Smith, I love you!" My own echo sounded distant, making it easy to believe that the wind would carry it to Amity. For a while, I stood there looking down at the Cumberland River winding though the valley like a snake. The wind felt like daggers on my face, but somehow that didn't matter. I owed Amity the time. After a while a kind of peace had washed over me, and my body felt as light as a feather. The feeling was almost surreal, and as if on cue, the wind ceased. "Thank God," I prayed. I knew somehow that Amity had heard me and that the hush of the wind had been a sign.

Once back in the truck Bonzelle commented on the serene look on my face. "Do you believe in ghosts?" My voice asked, almost without my permission.

"I don't know," she answered. "Why?"

"If you don't, you should," I whispered.

51 FLOYD WILKES IS DEAD

Bonzelle had sewn new curtains for the River House and had insisted we put them up before Christmas. On the twenty-first day of December, she suggested that we go to the back of the woods and cut a Christmas tree. She complained, "It ain't one bit Christmassy in here. There needs to be a big old tree right in front of the window."

"You better ask Daddy first. He might not want a tree. It might remind him too much of Rose. She loved Christmas and was the one who always put the star on top," I warned.

Bonzelle frowned and said, "I'm so sorry, Junie Mae. I wadn't thinkin'." After a few minutes of silence, though, she'd thought differently. "Maybe it would do you all good to have a Christmas tree. Don't you think Rose would want you to have a one? She wouldn't want you or your Daddy to miss out on celebratin' Christmas."

"It won't seem the same without her," I said blinking away the tears.

"I'll bet you're thinking about Amity, too," she said.

Nodding, I showed her the necklace I still wore around my neck and then the matching bracelet. "He worked real hard to buy the bracelet for my birthday."

"Oh honey. You've had so much to deal with. A girl your age should be thinking of school dances and proms and celebratin' Christmas. Why don't you and me take an axe, go down to them woods, and cut us a Christmas tree? We'll bring it in here and we'll decorate it. I got some big old orange and red bulbs in back of the house. We'll string them on there and it will look real pretty. We'll find some of Rose's favorite ornaments, too, and put them on the tree. If you want to we could we could put a little red ribbon near the top in remembrance of her. What do you say?"

I finally gave in. It was hard to say no to Bonzelle when she was so enthusiastic about everything. I remember trampling down that snowy field and into the woods in search of a tree. Bonzelle had donned a pair of Daddy's old work pants that she'd had to roll up several times in order to keep them off the ground. With Daddy's axe over her shoulder and her stocking cap, I thought she favored a miniature Paul Bunyan. Just watching her critically eyeing the trees had lightened my mood considerably. Laughing, I said, "You go at this tree huntin' like a doctor about to cut somebody open."

"Now Junie Mae, gettin' the right tree is important. You can't just drag in any old thing. You could help me look, you know," she suggested.

Walking over to the edge of the little woods, I studied the river. Unlike the river near the lodge, this body of water widened out and had no little islands or branches. Behind it, the steep flinty wall rose up out of the water, finally giving way to the barren hills. I had decided that this was a deeper fork of the Cumberland River, and I knew for sure that Daddy couldn't wait to sink his bait into the water.

As I walked back in the direction of the house, I felt something tugging on my hair. Thinking it was Bonzelle, I turned in time to see her walking down the hill toward the river. Automatically touching the back of my head, I thought of Floyd Wilkes' ghost. In front of me, there was a deadfall. Without warning, something big ascended out of it, awkwardly flapping its large wings before landing low on the ground. Startled, I jumped back before finally realizing that it was only a wild turkey. Still, something else was there. I'd felt it and realized that it was Floyd Wilkes' ghost. I knew all the signs. I had started to walk ahead when something moved in the brush near the deadfall. Looking around expectantly, I thought I'd seen something white flash through the little stand of trees to the left side of me. "Floyd Wilkes," I whispered, straining my ears in anticipation. Hearing nothing, I turned back in the direction of the river where I had seen Bonzelle walking; before I could make the first step something whizzed by my feet. Looking down I saw a small stick had landed on my boot. *Floyd Wilkes is playing with me.* Taking in a sharp, cool breath, I calmly spoke to the spiteful ghost. "Floyd Wilkes, you're dead. You need to go on to the light. I can't keep you here with me forever." Just as I said it, I heard something snap above me. Moving quickly, I turned to look backwards just in time to see a large tree branch come crashing down on the very spot where I'd been standing.

"What was that?" Bonzelle's voice echoed. When I didn't answer her immediately, she hollered again. "Junie Mae!"

"I'm up here," I yelled.

"Just stay where you are. I found a tree. I'll bring it up in a minute." In the distance, I could hear the echo of the axe chipping away at a bark.

Floyd Wilkes is angry with me. I could actually feel his fury all around me. Breathing steam, I stared at the downed tree branch and felt a chill.

He doesn't want to hear that he's dead. Suddenly all the good cheer of the day had fallen away, dropping a kind of gray curtain over any happiness I might have felt. It had suddenly occurred to me that I had kept his ghost around too long. But how could I send it away? It had been with me for as far back as I could remember.

Later, back at the house, Bonzelle and I filled the pretty branches of the Christmas tree with ornaments. After we put the star on top, we tied not one but two red ribbons near the star to remind us of Rose and Amity. "We'll just go to my house and get the lights, and then we'll start makin' some cookies and spiced cider," Bonzelle suggested. "It'll be a nice surprise for your Daddy." After we returned home with the Christmas lights, it had taken us both to string them around the tree. I had never seen lights on a tree before and thought how much Rose would have loved seeing the colored bulbs all lit up.

Daddy had come home that night to a kitchen that was full of delicious aromas. Bonzelle and I had baked several pans of assorted cookies after we finished with the tree. I loved how she had added various dried fruits and figs to the dough, which made them not only beautiful but delicious as well. Bracing myself for Daddy's reaction to the tree, I hunkered down in the big corner chair and watched. "We put some lights and two red ribbons as reminders of Amity Smith and Rose," she said. "We weren't sure how you'd take it, but we done it anyway," she said resolutely.

My eyes followed Daddy's gaze and then saw that he was smiling. "The tree is right pretty, Bonzelle. I reckon I can't say much to a woman who knows how to swing an axe," he joked.

Feeling relieved that he wasn't mad at us for putting up the tree, I got up from the chair and went to stand by him in the doorway. Turning to me, I could see his dark eyes had misted up. "I'll never stop missin' my Rose," he said with a tremor in voice.

"None of us will, Daddy. But I can promise you that she's at peace."

After the cider and cookies, Daddy brought up the subject of No. 5 mine. "I seen Harlan Ray and Harvey James this evenin' at Asher's store," he said. "I reckon things are goin' to hell in a bucket up there at the mine. Old Big Brock's stroke has hurt the business. Little Brock don't know what he's doin'. From what I hear, he's got two trucks down, and he ain't made a move to get 'em worked on. Old Purl's up there runnin' around like a chicken with his head cut off tryin' to order parts for the trucks and keep things in line."

Bonzelle nodded, and said, "Everybody knows Old Big Brock ran the show. Now that he's bedridden, Little Brock's lost. I hear Old Big Brock is in a real bad shape. I talked to Dan Stewart's wife yesterday morning and she said Joelyn told her she thought he was dyin'."

At the other end of the table, I sat listening impassively, remembering how Big Brock Asher had sat there behind his desk smugly denying that he'd ever touched Mama. But I'd cornered him with the truth and he couldn't take it -- couldn't take the fact that he had created such a mess. His intent was to destroy Mama, but in essence he had eventually destroyed himself. I thought of Bart and contemplated confronting him but then decided that God could handle him in His own way and time. I thought of Mama and realized that in time she would face her own kind of hell. A part of her had to know that how badly she had treated Rose. Mama may have been good at rearranging life to suit her needs, but I didn't see how she could hide from how she had treated Rose -- or Daddy, for that matter. Ironically, it would take a trip past the Daisy Mining Camp to open my eyes. Seeing where my Mama had lived as a small child had given me some insight as to why she had turned out as she did.

52 FACES TO REMEMBER

The three of us had celebrated Christmas at Granny Lee's house in Putney. Not one of Granny Lee's brood batted an eye when they saw Bonzelle. Granny Lee, of course, welcomed her into the house with a big hug. Like the rest of the family, Granny Lee appreciated the help and care that Bonzelle had shown Daddy after Mama left. Even Grandma Haley had gone to Bonzelle after the meal was over and thanked her for all she had done for Daddy and me. While at Granny Lee's house, I couldn't help but remember the Christmas before at the lodge. I pictured Rose sitting off by herself in the crowded kitchen looking as if the world had deserted her. I would never forget her woebegone expression. Bart Asher had caused that look with his false promises, and for that I hated him.

At the end of the day, as was the custom, Granny Lee had gathered us all together in prayer. With little Chester Harlan on her lap she prayed for peace and love, and she asked God to take care of our dear loved ones who had passed unto him. During the prayer, it was as if I had absorbed everyone's grief, and the weight of our loss had lain heavily upon my heart. I remember sitting there in that ratty chair in Granny Lee's cluttered living room and deciding that I must burn every dear face into my memory. Somehow, I would freeze the memory in time so I could take it out and look at it when trying to decide who I was and where I came from. One day they would all be gone, and it was important for me to remember them as they had looked that day.

53 THE DIVORCE

New Year's Day of 1950 brought about ice, snow, and cold howling winds. Harvey James and Harlan Ray helped Daddy put chains on his truck tires so that he could get to and from the sawmill. The cold blast and the ice lasted for almost two weeks. Since both the back roads and the main highways were covered with sheets of ice, the school bus was unable to pass the roads – especially up the hollers – and school was called off for two days. Housebound, I tried to read but found myself thinking of Floyd Wilkes' ghost, and how I'd not seen a vision since that day in the woods when I told it to go to the light. But even without a vision, I had felt the presence of the ghost all around me. A part of me still struggled with the idea that maybe I was the one holding Floyd Wilkes back from heaven, but saying goodbye to him was almost inconceivable. Still, a part of me knew that someday soon I would have to let him go.

During that last snow day, I cooked supper for Daddy and had the table set and waiting. I missed Bonzelle and hoped the snow would melt soon so that she could make it back to the River House. Daddy came home around six o'clock that night. I heard him stomping the snow off his boots. As soon as he entered the kitchen door, I saw the dismal look on his face and knew something was wrong. "What's the matter, Daddy?" I asked, hoping it wasn't something to do with the sawmill or No. 5 Mine. After taking his coat off and hanging it on a hook on the wall, he turned to me and asked, "Did you know that Larkin put Rhodie in an institution in late November?"

"No," I said honestly, reminding him that the last thing we got from Mama was a Christmas card. "She didn't even write nothin'…"

"She don't have Rhodie to take care of no more, and she never said a thing."

"Who told you, Daddy?" I asked curiously.

"Maw thought I already knowed." Daddy poured some of the warm water from the teakettle into a wash pan, then reached for the lye soap and started briskly lathering his hands. "I always thought she'd come back if Rhodie got put away. Don't look like she's comin' back," he added grimly.

Not wishing to darken Daddy's mood any more than it was already, I listened silently.

"She told me that her only reason for stayin' in Indianapolis was because Rhodie needed her. I reckon I wanted to believe that. I know better now. If she wanted to come home she would."

"I know that, Daddy," I finally said. "She never liked it here. I think the coal brings back too many bad memories for her."

"I reckon so," Daddy said, jerking the towel off the rack above the sink. "I guess it's time I see a lawyer and get some divorce papers fixed."

With mouth agape in astonishment, I could only nod my head. Daddy wants to divorce Mama. I knew he would never have said it if he hadn't meant it.

Daddy stood good on his promise. On the fourth day of January he saw an attorney he'd heard of in Harlan and had him draw up some divorce papers for Mama. I wouldn't have believed it had I not seen a copy of the papers for myself. Daddy had said of Mama, "If she wants to contest the divorce she'll have to come here and do it." One evening in the middle of January, I'd come home from school to find Bonzelle scrubbing the kitchen floor. On the table was a big stack of letters. "Your daddy asked me to get your all's mail," she said. Thumbing through the stack of mail, I came across a letter from Mama. I instantly recognized her neat handwriting on the face of the envelope. Tearing it open and unfolding it, I began to read her scorching words -- words which made it clear to me that she'd received the divorce papers. She'd written, "I knowed all along that your Daddy was seein' that Bonzelle Creech. That's the reason he is wantin' this divorce. If I really wanted to be mean I would come back there and demand some of that money he's got in the bank, rather than to let her have it. It wasn't her who slaved away all them years. It was me..." Feeling anger rise within me I wadded up the letter and threw it in the wood box.

"Is something wrong?" Bonzelle asked, placing the mop inside the bucket and then shoving it the corner with her foot.

"No," I lied.

"That was a letter from your Mama, wadn't it?"

"Yeah," I finally admitted, then added, "She's ragin' over the divorce papers."

"Oh, I see. I thought she'd probably have a fit when she got 'em. She's been married to your daddy for a long time. I can see why she'd be mad."

"Mama can't let go of nothin'. That's the way she is. If she wanted

Daddy, she would be here. Rhodie's been in an institution since before Christmas. Daddy found that out, and that's why he's divorcin' her."

"He loves her anyway, Junie Mae. I know this, and believe me -- it hurts me to the bone. But there ain't a lot you and me can do about it."

"He'll get over her," I promised her. "You're good for Daddy in a way Mama could never be."

From that day forward, I had taken it upon myself to get the mail so that I could intercept any letters Mama might send. The last thing I wanted was for Daddy to read her rants. Luckily, no more came and Mama eventually signed the divorce papers without a hitch.

Bonzelle was thrilled when she learned Mama had signed the divorce papers. "Now I don't have to feel like I'm cleanin' up another woman's house," she said. I had hoped Daddy would ask Bonzelle to marry him soon, but he had shown no sign of doing so even after the divorce from Mama was finalized. I'd also suspected that he'd had sent Mama more of the money he'd received from Uncle Corbin's will; it wasn't so much a payoff but more because he believed she had earned it. That's the way Daddy thought, being the honest man he was. In watching Daddy for the next few months I had realized how much Mama had hurt him, and sadly, no matter what she had done, he would always love her.

54 THE RETURN OF FLOYD WILKES' GHOST

The winter months crawled by at a snail's pace. More snow fell in February, causing hazardous conditions on the roadway. March brought cold winds and a rain, which caused many lowlands to flood. I recall standing on our back porch and looking down toward the river where the floodwaters had spilled over into the lower part of the woods. All my life I had seen flooding and the mounds of debris left behind once the tide had fallen. Daddy had called the debris "drifts," and those drifts were sometimes as much as ten feet tall. When Rose and I were small, Daddy would take us down to the river and allow us to root through the drifts. Sometimes we would find wonderful things like pretty perfume bottles, baseball bats, and even plastic beach balls. Once, Daddy had unearthed a rowboat that was in surprisingly good condition. It had taken him a week to dig it out of the rubble. I remember how badly I'd wanted him to take me and Rose out in that boat, but he'd refused, saying that it probably belonged to somebody up the river. He'd said, "I'll tell you what: I'll look the boat over for leaks. Then I'll tie it up on the bank and we'll wait a week or so. If nobody claims it then we'll call it ours." A week had passed, and lucky for us nobody claimed the boat. I remember how excited we were just waiting for the week to pass. When it finally did, Daddy had celebrated owning the boat by taking us out on the river. I can still hear Rose's happy squeals echoing off the flinty walls.

By the time the month of April arrived, the Cumberland River had shrunk back to its normal size, but its shrinkage was not to last. The warmer rains soon came and brought high tides, swollen hollers, and bulging creeks. Boats were a common sight on the river. It seemed everybody owned one or two. The month of May brought warmer weather as well as the end of school. During the latter part of the month, Bonzelle decided it was time to air out the house and had raised all the windows. "If the flies come in we'll just kill 'em. Every home needs a good airin' in the spring," she said decidedly. Later in my room, I started the task of putting my schoolbooks away. Granny Lee had given me a hope chest for my twelfth birthday, and each year after school was finished I would store my books in the chest. I had just opened the lid when something crashed loudly behind me. Startled, I jumped up and automatically scanned the room for any fallen objects, but everything seemed strangely in place. Turning to the window, I noticed that it was no longer open. "So the window crashed," I thought. Before I could make an effort to raise it, I heard another crash coming from the living room, followed by a third crash that sounded like it was coming from the kitchen. Bonzelle, who was outside, came running up to the kitchen door looking startled and said, "It sounds like the whole house is coming down. What fell?"

"You heard the noise?" I asked in surprise. I was remembering the night at the lodge when Floyd Wilkes had caused the living room door to fly open and the clock to come crashing off the mantle. Oddly, neither Mama nor Daddy had woken up. But Bonzelle had heard the crashes.

"Who could miss hearin' it?" she answered, and then asked, "What caused it?"

"The windows in the bedroom, living room, and kitchen fell," I answered.

"Dang it! I knowed I should've propped them all open with window sticks," she said regretfully, as if what had happened with the windows was the most natural thing in the world. "Just leave 'em closed for now. I'll have your daddy cut me some sticks to prop 'em up again. I hope none of the glass broke."

I'd known it was the ghost of Floyd Wilkes trying to get my attention. But why? Fear loomed inside me at the thought that something bad was about happen. I remembered the incident with the fallen tree branch in the woods before Christmas, and nothing bad had occurred afterward. Nevertheless, I could still never be sure. One part of me had learned to fear the ghost of Floyd Wilkes, while the other part continued to hold onto it out of some kind of love and need.

55 GOD GIVES US WHAT WE NEED

My sixteenth birthday was coming up on the 14th day of May. Two days before it, Bonzelle had asked me how I would celebrate it. My answer came quickly. "I want to go to the plank bridge near the old Daisy Mining Camp."

"You want to see the old plank bridge?" she asked, looking puzzled.

"Yes," I answered solemnly.

Bonzelle had bought new wallpaper for the kitchen and was cutting long strips on the table. "What's on the bridge, Junie Mae?"

"Something I need to say goodbye to," I answered.

"It's your birthday. I reckon you oughta get what you ask for. When might you want to go?"

"Soon – tomorrow, maybe."

"All right," she agreed. "We can go before noonday if you want to." Changing the subject abruptly, she grouched, "Would you look at this! I've cut this strip too short. I guess it don't matter much. He won't notice it anyways."

I could hear the frustration in her voice and knew the reason for it was Daddy's apprehension toward marriage. However, Bonzelle spoke her mind; she wasn't one to keep her feelings bundled up inside. "Your Daddy ain't never gonna marry me. It's just a waste of my time and energy hopin' he will. I do anything and everything for that man and I barely get a thank you. I can't go on this way much longer."

I had wanted to comfort her and promise her Daddy would eventually come around, but my honesty would not allow me to paint her a pretty picture. I wasn't Mama.

Bonzelle went on, "I don't think your Daddy really wanted to divorce your Mama. I believe he was hopin' she'd come back if he sent her the divorce papers."

"I don't know, Bonzelle," I admitted uncomfortably. I had come to love Bonzelle and couldn't stand the thought of losing her. But I couldn't speak for Daddy.

"I'll just finish up here and go on home," she said in a depressed tone. Just as she finished speaking, the kitchen door opened and Daddy walked in. Looking grave, he told us that Big Brock Asher had died in the night. Maybe I should have felt responsible for his death. Daddy's declaration had brought back memories of the day I had told Big Brock Asher about Rose. I recalled how pale he looked and how he kept tugging at his tie, as if it was strangling him. In retrospect, I had felt no guilt. In fact, I was relieved in knowing that he had finally gone on to face the eternal flames of hell that Granny Lee claimed was ten times hotter than the normal fire. Daddy, though, feared the effect his death would have on the running of No. 5 Mine. According to what he had heard from his brothers, Uncle Purl was keeping things going.

Daddy said, "Harvey James told me that Little Brock Asher ain't been to the mine in days. Maybe he's been sittin' with his sick Daddy, but things are gettin' bad up there. Purl might be good at keepin' the trucks on the road, but he ain't worth diddly when it comes to gettin' along with the miners, or keepin' things in good repair. Ain't nobody cares what he says. The men hate him -- always have."

I was thinking that maybe Little Brock might eventually force Bart to forego his schooling and take over Mine No. 5 the way his daddy had forced him to take over his coal business. I decided it would serve Bart right if this happened. In truth, I had wanted Bart to suffer the way he'd made Rose suffer. Granny Lee, of course, wouldn't have approved of my vengeful thinking had she known of it, but I couldn't help how I felt.

After Bonzelle left that day, Daddy told me something that he felt he couldn't say around Bonzelle. It concerned the men who had beaten up Uncle Corbin for crossing the picket line. "Junie Mae, I heard today that Seth Couch and Les Hensley was found beaten half to death behind a tavern in Hazard. I don't know about Seth, but Les is in a real bad shape." Daddy's voice sounded grim.

I had heard about the tavern and knew that it was a bad place. He went on, "I reckon they'll both live, but neither of 'em's got a tooth left in their heads."

"Who done it?"

"Well, that's the thing. The law is tryin' to blame Harlan Ray, but he had an alibi. It was lucky that he stopped over at the Billiard Hall last night. I reckon he was shootin' billiards at the time the men was beat up." Daddy chuckled and then admitted that he knew who had done it.

"Who?" I asked incredulously.

"I heard through the grapevine that it was your Uncles Coy and Noah that done it. You know they go to that tavern every Saturday night. The boys loved Corbin. I think they was just waitin' for the right time to pay them men back for what they done to him."

"The law will come lookin' for them," I said.

Daddy shook his head. "I doubt them men will say a word. The Haley boys have got a bad reputation and a lot of people are afraid of 'em. Don't you worry none. I probably shouldn't have told you," he admitted sheepishly.

"I'd have knowed about it eventually," I said.

"I don't doubt it," he laughed, and then added, "Ain't a lot that escapes you."

"Are you goin' to ask Bonzelle to marry you?" I said without thinking.

Daddy's amused expression changed abruptly into a frown. "Why would you ask me somethin' like that? I ain't in no real hurry for a wife," he said sullenly.

Realizing it was too late to take back what I asked, I went on, "Bonzelle's getting tired of waitin' for you to make up your mind about her. She thinks it's because you still love Mama."

After pulling off his billed hat and then hanging it on a hook behind the door, he turned to me with a sincere look. "I do love your Mama, Junie Mae. You can hate me for feelin' that way if you want to. It's just somethin' that I can't help. I care for Bonzelle, but I don't know as I'm ready to make her my wife."

Using one of Granny Lee's favorite teachings, I told Daddy, "God don't give people what they want. He gives them what they need." I thought of how Mama and Rose had wasted themselves on people who would never give them anything but grief. I realized with disgust that Daddy wasn't any different and would probably waste his life away wanting someone that would never want him back. "You do what you want to, Daddy. If you decide to sit here and pine your life away, there ain't a thing I can do about it. I think it's a shame, though. Bonzelle is good woman who loves you. Mama never will."

56 GOODBYE, FLOYD WILKES

On the day I visited the plank bridge I had decided to remember it with as much clarity as possible. However, the lonely sight of the plank bridge wasn't the only thing that stuck in my head. The abandoned Daisy Mining Camp had struck something deep within me that made sure I would never forget it. As promised, Bonzelle had arrived at River House at exactly noonday, but I had been ready for hours. I had half-expected Floyd Wilkes' ghost to kick up some kind of fuss by slinging open a door or crashing a clock to the floor, but neither happened. On the contrary, things had remained eerily quiet -- almost too quiet. I felt like a mourner that day. I was for all intents and purposes planning a funeral. As Bonzelle steered her daddy's old truck down the winding road and in the direction of the old Daisy Mining Camp, I felt a kind of dismal finality sink in. My mind was hit hard by the notion that I was about to say goodbye to something that had been a part of me since I was five years old. I knew that children often held on to tattered blankets and chewed up toys for as long as they could before their parents finally took the beloved thing away. I suddenly understood the pain of separation.

Bonzelle's kindly voice had brought me out of my reverie. "Junie Mae, I don't aim to be nosey, but I was wonderin' why we're goin' to the plank bridge."

"Mama's little brother was killed there years ago. A drunken college student ran him over."

"I didn't know that," she said in a sympathetic voice.

"Mama never talked about it. My Grandma Haley said she never got over what she seen that day."

"I know what it's like to lose the most important person in your life," she choked, and then pointed toward the valley. "There's the old Daisy Mining Camp." Leaning forward, I asked her to pull over to the side of the road. I need not have worried, for the highway had given way to a bumpy dirt road that was full of holes. While we were there, not one car passed us.

The Daisy Mining Camp was made up of several rows of small, dilapidated houses. Some had windows missing while others had no doors. The crude front porches were missing planks, and a few vines had trailed up the sides of the houses nearest the creek. In the distance stood a red brick building that had once been the Company Store. Surprisingly, it was in a much better state than the cheaply built homes. My eyes roamed the rutted valley where only a few patches of grass had managed to push through the scarred ground. "Desolate" was the only fitting word to describe the camp. In seeing what was left of the tall skinny outhouses, I remembered Mama once saying that there were never enough outhouses, and that sometimes she would pee on herself while waiting for one to come empty.

"This place ain't changed a lot," Bonzelle whispered. "Daddy moved us here when I was around nine years old. We didn't stay long, though. It was just too awful here. Daddy said he'd had nightmares about this camp."

Nodding I said, "I can see why. Mama never got over it, either. She talked about this place all the time. She just couldn't get it out of her mind even after she growed up and married."

I recall getting out and standing on the hill overlooking the camp and thinking that it was nothing more than a graveyard full of tragedy and broken dreams. I remember Granny Lee saying that if bad things happen in a place then the ugliness of it all stays right there in the air forever. I knew she was right because I could see ugliness and poverty all over the camp. Its very air reeked of the past oppression. Staring hard at the camp, I began to see it as it was years before. Thin, hollow-cheeked men dressed in heavy coats and worn out brogan boots walked up the long road leading to the coalmine. The miners wore scarred mining caps with heavy headlamps, and they carried their dinner pails protectively underneath their arms. It was hard to tell one man from the next. The coalmine had taken away their youth early on. It was impossible to miss the stoop in their backs caused from being on their knees shoveling coal for hours. The women weren't much better; all of them wore tired expressions as they went about their daily chores. I saw them on their back porches slinging pans of dirty dishwater out onto the muddy ground, simply because it didn't matter. There wasn't a clean grassy spot in the place, anyway, and the women had lost heart long ago. Accustomed to the dirt, the children ran through it barefooted as if it were a field of soft clover. The hordes of flies no longer bothered them, for they had learned to live with the ones their mother's couldn't kill. I have heard some say that the people in the mining camps were dirty and didn't care about hygiene. To me, this is a ridiculous assumption. My mother and many of the women I had known in the Asher

Mining Camp were exceptional housekeepers. However, when several families are crowded together in small cramped houses and separated by a filthy drainage ditch, there is very little one can do to keep things clean. In seeing the Daisy Mining Camp, I felt a stab of deep sorrow for not just Mama, but for every family that had ever lived there. Although the Asher Camp was bad, this went beyond the word "bad." Tears welled up in my eyes and blinded my vision; wiping them away with my sleeve, I told Bonzelle that I was ready to go to the plank bridge.

Not even a mile from the Daisy Camp, the weathered plank bridge looked every bit as desolate as Daisy Camp had looked. I could feel the overwhelming isolation the minute I saw it. Swallowing hard, I said, "It feels so lonely here."

"Well, it ain't much traveled since they built the new bridge," she offered. The bridge was wide and stood high over a little branch of the Cumberland River. Its wrought iron railing was badly rusted in places, and the planks were thin and badly worn. It was plain to me that nobody had cared about the bridge in a long time.

Sensing my need to be alone, Bonzelle pointed to a wide spot just a little ways past the bridge, and said softly, "I'll just be a few feet away."

Taking in a deep shuddering breath, my eyes scanned the length of the bridge and realized that it was the bridge in my dreams. Standing perfectly still, I called Floyd Wilkes' name and waited. All around me a warm wind blew, and the trees bent over the creek bank were in full bloom. I remember the sweet scent of the honeysuckle vines that clung to the railing at the base of the bridge. I wondered if the honeysuckle vines were there the day Floyd Wilkes had died. Somehow, I had known they were. Walking the length of the bridge, I started talking in a soft voice. I told Floyd Wilkes the story of how one day a young boy had decided to sell two buckets of blackberries so that he could earn money to buy his sister some pretty butterfly print material.

"She was going to make a dress out of that material," I told him. "The boy loved his sister so much, and she was always makin' him special food and dotin' on him. He just wanted to do something special for her. On that day, he had walked in the sun and his tattered clothes were soaked from sweat. He was glad to see the bridge because it meant Harlan was only a few minutes away. Walkin' beside him was a little black boy from Daisy Camp who had followed him. The two of them were talkin' and didn't even hear the car come up behind them. The man drivin' probably didn't see the boys, either, because the way the road bends causes a blind spot on the bridge." Feeling sick to my stomach and full of unspent emotion, I tried to keep the tremor out of my voice. "The car hit the boy holdin' the berries. He died right here on the bridge. That boy was you, Floyd Wilkes. You should have gone off to heaven, but you stayed here because you wanted to be near Mama and protect her. You can't protect her, Floyd Wilkes. You can't protect me no more, either. You brought me back only because God let you. It wadn't my time to go. You couldn't save Rose or Uncle Corbin, or Amity Smith. Your warnings come too late. I know you tried," I sobbed.

Inside, I mourned his death as if it had happened only yesterday. Saying goodbye to a ghost that had been with me since I was five years old was almost as hard as saying goodbye to Rose and Amity. Closing my eyes against the full glare of the sun, I instantly saw darkness and then a succession of bright flashes that showed various images of Floyd Wilkes in death. In front of me, his broken body lay face down against the wooden planks with blood trickling from his mouth and streaking the lightness of his hair. I saw the little colored boy crying as he gently cradled Floyd Wilkes' head in his lap. Mama had seen all these heartbreaking images that day – and the sight of the scattered berries smashed and streaming juice like blood all over the wood. She had heard the warm breeze rattling the empty buckets. Now Floyd Wilkes' ghost stood over his own body curiously looking down on it as if he wasn't sure what it was. After a while, his eyes met mine ever so briefly, and then I was back in the present. Opening my eyes, I saw only the weathered planks where Floyd Wilkes' body had lain only minutes before. Feeling a sudden lightness within myself, I realized that the spirit of Floyd Wilkes was gone. In the woods, a bird chirped happily. Down below me the water hissed and rushed over rocks. My nose took in the sweet scent of the honeysuckle, and for a little space of time, I felt a deep sense of peace.

 I would think of that day on the bridge many times over the course of my life. My decision to say goodbye to the ghost of Floyd Wilkes had seemed like the only sensible thing to do, then. Even now, I understand why I did it. A part of me had held on to the ghost for comfort and assurance. Somewhere inside myself, I believed that the ghost had the power to change the course of life, or make it better. But it never did, because it couldn't. Only God had the awesome power to change things. Age and death had taught me that nothing lasts forever, and that life is just a game of hit and miss. Sometimes you win the game and sometimes you lose, but you can't hold on too tightly to things and people.

 Mama and Rose had taught me what can happen when people hold onto things for too long -- especially things that do not and never will belong to you. The ghost of Floyd Wilkes had belonged to God, and I had kept it from him. In retrospect, Mama had become the scapegoat, and it was easy for me to believe that she was the one who had held on to the ghost when in reality I was the one who had held it back. Maybe, though, it was the deaths of Amity and Rose that had taught me to finally let go. I'd had to. Daddy's dependence on me had demanded that I grow up and move forward.

Some may say that my intuitive nature was nothing out of the ordinary, and that my ability to sense things came from having grown up to fast and having learned the predictable natures of those around me. Perhaps this is true concerning Rose, but Mama's nature was never that tractable. As of this writing, she remains a mystery to me.

57 GHOSTS AT PEACE

Two years after I had said goodbye to Floyd Wilkes' ghost, Daddy married Bonzelle Creech. It was a small affair with only family attending. Bonzelle was a happy bride and Daddy seemed pleased, too, but my intuition told me that a part of Daddy's heart would always belong to Mama.

Ironically, Mama would wait twenty years before marrying Uncle Larkin. By then, Rhodie, Daddy, and Granny Lee had died. Thankfully, Grandma Haley was eleven years gone and would never have to face the shame associated with her daughter having married the brother of her ex-husband. I suppose waiting was Mama's idea of doing the decent thing. However, I saw her actions as both hypocritical and cowardly.

Not long after I turned twenty-one, I traveled by bus to Indianapolis in order to see Mama. I suppose I was curious to see how she had fared over the years. As with any small-town girl, I was taken aback by the awesome size of the city with its many tall buildings and heavy traffic. While wandering its streets on foot, I took in the many coffee shops and restaurants, as well as the various boutiques and clothing stores.

Uncle Larkin had met me at the bus station. Upon seeing him, I was amazed as to how much he favored Daddy, save for his straight back and generous amount of hair that had grayed near his temples. There was a natural easiness between us that had begun a long time ago. Hugging me tightly he said, "I'm glad to see you. I know your Mama is anxious, too."

Mama and Uncle Larkin's farm was nestled in a little valley. Summer was at its peak and the rolling fields surrounding the house, barn, and outbuildings were lush green and almost looked surreal. All around me, the lands dipped in places but were flat for the most part. Never having seen anything but mountains and hills, I found the farm a kind of paradise. The inside of the two-storied house was modern and beautifully furnished. I wondered if Rhodie had been the decorator. Mama, however, was quick to inform me that she had refurbished the house after Rhodie was hospitalized.

She said of Rhodie, "It's just a matter of time before she dies. Larkin says she won't eat and is as skinny as a beanpole." Uncle Larkin had left for Whitesburg, Kentucky, that same night, allowing me a chance to study Mama.

We were sitting at the table sipping orange chamomile tea and nibbling vanilla wafers. The orangey smell of the tea had reminded me of the night of the blizzard when Mama had warned me about Amity Smith. When I mentioned that night, she said, "That was so long ago, Junie Mae. I can barely remember it."

Mama's appearance had changed but in a subtle way. She had kept her hair shoulder length and dyed a medium black. Her skin was as smooth as always save for the tiny lines about the corners of her eyes and mouth, but her eyes were different. Though still pretty and dark, a look of wariness had replaced their old furtiveness. Mama had picked up the habit of smoking, and her choice of cigarettes was the Eve brand. Lighting one and then taking a long drag she said, "So how's your life, Junie Mae?"

Shrugging, I said, "I am thinking of enrolling in college but don't have the money to do it."

Mama said, in a breezy tone, "Ask your Uncle Larkin. I'm sure he would give you enough to get started."

"I couldn't do that," I said, feeling both embarrassed and crestfallen with the fact that Mama believed that I was only there for money.

"I'll write you a check," she offered. Taking another long drag off her cigarette, she eyed me sharply and said, "You did come here for the money, didn't you?"

Feeling both hurt and angry, I shook my head no. My throat was too swollen with emotion to talk.

"You don't want money? Then why are you here?"

No longer able to hold my tears back, I rose quickly from the table and said, "This was a mistake. I'm sorry I came."

"Sit back down!" she gently commanded, and then asked, "Why on earth are you cryin'?"

"I thought we could have a conversation. I thought maybe you wanted to be my mother."

Up went her eyes. I saw a kind of spark in them. "When did you decide that?" she snapped. "You've hated me for years. Why would I think you'd come here for anything besides money? Don't tell me that woman has already run through your Daddy's money."

"Bonzelle loves Daddy. She didn't run through his money," I said defensively. I could feel her dark eyes boring a hole though me. Finally I spoke again. "I didn't come here for money, Mama. I did hate you, but mostly because you never loved or needed any of us."

Stubbing her cigarette into an ashtray and then lighting a fresh one she said, "Big Brock Asher murdered me that night in his morgue. After he done what he done to me, I was as dead as that corpse on the slab. I know it wadn't your or Rose's fault, but it wadn't all my fault, either. I gave Daddy and you girls all I had left."

"I'm certain that Big Brock got what he deserved in the end," I said cryptically.

"What do you want from me, Junie Mae?" she asked pointedly.

"I don't know," I answered truthfully.

"Would it satisfy you to know that I've paid for my sins? Granny Lee's lovin' God made sure of that. He may not give you what you want, but he's quick to give you what He wants. I found that out when your Uncle Floyd was killed. I remember standin' there in front of that bridge and seein' that poor little boy all broke and bleedin'. I was wonderin' how in the world God could take him from me. I know now that He took him because he was good. God can't leave the good ones alone."

"Oh, Mama," I said, tenderly placing my hand on hers. I thought she might snatch her hand back but she didn't. "Maybe it's time for us to forgive each other," I whispered.

Her eyes searched mine. I had never seen them look so wounded and tired. "All my life, I've tried to forget everything bad that's ever happened to me. That's why I left Harlan. How could I forget somethin' that I seen every day?" She laughed bitterly, and then added, "You can leave a place, but you can't leave your memories. I brought them all here and dumped them on Larkin's lap. But he had enough of his mama in him to understand. I guess I should be more grateful to him. I've tried..." Her voice trailed off.

"You love Uncle Larkin, don't you, Mama?" It was more of a hope than question.

"I stopped lovin' with my heart the day I lost Little Brock Asher. I decided that I would never let myself hurt that way again. I guess I appreciate Larkin more than anyone I've ever met. I reckon he deserves some kind of medal for what I've put him through."

"You got the money and the nice house Mama. Ain't these the things you always dreamed of?"

"You'd think I'd be in some kind of seventh heaven, wouldn't you? Well, I'm not, Junie Mae. In a way, I traded you and your Daddy and Rose for what I got here. Maybe in the long run I realized the trade-off wadn't worth it."

"Granny Lee told me once that people do things not always because they want to but because they have to. Maybe you had to do what you done, Mama."

Mama laughed and lit another cigarette. "Your Granny Lee is a lot like God. She's got an answer for everything in this world. I never understood how she could just accept whatever and be happy about it. If someone killed her whole family she'd say it was God's will."

"There's nobody like Granny Lee," I said.

Mama agreed and said, "I reckon not. Your daddy and Larkin puts a lot of store in her and what she says. Both of 'em turned out to be good men so I guess she done somethin' right."

"I seen Daisy Camp," I blurted out. "It was an awful place, Mama. I'm sorry you ever had to live there."

Looking up at me in surprise she asked, "When did you go there?"

"Years ago. It was right after Amity Smith died. I guess I just wanted to see what you had been talkin' about for so many years."

"I doubt you was disappointed. It was a real sewer hole, wadn't it? Poor Daddy. I can see him walkin' up that hill toward the mine. I still have nightmares about the camp."

That night Mama and I had talked until well into the wee hours of the morning. I told her something of my life at the River House, and she showed me several albums of pictures that she and Uncle Larkin had taken of their trips to Florida and California. The one person she failed to mention was Rose, but I wasn't surprised. Mama could never talk about the things that cut her the deepest. It would take me years to break though Mama's walls where Rose was concerned.

Shortly after I turned twenty-two I left River House and moved to Indianapolis, where I enrolled in a secretarial school. Uncle Larkin had gladly paid my tuition and had encouraged me to learn all I could. I lived in their guest house for the next three years. During that time, many things happened, beginning with the strange death of Little Brock Asher. According to Uncle Harvey James, Uncle Purl had gone up into his office one morning and found him slumped over his desk with his gun still in his hand. The police had called it suicide, but many - including Mama - thought that maybe someone might have murdered him. The news of Little Brock's death had hit Mama hard. She looked as if a light had gone out of her. Time had somehow worn away the layers of her protective walls, leaving her naked and vulnerable. Seeing her cry with such abandonment had both shaken and mystified me. I remembered how well she'd held herself together when Rose died. I hadn't seen her shed a tear. It had occurred to me then that perhaps Little Brock's death had opened up some kind of floodgate in her, and maybe she was crying for Rose, too.

"You really loved him, didn't you Mama?" I whispered.

She nodded and said, "I really did. I hate to think that he done himself in. Somebody probably killed him. God knows enough people hated him." Sighing, she added, "After we got older I thought about goin' to him and tellin' him what his Daddy done to me. I didn't, though, because I was afraid that he might not believe me. Now it's too late. " Mama turned toward the living room window that looked out onto the wide front yard. I could no longer see her face but knew she was crying. Reaching into the pocket of her sweater, she retrieved her cigarettes, lit one, and then exhaled a long plume of smoke. "I'll never cry like this again. Cryin' ain't done me a bit of good. It won't bring Rose or Little Brock back. I have to go on," she said to the window. It was as if she had forgotten I was standing behind her. I felt suddenly like an eavesdropper. To stand there and listen to her rearranging things so she could bear up allowed me a rare glimpse into her mind how she thought.

Mama had kept her promise of never crying again -- at least in my presence. Even after the deaths of her own mama, Granny Lee, and finally Daddy, she remained dry-eyed and strangely detached. Her eyes betrayed her, though. I had learned to gauge her by the way she looked out of them. I often saw a kind of torture in their expressions, and would soon realize that she was paying for her sins of loving one too much and others too little.

My own life would take many twists and turns throughout the years. I would divorce twice and birth four children before I came to fully realize how cruel and uncertain life could be. After Uncle Larkin and then Mama passed away, I'd felt completely alone, and for months I stayed locked inside the little guest house avoiding everyone, including my adult children. I had dreaded going inside the main house because it looked so empty and forlorn with its drawn shades and high grass. I hadn't the heart to open up the house or hire someone to mow the yard. A part of me wanted to sell the house while another part believed selling it would be like selling Mama's dreams of a better life. Thankfully, I had made my peace with Mama before she lost her battle with cancer in 1999. I prayed that she found peace in the afterlife, because life on earth had been hard on her. In time, I would conclude that Mama was merely a product of time, place, and circumstance, and though she had made many mistakes, hers weren't much worse than mine or anyone else's. Granny Lee once said that one little sin was as bad as a big sin. In that case, people are all the same if you consider that everyone sins in the eyes of God.

I remember the day I finally opened Mama's house. I had raised the shades and had sat in her favorite chair by the sliding glass door that looked out into her rose garden that was in full bloom. A variety of roses grew along the fence line, with one wild red rosebush centering the garden. Mama had once told me that while visiting Granny Lee that Uncle Larkin had dug up that bush on the banks of the Cumberland River not far from the lodge. Sliding back the door, I walked out onto the patio and admired the beauty while inhaling the sweet fragrance. I had never seen the roses look so full and colorful, especially the wild red ones. Mama never said it, but I knew she had planted the garden in memory of Rose. In the months before she died, Mama would sit on the little bench in the center of the garden, sometimes for hours. In studying her, I realized for the first time in my life that she was old, and that a part of her had already died a long time ago. Seeing her so sick and miserable had made want to rush out there and assure her that Rose had forgiven her, but I wasn't sure that was true. Only God could tell her that. Looking about the garden and the house, I realized that its spirit was gone, and that it was up to me to put life back into it. I started cleaning and dusting and rearranging that day. As long as I kept busy, I wouldn't have to think. I had slept in Uncle Larkin and Mama's bed that night. I had expected it to be an awful experience, but, as it turned out, sleeping there had filled me with sense of peace. On other nights, however, I would lie awake thinking of the past and wondering where I might have been had Mama not left us, and Amity Smith hadn't died. One night, I dreamed of Amity Smith. He was standing by the fence near the baseball field where we had stood years before. The wind ruffled though his blonde hair and his dimples showed when he laughed. His blue eyes sought mine for an answer, but I found I couldn't answer because I had forgotten his question. I had awakened with tears in my eyes. That would be my first and last dream of Amity Smith.

One night the following winter, I received a phone call from Violet Elizabeth Smith, now Parsons. Violet and her husband were both schoolteachers and lived in a house with Mrs. Smith, whose husband had died a few years before. Violet and I had kept up over the years, and a late night phone call from her was not that uncommon. On the other end of the phone, Violet said, "Did you know that the Asher house burned down last night? The inside was gone even before the firefighters got there. Thank God it was empty at the time." Violet went on to tell me that after Miss Joelyn died the house had remained empty for years. "All three of the Asher children live out of state. They finally put a 'For Sale' sign on it, but nobody could afford to buy it with the sad shape of things around here."

I thought of the time I'd wanted the Asher house to burn. I had felt such a hatred for it as well as for the Ashers themselves. I pictured the big house with its steeped roof, jutting chimneys, and eyebrow shaped shutters. I could almost smell the green grass on its sloping hillside and touch the feathery pink flowers of the Formosa trees. Granny Lee had said the place was cursed. I was sure she was right. Granny Lee was always right. That same night I had a dream that I was standing on the Wilder Creek Bridge watching the Creekstone House burn. The orange and red flames flicked and danced high into the night sky. The Formosa trees caught quickly; their pink flowers shriveled and seemingly melted while their branches crackled and popped like gunshots bouncing off the distant cliffs. Watching the fire, I noticed odd, dark shapes snaking out of the high flames. Somewhere in the distance, I heard what sounded like cries and moans all mingled together. The ghosts of the Creekstone House were finally free.

ABOUT THE AUTHOR

Sandi Knapp was born in Salem, Indiana. She spent most of her childhood in Hyden, Kentucky, and she was raised with the stories and lives of coal miners. She now lives and writes in Indiana.

Made in the USA
Coppell, TX
11 January 2021